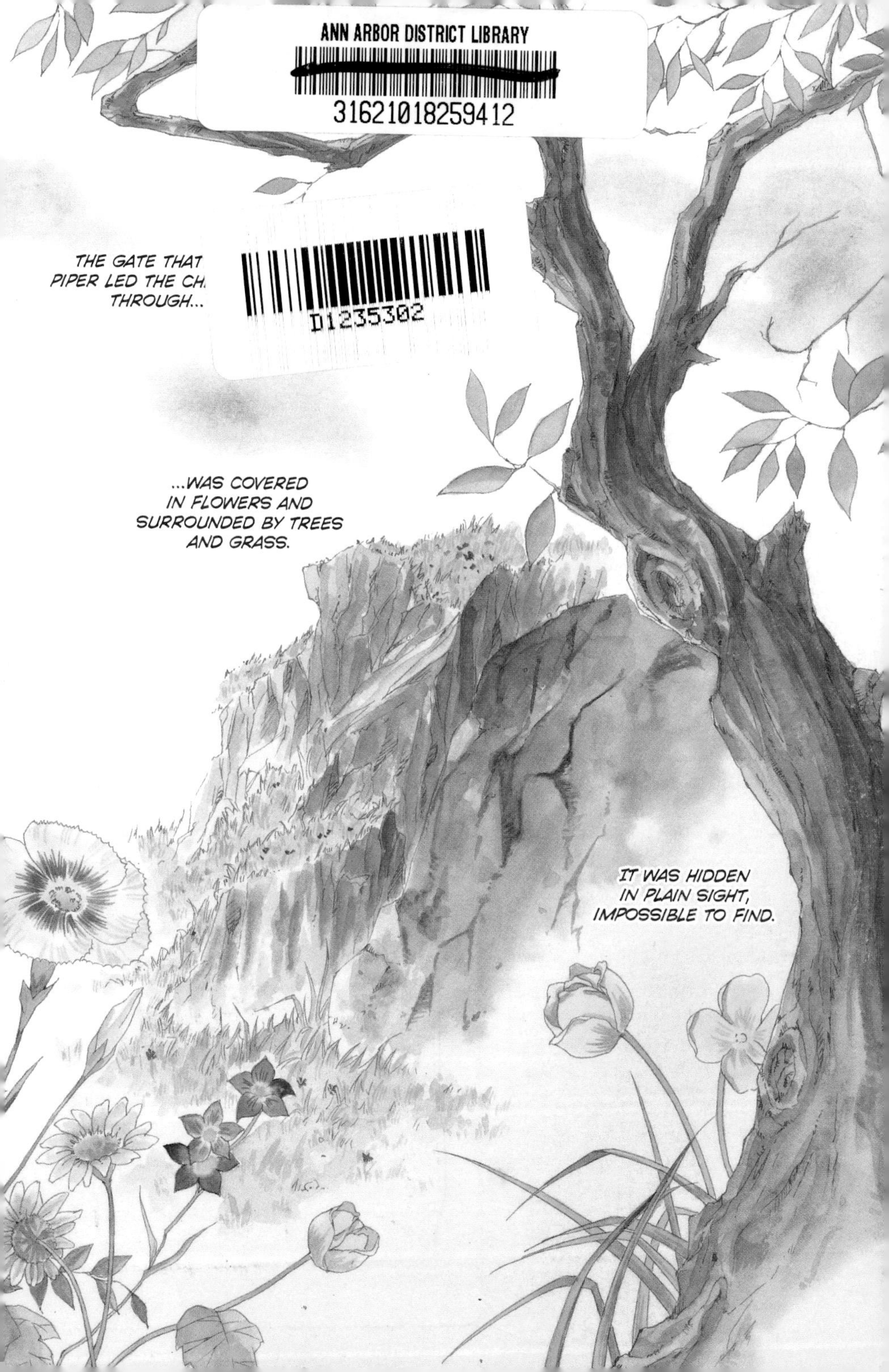
THE GATE THAT
PIPER LED THE CH
THROUGH...
...WAS COVERED IN FLOWERS AND SURROUNDED BY TREES AND GRASS.
IT WAS HIDDEN IN PLAIN SIGHT, IMPOSSIBLE TO FIND.

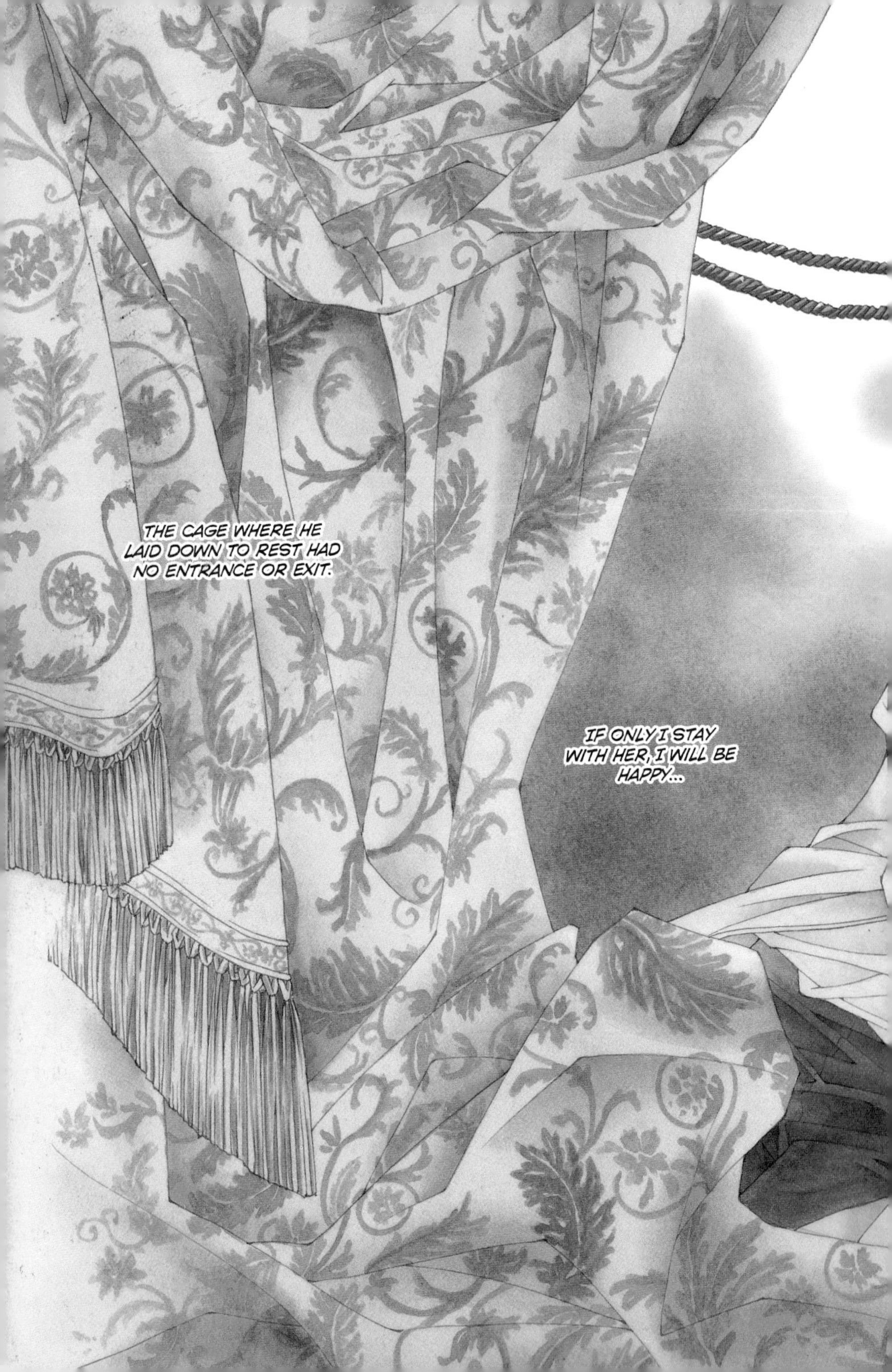
THE CAGE WHERE HE LAID DOWN TO REST HAD NO ENTRANCE OR EXIT.
IF ONLY I STAY WITH HER, I WILL BE HAPPY...

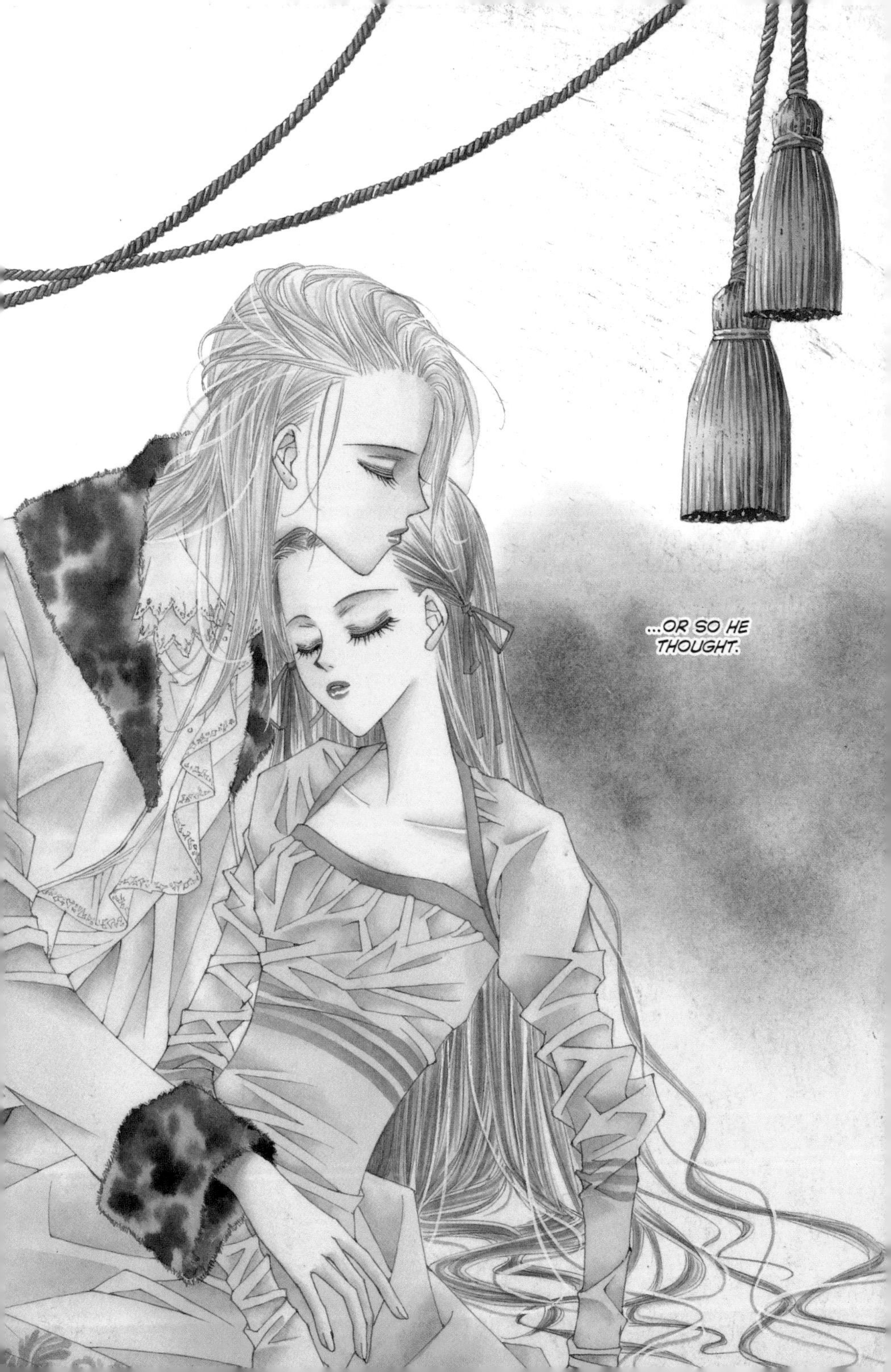
...OR SO HE THOUGHT.

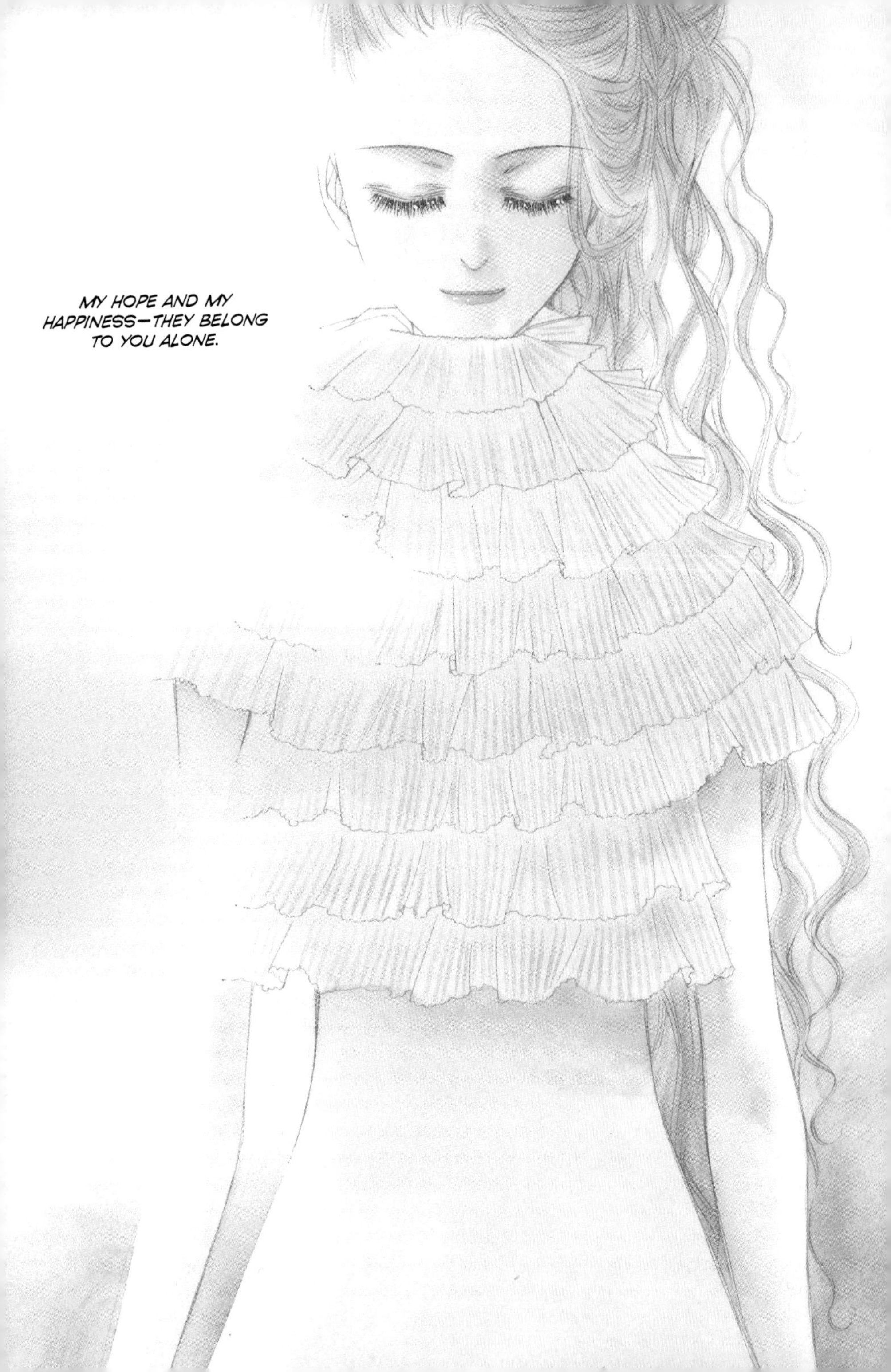
MY HOPE AND MY HAPPINESS—THEY BELONG TO YOU ALONE.

Cynical Orange

Vol. 5

Yun JiUn

Yen Press

About the Creator

Cynical Orange

JiUn Yun

JiUn Yun made her professional debut in 2000 by placing second in a Manhwa competition with her short story <Are you? I am!>. However, she was already famous among amateur Manhwa clubs in Korea for her delicate drawings, unique heroines, and distinctive plots. Her special style of combining artistic creativity with beautiful composition has led to an enormous fan base in Asia.

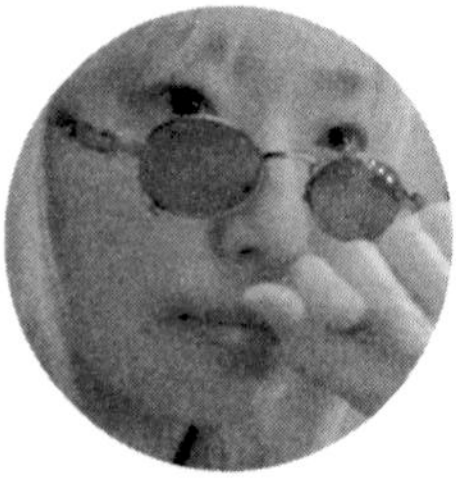

Other major works
<Afterimage of the Red Shoes>, <Hush>, <Are you? I am!>, <The Doll's Request>, <Happy End>, <Excel>, <Cynical Orange>, <Dear Waltz>, <Pa-Han-Zip>

When I was in elementary school,
there was a well near my family's
house. The well was rather huge, and
it even had a roof on it. It was in an area
where sunlight couldn't reach, so it was very
dark inside. When I looked down into the well,
I couldn't see anything, and it made me scared.
I imagined some kind of monsters lived there,
like out of an old story. I thought a ghost would
show me its frightening face or a monster would
pull me down the hole. I thought a well was
like a gateway to different worlds. It
was really scary, but at the same
time I also really wanted to
jump in and see what was
below the surface.

--JiUn Yun

C O N T E N T S

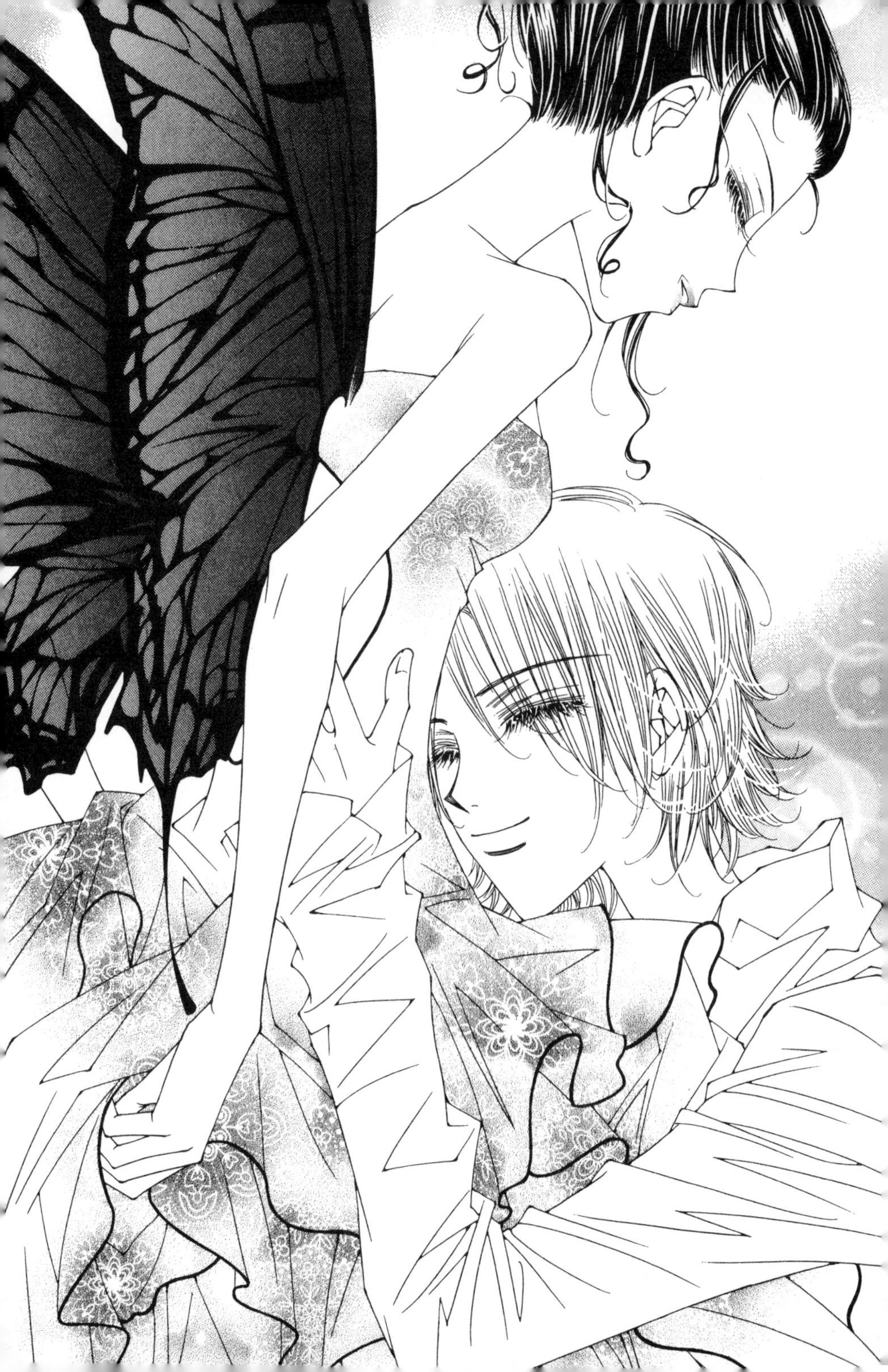

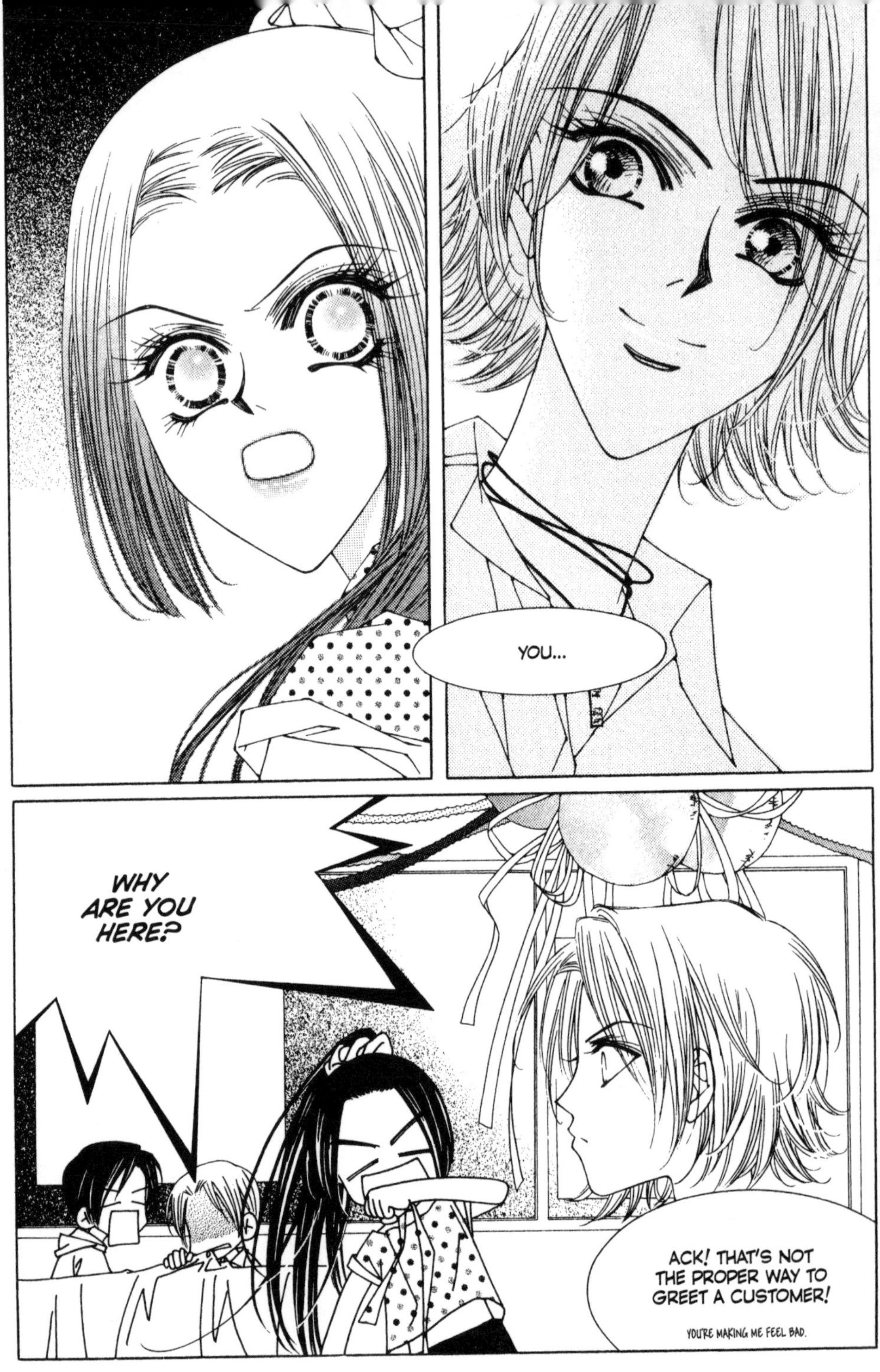
YOU...
WHY ARE YOU HERE?
ACK! THAT'S NOT THE PROPER WAY TO GREET A CUSTOMER!
YOU'RE MAKING ME FEEL BAD.

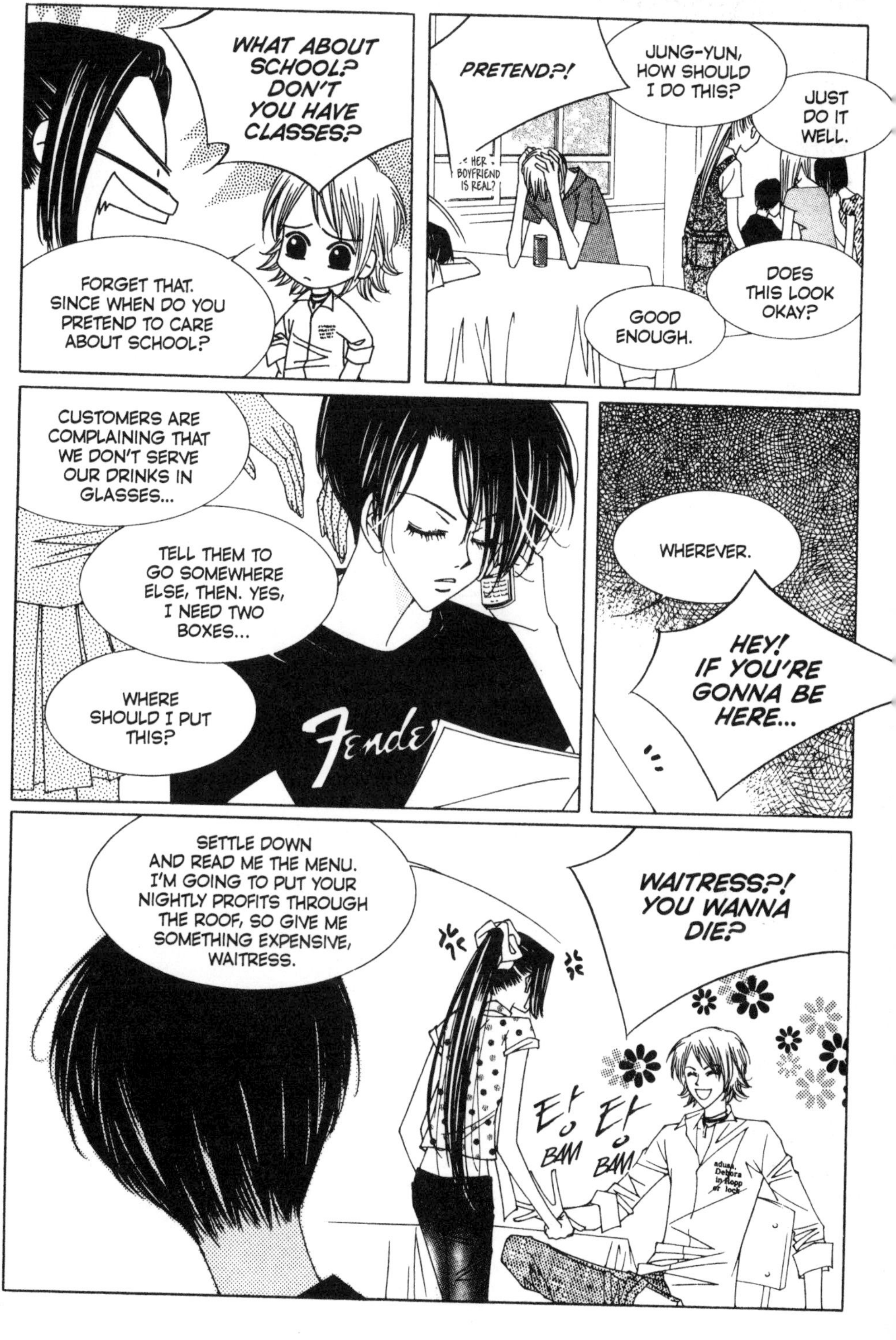
WHAT ABOUT SCHOOL? DON'T YOU HAVE CLASSES?
FORGET THAT. SINCE WHEN DO YOU PRETEND TO CARE ABOUT SCHOOL?
PRETEND?!
JUNG-YUN, HOW SHOULD I DO THIS?
JUST DO IT WELL.
HER BOYFRIEND IS REAL?
DOES THIS LOOK OKAY?
GOOD ENOUGH.
CUSTOMERS ARE COMPLAINING THAT WE DON'T SERVE OUR DRINKS IN GLASSES...
TELL THEM TO GO SOMEWHERE ELSE, THEN. YES, I NEED TWO BOXES...
WHERE SHOULD I PUT THIS?
WHEREVER.
HEY! IF YOU'RE GONNA BE HERE...
SETTLE DOWN AND READ ME THE MENU. I'M GOING TO PUT YOUR NIGHTLY PROFITS THROUGH THE ROOF, SO GIVE ME SOMETHING EXPENSIVE, WAITRESS.
WAITRESS?! YOU WANNA DIE?
탕 BAM
탕 BAM

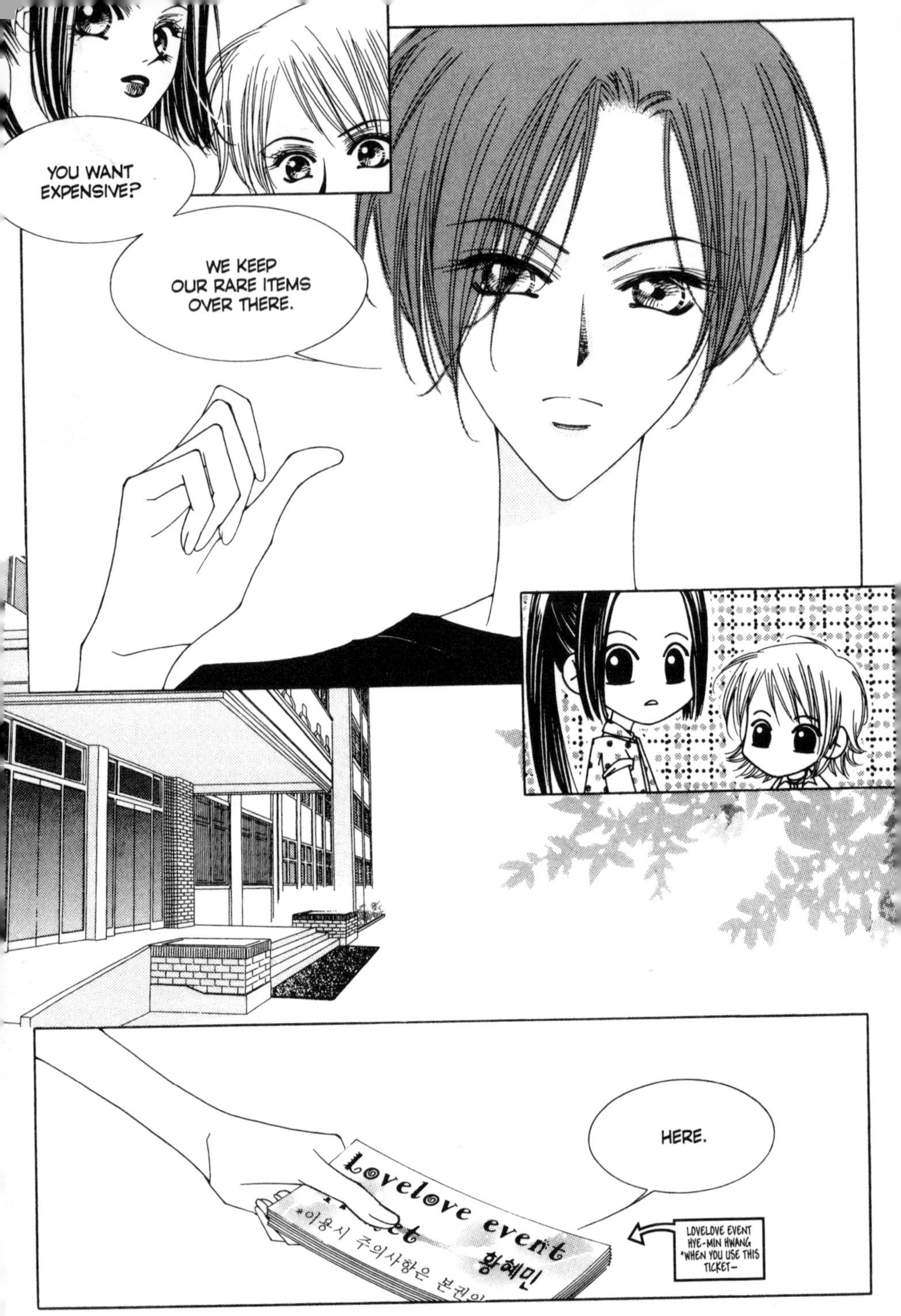
YOU WANT EXPENSIVE?
WE KEEP OUR RARE ITEMS OVER THERE.
HERE.
Lovelove event
황혜민
*이용시 주의사항은 본권의
LOVELOVE EVENT HYE-MIN HWANG *WHEN YOU USE THIS TICKET—

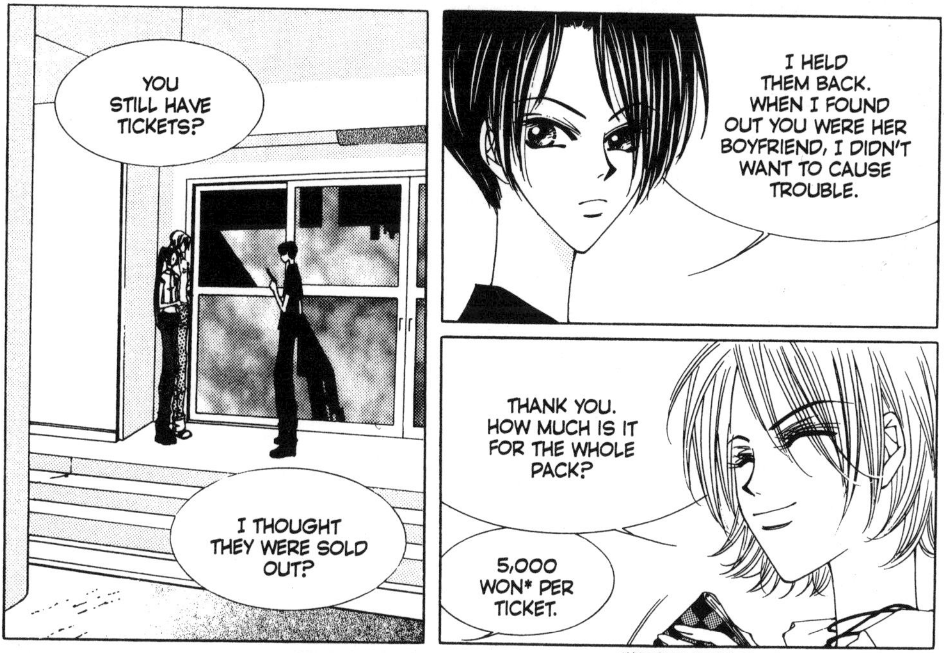
YOU STILL HAVE TICKETS?
I THOUGHT THEY WERE SOLD OUT?
I HELD THEM BACK. WHEN I FOUND OUT YOU WERE HER BOYFRIEND, I DIDN'T WANT TO CAUSE TROUBLE.
THANK YOU. HOW MUCH IS IT FOR THE WHOLE PACK?
5,000 WON* PER TICKET.

*KOREAN MONETARY UNIT. 5,000 WON = $5.34

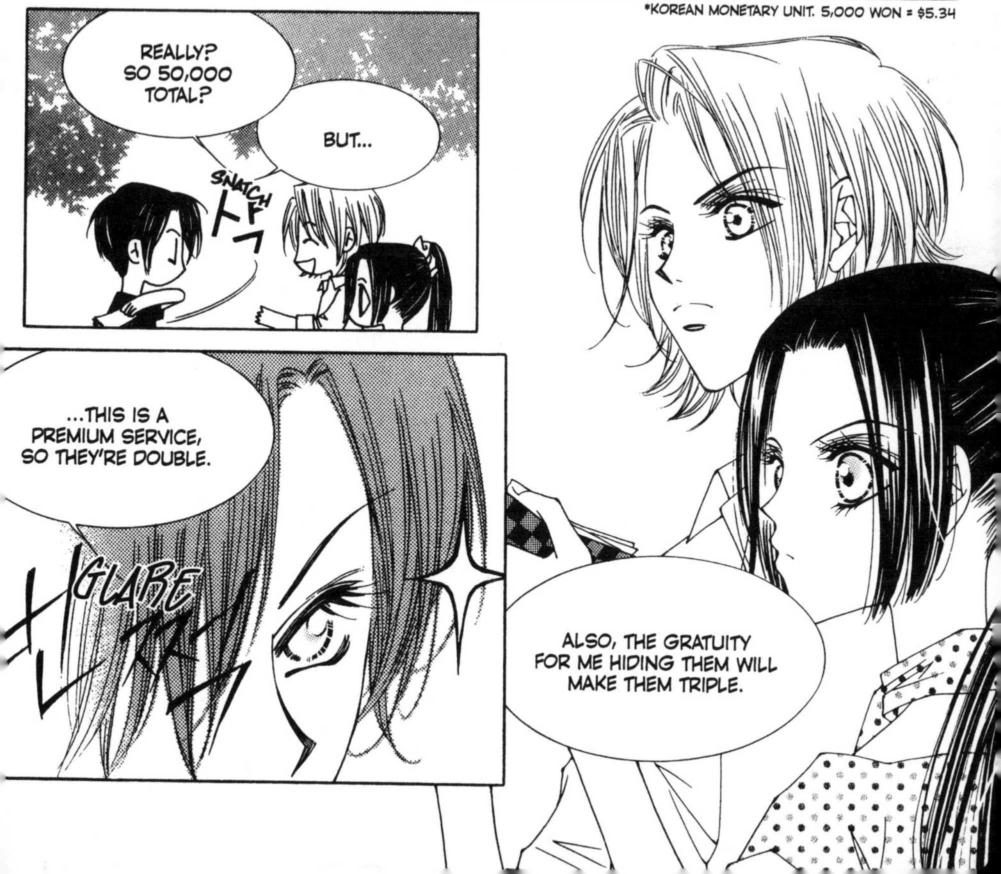
REALLY? SO 50,000 TOTAL?
BUT...
SNATCH
...THIS IS A PREMIUM SERVICE, SO THEY'RE DOUBLE.
GLARE
ALSO, THE GRATUITY FOR ME HIDING THEM WILL MAKE THEM TRIPLE.

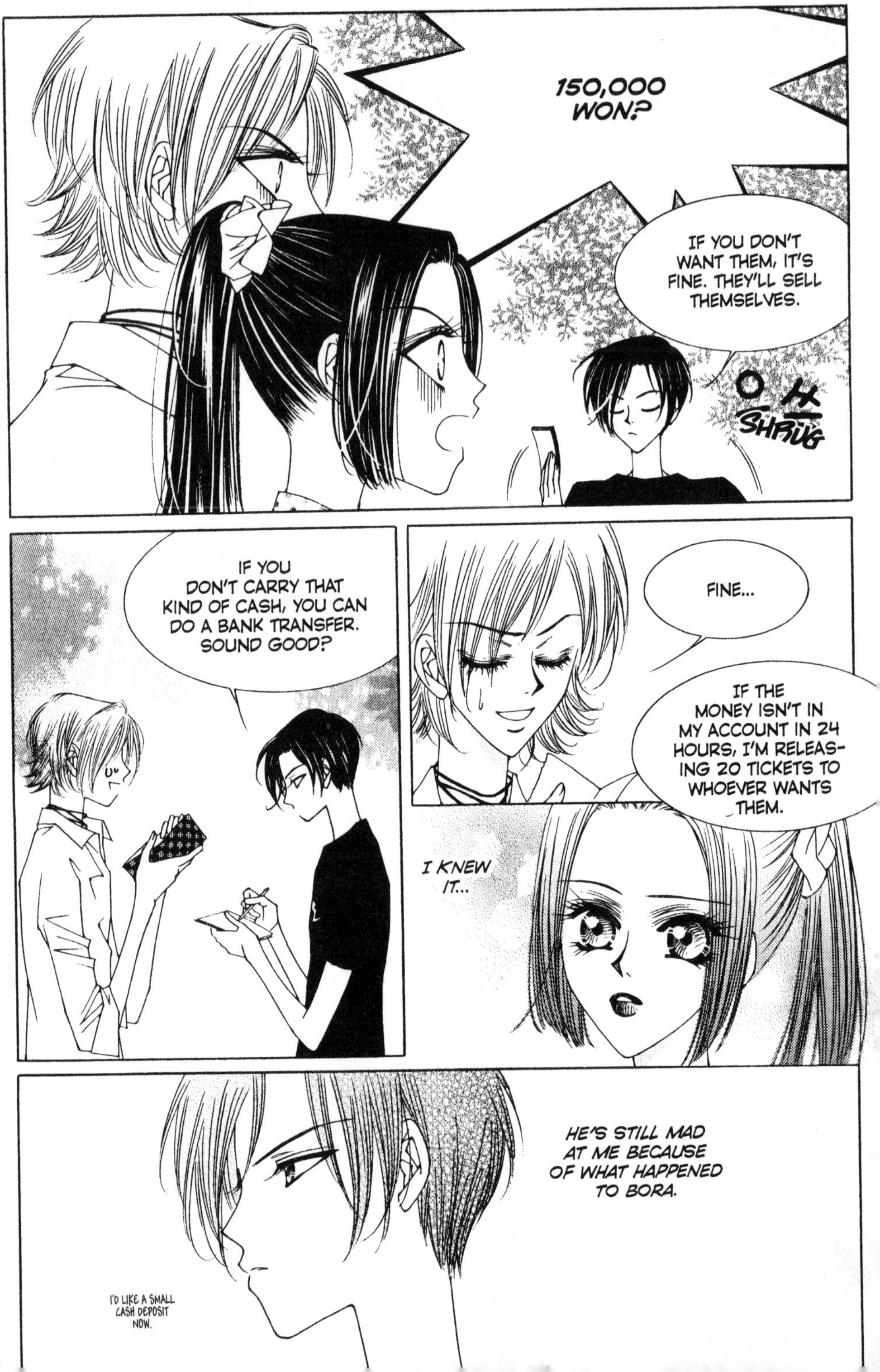
150,000 WON?
IF YOU DON'T WANT THEM, IT'S FINE. THEY'LL SELL THEMSELVES.
으쓱
SHRUG
IF YOU DON'T CARRY THAT KIND OF CASH, YOU CAN DO A BANK TRANSFER. SOUND GOOD?
FINE...
IF THE MONEY ISN'T IN MY ACCOUNT IN 24 HOURS, I'M RELEASING 20 TICKETS TO WHOEVER WANTS THEM.
I KNEW IT...
HE'S STILL MAD AT ME BECAUSE OF WHAT HAPPENED TO BORA.
I'D LIKE A SMALL CASH DEPOSIT NOW.

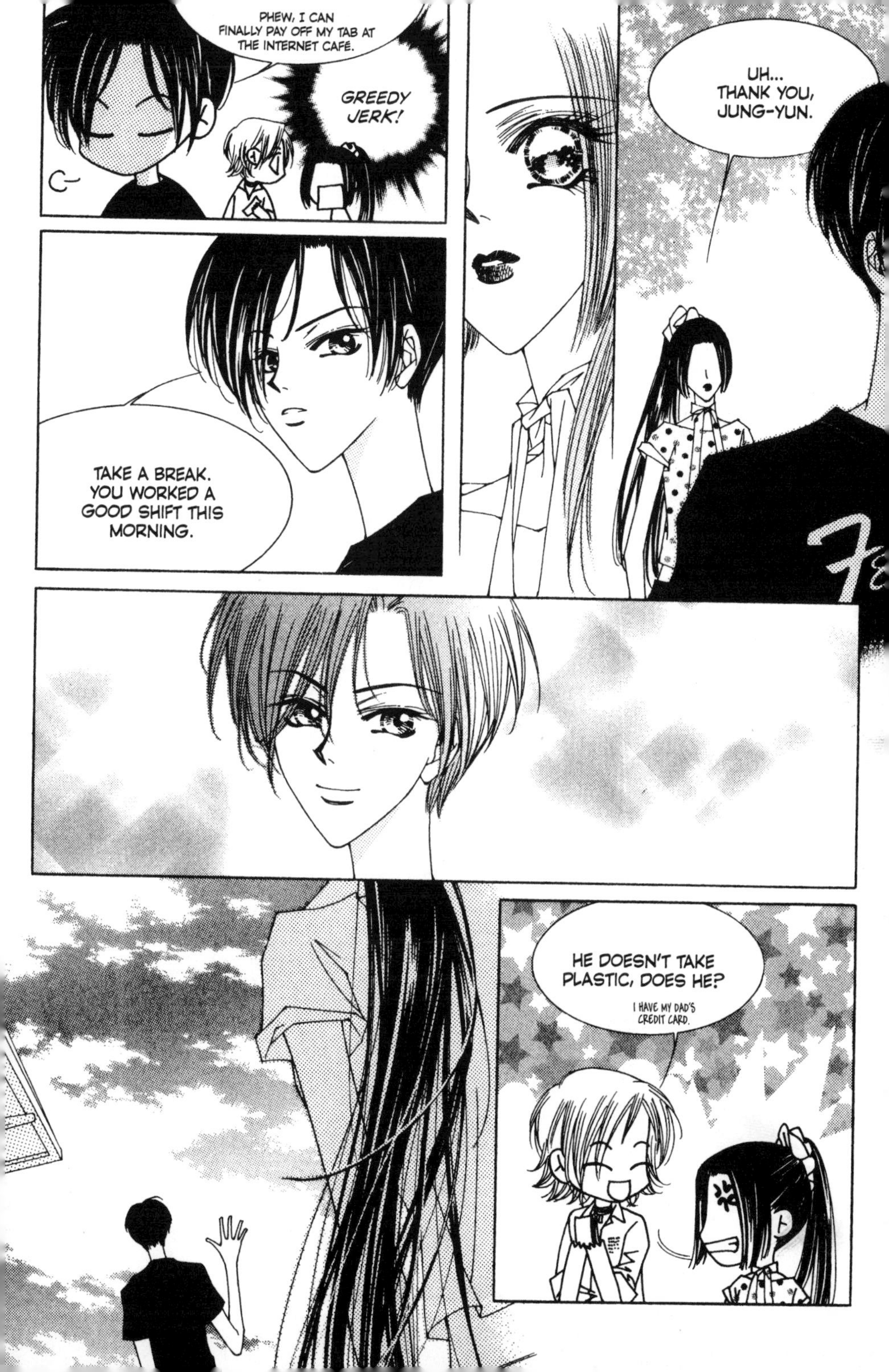

PHEW, I CAN FINALLY PAY OFF MY TAB AT THE INTERNET CAFÉ.
GREEDY JERK!
TAKE A BREAK. YOU WORKED A GOOD SHIFT THIS MORNING.
UH... THANK YOU, JUNG-YUN.
HE DOESN'T TAKE PLASTIC, DOES HE?
I HAVE MY DAD'S CREDIT CARD.

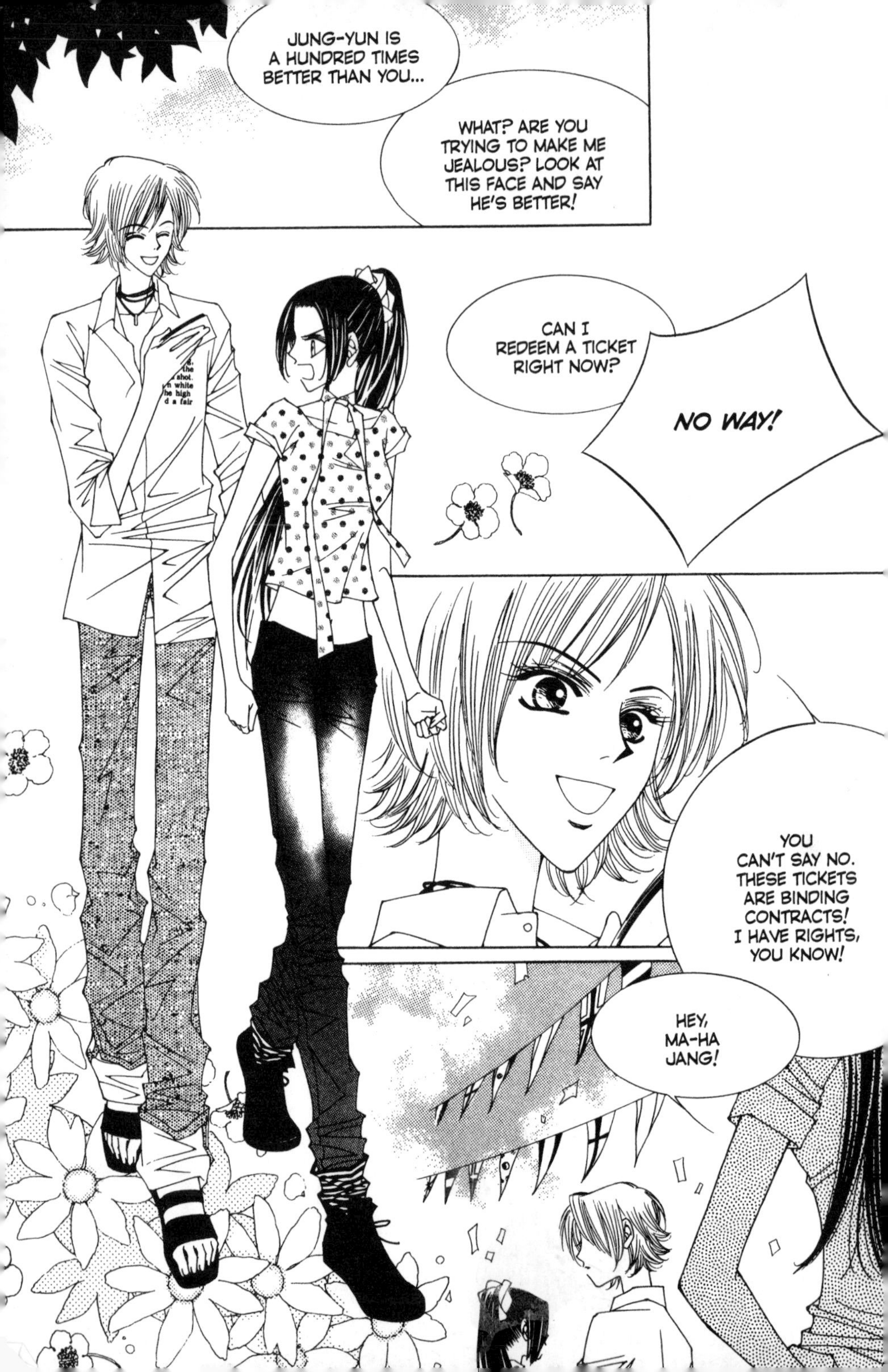
JUNG-YUN IS A HUNDRED TIMES BETTER THAN YOU...
WHAT? ARE YOU TRYING TO MAKE ME JEALOUS? LOOK AT THIS FACE AND SAY HE'S BETTER!
CAN I REDEEM A TICKET RIGHT NOW?
NO WAY!
YOU CAN'T SAY NO. THESE TICKETS ARE BINDING CONTRACTS! I HAVE RIGHTS, YOU KNOW!
HEY, MA-HA JANG!

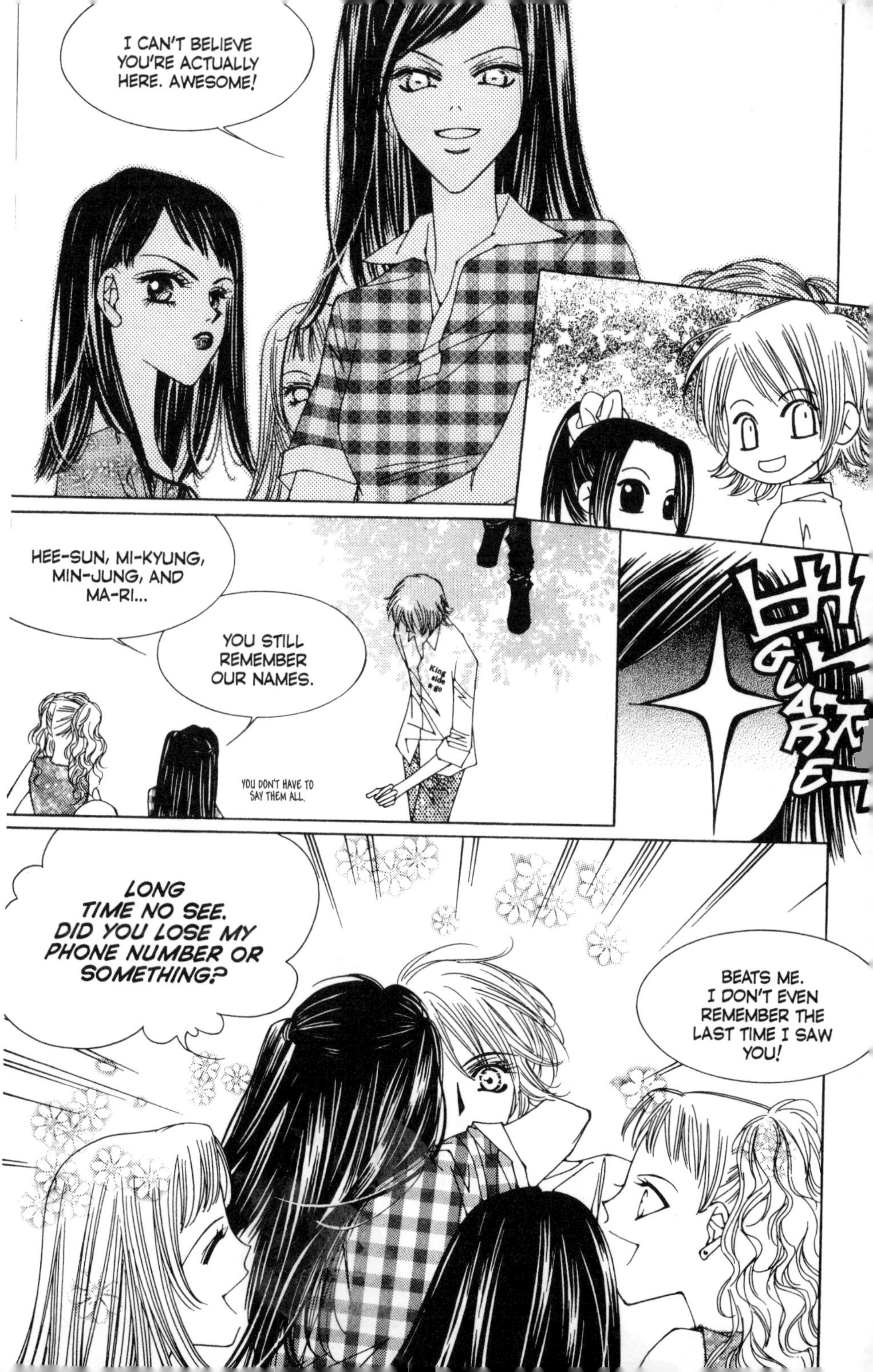
I CAN'T BELIEVE YOU'RE ACTUALLY HERE. AWESOME!
HEE-SUN, MI-KYUNG, MIN-JUNG, AND MA-RI...
YOU STILL REMEMBER OUR NAMES.
YOU DON'T HAVE TO SAY THEM ALL.
King side a-go
GLARE
LONG TIME NO SEE. DID YOU LOSE MY PHONE NUMBER OR SOMETHING?
BEATS ME. I DON'T EVEN REMEMBER THE LAST TIME I SAW YOU!

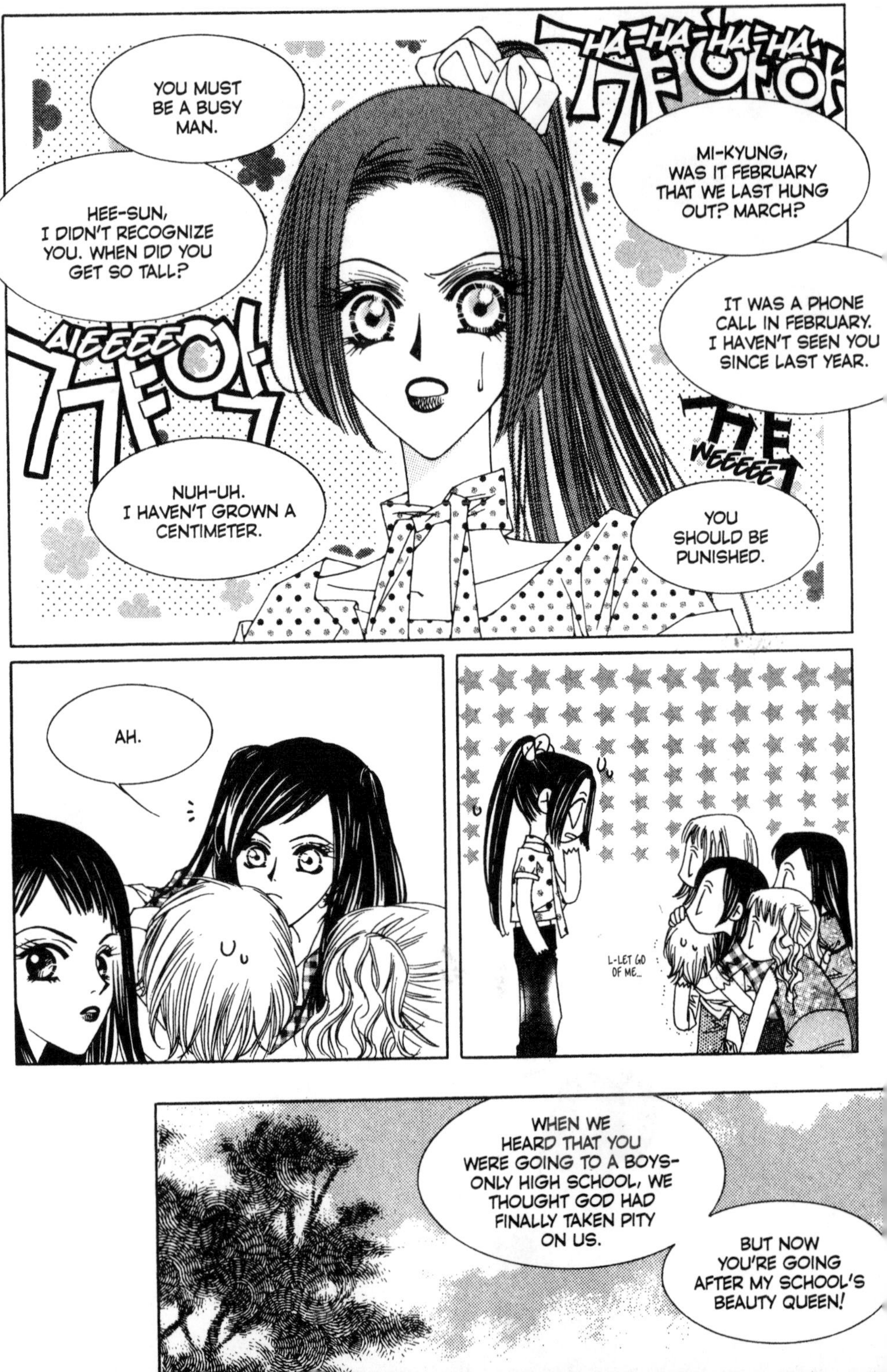

YOU MUST BE A BUSY MAN.
HA-HA-HA-HA
MI-KYUNG, WAS IT FEBRUARY THAT WE LAST HUNG OUT? MARCH?
HEE-SUN, I DIDN'T RECOGNIZE YOU. WHEN DID YOU GET SO TALL?
IT WAS A PHONE CALL IN FEBRUARY. I HAVEN'T SEEN YOU SINCE LAST YEAR.
AIEEEE
WEEEEE
NUH-UH. I HAVEN'T GROWN A CENTIMETER.
YOU SHOULD BE PUNISHED.
AH.
L-LET GO OF ME...
WHEN WE HEARD THAT YOU WERE GOING TO A BOYS-ONLY HIGH SCHOOL, WE THOUGHT GOD HAD FINALLY TAKEN PITY ON US.
BUT NOW YOU'RE GOING AFTER MY SCHOOL'S BEAUTY QUEEN!

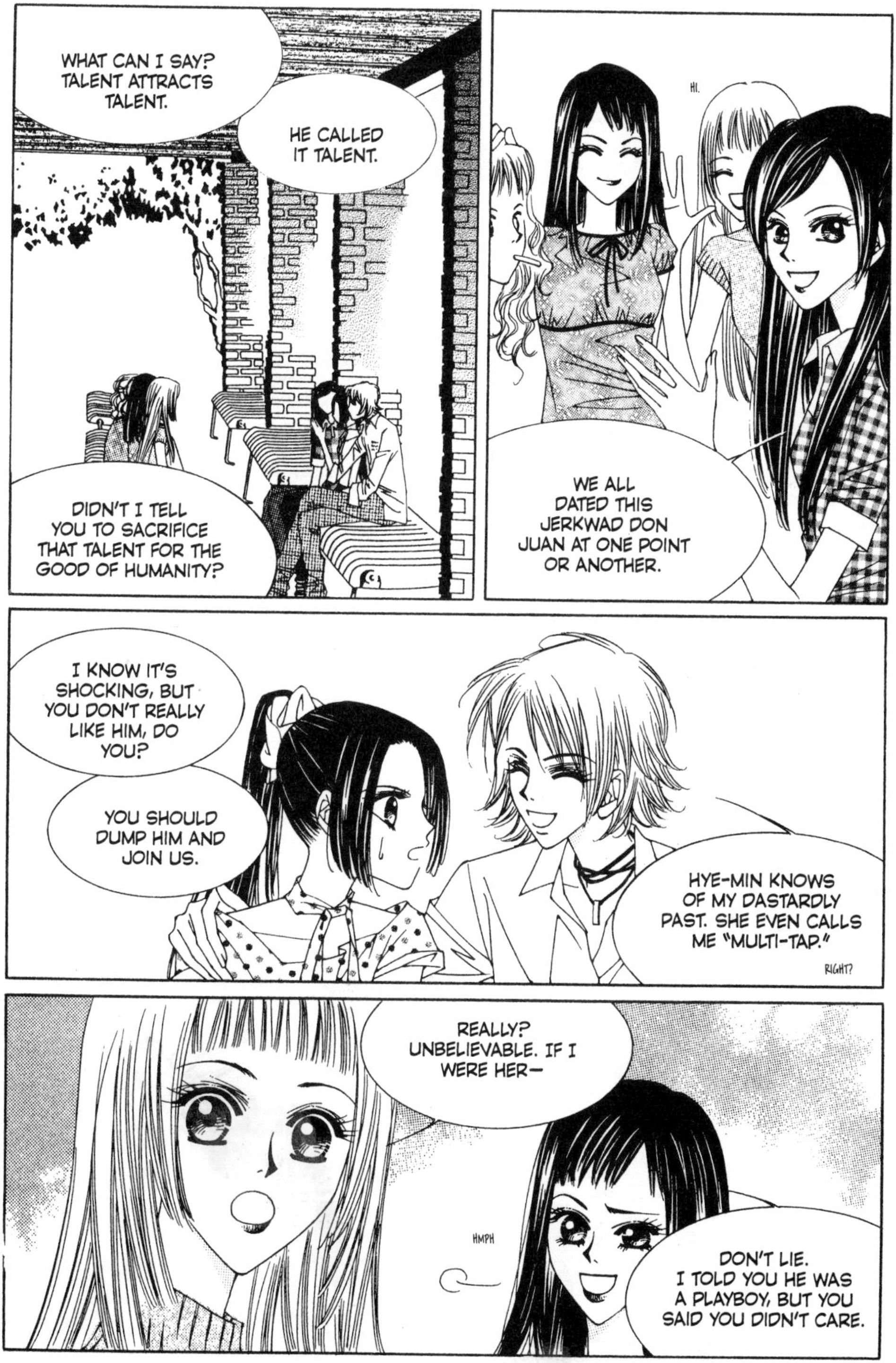
WHAT CAN I SAY? TALENT ATTRACTS TALENT.
HE CALLED IT TALENT.
DIDN'T I TELL YOU TO SACRIFICE THAT TALENT FOR THE GOOD OF HUMANITY?
HI.
WE ALL DATED THIS JERKWAD DON JUAN AT ONE POINT OR ANOTHER.
I KNOW IT'S SHOCKING, BUT YOU DON'T REALLY LIKE HIM, DO YOU?
YOU SHOULD DUMP HIM AND JOIN US.
HYE-MIN KNOWS OF MY DASTARDLY PAST. SHE EVEN CALLS ME "MULTI-TAP."
RIGHT?
REALLY? UNBELIEVABLE. IF I WERE HER—
HMPH
DON'T LIE. I TOLD YOU HE WAS A PLAYBOY, BUT YOU SAID YOU DIDN'T CARE.

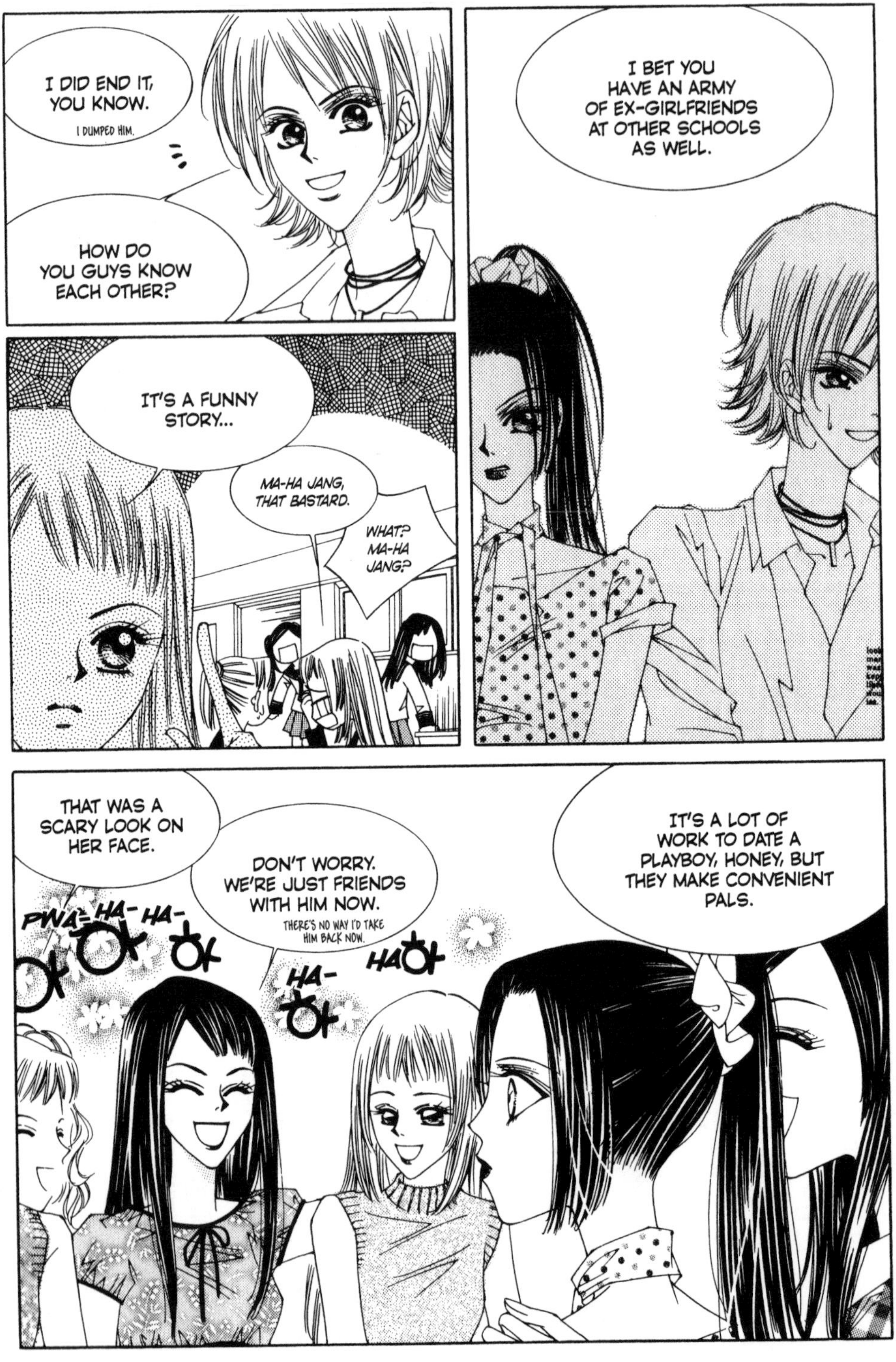
I DID END IT, YOU KNOW.
I DUMPED HIM.
HOW DO YOU GUYS KNOW EACH OTHER?
IT'S A FUNNY STORY...
MA-HA JANG, THAT BASTARD.
WHAT? MA-HA JANG?
I BET YOU HAVE AN ARMY OF EX-GIRLFRIENDS AT OTHER SCHOOLS AS WELL.
THAT WAS A SCARY LOOK ON HER FACE.
PWA- HA- HA-
DON'T WORRY. WE'RE JUST FRIENDS WITH HIM NOW.
THERE'S NO WAY I'D TAKE HIM BACK NOW.
HA- HA
IT'S A LOT OF WORK TO DATE A PLAYBOY, HONEY, BUT THEY MAKE CONVENIENT PALS.

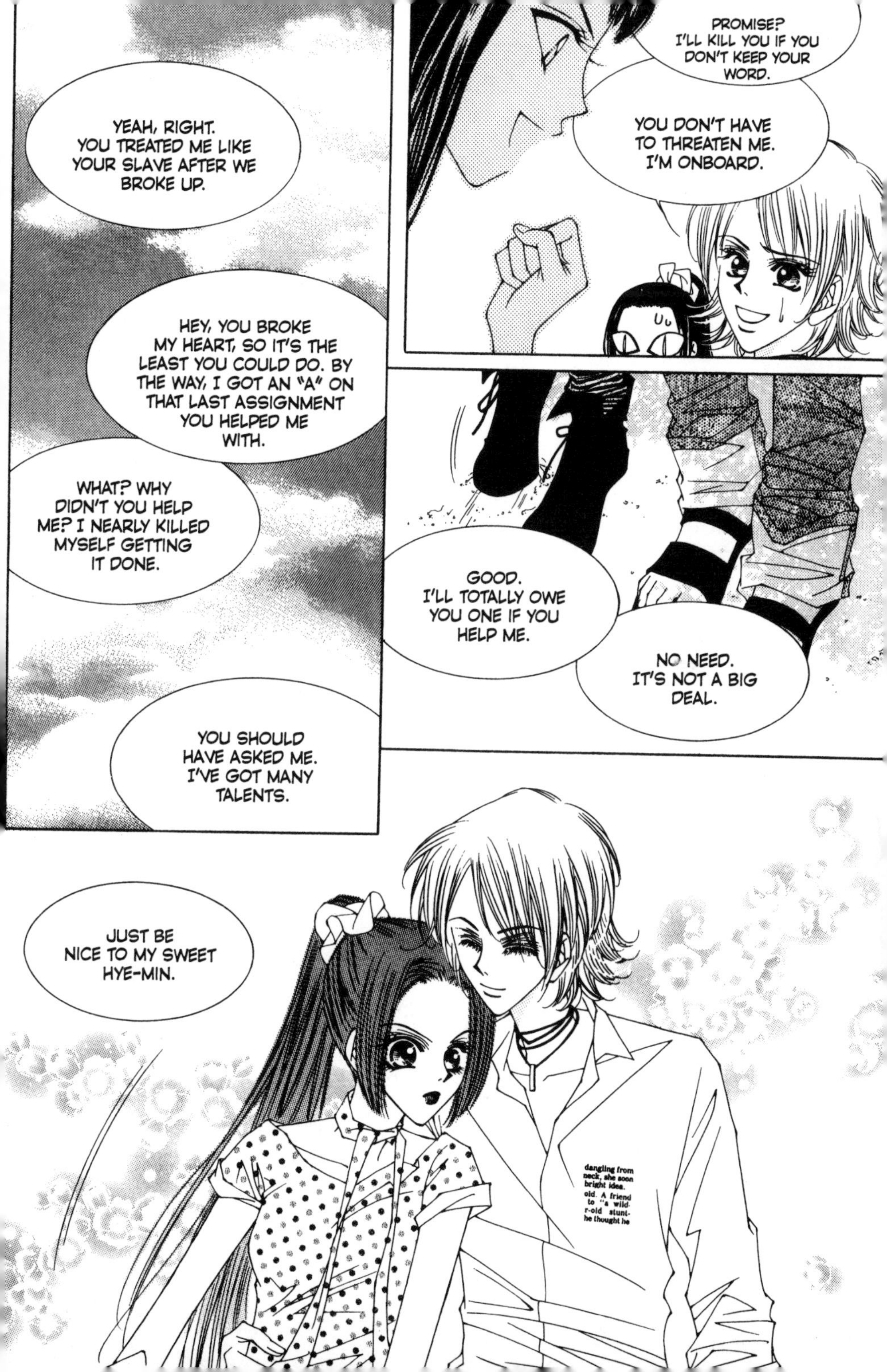
YEAH, RIGHT. YOU TREATED ME LIKE YOUR SLAVE AFTER WE BROKE UP.
HEY, YOU BROKE MY HEART, SO IT'S THE LEAST YOU COULD DO. BY THE WAY, I GOT AN "A" ON THAT LAST ASSIGNMENT YOU HELPED ME WITH.
WHAT? WHY DIDN'T YOU HELP ME? I NEARLY KILLED MYSELF GETTING IT DONE.
YOU SHOULD HAVE ASKED ME. I'VE GOT MANY TALENTS.
PROMISE? I'LL KILL YOU IF YOU DON'T KEEP YOUR WORD.
YOU DON'T HAVE TO THREATEN ME. I'M ONBOARD.
GOOD. I'LL TOTALLY OWE YOU ONE IF YOU HELP ME.
NO NEED. IT'S NOT A BIG DEAL.
JUST BE NICE TO MY SWEET HYE-MIN.
dangling from neck, she soon bright idea. old. A friend to "a wild- r-old stunt- he thought he

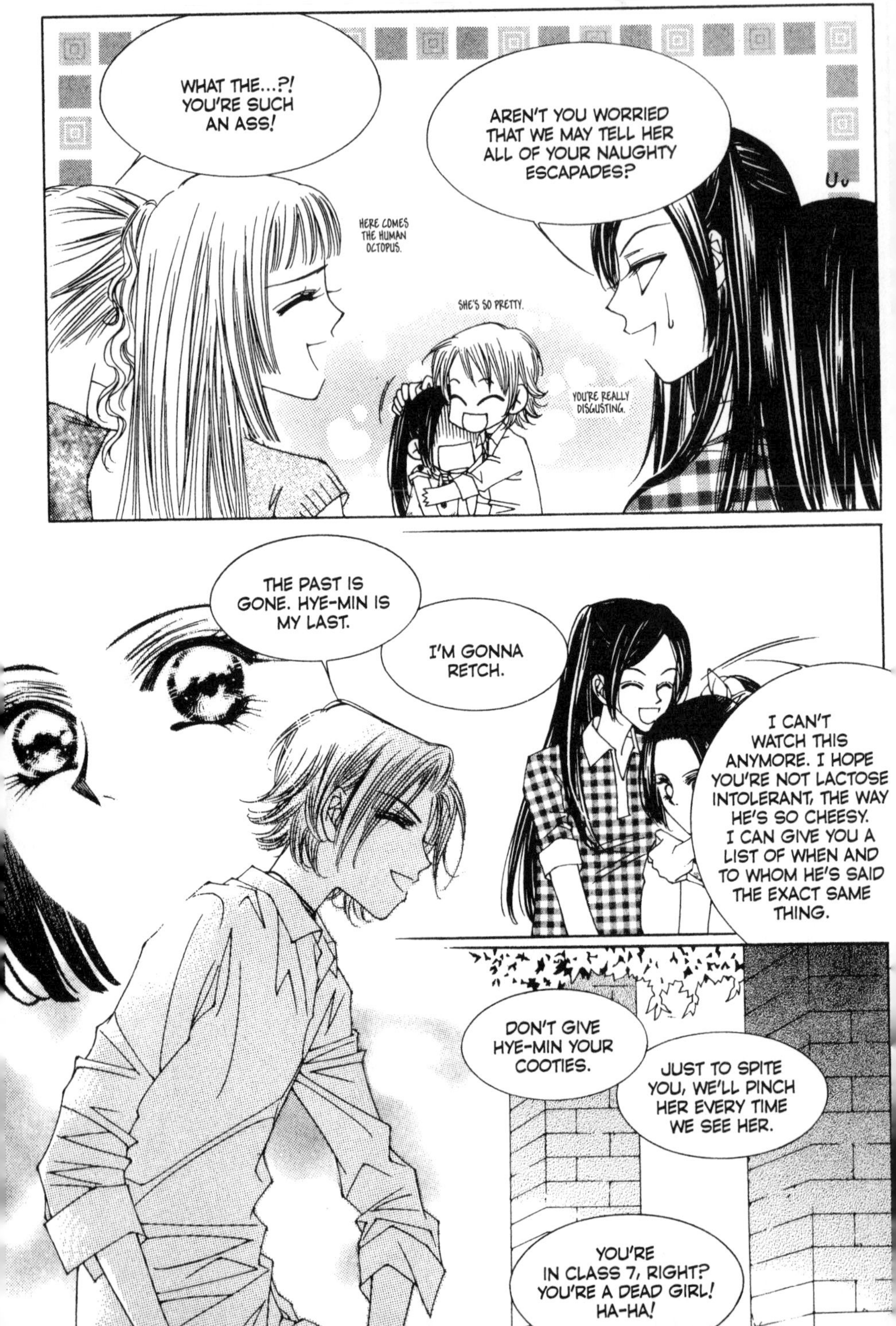
WHAT THE...?! YOU'RE SUCH AN ASS!
AREN'T YOU WORRIED THAT WE MAY TELL HER ALL OF YOUR NAUGHTY ESCAPADES?
HERE COMES THE HUMAN OCTOPUS.
SHE'S SO PRETTY.
YOU'RE REALLY DISGUSTING.
THE PAST IS GONE. HYE-MIN IS MY LAST.
I'M GONNA RETCH.
I CAN'T WATCH THIS ANYMORE. I HOPE YOU'RE NOT LACTOSE INTOLERANT, THE WAY HE'S SO CHEESY. I CAN GIVE YOU A LIST OF WHEN AND TO WHOM HE'S SAID THE EXACT SAME THING.
DON'T GIVE HYE-MIN YOUR COOTIES.
JUST TO SPITE YOU, WE'LL PINCH HER EVERY TIME WE SEE HER.
YOU'RE IN CLASS 7, RIGHT? YOU'RE A DEAD GIRL! HA-HA!

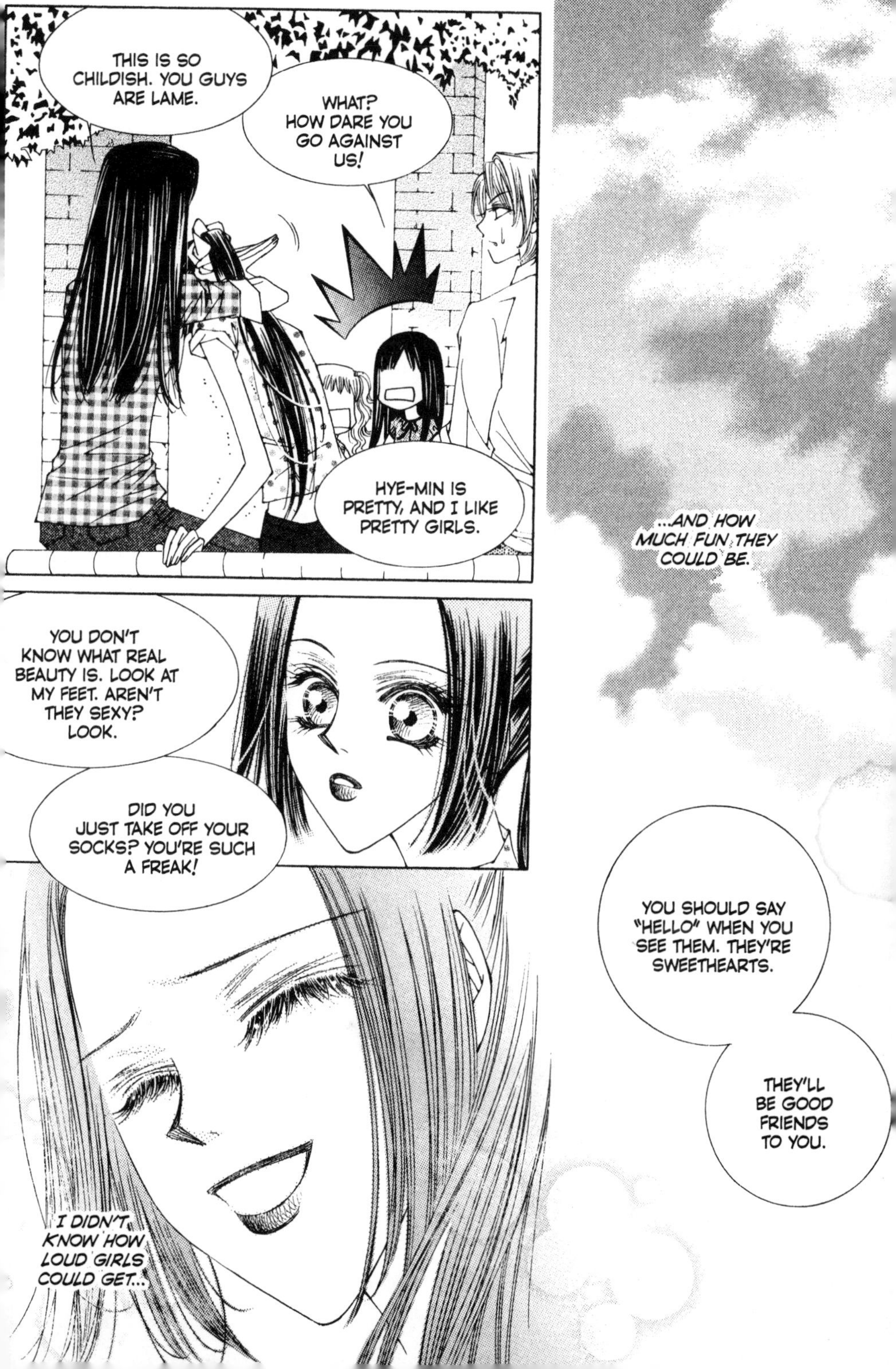
THIS IS SO CHILDISH. YOU GUYS ARE LAME.
WHAT? HOW DARE YOU GO AGAINST US!
HYE-MIN IS PRETTY, AND I LIKE PRETTY GIRLS.
YOU DON'T KNOW WHAT REAL BEAUTY IS. LOOK AT MY FEET. AREN'T THEY SEXY? LOOK.
DID YOU JUST TAKE OFF YOUR SOCKS? YOU'RE SUCH A FREAK!
I DIDN'T KNOW HOW LOUD GIRLS COULD GET...
...AND HOW MUCH FUN THEY COULD BE.
YOU SHOULD SAY "HELLO" WHEN YOU SEE THEM. THEY'RE SWEETHEARTS.
THEY'LL BE GOOD FRIENDS TO YOU.

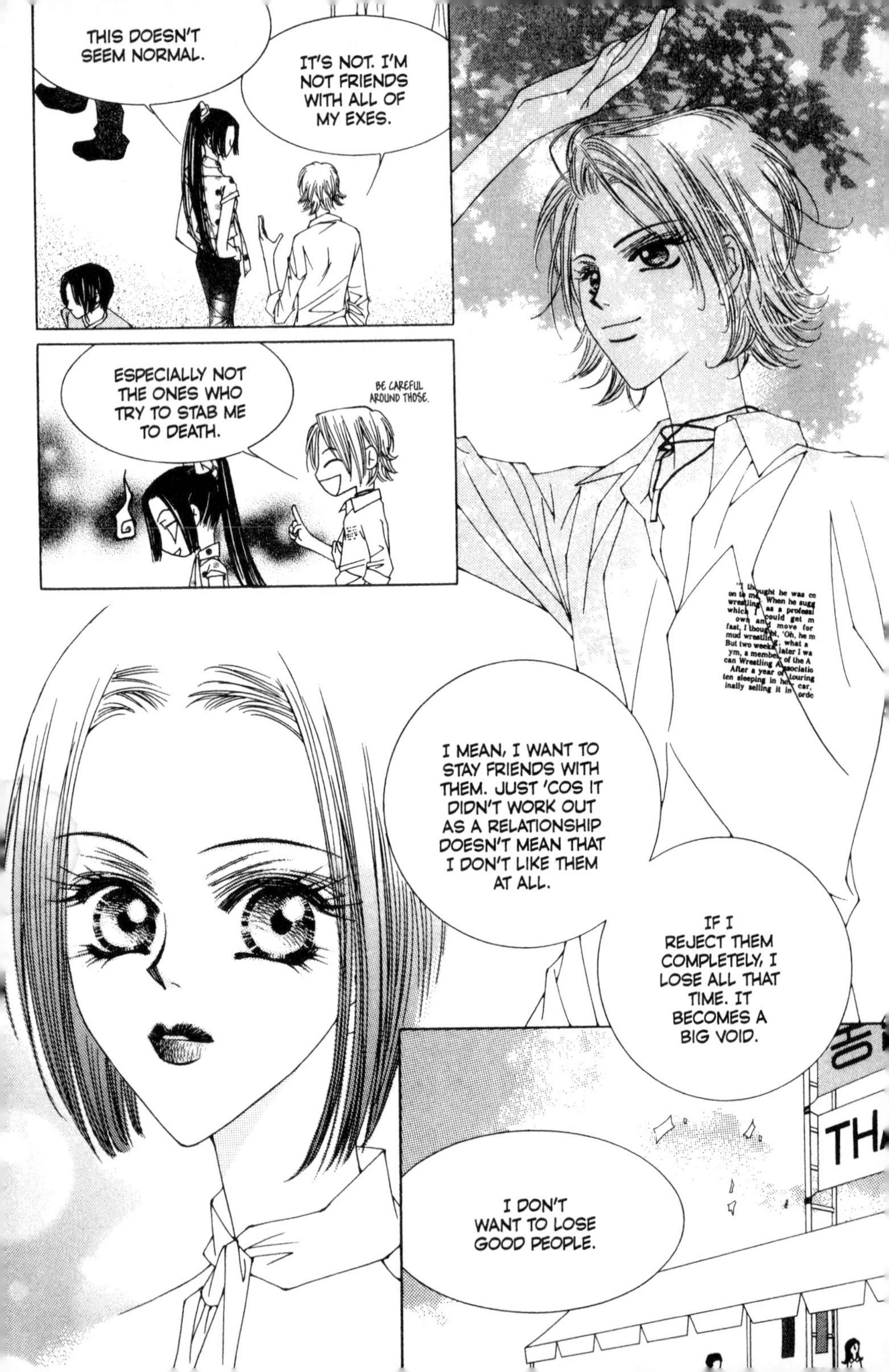
THIS DOESN'T SEEM NORMAL.
IT'S NOT. I'M NOT FRIENDS WITH ALL OF MY EXES.
ESPECIALLY NOT THE ONES WHO TRY TO STAB ME TO DEATH.
BE CAREFUL AROUND THOSE.
I MEAN, I WANT TO STAY FRIENDS WITH THEM. JUST 'COS IT DIDN'T WORK OUT AS A RELATIONSHIP DOESN'T MEAN THAT I DON'T LIKE THEM AT ALL.
IF I REJECT THEM COMPLETELY, I LOSE ALL THAT TIME. IT BECOMES A BIG VOID.
I DON'T WANT TO LOSE GOOD PEOPLE.

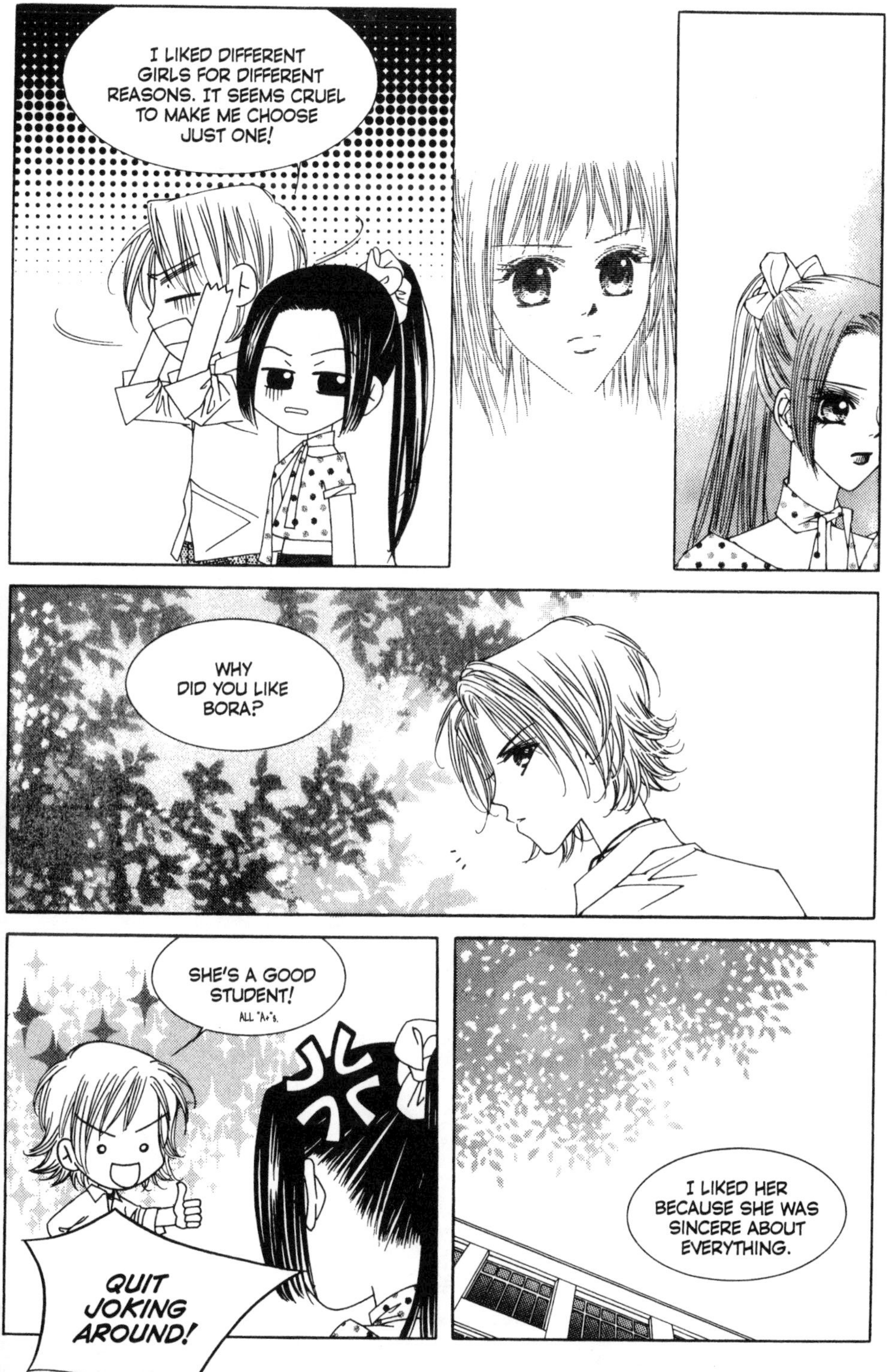
I LIKED DIFFERENT GIRLS FOR DIFFERENT REASONS. IT SEEMS CRUEL TO MAKE ME CHOOSE JUST ONE!
WHY DID YOU LIKE BORA?
SHE'S A GOOD STUDENT!
ALL "A+"s.
QUIT JOKING AROUND!
I LIKED HER BECAUSE SHE WAS SINCERE ABOUT EVERYTHING.

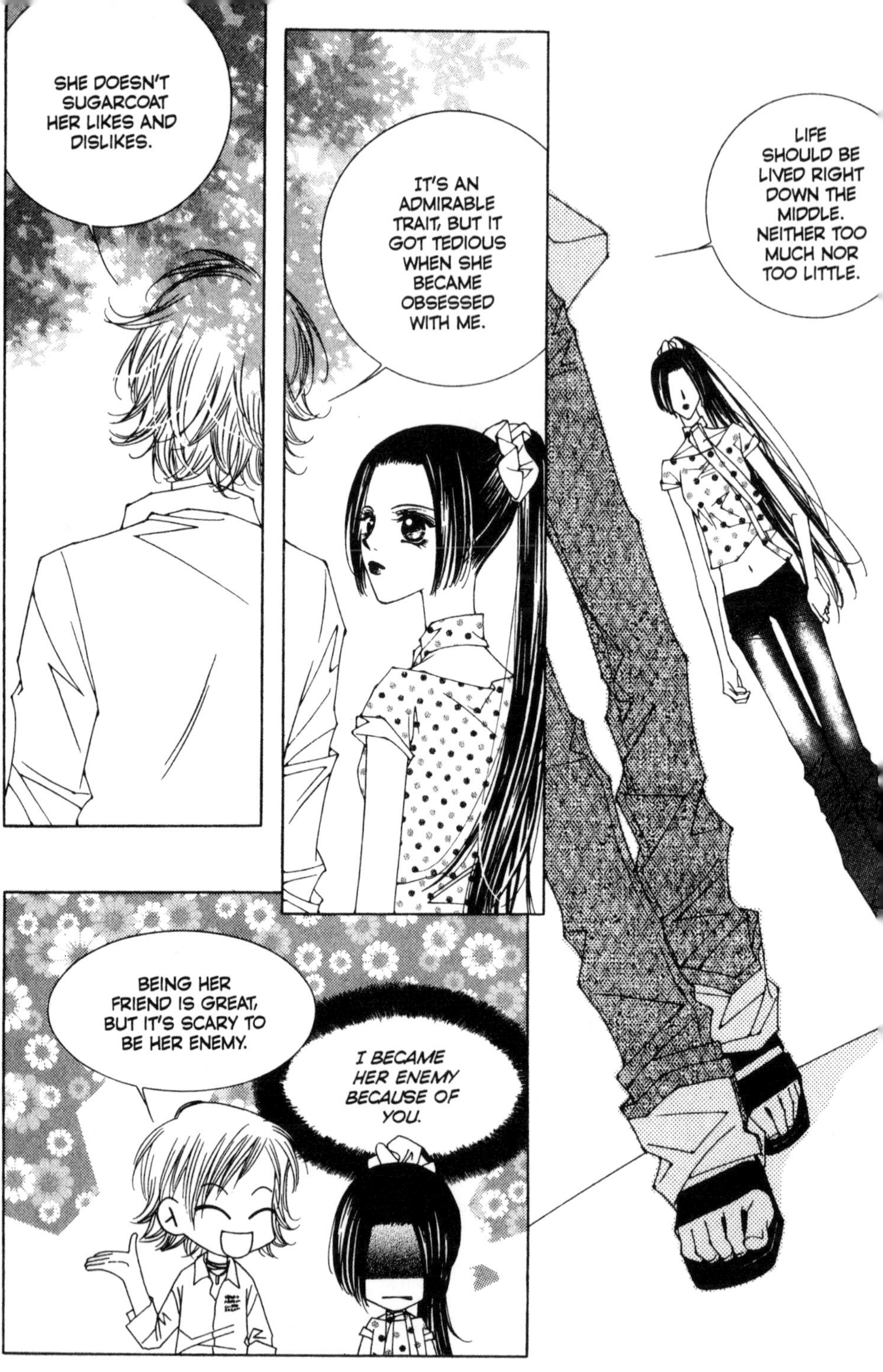
SHE DOESN'T SUGARCOAT HER LIKES AND DISLIKES.
IT'S AN ADMIRABLE TRAIT, BUT IT GOT TEDIOUS WHEN SHE BECAME OBSESSED WITH ME.
LIFE SHOULD BE LIVED RIGHT DOWN THE MIDDLE. NEITHER TOO MUCH NOR TOO LITTLE.
BEING HER FRIEND IS GREAT, BUT IT'S SCARY TO BE HER ENEMY.
I BECAME HER ENEMY BECAUSE OF YOU.

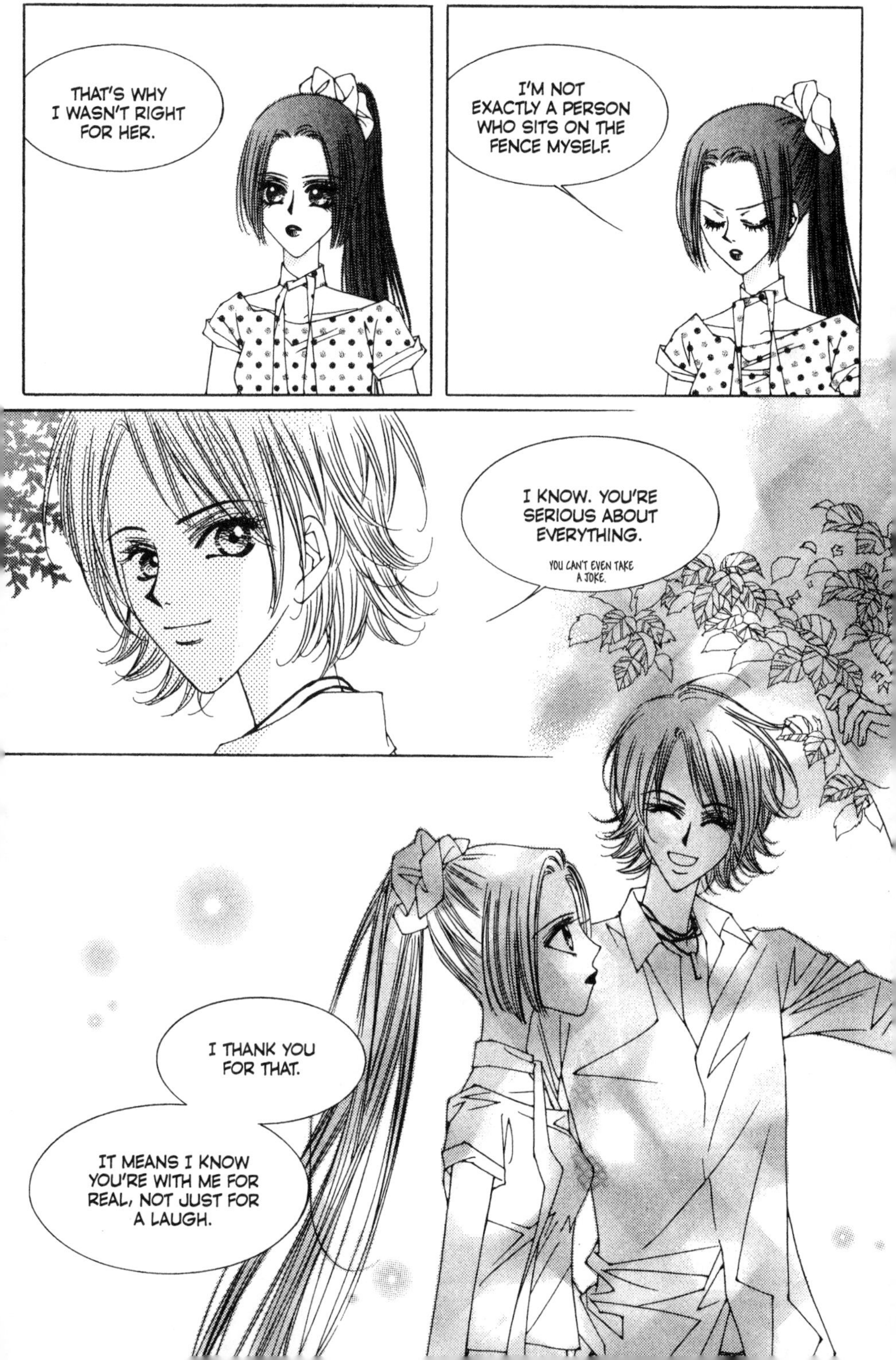
THAT'S WHY I WASN'T RIGHT FOR HER.
I'M NOT EXACTLY A PERSON WHO SITS ON THE FENCE MYSELF.
I KNOW. YOU'RE SERIOUS ABOUT EVERYTHING.
YOU CAN'T EVEN TAKE A JOKE.
I THANK YOU FOR THAT.
IT MEANS I KNOW YOU'RE WITH ME FOR REAL, NOT JUST FOR A LAUGH.

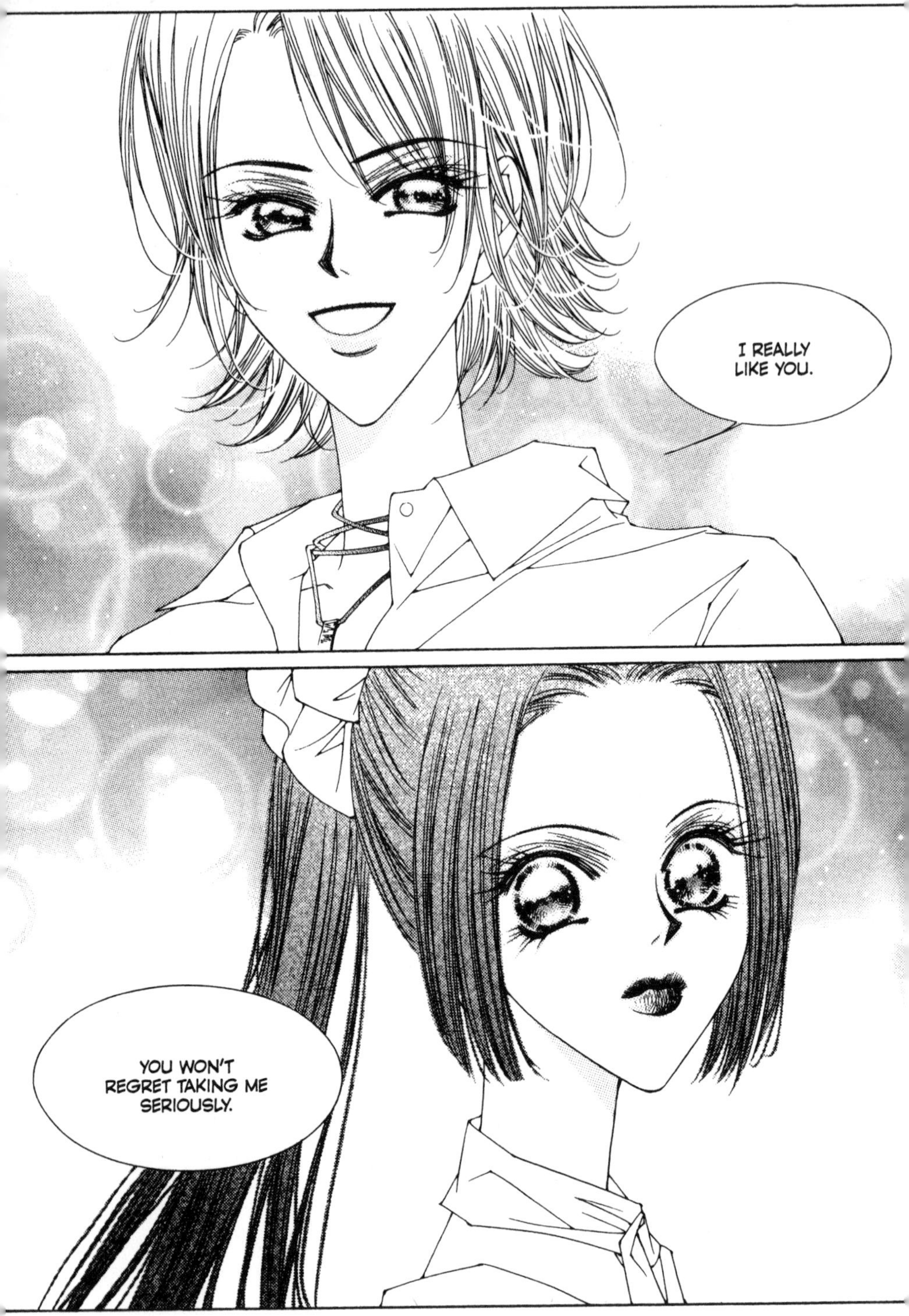
I REALLY LIKE YOU.
YOU WON'T REGRET TAKING ME SERIOUSLY.

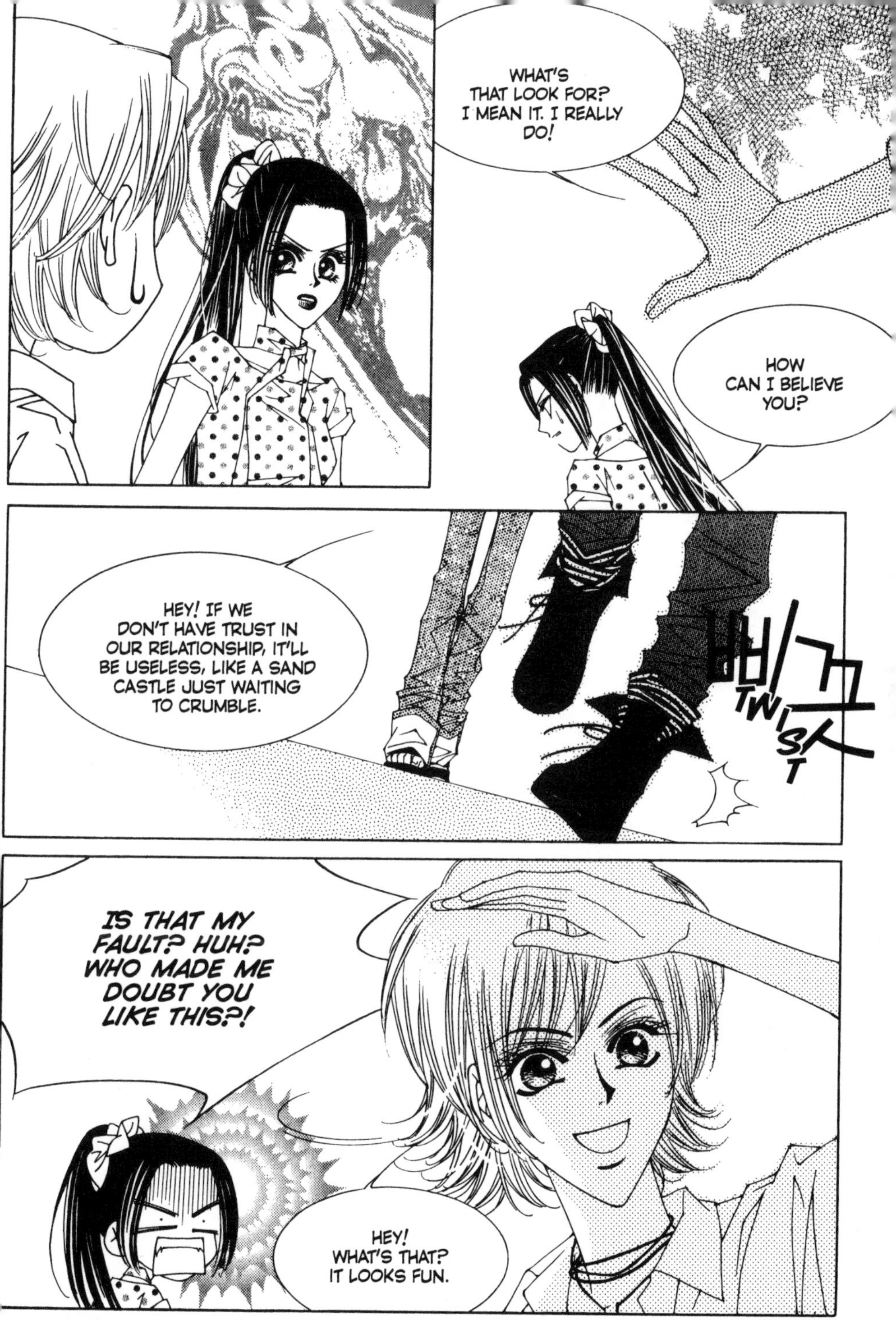
WHAT'S THAT LOOK FOR? I MEAN IT. I REALLY DO!
HOW CAN I BELIEVE YOU?
HEY! IF WE DON'T HAVE TRUST IN OUR RELATIONSHIP, IT'LL BE USELESS, LIKE A SAND CASTLE JUST WAITING TO CRUMBLE.
삐끗
TWIST
IS THAT MY FAULT? HUH? WHO MADE ME DOUBT YOU LIKE THIS?!
HEY! WHAT'S THAT? IT LOOKS FUN.

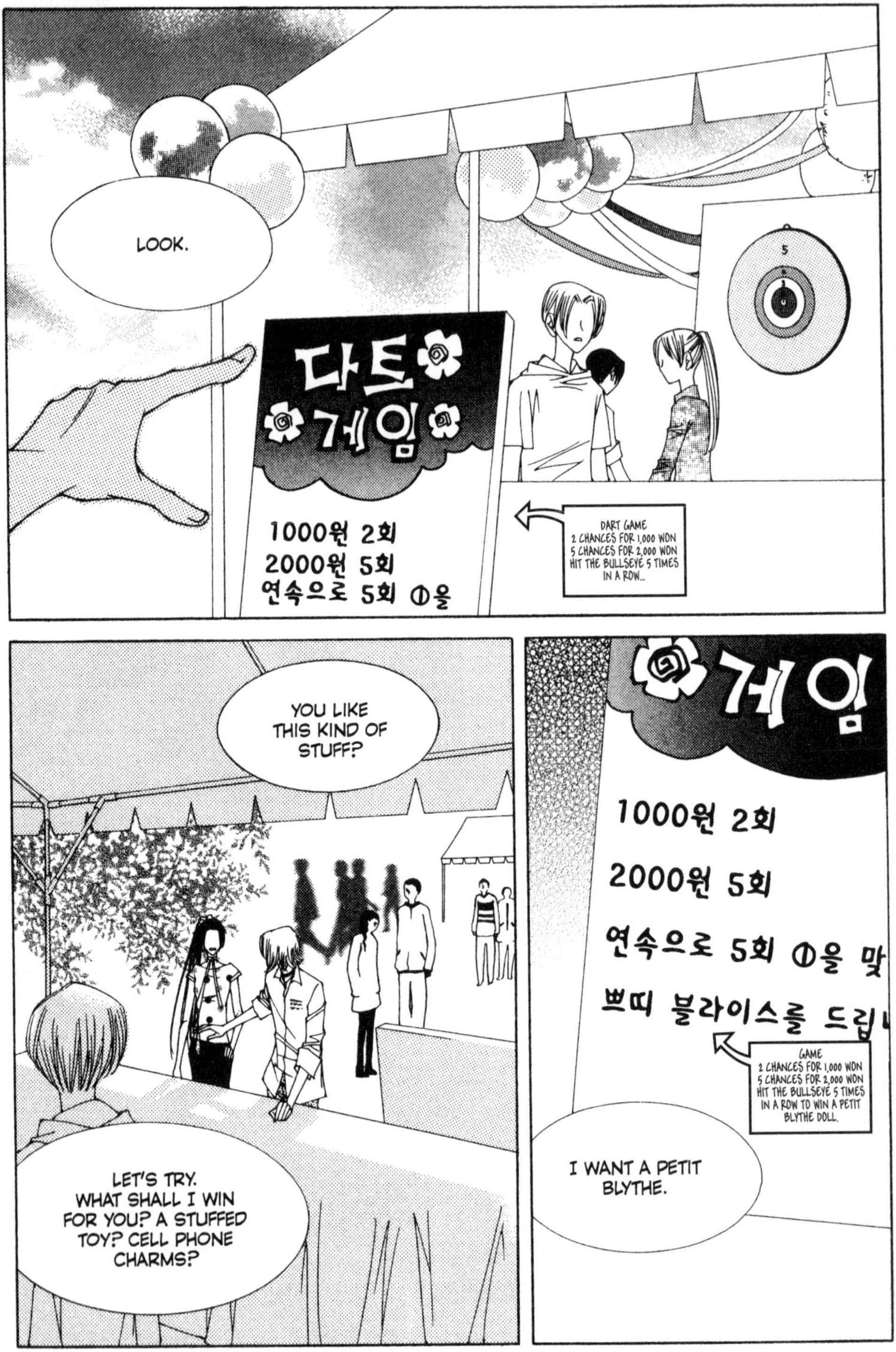
LOOK.
다트 게임
1000원 2회
2000원 5회
연속으로 5회 ①을
DART GAME 2 CHANCES FOR 1,000 WON 5 CHANCES FOR 2,000 WON HIT THE BULLSEYE 5 TIMES IN A ROW...
YOU LIKE THIS KIND OF STUFF?
LET'S TRY. WHAT SHALL I WIN FOR YOU? A STUFFED TOY? CELL PHONE CHARMS?
게임
1000원 2회
2000원 5회
연속으로 5회 ①을 맞
쁘띠 블라이스를 드립
GAME 2 CHANCES FOR 1,000 WON 5 CHANCES FOR 2,000 WON HIT THE BULLSEYE 5 TIMES IN A ROW TO WIN A PETIT BLYTHE DOLL.
I WANT A PETIT BLYTHE.

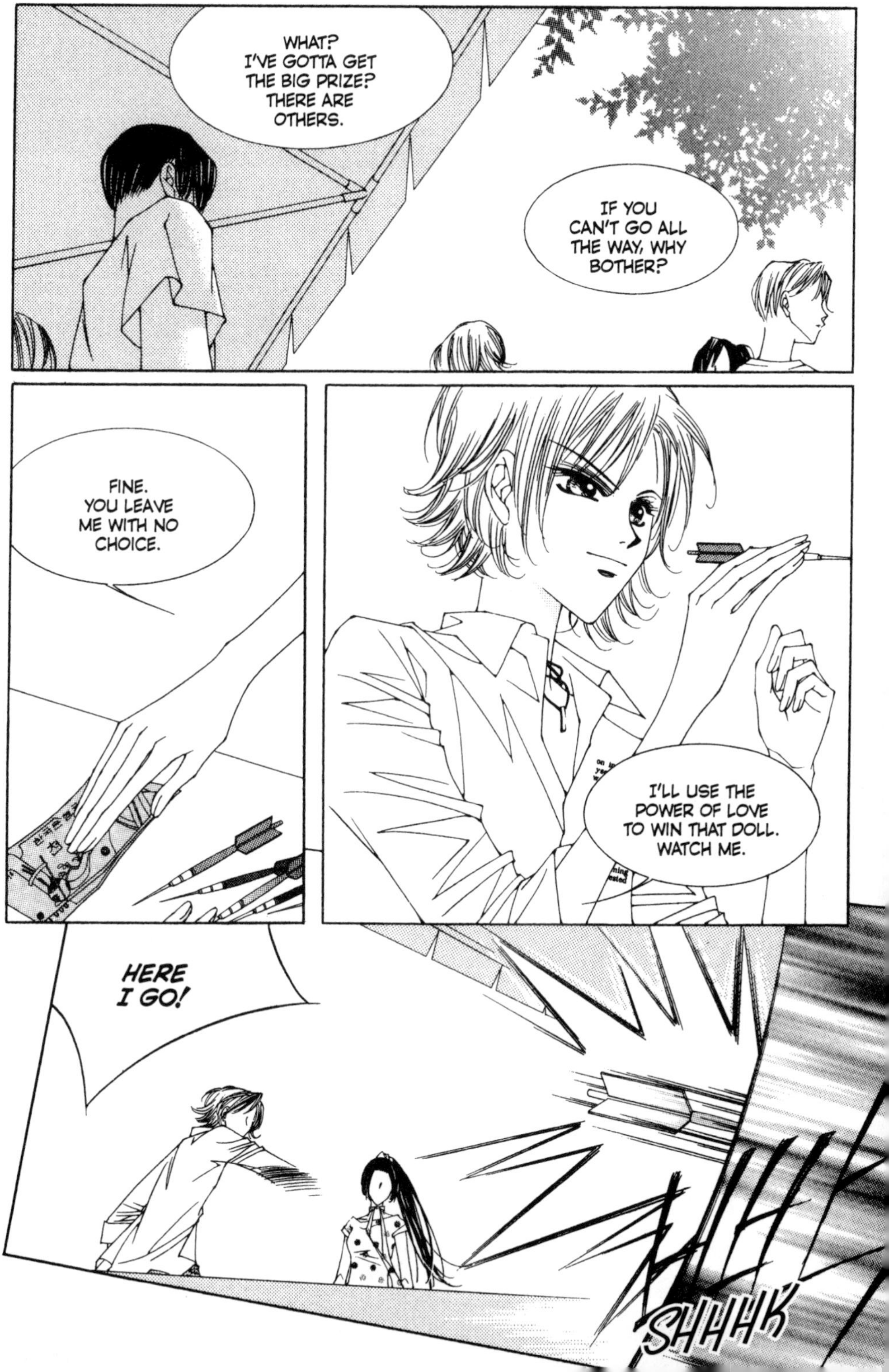
WHAT? I'VE GOTTA GET THE BIG PRIZE? THERE ARE OTHERS.
IF YOU CAN'T GO ALL THE WAY, WHY BOTHER?
FINE. YOU LEAVE ME WITH NO CHOICE.
I'LL USE THE POWER OF LOVE TO WIN THAT DOLL. WATCH ME.
HERE I GO!
SHHHK

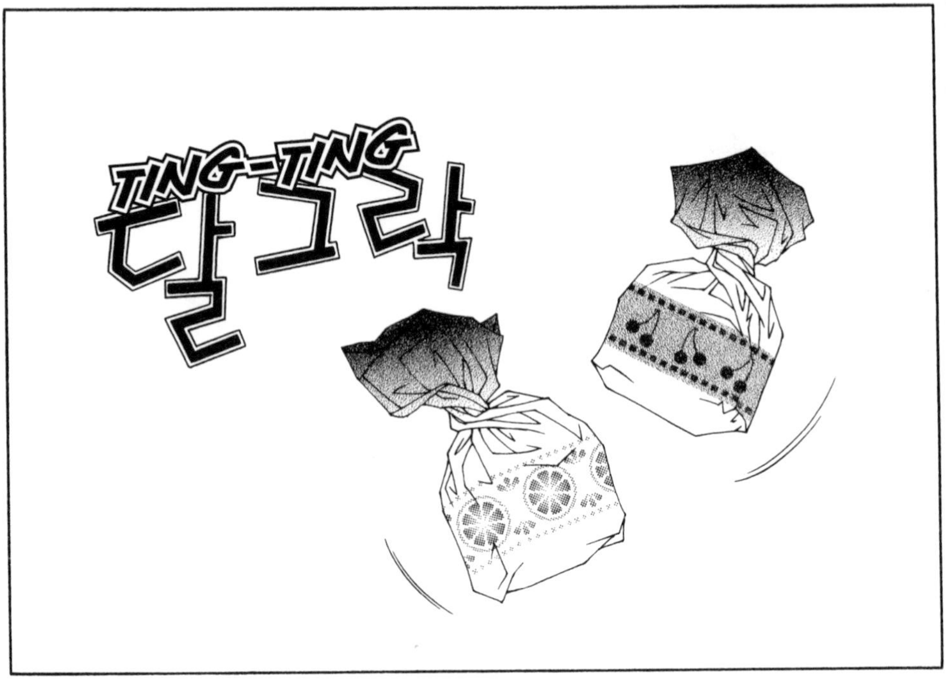
TING-TING
달그락

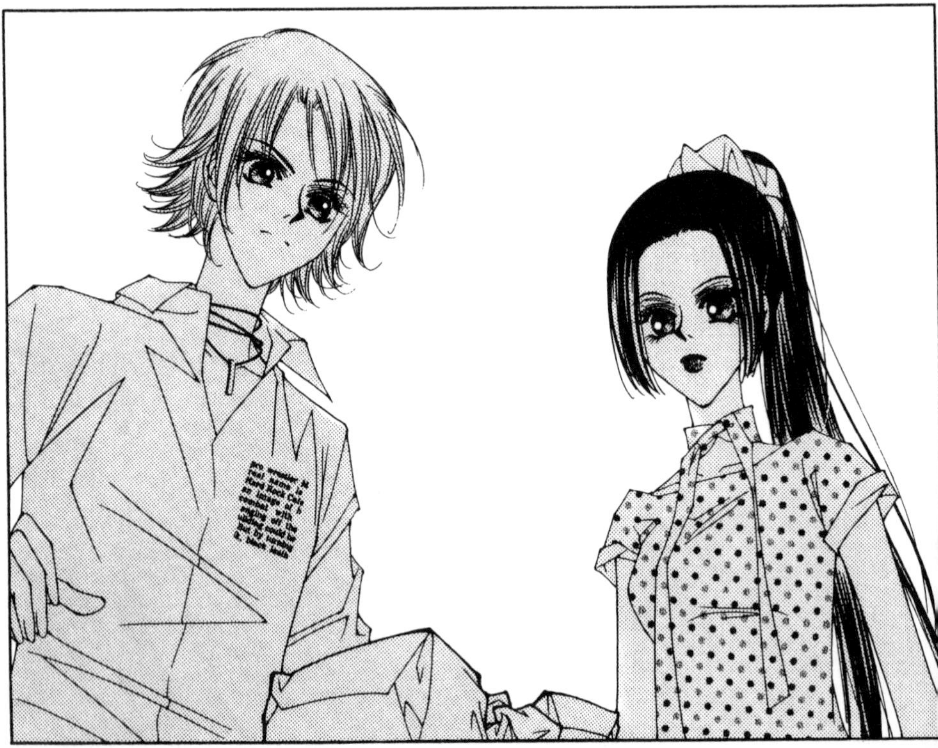

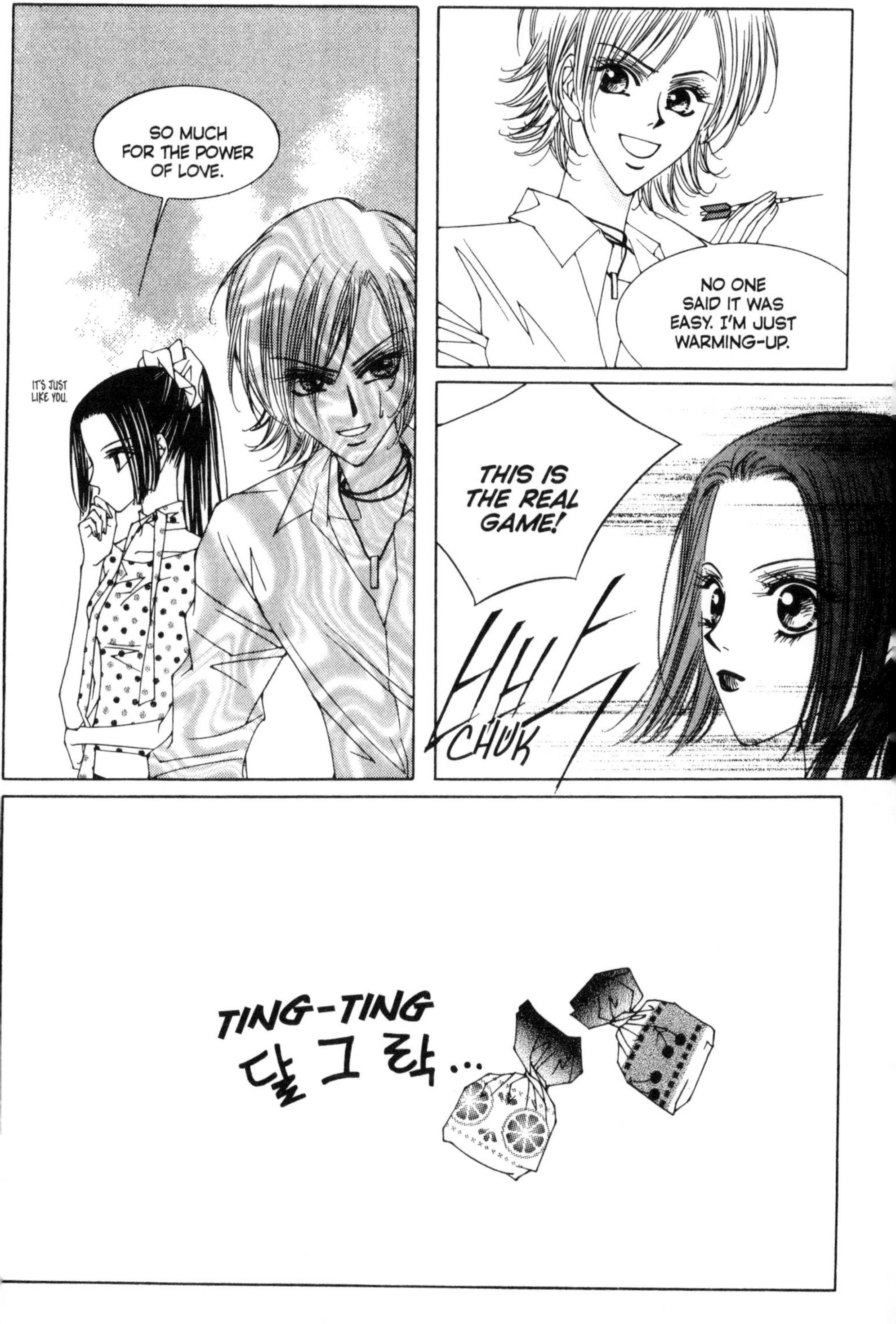
SO MUCH FOR THE POWER OF LOVE.
IT'S JUST LIKE YOU.
NO ONE SAID IT WAS EASY. I'M JUST WARMING-UP.
THIS IS THE REAL GAME!
CHUK
TING-TING
달그락...

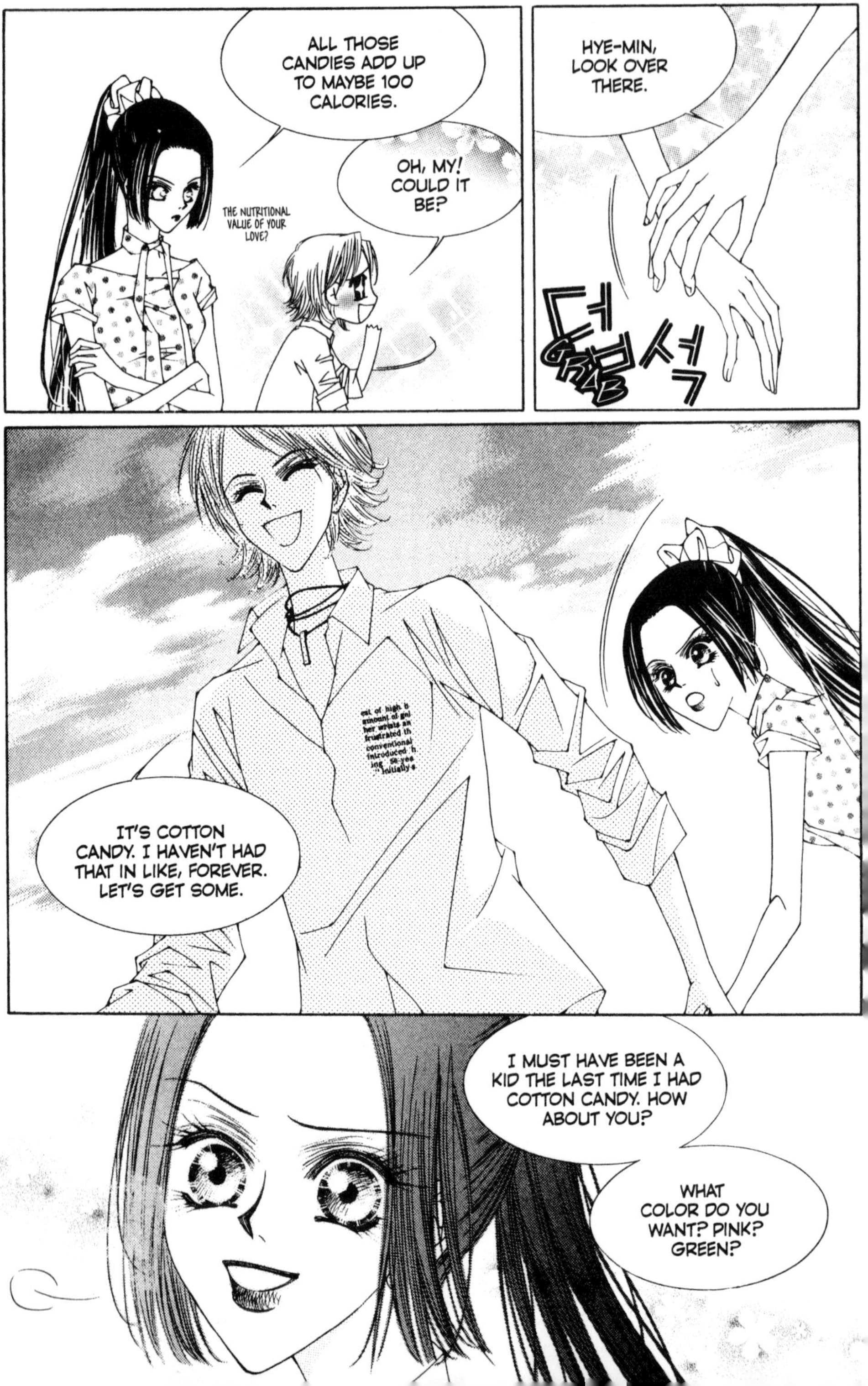
ALL THOSE CANDIES ADD UP TO MAYBE 100 CALORIES.
THE NUTRITIONAL VALUE OF YOUR LOVE?
OH, MY! COULD IT BE?
HYE-MIN, LOOK OVER THERE.
덥석
GRAB
IT'S COTTON CANDY. I HAVEN'T HAD THAT IN LIKE, FOREVER. LET'S GET SOME.
I MUST HAVE BEEN A KID THE LAST TIME I HAD COTTON CANDY. HOW ABOUT YOU?
WHAT COLOR DO YOU WANT? PINK? GREEN?

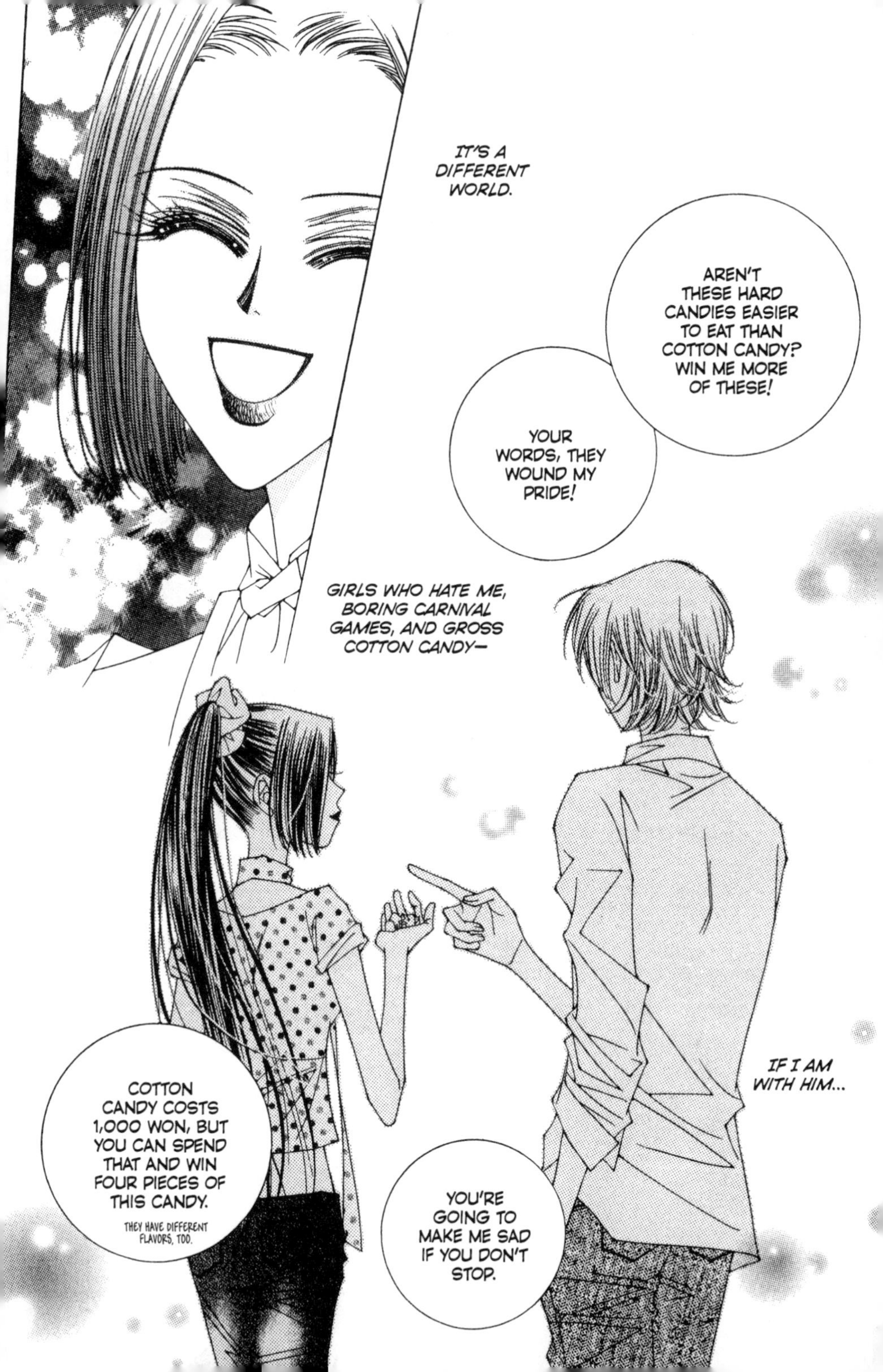
IT'S A DIFFERENT WORLD.
AREN'T THESE HARD CANDIES EASIER TO EAT THAN COTTON CANDY? WIN ME MORE OF THESE!
YOUR WORDS, THEY WOUND MY PRIDE!
GIRLS WHO HATE ME, BORING CARNIVAL GAMES, AND GROSS COTTON CANDY—
IF I AM WITH HIM...
COTTON CANDY COSTS 1,000 WON, BUT YOU CAN SPEND THAT AND WIN FOUR PIECES OF THIS CANDY.
THEY HAVE DIFFERENT FLAVORS, TOO.
YOU'RE GOING TO MAKE ME SAD IF YOU DON'T STOP.

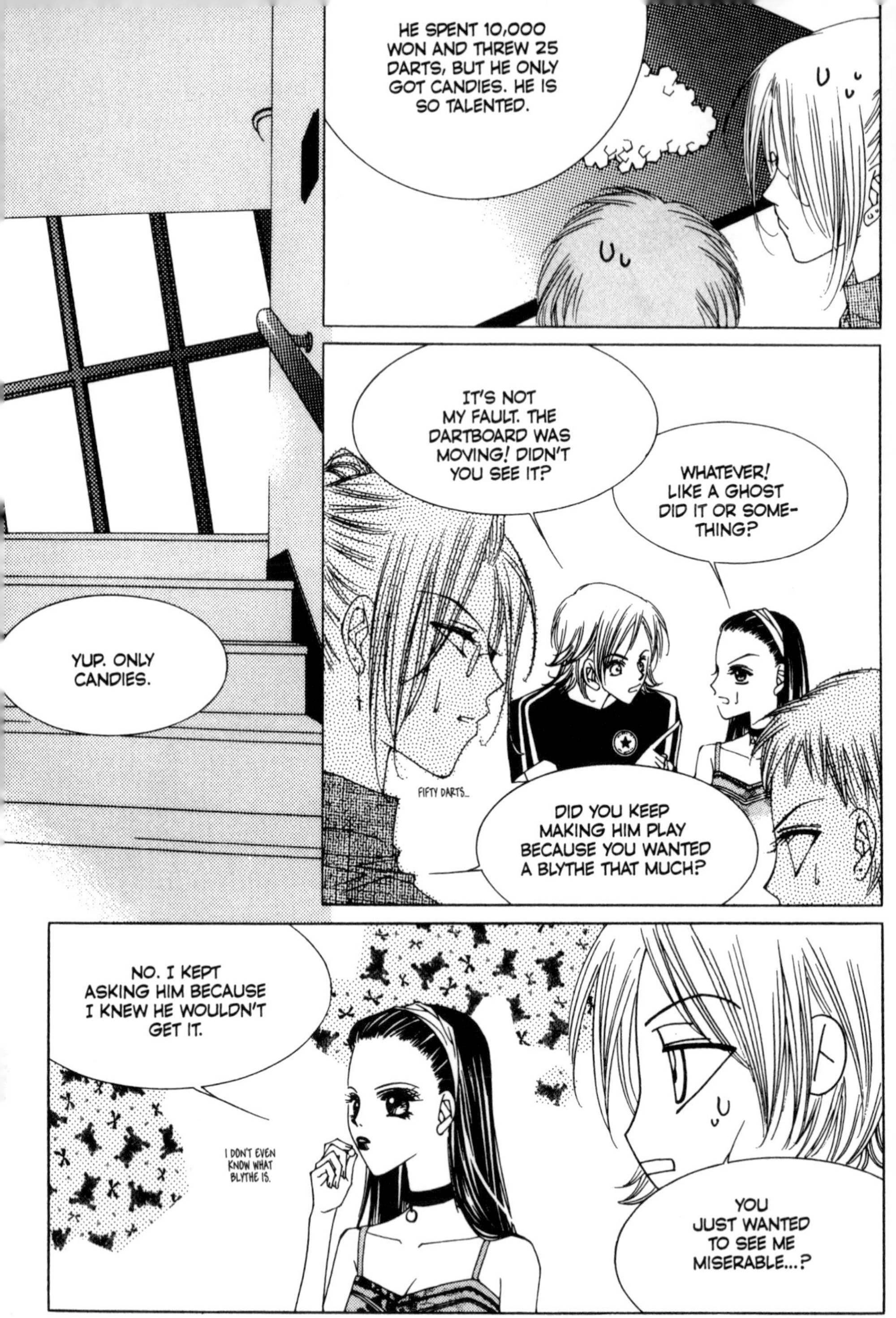
YUP. ONLY CANDIES.
HE SPENT 10,000 WON AND THREW 25 DARTS, BUT HE ONLY GOT CANDIES. HE IS SO TALENTED.
IT'S NOT MY FAULT. THE DARTBOARD WAS MOVING! DIDN'T YOU SEE IT?
WHATEVER! LIKE A GHOST DID IT OR SOME-THING?
FIFTY DARTS...
DID YOU KEEP MAKING HIM PLAY BECAUSE YOU WANTED A BLYTHE THAT MUCH?
NO. I KEPT ASKING HIM BECAUSE I KNEW HE WOULDN'T GET IT.
I DON'T EVEN KNOW WHAT BLYTHE IS.
YOU JUST WANTED TO SEE ME MISERABLE...?

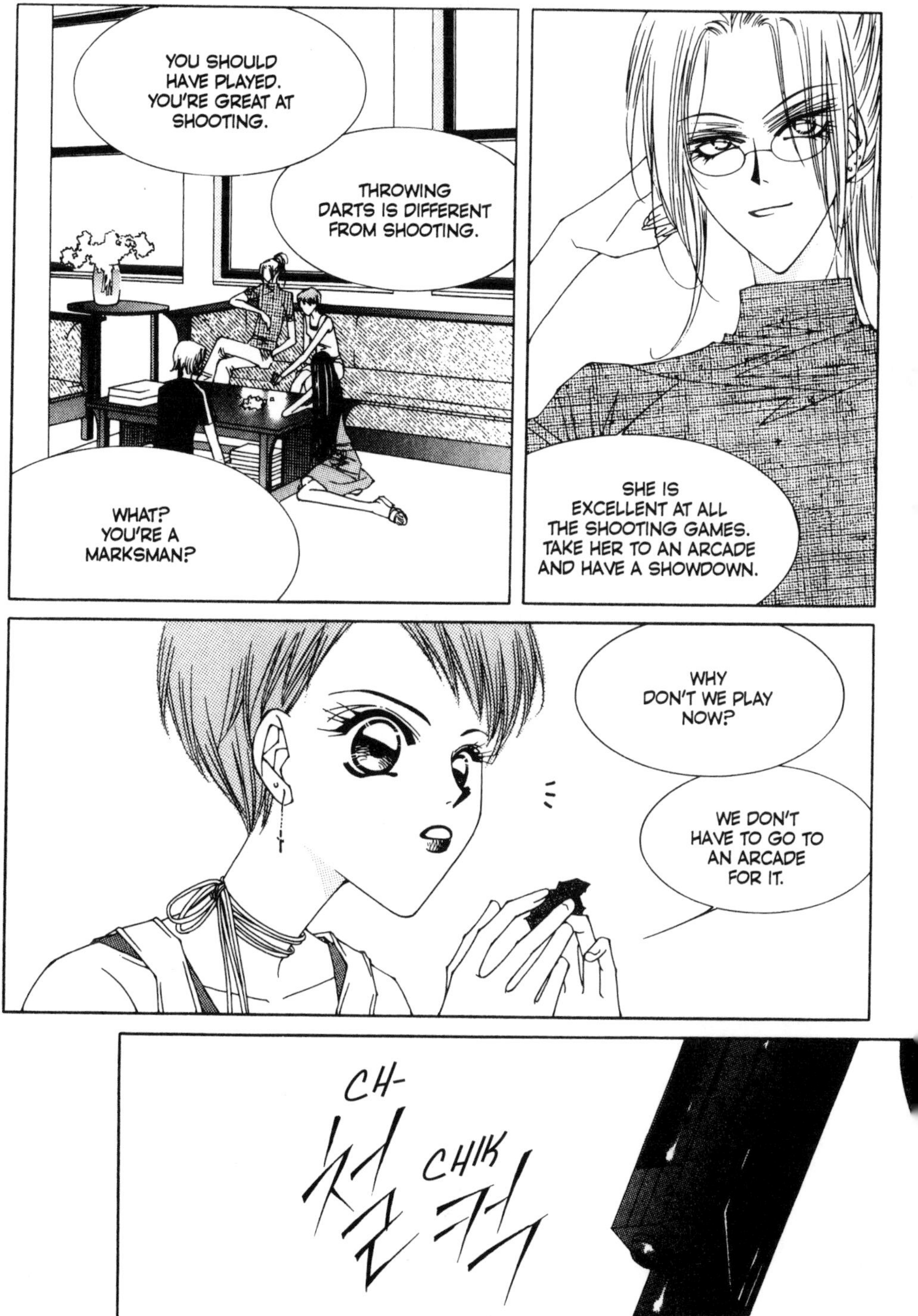
YOU SHOULD HAVE PLAYED. YOU'RE GREAT AT SHOOTING.
THROWING DARTS IS DIFFERENT FROM SHOOTING.
WHAT? YOU'RE A MARKSMAN?
SHE IS EXCELLENT AT ALL THE SHOOTING GAMES. TAKE HER TO AN ARCADE AND HAVE A SHOWDOWN.
WHY DON'T WE PLAY NOW?
WE DON'T HAVE TO GO TO AN ARCADE FOR IT.
CH-
CHIK
철컥

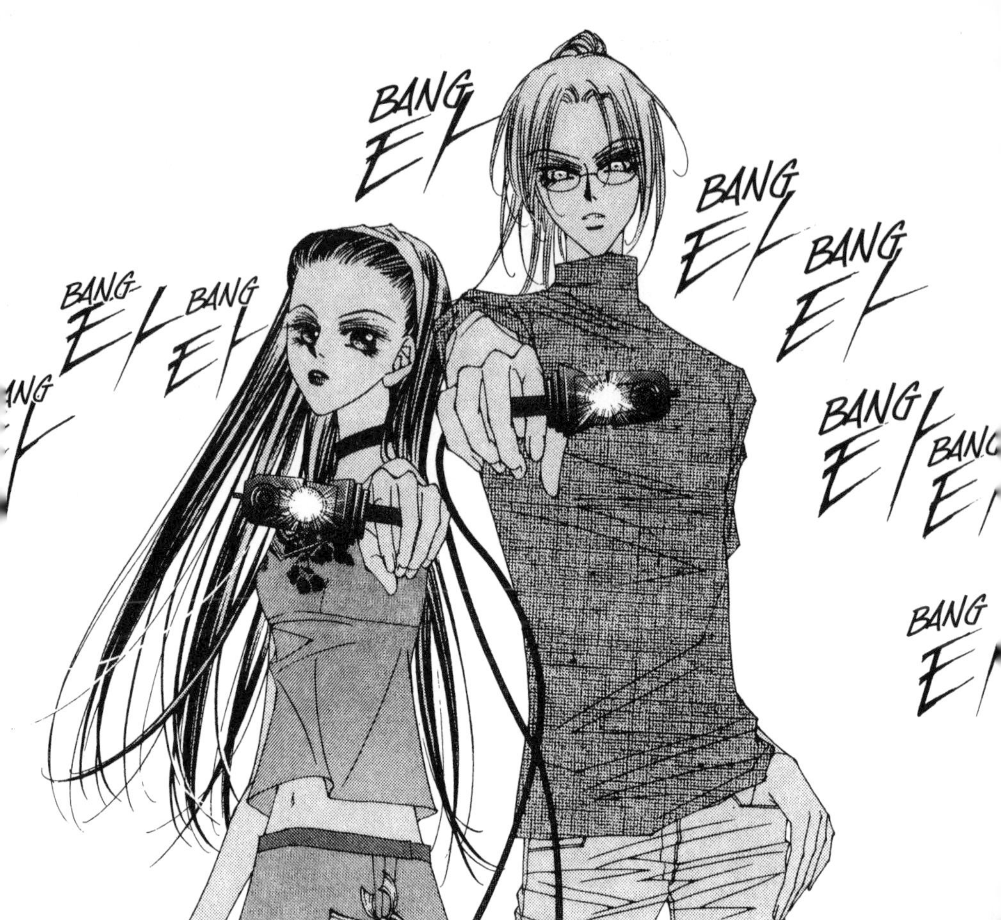
BANG
BANG
BANG
BANG
BANG
BANG
BANG
BANG

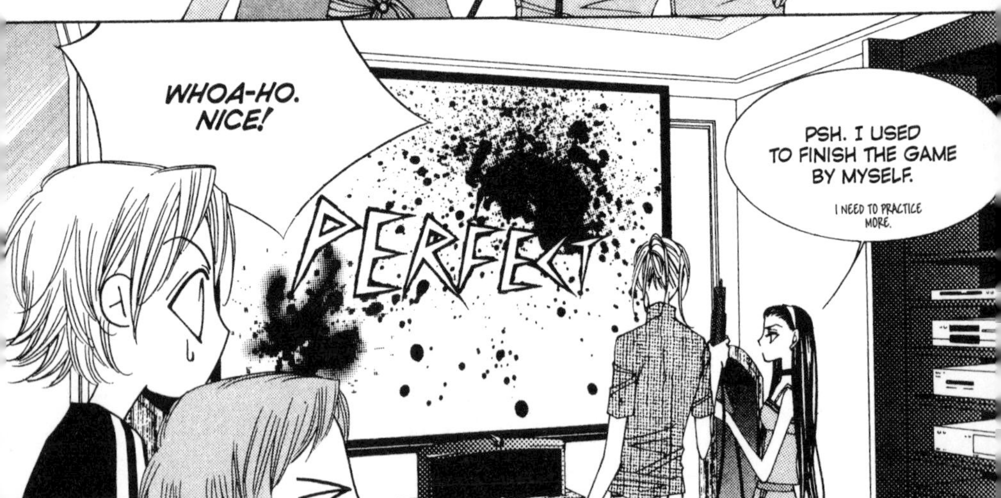
WHOA-HO. NICE!
PERFECT
PSH. I USED TO FINISH THE GAME BY MYSELF.
I NEED TO PRACTICE MORE.

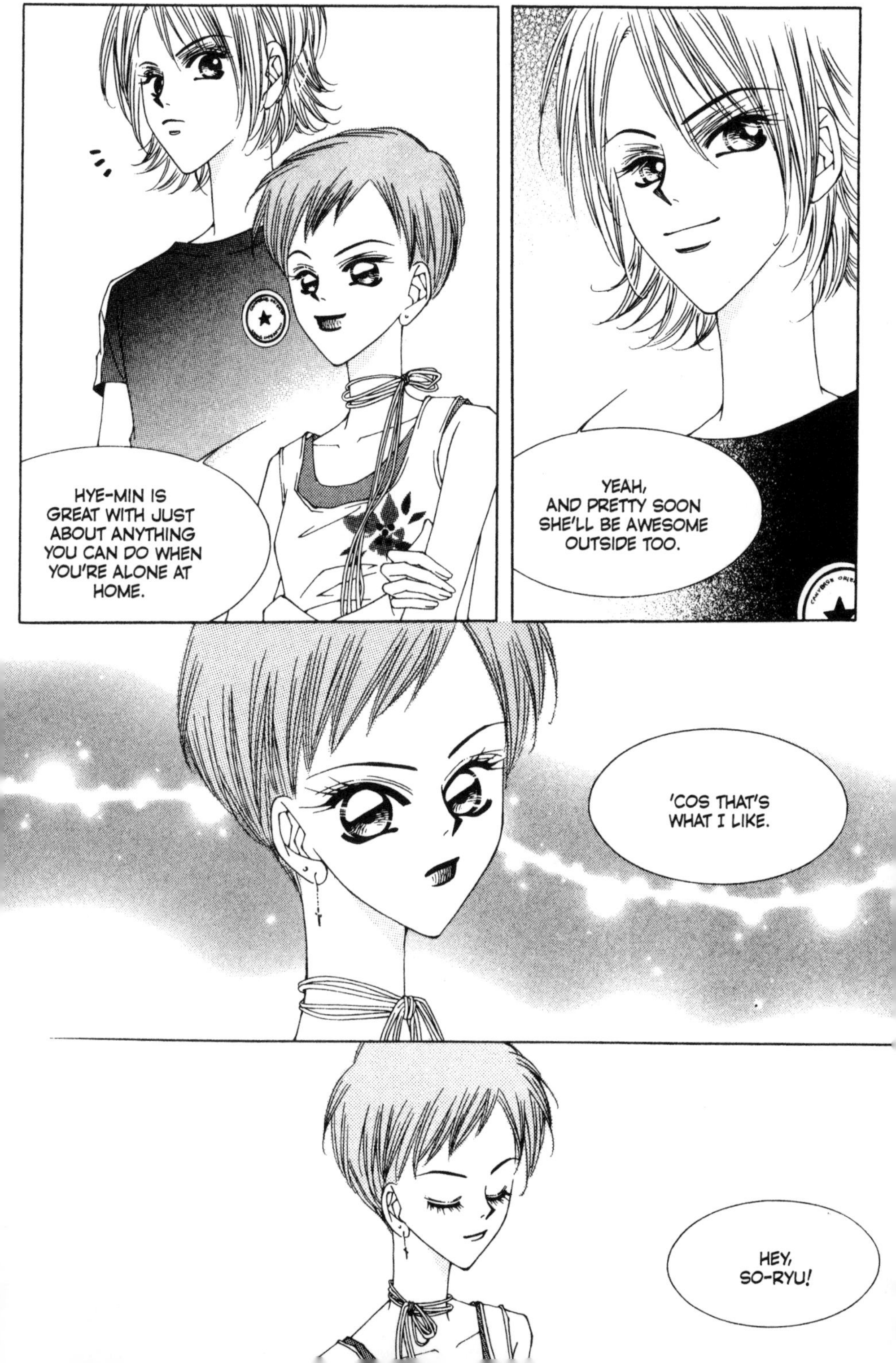
HYE-MIN IS GREAT WITH JUST ABOUT ANYTHING YOU CAN DO WHEN YOU'RE ALONE AT HOME.
YEAH, AND PRETTY SOON SHE'LL BE AWESOME OUTSIDE TOO.
'COS THAT'S WHAT I LIKE.
HEY, SO-RYU!

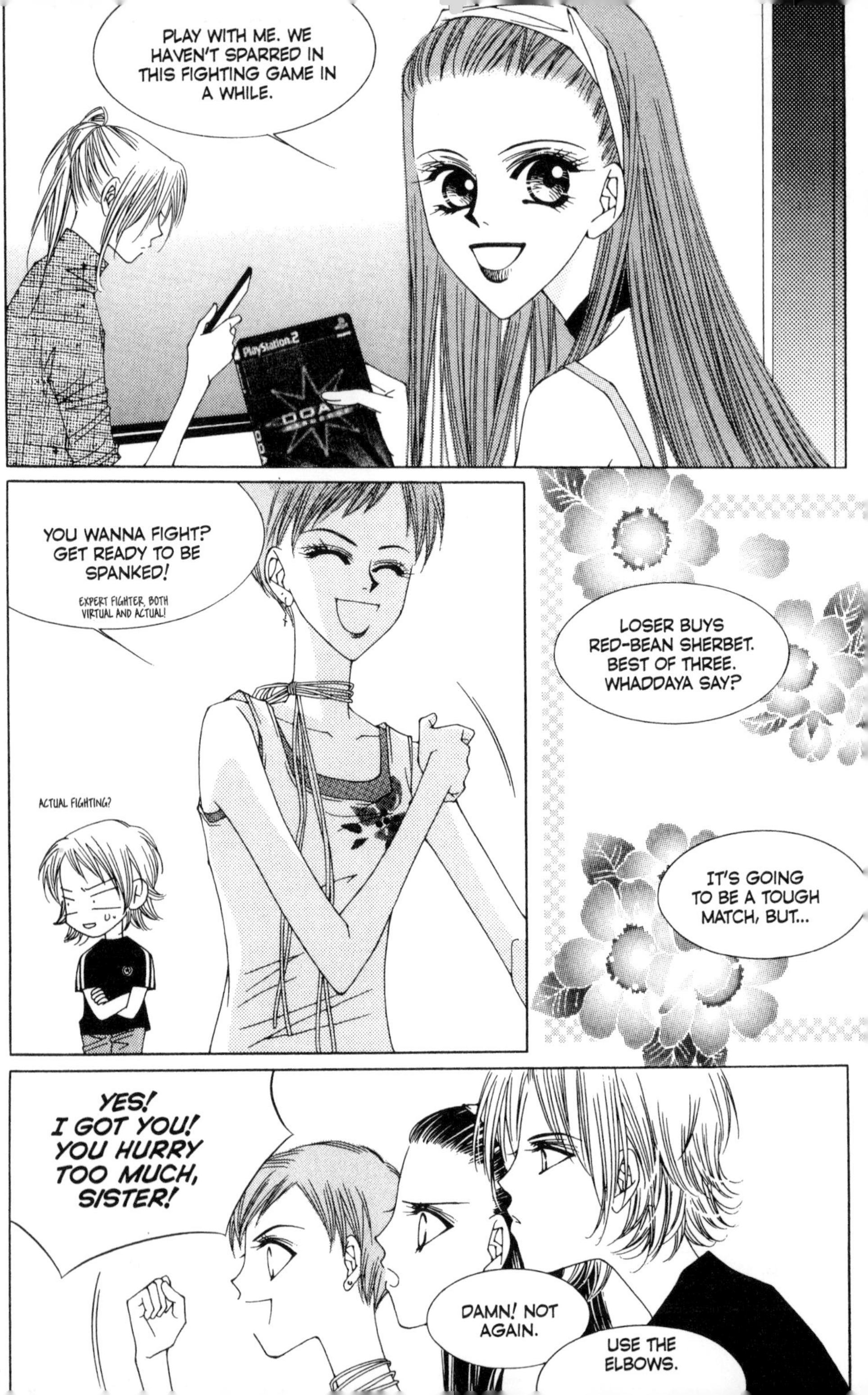
PLAY WITH ME. WE HAVEN'T SPARRED IN THIS FIGHTING GAME IN A WHILE.
PlayStation 2
YOU WANNA FIGHT? GET READY TO BE SPANKED!
EXPERT FIGHTER, BOTH VIRTUAL AND ACTUAL!
ACTUAL FIGHTING?
LOSER BUYS RED-BEAN SHERBET. BEST OF THREE. WHADDAYA SAY?
IT'S GOING TO BE A TOUGH MATCH, BUT...
YES! I GOT YOU! YOU HURRY TOO MUCH, SISTER!
DAMN! NOT AGAIN.
USE THE ELBOWS.

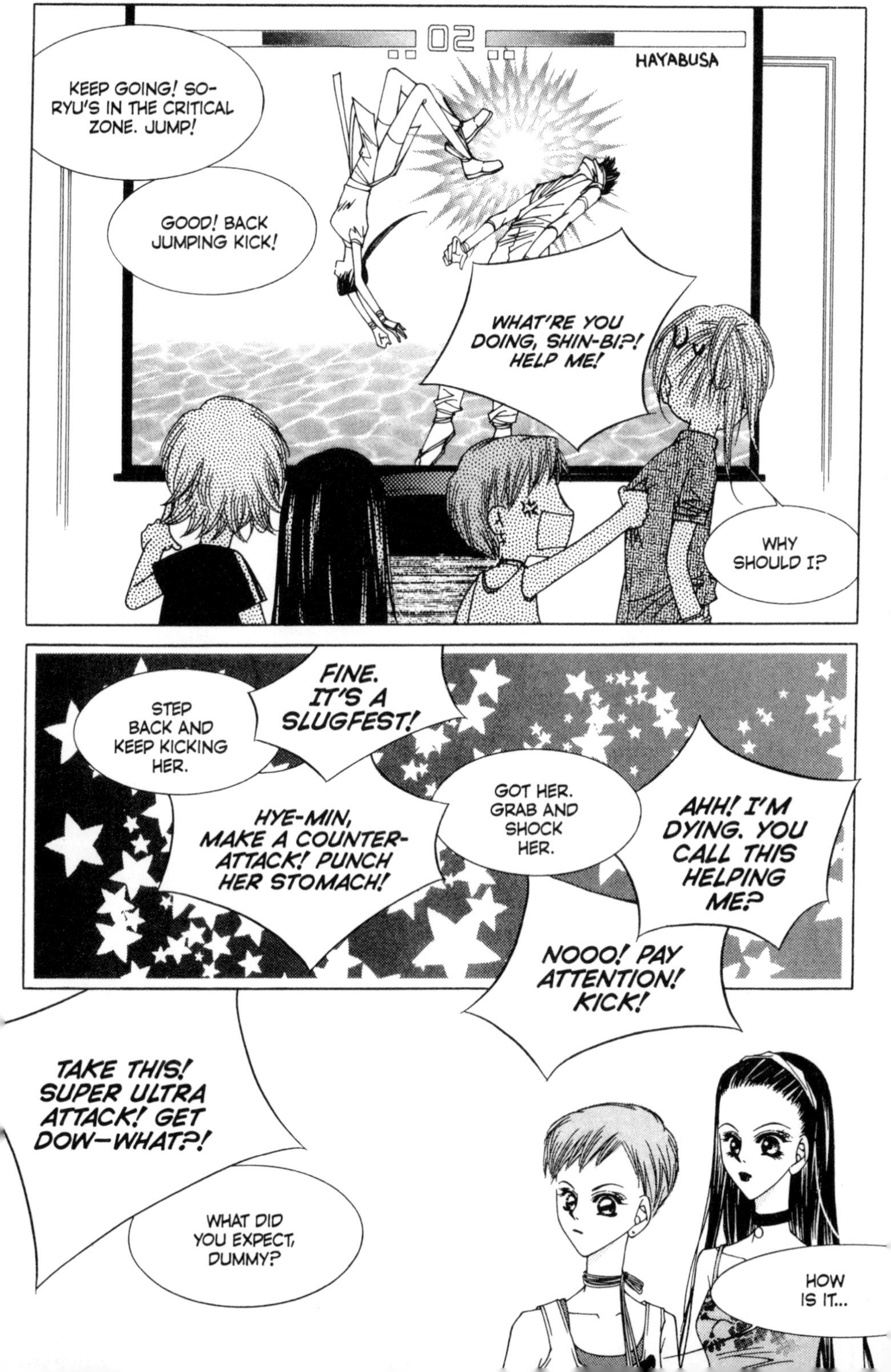
02
HAYABUSA
KEEP GOING! SO-RYU'S IN THE CRITICAL ZONE. JUMP!
GOOD! BACK JUMPING KICK!
WHAT'RE YOU DOING, SHIN-BI?! HELP ME!
WHY SHOULD I?
STEP BACK AND KEEP KICKING HER.
FINE. IT'S A SLUGFEST!
HYE-MIN, MAKE A COUNTER-ATTACK! PUNCH HER STOMACH!
GOT HER. GRAB AND SHOCK HER.
AHH! I'M DYING. YOU CALL THIS HELPING ME?
NOOO! PAY ATTENTION! KICK!
TAKE THIS! SUPER ULTRA ATTACK! GET DOW—WHAT?!
WHAT DID YOU EXPECT, DUMMY?
HOW IS IT...

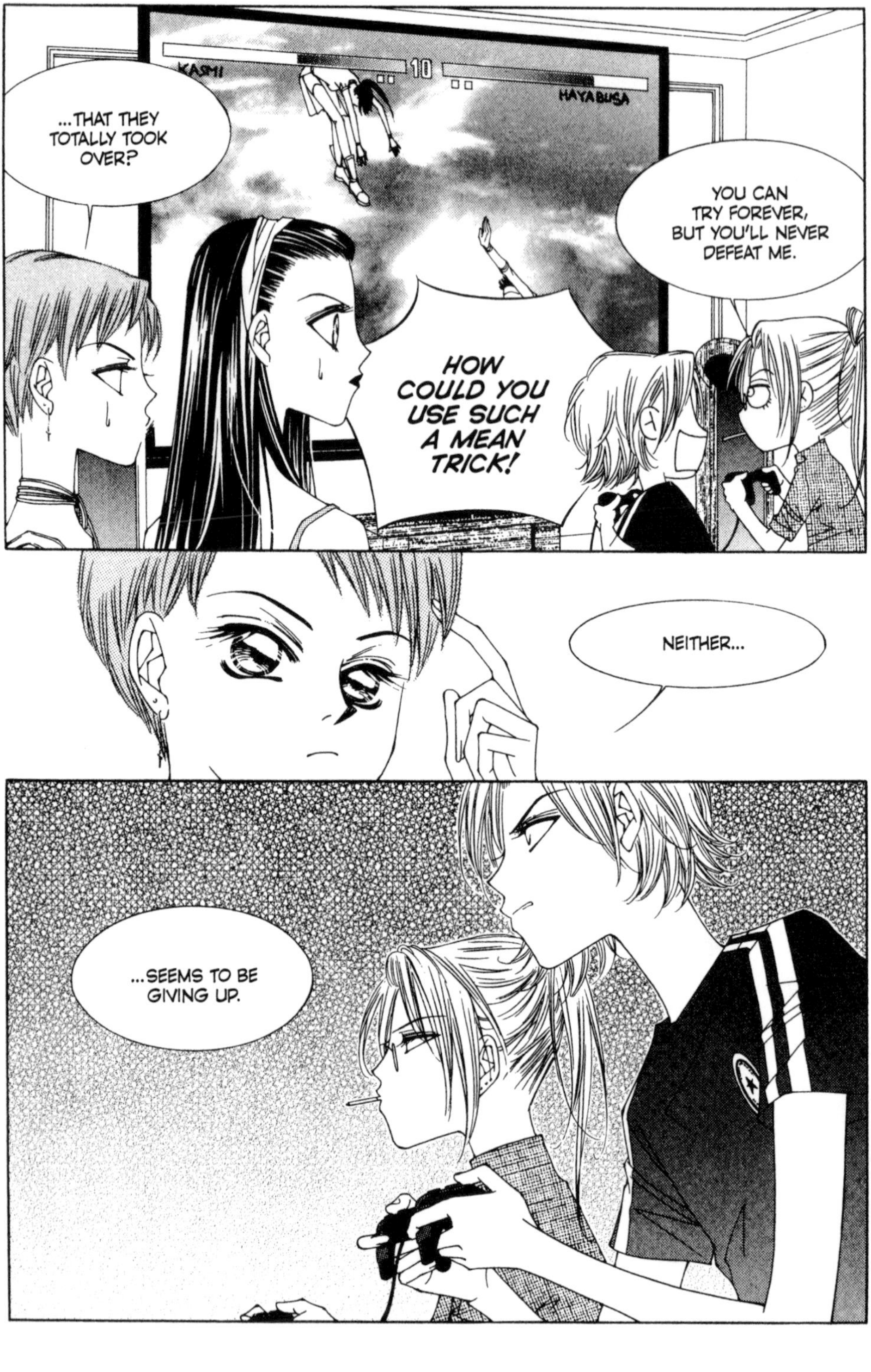
KASMI
10
HAYABUSA
...THAT THEY TOTALLY TOOK OVER?
HOW COULD YOU USE SUCH A MEAN TRICK!
YOU CAN TRY FOREVER, BUT YOU'LL NEVER DEFEAT ME.
NEITHER...
...SEEMS TO BE GIVING UP.

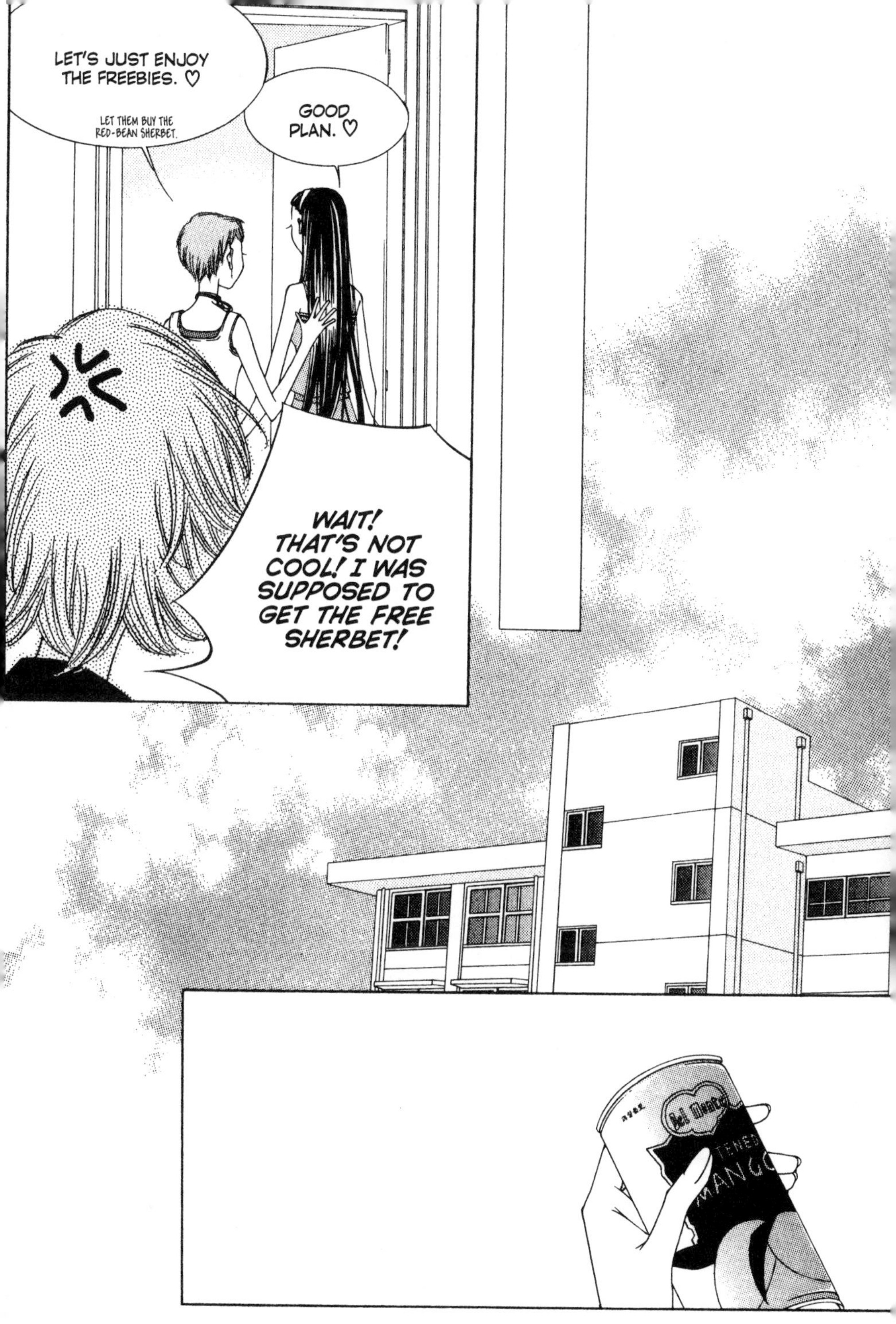
LET'S JUST ENJOY THE FREEBIES. ♡
LET THEM BUY THE RED-BEAN SHERBET.
GOOD PLAN. ♡
WAIT! THAT'S NOT COOL! I WAS SUPPOSED TO GET THE FREE SHERBET!

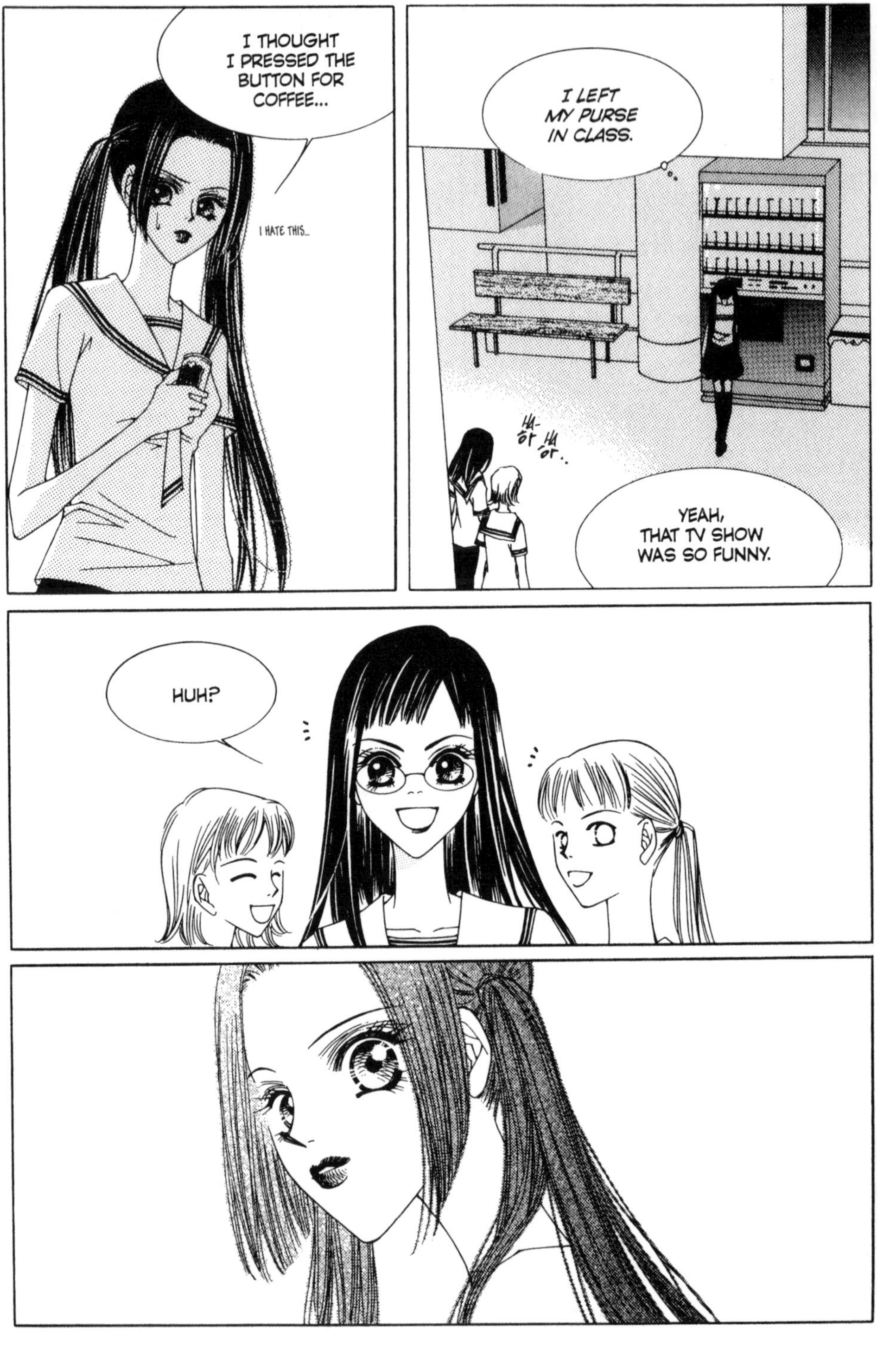
I THOUGHT I PRESSED THE BUTTON FOR COFFEE...
I HATE THIS...
I LEFT MY PURSE IN CLASS.
HA- HA..
YEAH, THAT TV SHOW WAS SO FUNNY.
HUH?

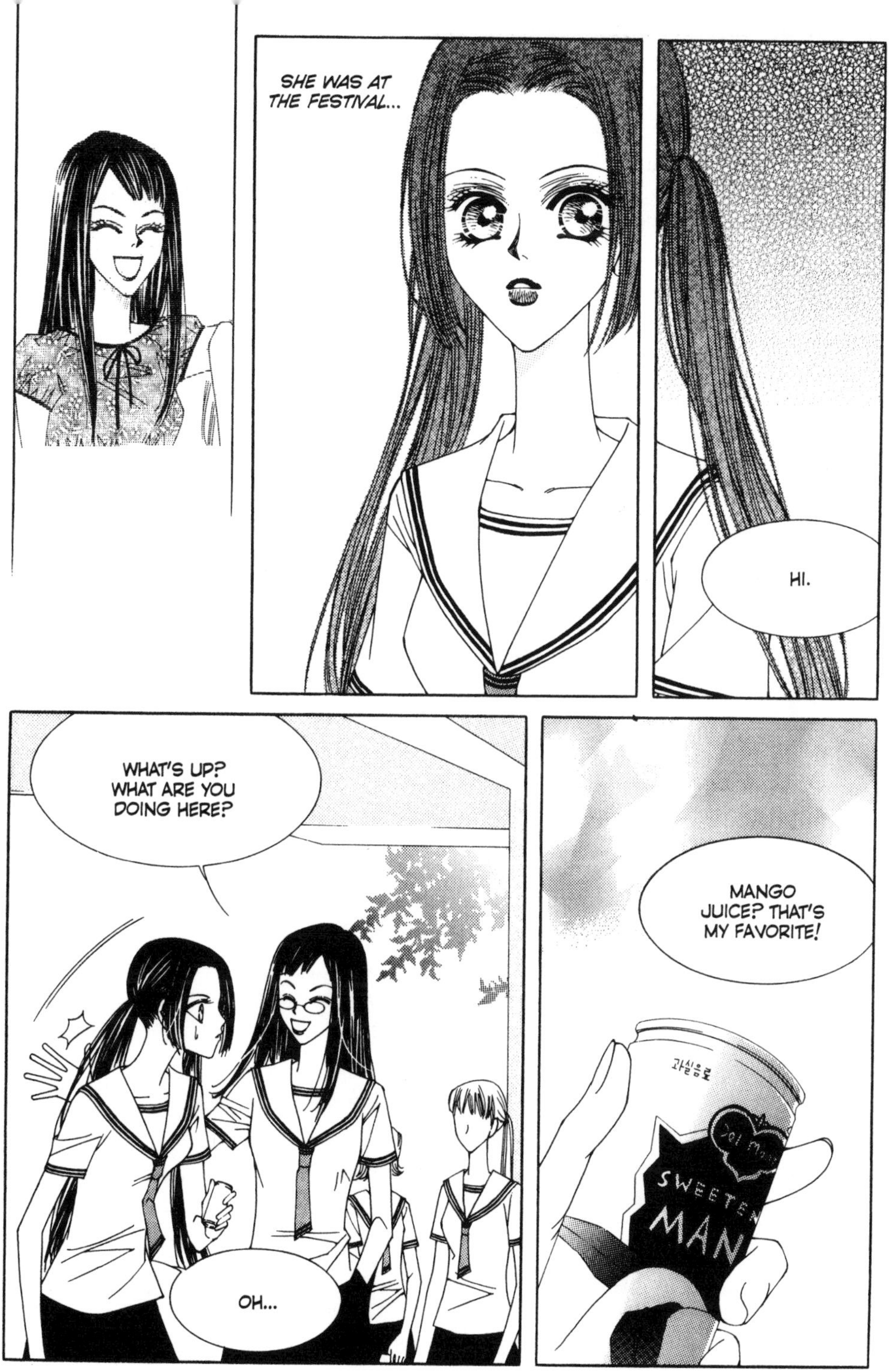
SHE WAS AT THE FESTIVAL...
HI.
WHAT'S UP? WHAT ARE YOU DOING HERE?
OH...
MANGO JUICE? THAT'S MY FAVORITE!

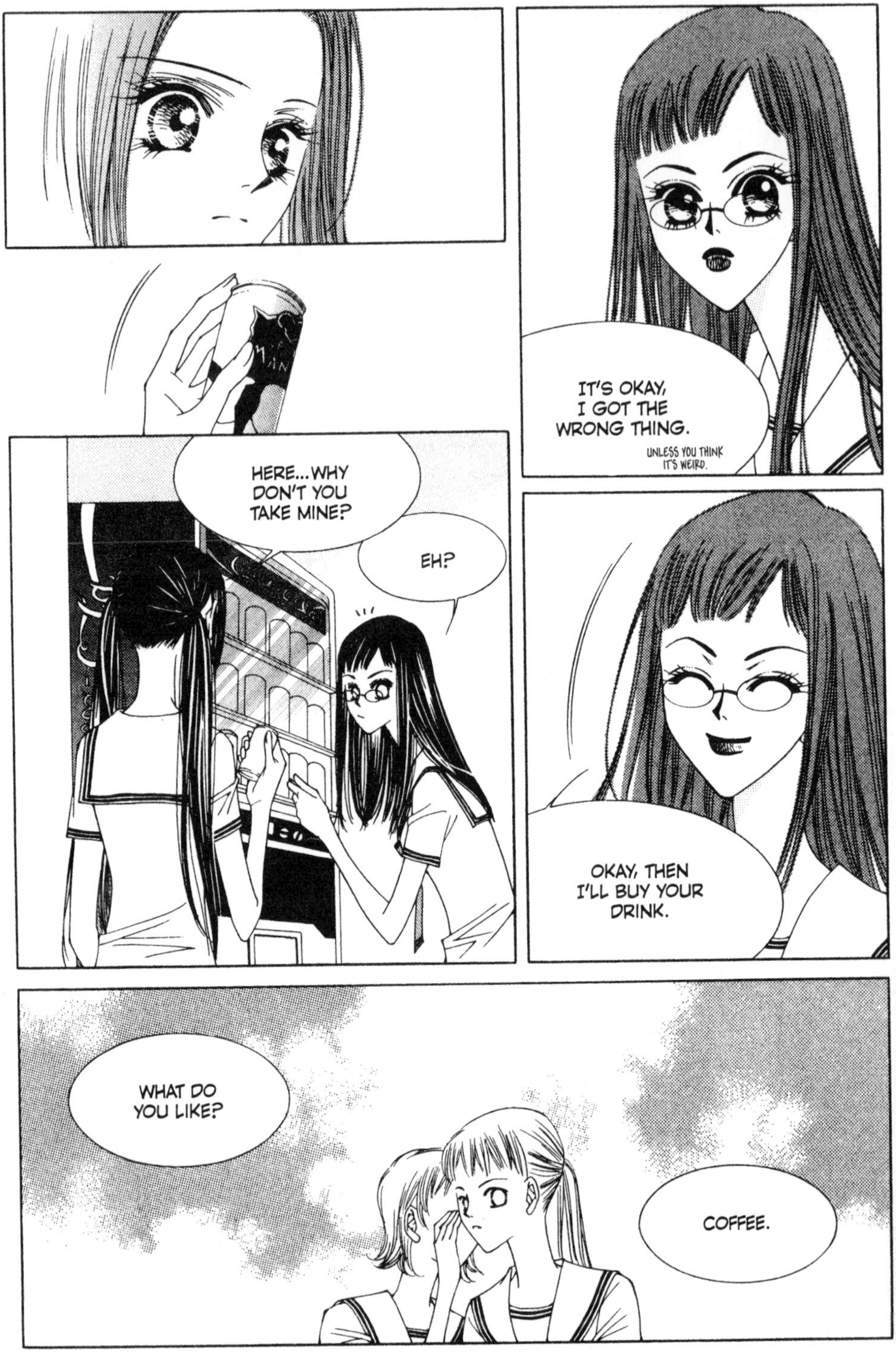
HERE...WHY DON'T YOU TAKE MINE?
EH?
IT'S OKAY, I GOT THE WRONG THING.
UNLESS YOU THINK IT'S WEIRD.
OKAY, THEN I'LL BUY YOUR DRINK.
WHAT DO YOU LIKE?
COFFEE.

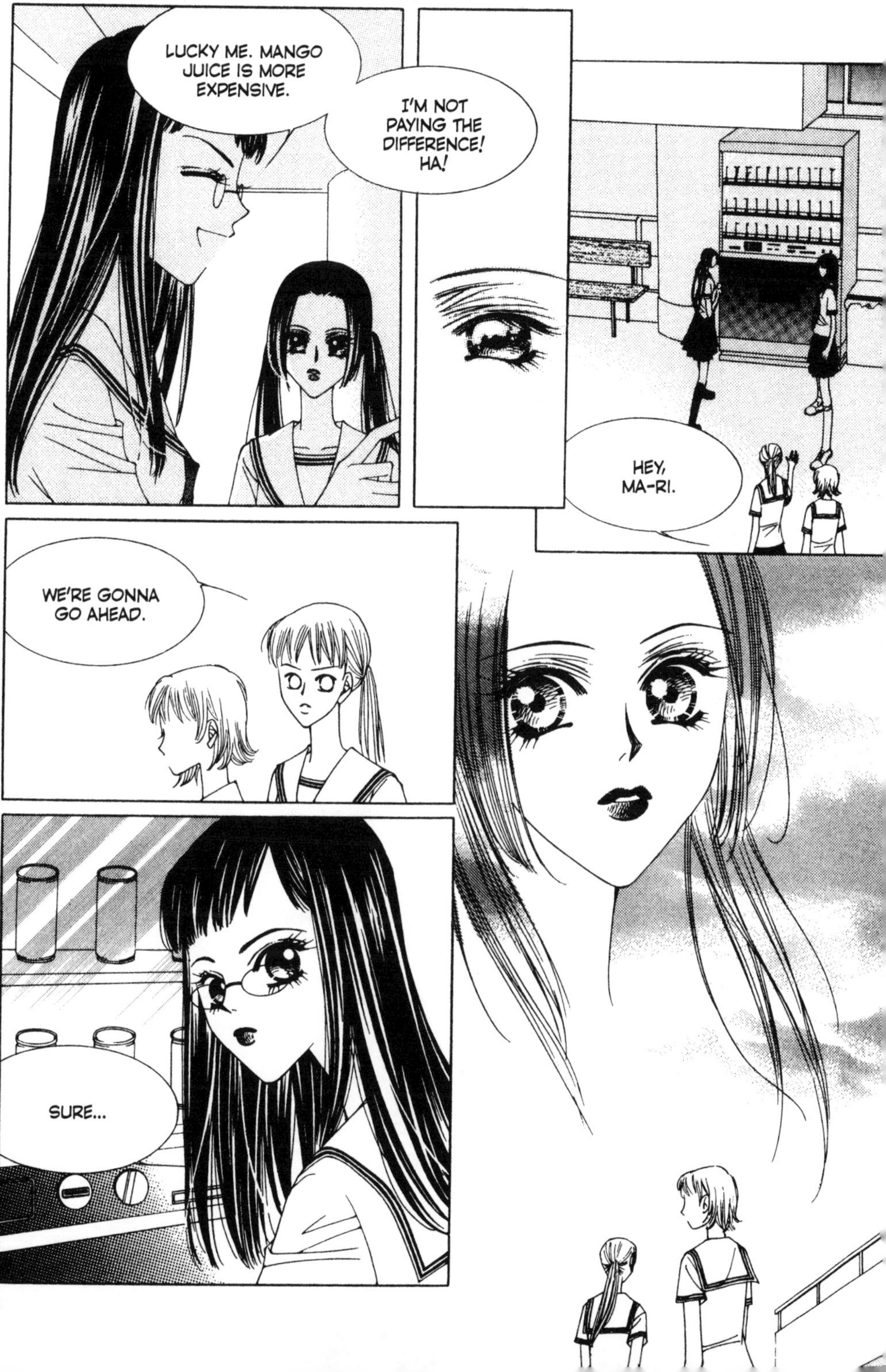
LUCKY ME. MANGO JUICE IS MORE EXPENSIVE.
I'M NOT PAYING THE DIFFERENCE! HA!
HEY, MA-RI.
WE'RE GONNA GO AHEAD.
SURE...

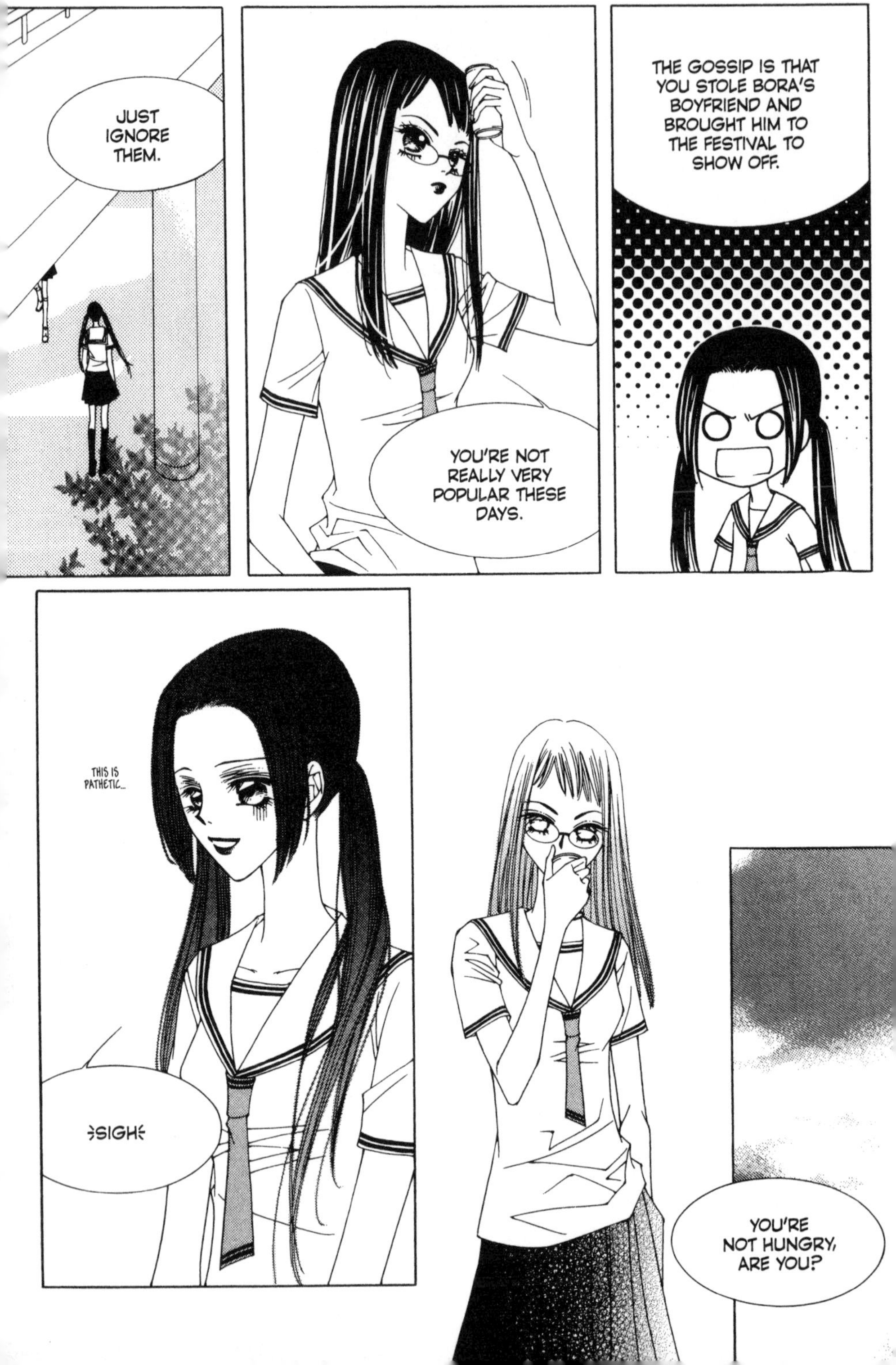
JUST IGNORE THEM.
YOU'RE NOT REALLY VERY POPULAR THESE DAYS.
THE GOSSIP IS THAT YOU STOLE BORA'S BOYFRIEND AND BROUGHT HIM TO THE FESTIVAL TO SHOW OFF.
THIS IS PATHETIC...
SIGH
YOU'RE NOT HUNGRY, ARE YOU?

HUH?

I DIDN'T EAT BREAKFAST AND I'M STARVING. I CAN'T WAIT UNTIL LUNCHTIME. LET'S DITCH.

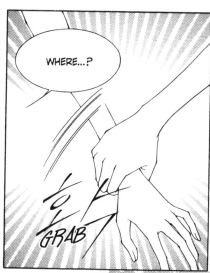

WHERE...?

GRAB

HURRY. I'M REALLY HUNGRY.

BUT CLASS...?

DON'T BE SUCH A WUSS. HURRY UP.

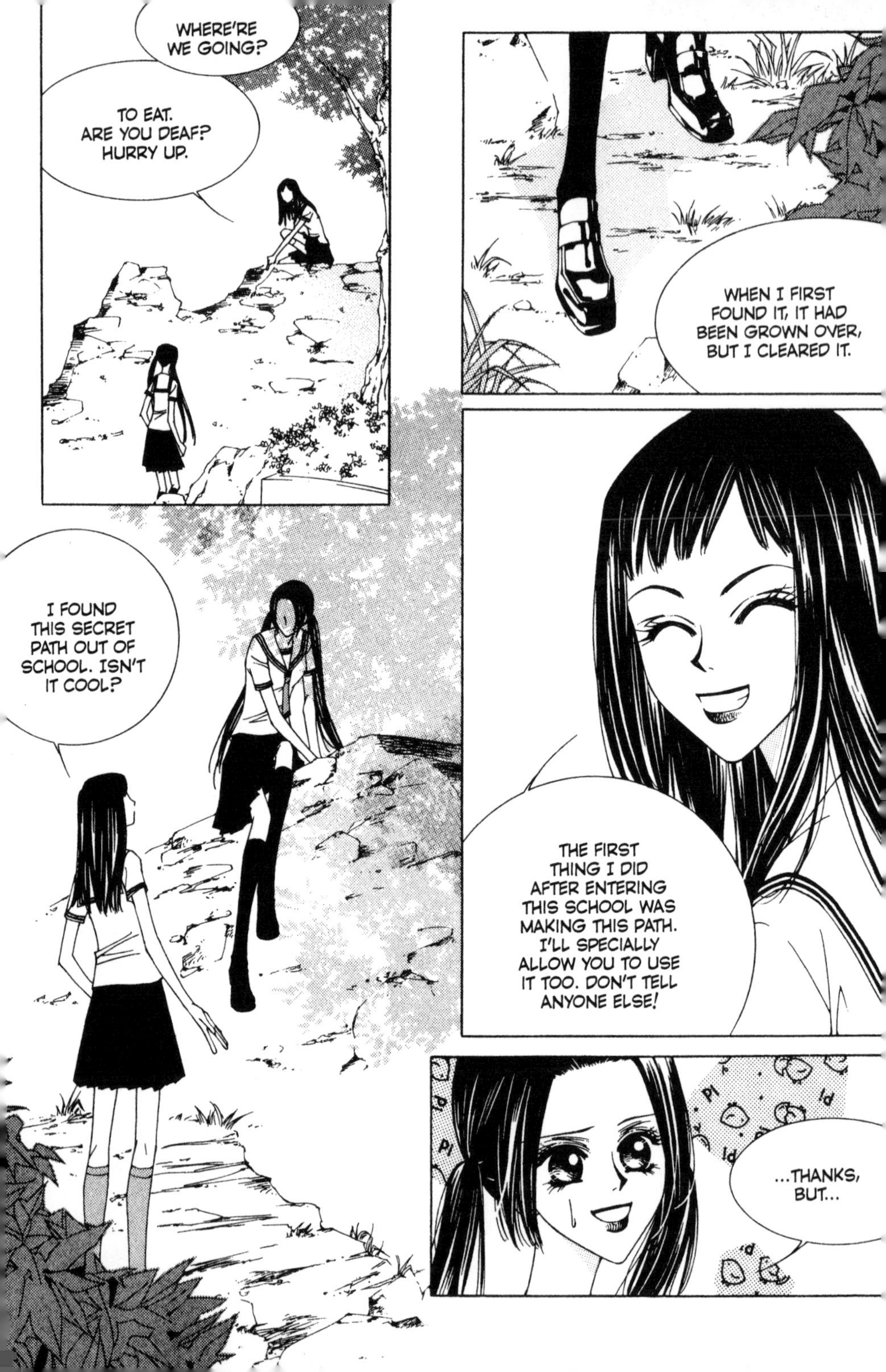
WHERE'RE WE GOING?
TO EAT. ARE YOU DEAF? HURRY UP.
WHEN I FIRST FOUND IT, IT HAD BEEN GROWN OVER, BUT I CLEARED IT.
I FOUND THIS SECRET PATH OUT OF SCHOOL. ISN'T IT COOL?
THE FIRST THING I DID AFTER ENTERING THIS SCHOOL WAS MAKING THIS PATH. I'LL SPECIALLY ALLOW YOU TO USE IT TOO. DON'T TELL ANYONE ELSE!
...THANKS, BUT...

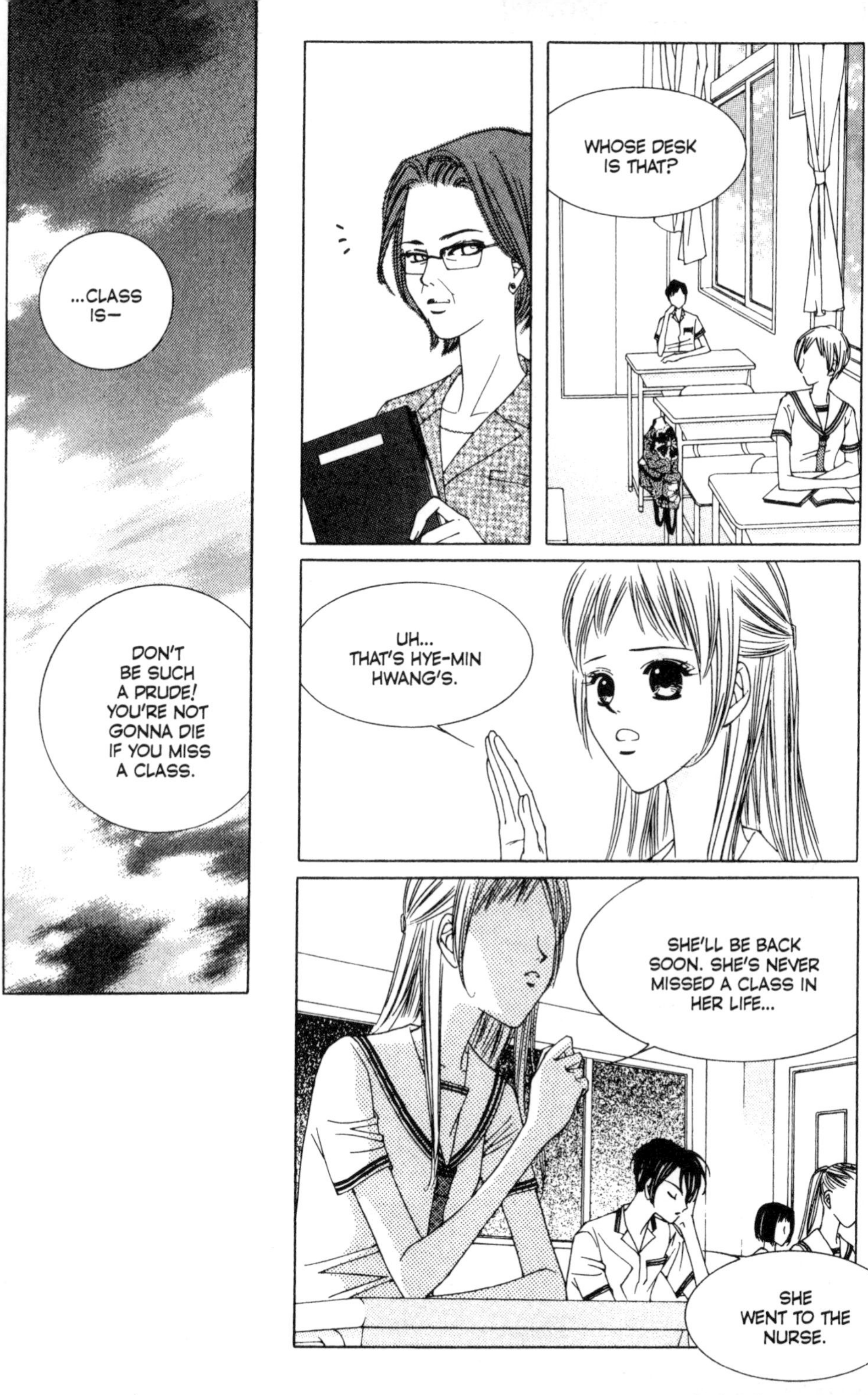
...CLASS IS—
DON'T BE SUCH A PRUDE! YOU'RE NOT GONNA DIE IF YOU MISS A CLASS.
WHOSE DESK IS THAT?
UH... THAT'S HYE-MIN HWANG'S.
SHE'LL BE BACK SOON. SHE'S NEVER MISSED A CLASS IN HER LIFE...
SHE WENT TO THE NURSE.

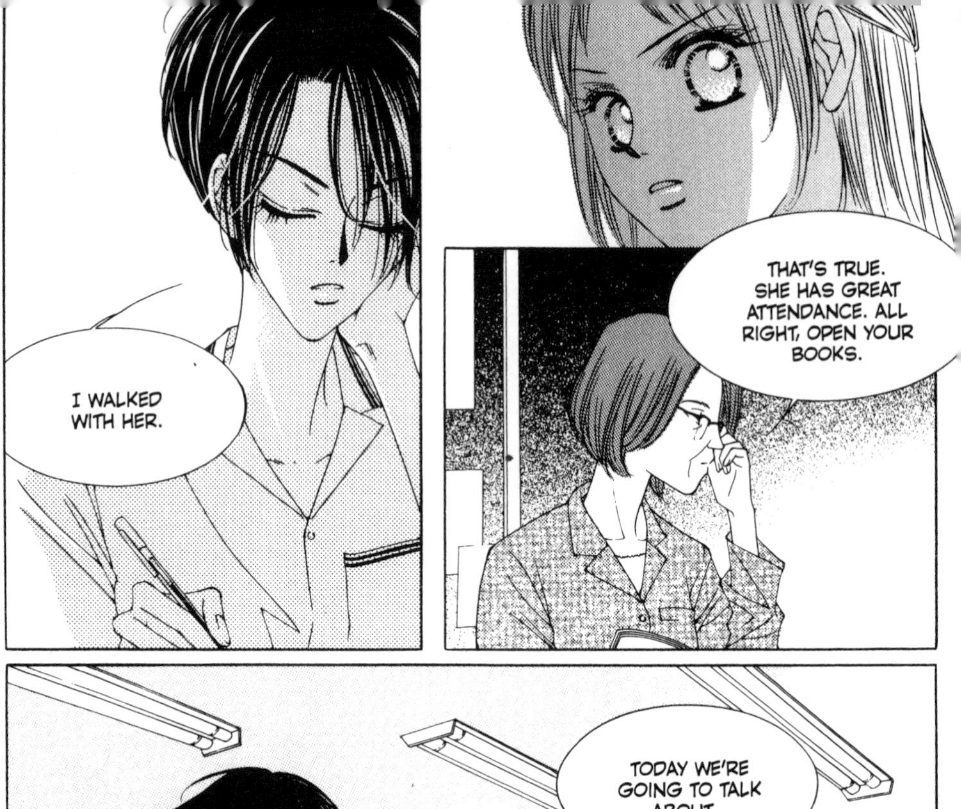
I WALKED WITH HER.
THAT'S TRUE. SHE HAS GREAT ATTENDANCE. ALL RIGHT, OPEN YOUR BOOKS.
TODAY WE'RE GOING TO TALK ABOUT...

* OLDER LADY. COULD BE EITHER CONDESCENDING OR ENDEARING.

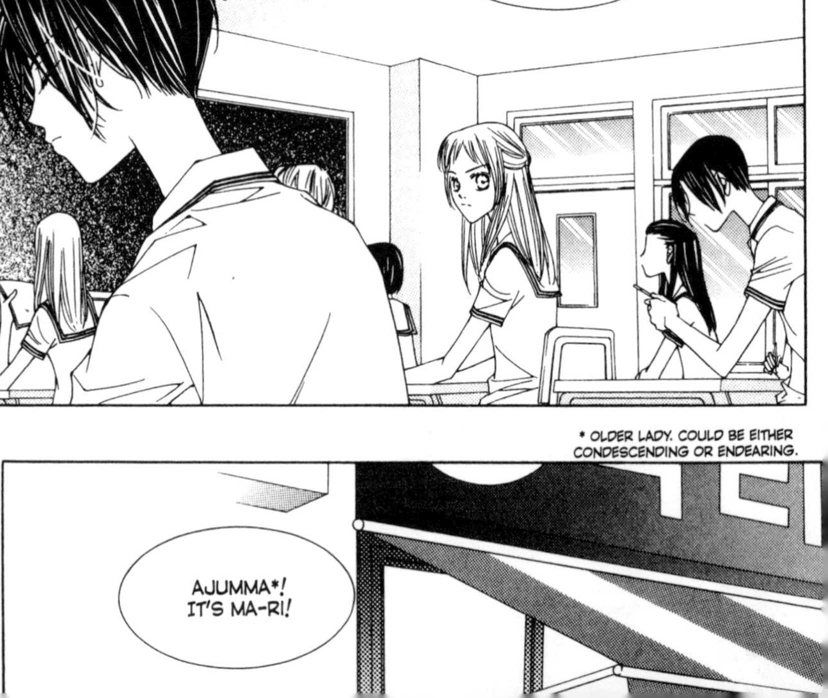
AJUMMA*! IT'S MA-RI!

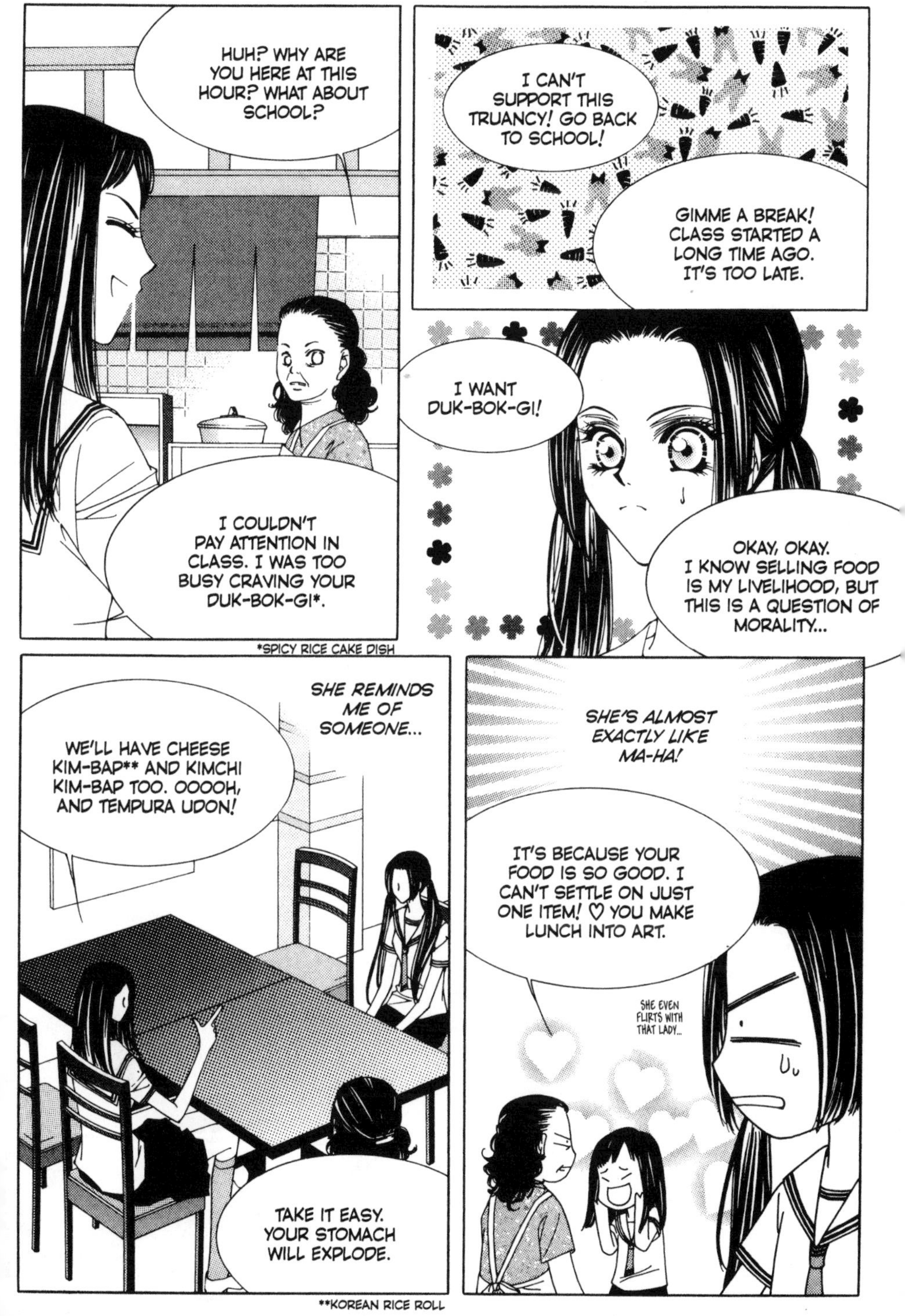
HUH? WHY ARE YOU HERE AT THIS HOUR? WHAT ABOUT SCHOOL?
I COULDN'T PAY ATTENTION IN CLASS. I WAS TOO BUSY CRAVING YOUR DUK-BOK-GI*.
I CAN'T SUPPORT THIS TRUANCY! GO BACK TO SCHOOL!
GIMME A BREAK! CLASS STARTED A LONG TIME AGO. IT'S TOO LATE.
I WANT DUK-BOK-GI!
OKAY, OKAY. I KNOW SELLING FOOD IS MY LIVELIHOOD, BUT THIS IS A QUESTION OF MORALITY...
SHE REMINDS ME OF SOMEONE...
WE'LL HAVE CHEESE KIM-BAP** AND KIMCHI KIM-BAP TOO. OOOOH, AND TEMPURA UDON!
TAKE IT EASY. YOUR STOMACH WILL EXPLODE.
SHE'S ALMOST EXACTLY LIKE MA-HA!
IT'S BECAUSE YOUR FOOD IS SO GOOD. I CAN'T SETTLE ON JUST ONE ITEM! ♡ YOU MAKE LUNCH INTO ART.
SHE EVEN FLIRTS WITH THAT LADY...

*SPICY RICE CAKE DISH

**KOREAN RICE ROLL

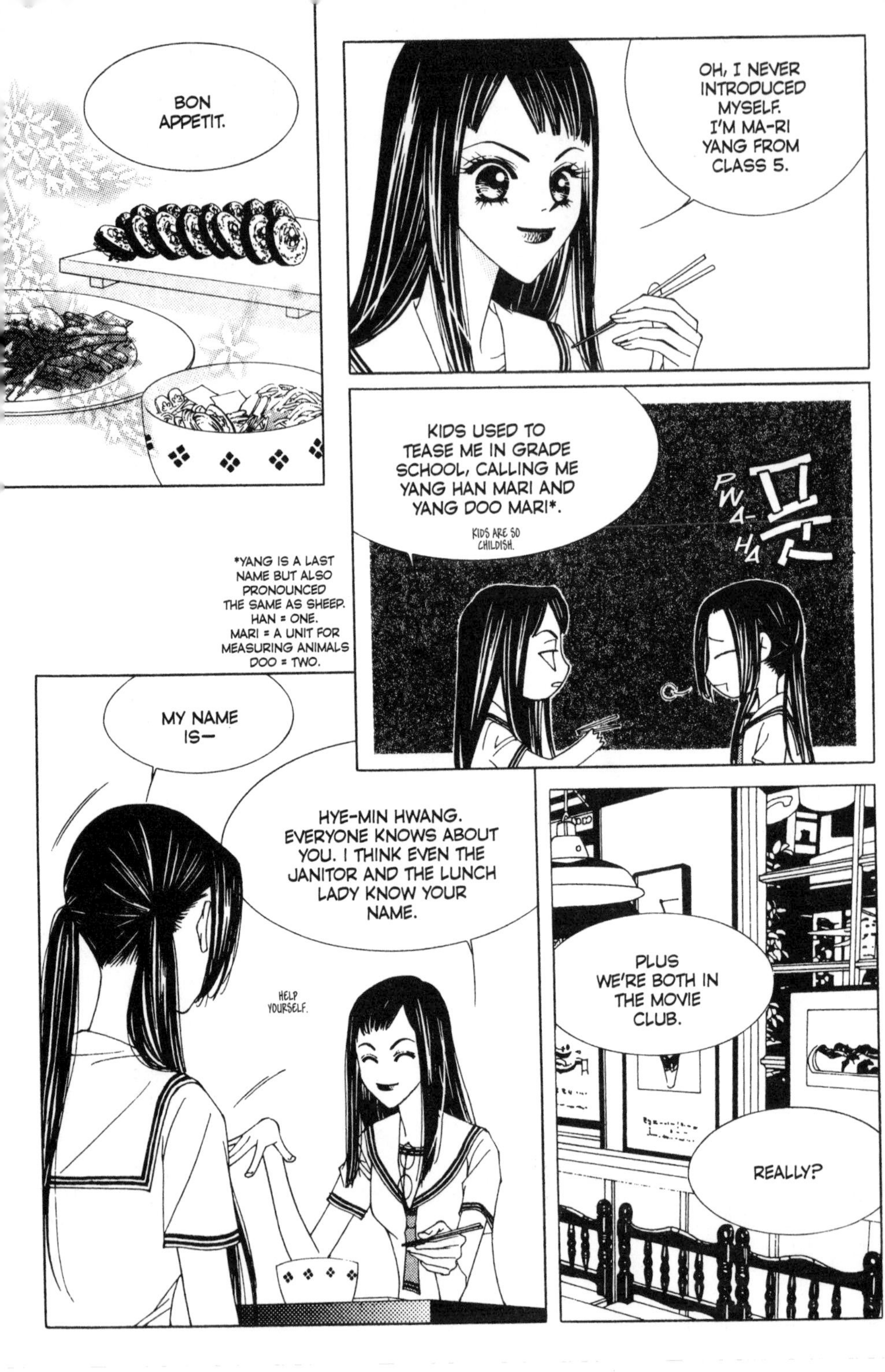
BON APPETIT.
OH, I NEVER INTRODUCED MYSELF. I'M MA-RI YANG FROM CLASS 5.
KIDS USED TO TEASE ME IN GRADE SCHOOL, CALLING ME YANG HAN MARI AND YANG DOO MARI*.
KIDS ARE SO CHILDISH.
PWA-HA
*YANG IS A LAST NAME BUT ALSO PRONOUNCED THE SAME AS SHEEP. HAN = ONE. MARI = A UNIT FOR MEASURING ANIMALS DOO = TWO.
MY NAME IS—
HYE-MIN HWANG. EVERYONE KNOWS ABOUT YOU. I THINK EVEN THE JANITOR AND THE LUNCH LADY KNOW YOUR NAME.
HELP YOURSELF.
PLUS WE'RE BOTH IN THE MOVIE CLUB.
REALLY?

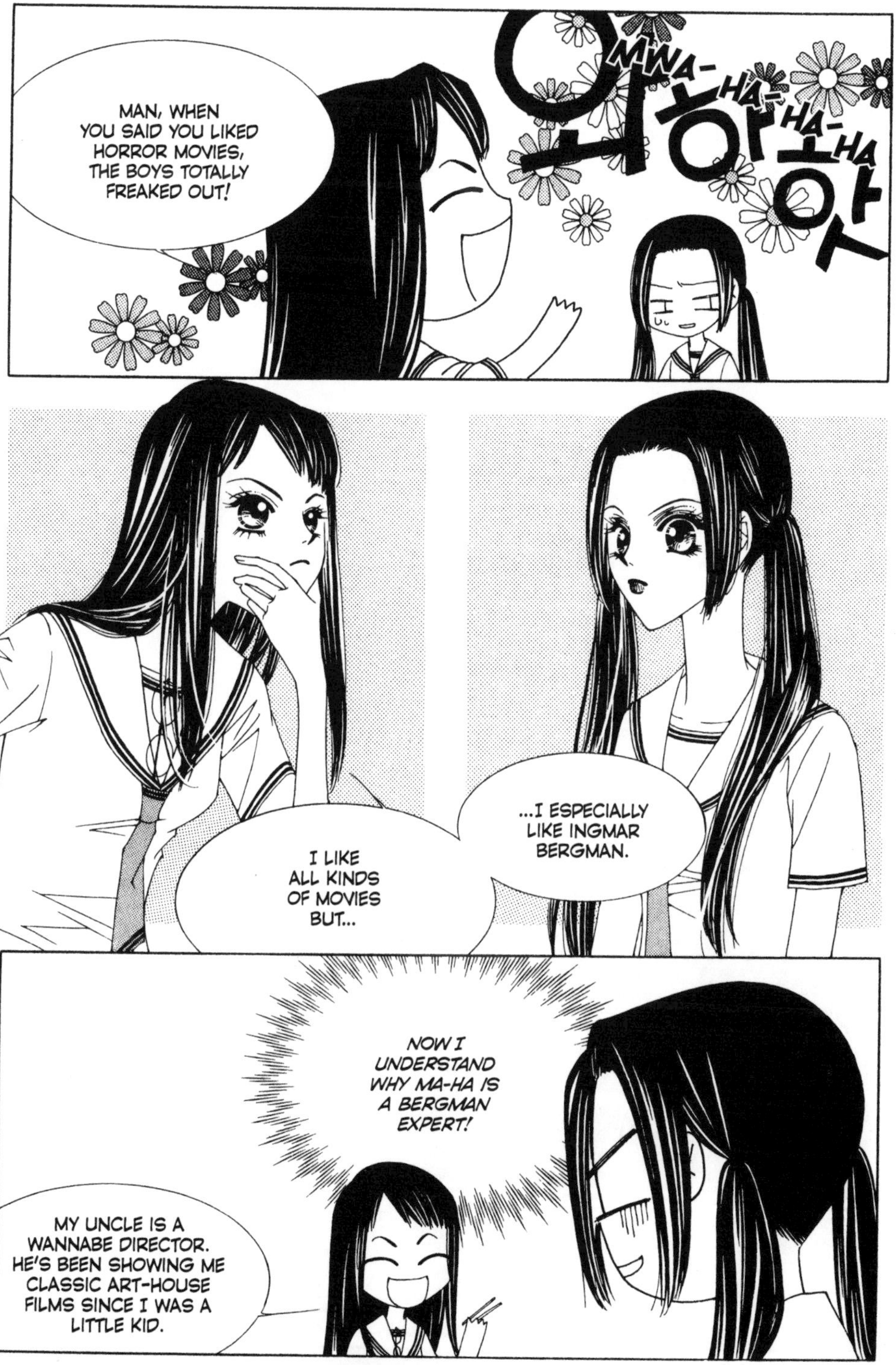
MAN, WHEN YOU SAID YOU LIKED HORROR MOVIES, THE BOYS TOTALLY FREAKED OUT!
MWA-HA-HA-HA
I LIKE ALL KINDS OF MOVIES BUT...
...I ESPECIALLY LIKE INGMAR BERGMAN.
NOW I UNDERSTAND WHY MA-HA IS A BERGMAN EXPERT!
MY UNCLE IS A WANNABE DIRECTOR. HE'S BEEN SHOWING ME CLASSIC ART-HOUSE FILMS SINCE I WAS A LITTLE KID.

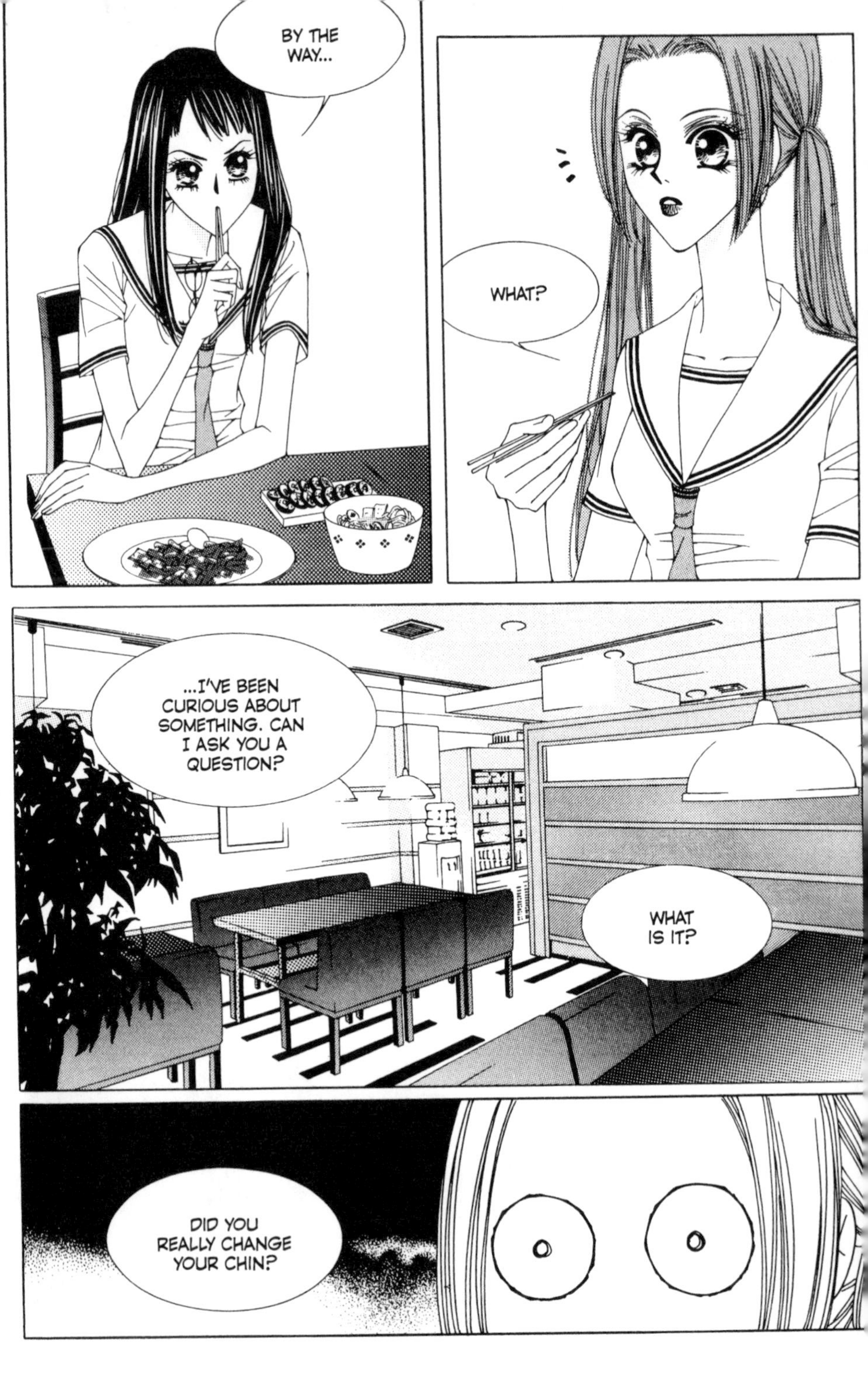
BY THE WAY...
WHAT?
...I'VE BEEN CURIOUS ABOUT SOMETHING. CAN I ASK YOU A QUESTION?
WHAT IS IT?
DID YOU REALLY CHANGE YOUR CHIN?

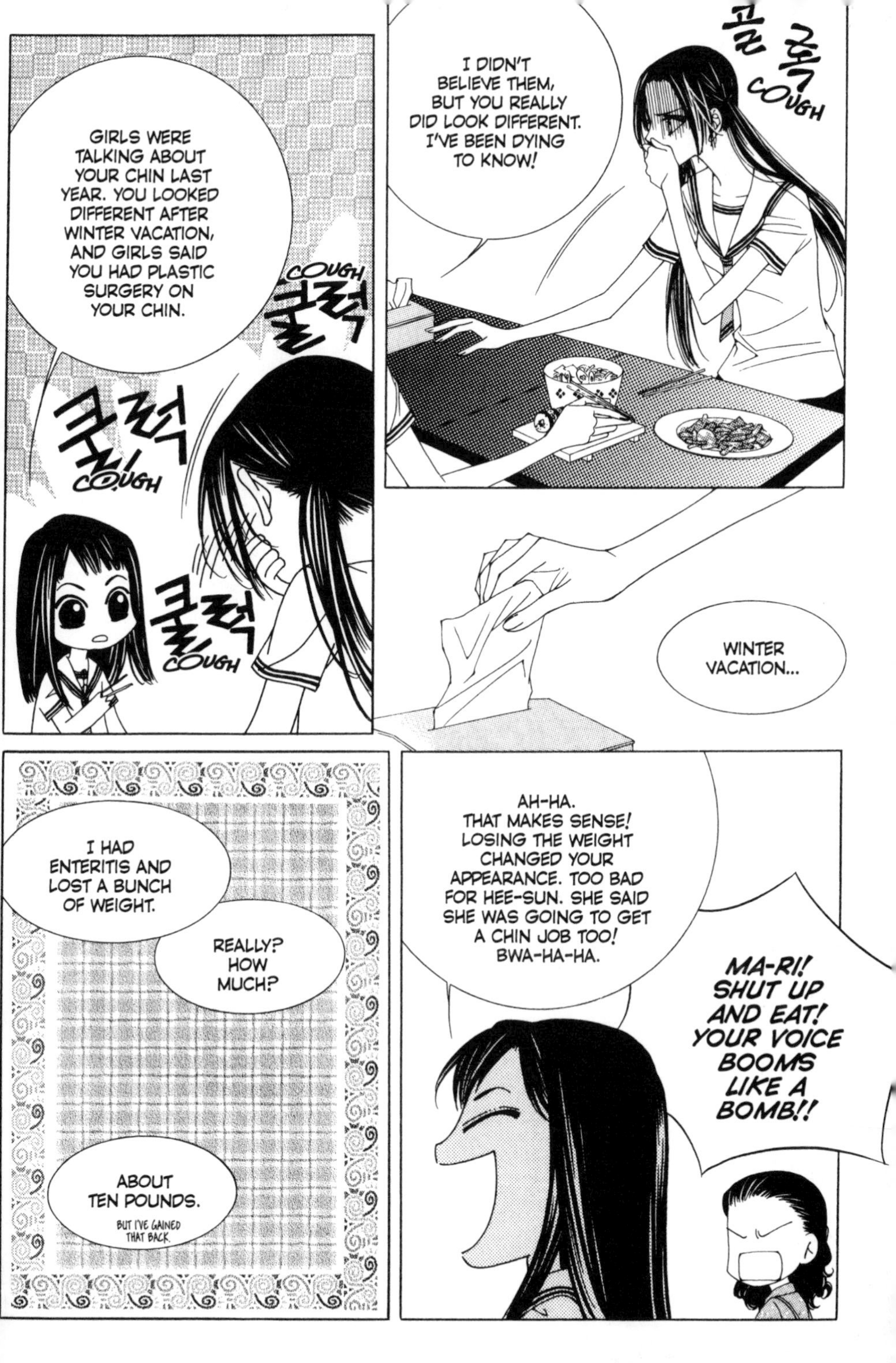
GIRLS WERE TALKING ABOUT YOUR CHIN LAST YEAR. YOU LOOKED DIFFERENT AFTER WINTER VACATION, AND GIRLS SAID YOU HAD PLASTIC SURGERY ON YOUR CHIN.
COUGH
COUGH
COUGH
I DIDN'T BELIEVE THEM, BUT YOU REALLY DID LOOK DIFFERENT. I'VE BEEN DYING TO KNOW!
COUGH
WINTER VACATION...
I HAD ENTERITIS AND LOST A BUNCH OF WEIGHT.
REALLY? HOW MUCH?
ABOUT TEN POUNDS.
BUT I'VE GAINED THAT BACK.
AH-HA. THAT MAKES SENSE! LOSING THE WEIGHT CHANGED YOUR APPEARANCE. TOO BAD FOR HEE-SUN. SHE SAID SHE WAS GOING TO GET A CHIN JOB TOO! BWA-HA-HA.
MA-RI! SHUT UP AND EAT! YOUR VOICE BOOMS LIKE A BOMB!!

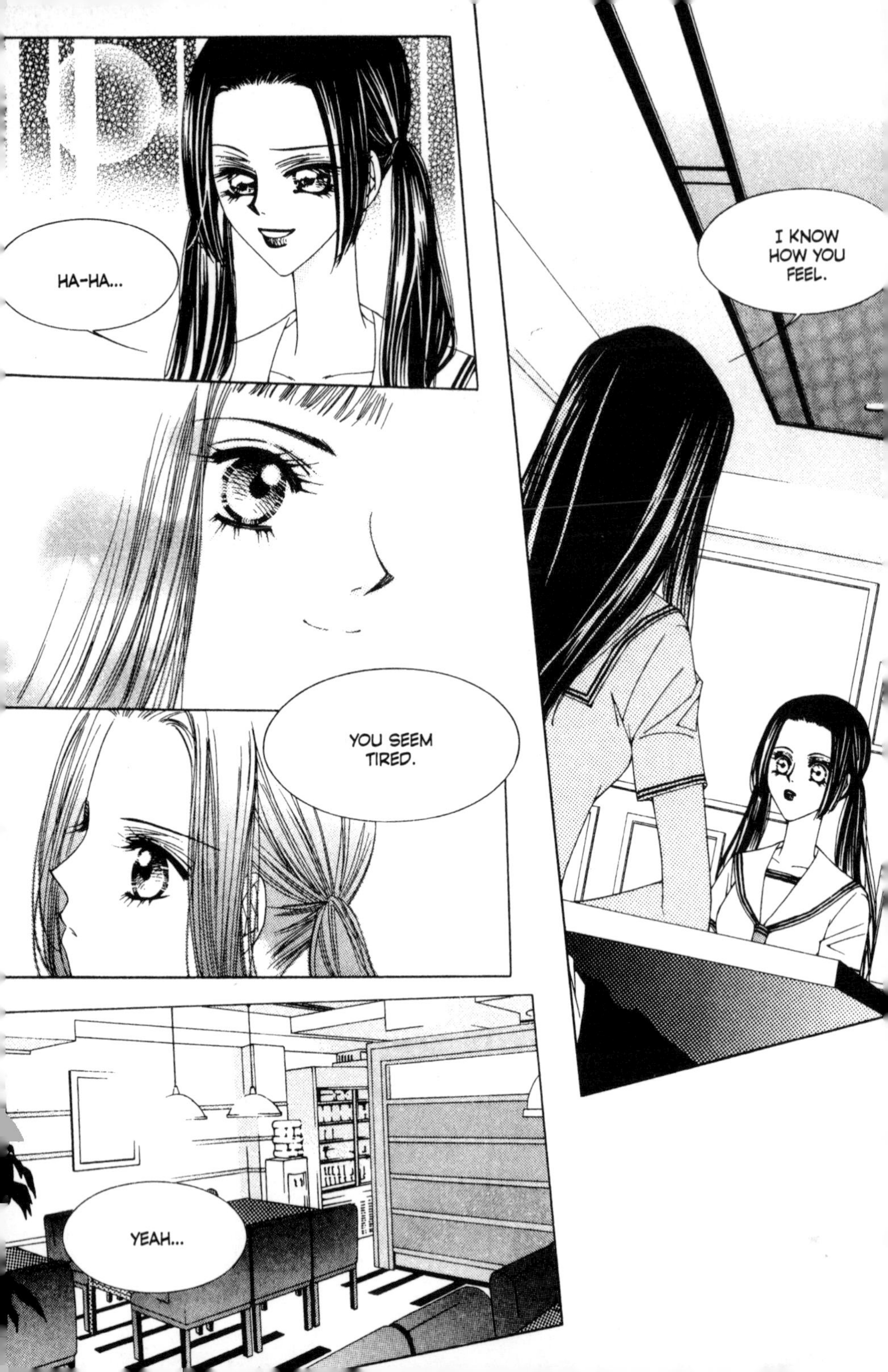
HA-HA...
YOU SEEM TIRED.
YEAH...
I KNOW HOW YOU FEEL.

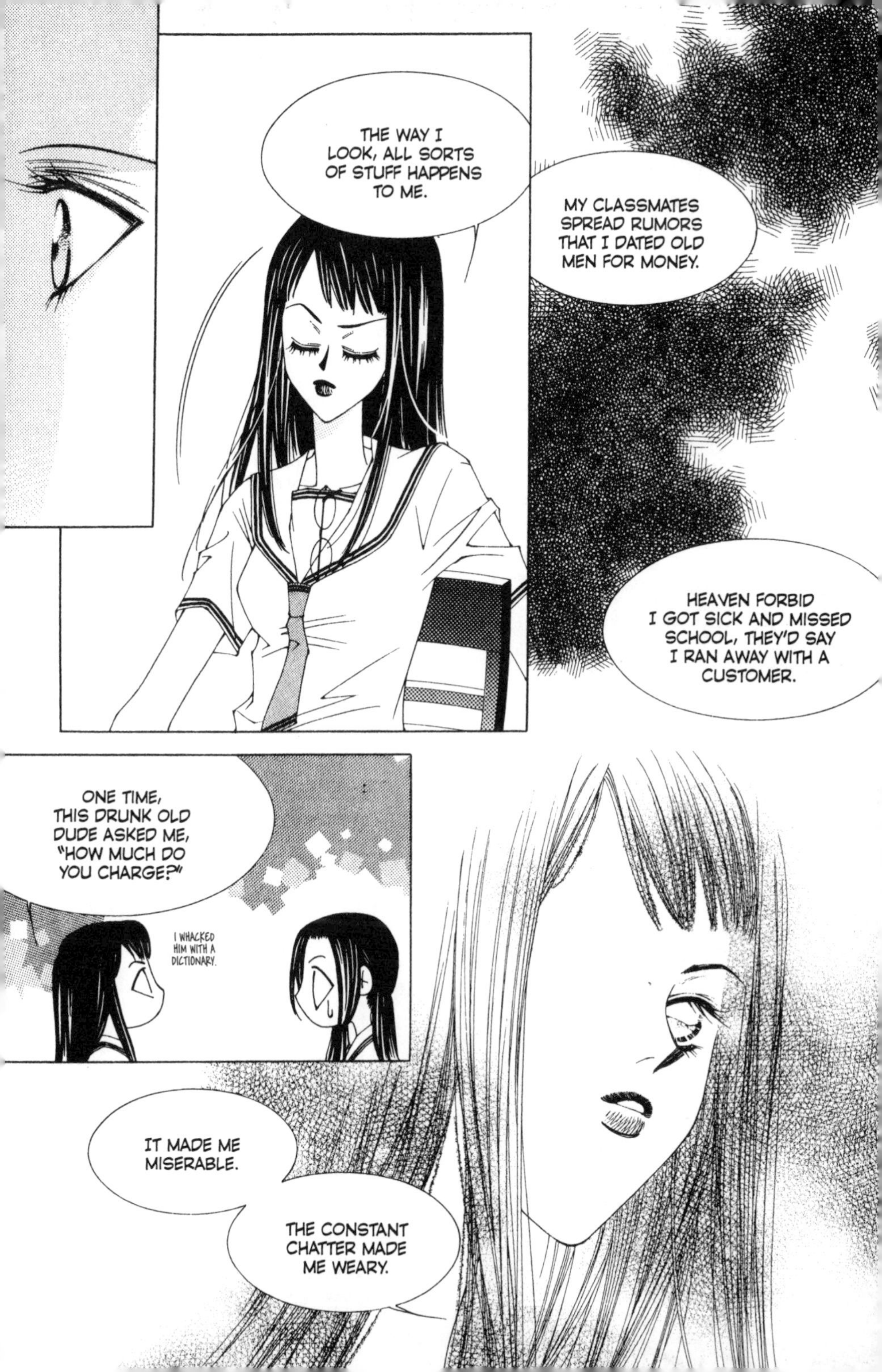
THE WAY I LOOK, ALL SORTS OF STUFF HAPPENS TO ME.
MY CLASSMATES SPREAD RUMORS THAT I DATED OLD MEN FOR MONEY.
HEAVEN FORBID I GOT SICK AND MISSED SCHOOL, THEY'D SAY I RAN AWAY WITH A CUSTOMER.
ONE TIME, THIS DRUNK OLD DUDE ASKED ME, "HOW MUCH DO YOU CHARGE?"
I WHACKED HIM WITH A DICTIONARY.
IT MADE ME MISERABLE.
THE CONSTANT CHATTER MADE ME WEARY.

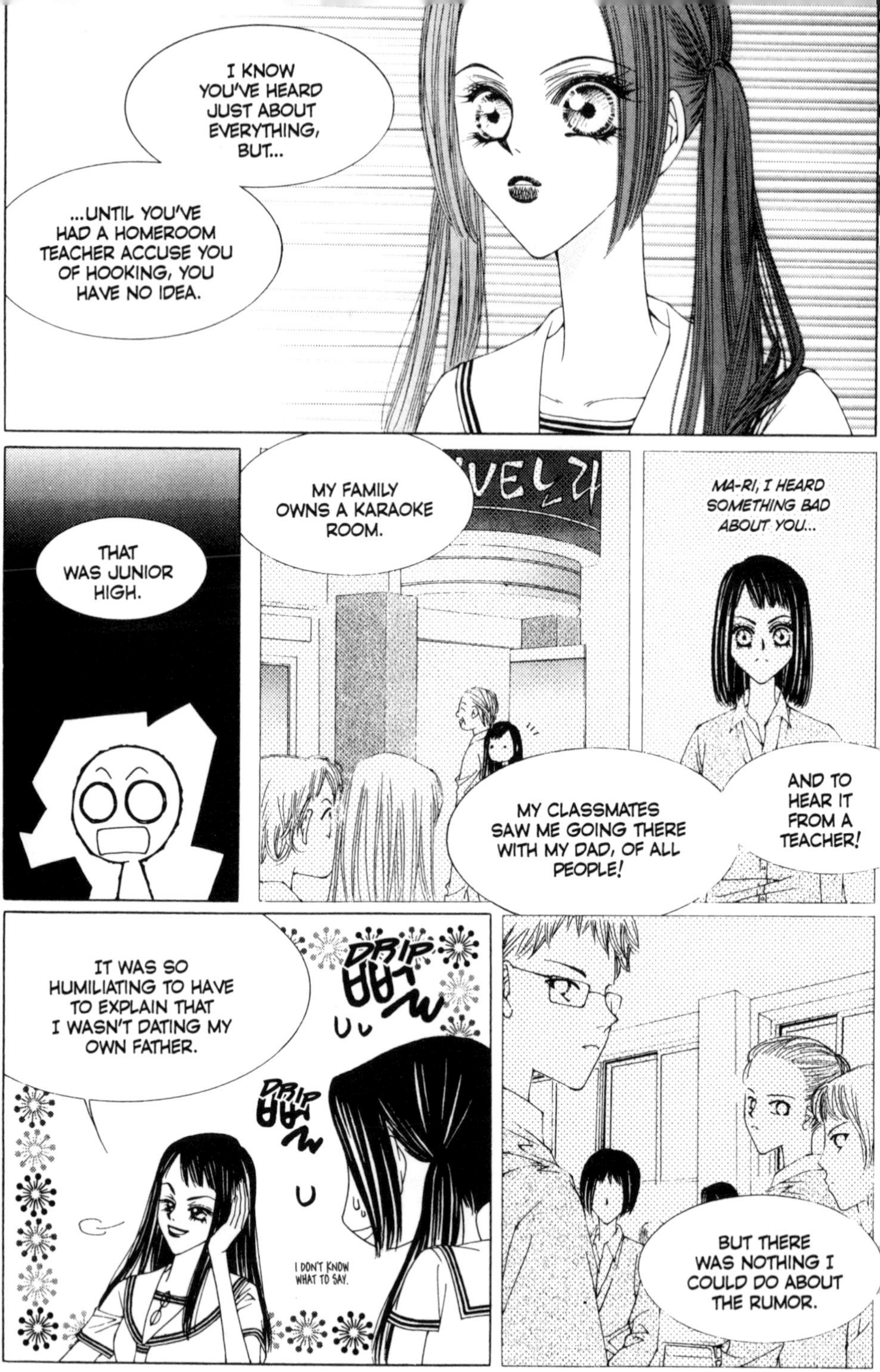
I KNOW YOU'VE HEARD JUST ABOUT EVERYTHING, BUT...
...UNTIL YOU'VE HAD A HOMEROOM TEACHER ACCUSE YOU OF HOOKING, YOU HAVE NO IDEA.
THAT WAS JUNIOR HIGH.
MY FAMILY OWNS A KARAOKE ROOM.
MY CLASSMATES SAW ME GOING THERE WITH MY DAD, OF ALL PEOPLE!
MA-RI, I HEARD SOMETHING BAD ABOUT YOU...
AND TO HEAR IT FROM A TEACHER!
IT WAS SO HUMILIATING TO HAVE TO EXPLAIN THAT I WASN'T DATING MY OWN FATHER.
DRIP
DRIP
I DON'T KNOW WHAT TO SAY.
BUT THERE WAS NOTHING I COULD DO ABOUT THE RUMOR.

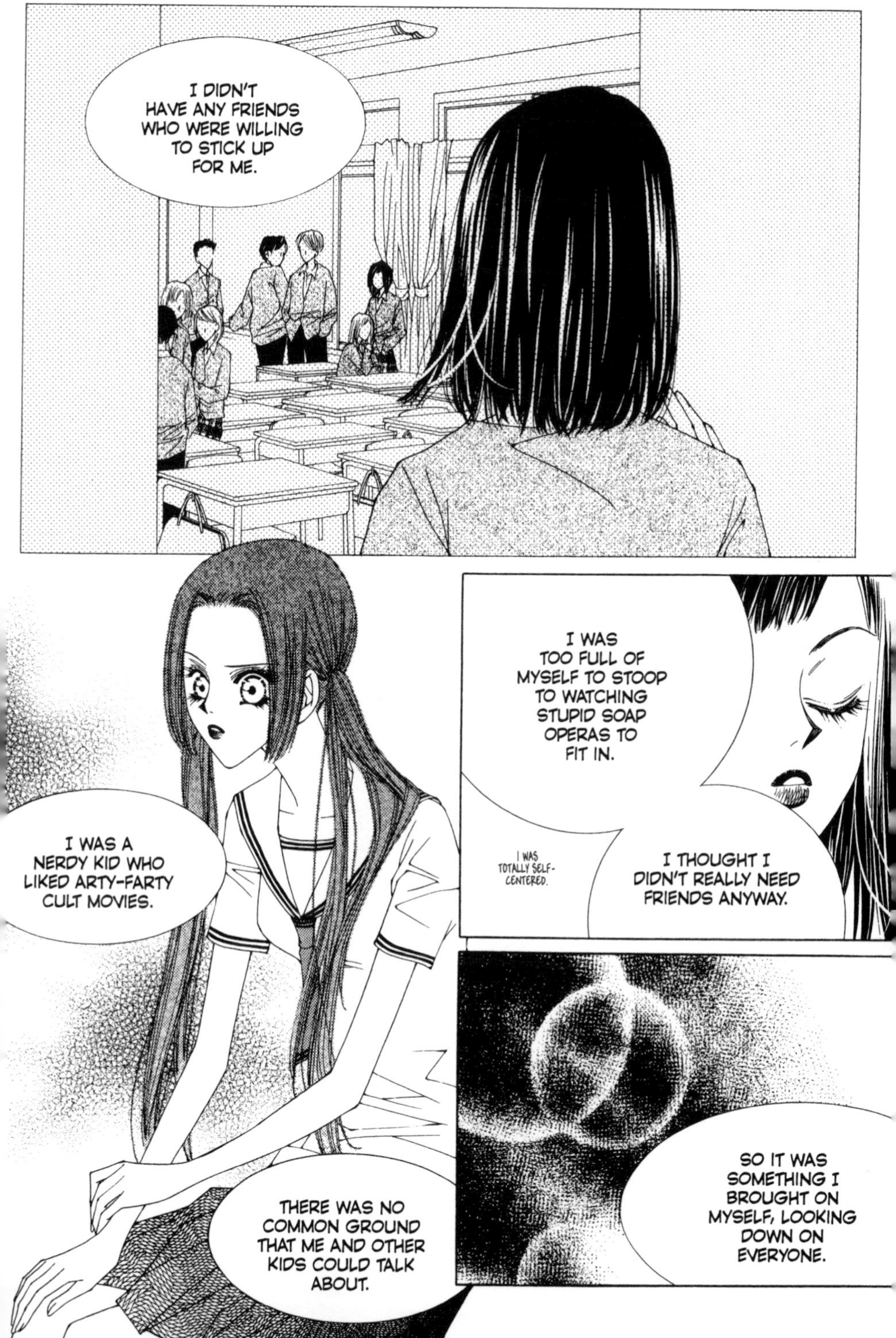
I DIDN'T HAVE ANY FRIENDS WHO WERE WILLING TO STICK UP FOR ME.
I WAS A NERDY KID WHO LIKED ARTY-FARTY CULT MOVIES.
THERE WAS NO COMMON GROUND THAT ME AND OTHER KIDS COULD TALK ABOUT.
I WAS TOO FULL OF MYSELF TO STOOP TO WATCHING STUPID SOAP OPERAS TO FIT IN.
I WAS TOTALLY SELF-CENTERED.
I THOUGHT I DIDN'T REALLY NEED FRIENDS ANYWAY.
SO IT WAS SOMETHING I BROUGHT ON MYSELF, LOOKING DOWN ON EVERYONE.

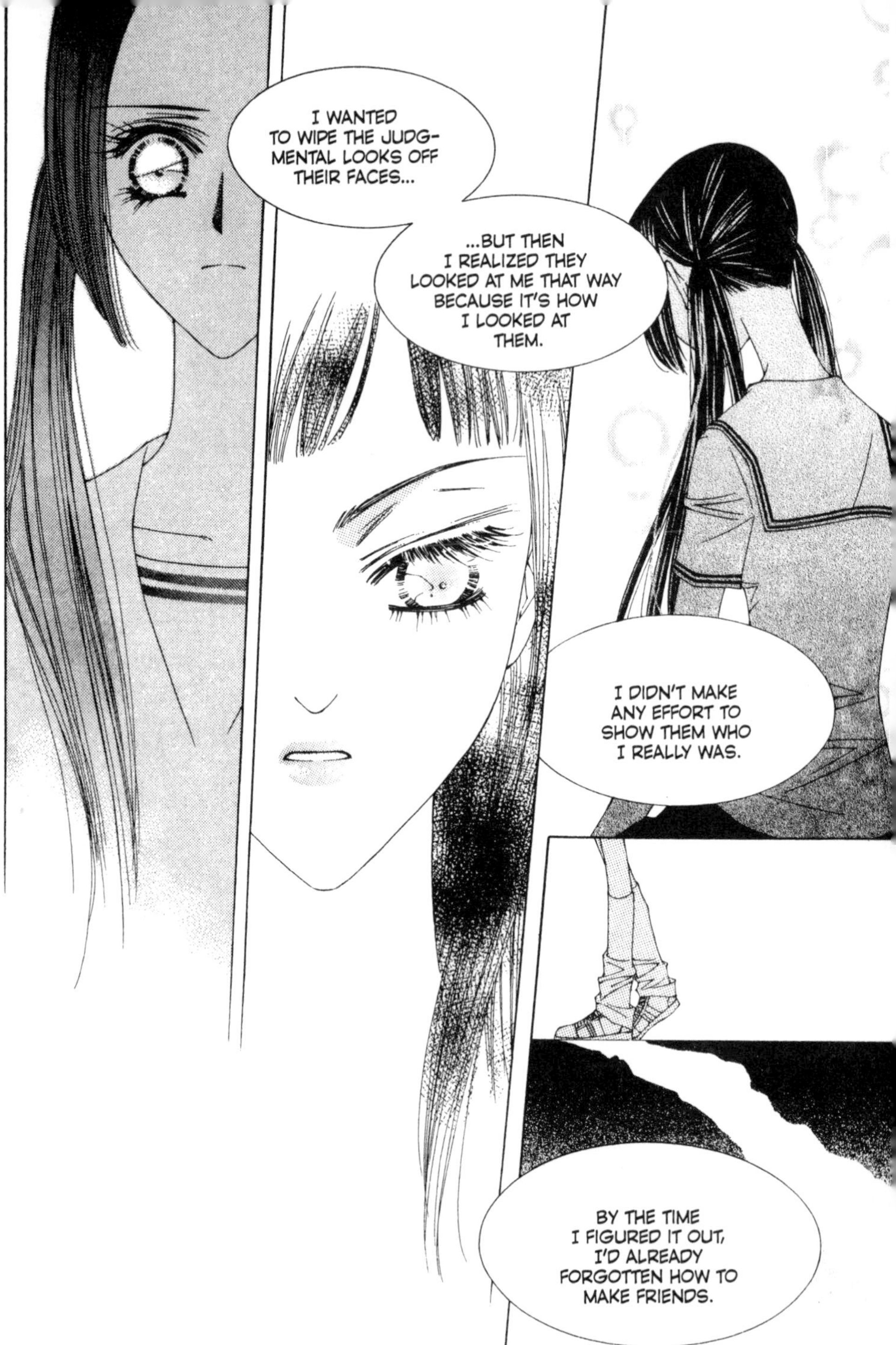
I WANTED TO WIPE THE JUDG- MENTAL LOOKS OFF THEIR FACES...
...BUT THEN I REALIZED THEY LOOKED AT ME THAT WAY BECAUSE IT'S HOW I LOOKED AT THEM.
I DIDN'T MAKE ANY EFFORT TO SHOW THEM WHO I REALLY WAS.
BY THE TIME I FIGURED IT OUT, I'D ALREADY FORGOTTEN HOW TO MAKE FRIENDS.

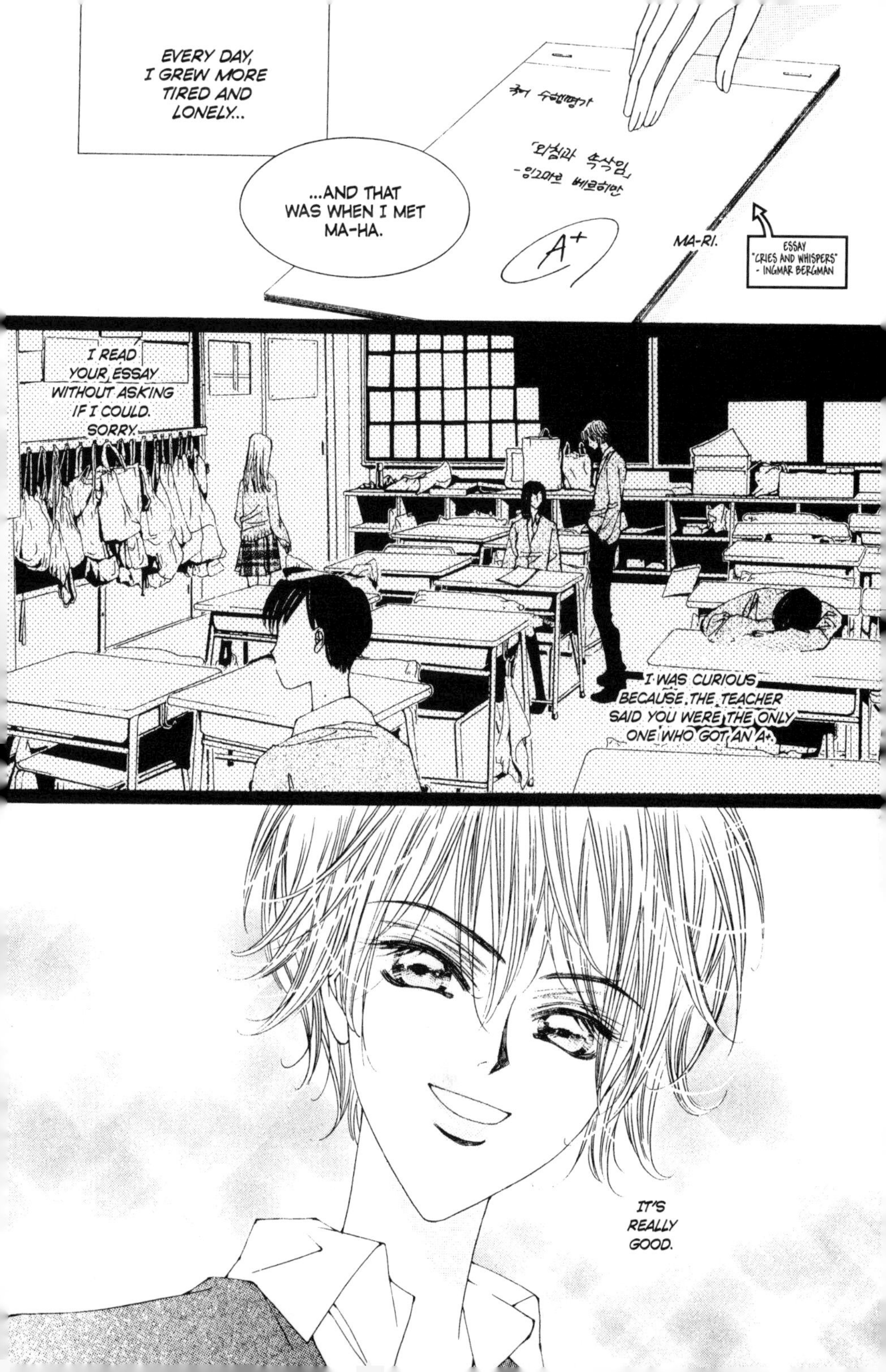
EVERY DAY, I GREW MORE TIRED AND LONELY...
...AND THAT WAS WHEN I MET MA-HA.
「외침과 속삭임」
-잉그마르 베르히만
A+
MA-RI.
ESSAY "CRIES AND WHISPERS" - INGMAR BERGMAN
I READ YOUR ESSAY WITHOUT ASKING IF I COULD. SORRY.
I WAS CURIOUS BECAUSE THE TEACHER SAID YOU WERE THE ONLY ONE WHO GOT AN A+.
IT'S REALLY GOOD.

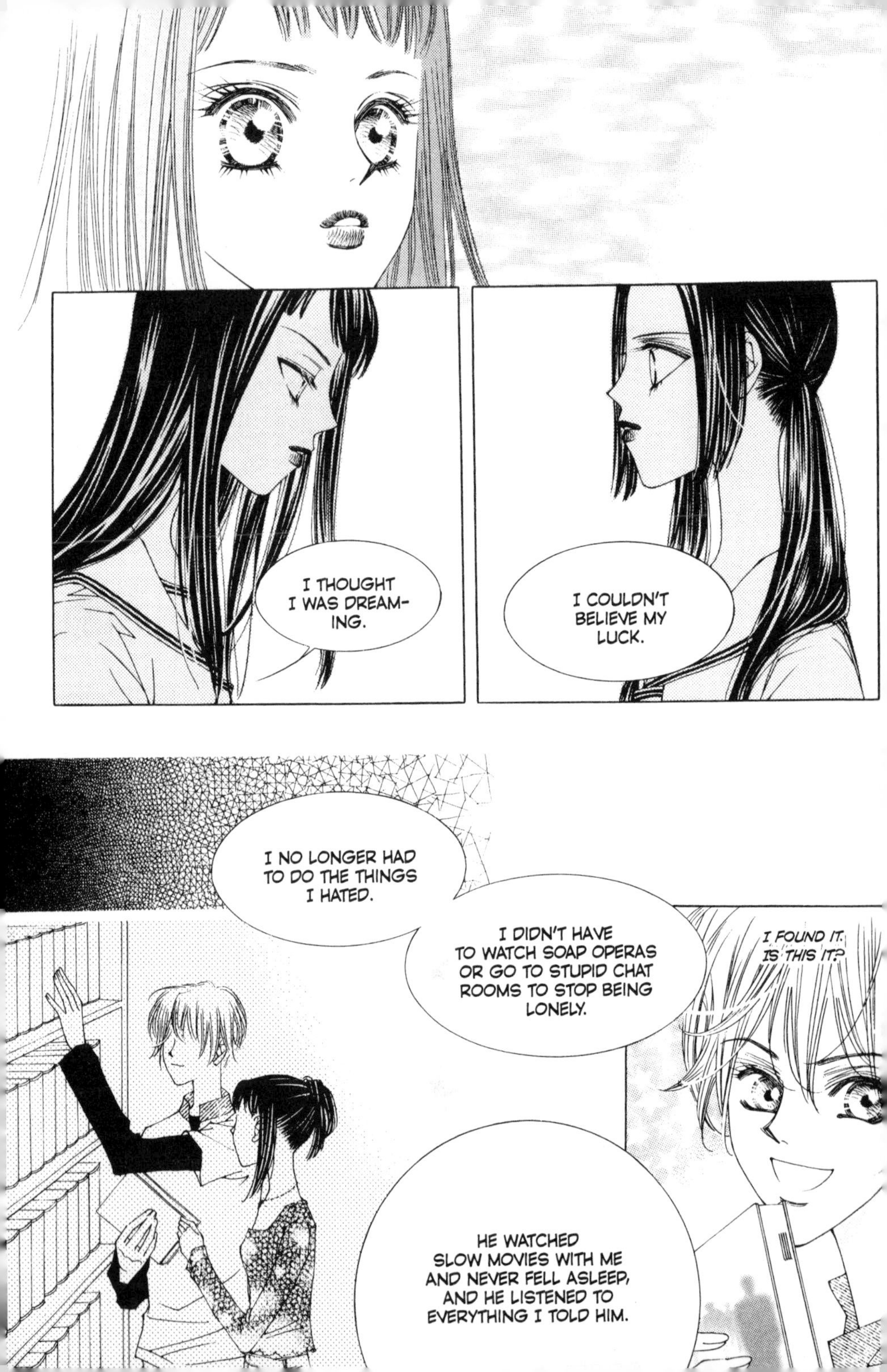
I THOUGHT I WAS DREAM-ING.
I COULDN'T BELIEVE MY LUCK.
I NO LONGER HAD TO DO THE THINGS I HATED.
I DIDN'T HAVE TO WATCH SOAP OPERAS OR GO TO STUPID CHAT ROOMS TO STOP BEING LONELY.
I FOUND IT. IS THIS IT?
HE WATCHED SLOW MOVIES WITH ME AND NEVER FELL ASLEEP, AND HE LISTENED TO EVERYTHING I TOLD HIM.

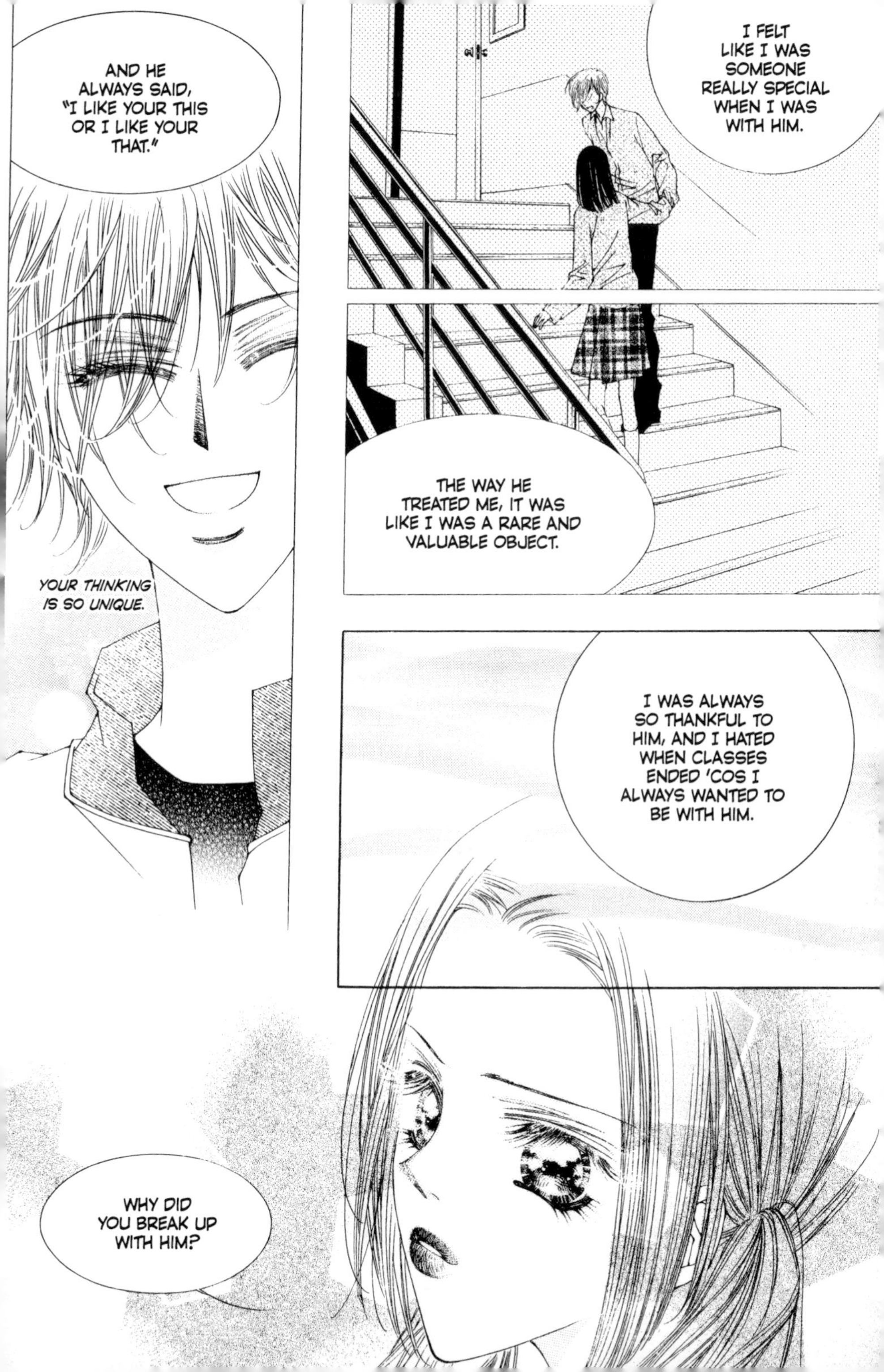
AND HE ALWAYS SAID, "I LIKE YOUR THIS OR I LIKE YOUR THAT."
YOUR THINKING IS SO UNIQUE.
I FELT LIKE I WAS SOMEONE REALLY SPECIAL WHEN I WAS WITH HIM.
THE WAY HE TREATED ME, IT WAS LIKE I WAS A RARE AND VALUABLE OBJECT.
I WAS ALWAYS SO THANKFUL TO HIM, AND I HATED WHEN CLASSES ENDED 'COS I ALWAYS WANTED TO BE WITH HIM.
WHY DID YOU BREAK UP WITH HIM?

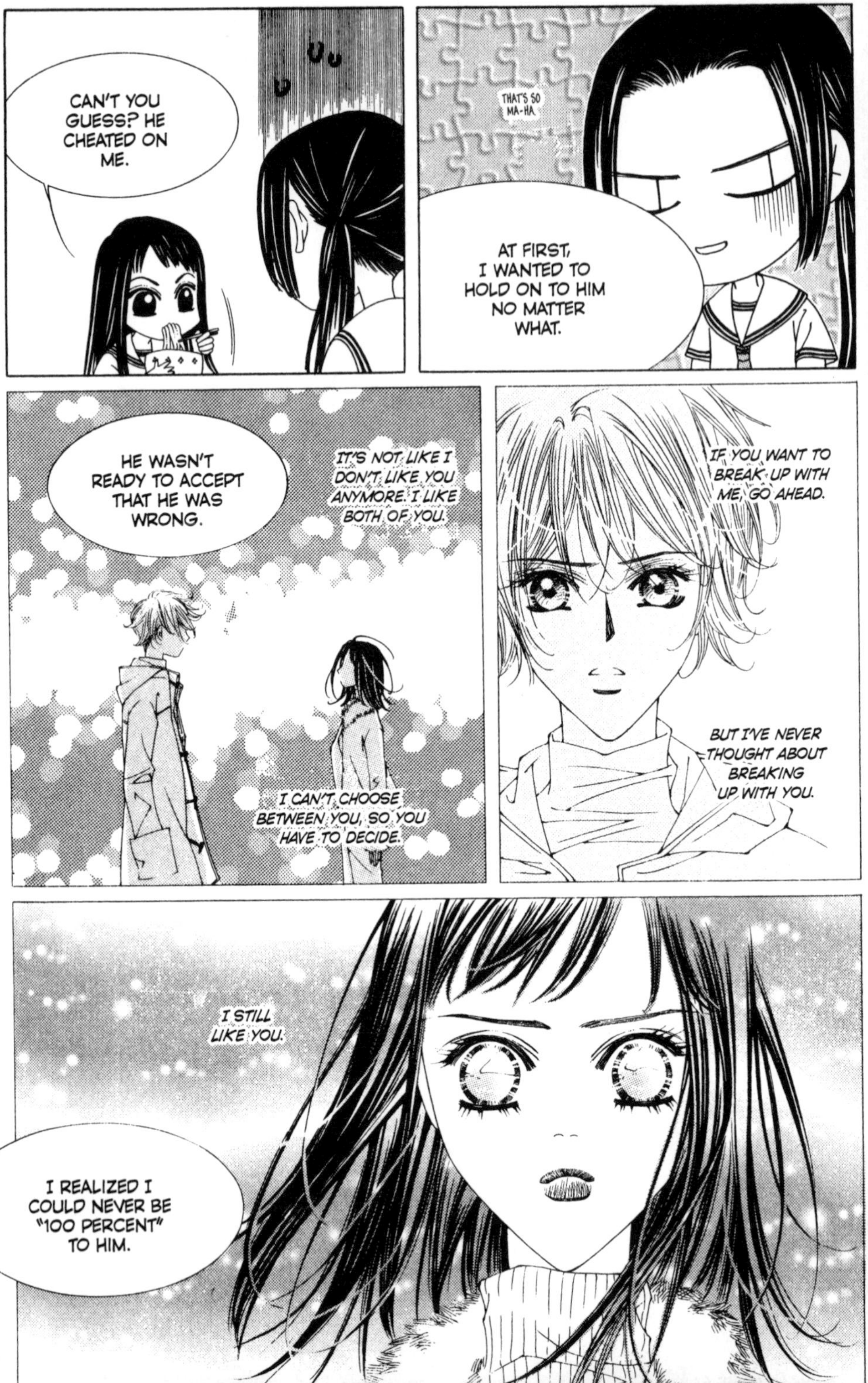
CAN'T YOU GUESS? HE CHEATED ON ME.
THAT'S SO MA-HA.
AT FIRST, I WANTED TO HOLD ON TO HIM NO MATTER WHAT.
HE WASN'T READY TO ACCEPT THAT HE WAS WRONG.
IT'S NOT LIKE I DON'T LIKE YOU ANYMORE. I LIKE BOTH OF YOU.
I CAN'T CHOOSE BETWEEN YOU, SO YOU HAVE TO DECIDE.
IF YOU WANT TO BREAK UP WITH ME, GO AHEAD.
BUT I'VE NEVER THOUGHT ABOUT BREAKING UP WITH YOU.
I STILL LIKE YOU.
I REALIZED I COULD NEVER BE "100 PERCENT" TO HIM.

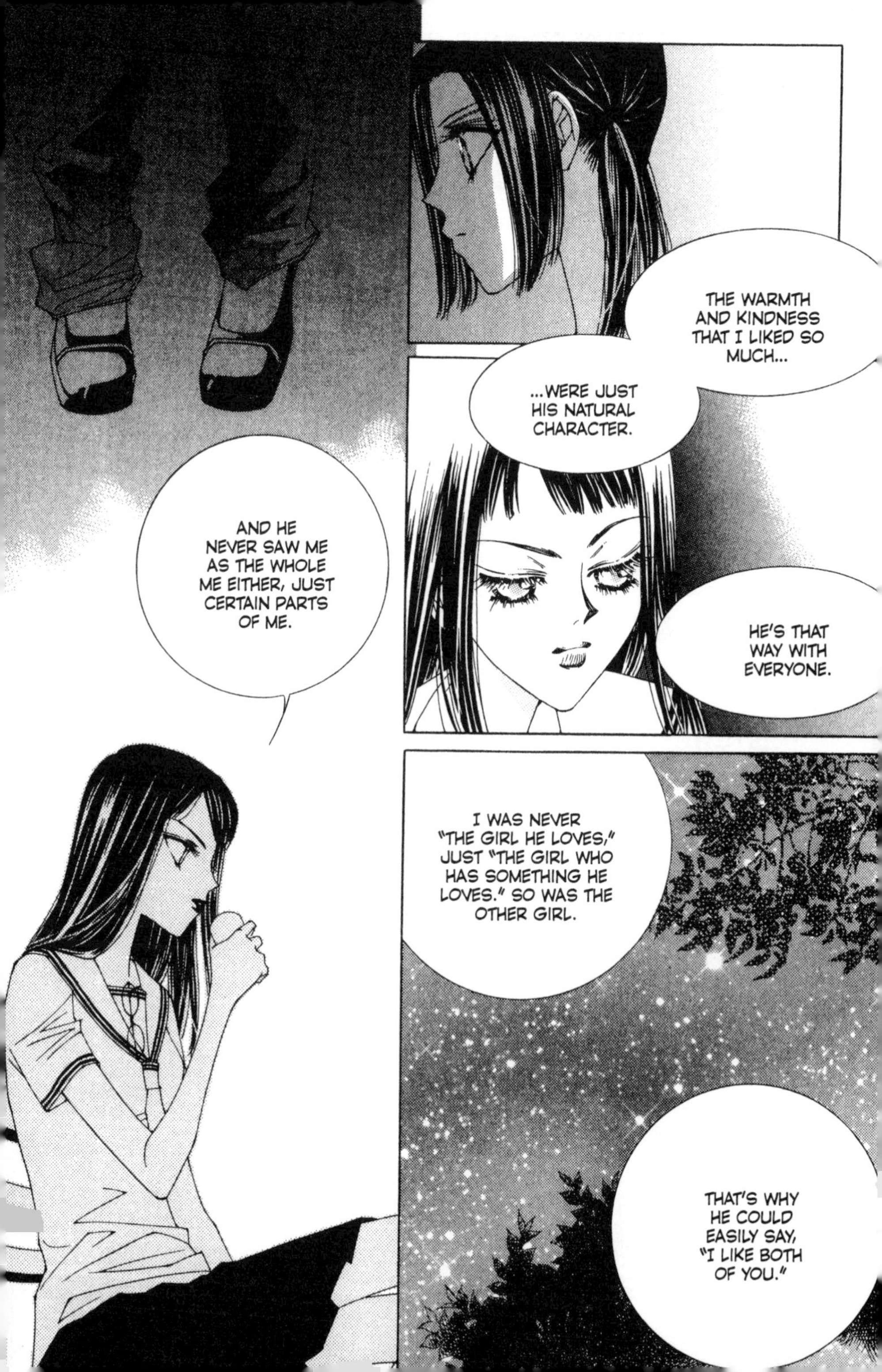
THE WARMTH AND KINDNESS THAT I LIKED SO MUCH...
...WERE JUST HIS NATURAL CHARACTER.
HE'S THAT WAY WITH EVERYONE.
AND HE NEVER SAW ME AS THE WHOLE ME EITHER, JUST CERTAIN PARTS OF ME.
I WAS NEVER "THE GIRL HE LOVES," JUST "THE GIRL WHO HAS SOMETHING HE LOVES." SO WAS THE OTHER GIRL.
THAT'S WHY HE COULD EASILY SAY, "I LIKE BOTH OF YOU."

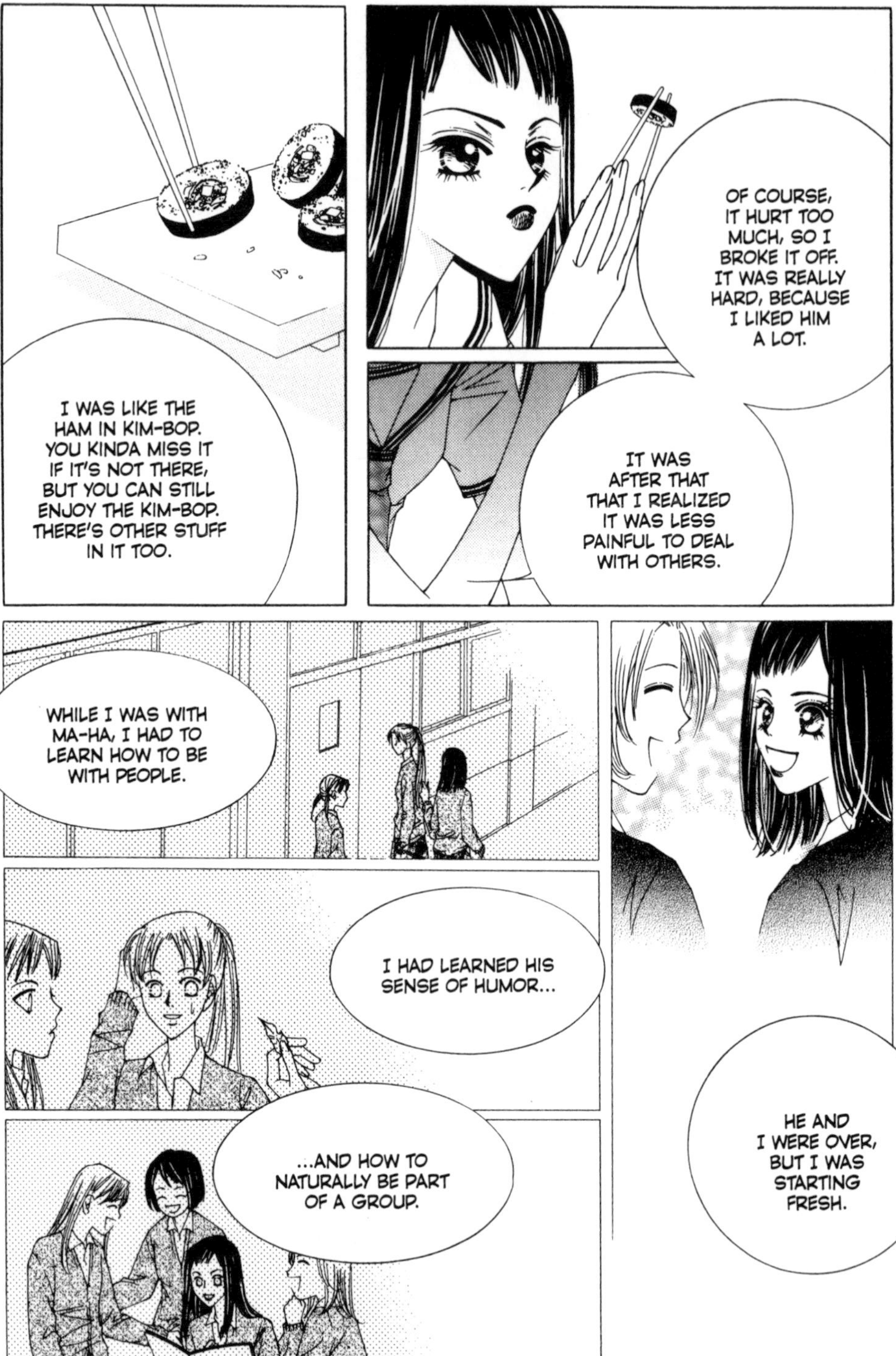
I WAS LIKE THE HAM IN KIM-BOP. YOU KINDA MISS IT IF IT'S NOT THERE, BUT YOU CAN STILL ENJOY THE KIM-BOP. THERE'S OTHER STUFF IN IT TOO.
OF COURSE, IT HURT TOO MUCH, SO I BROKE IT OFF. IT WAS REALLY HARD, BECAUSE I LIKED HIM A LOT.
IT WAS AFTER THAT THAT I REALIZED IT WAS LESS PAINFUL TO DEAL WITH OTHERS.
WHILE I WAS WITH MA-HA, I HAD TO LEARN HOW TO BE WITH PEOPLE.
I HAD LEARNED HIS SENSE OF HUMOR...
...AND HOW TO NATURALLY BE PART OF A GROUP.
HE AND I WERE OVER, BUT I WAS STARTING FRESH.

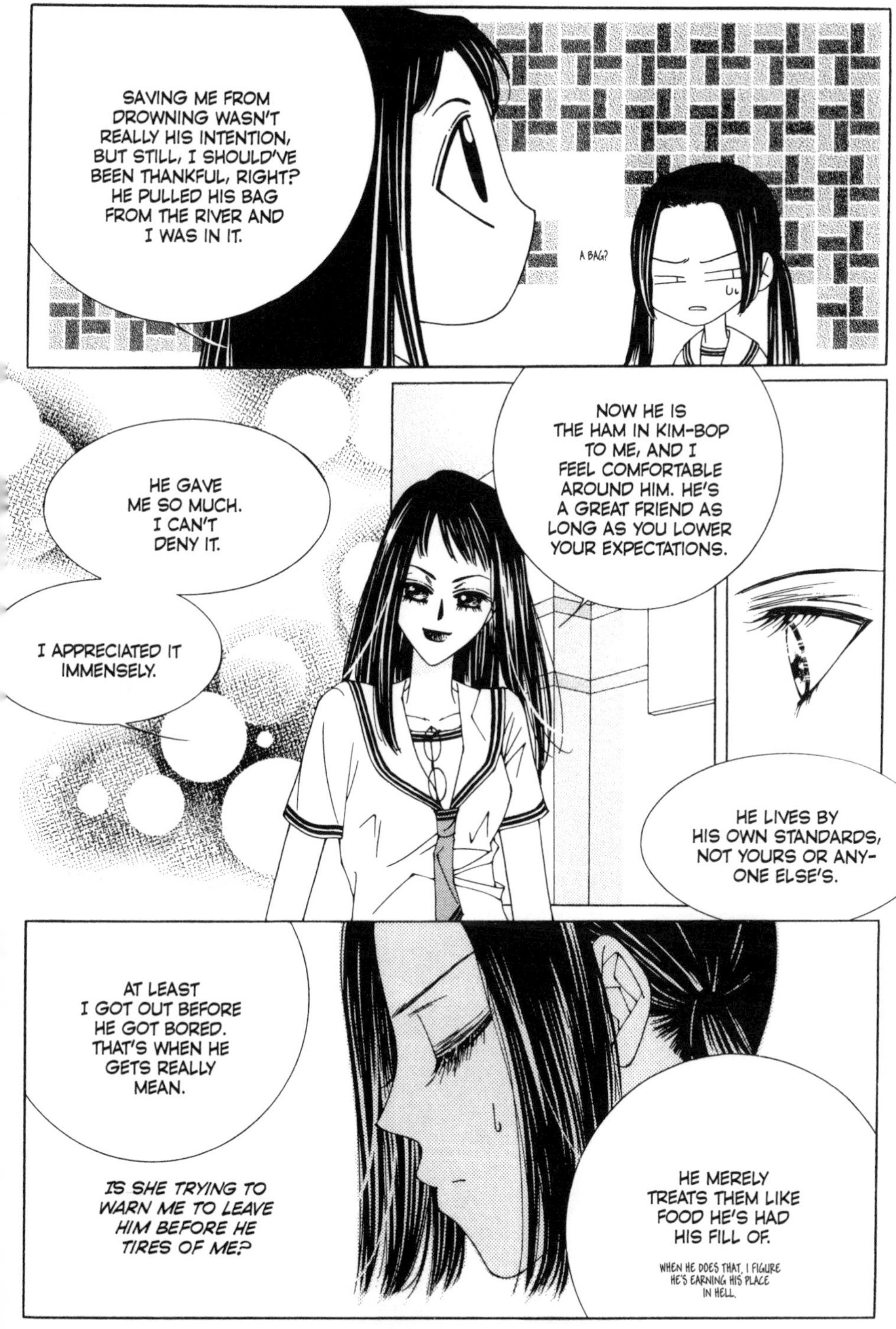
SAVING ME FROM DROWNING WASN'T REALLY HIS INTENTION, BUT STILL, I SHOULD'VE BEEN THANKFUL, RIGHT? HE PULLED HIS BAG FROM THE RIVER AND I WAS IN IT.
A BAG?
HE GAVE ME SO MUCH. I CAN'T DENY IT.
I APPRECIATED IT IMMENSELY.
NOW HE IS THE HAM IN KIM-BOP TO ME, AND I FEEL COMFORTABLE AROUND HIM. HE'S A GREAT FRIEND AS LONG AS YOU LOWER YOUR EXPECTATIONS.
HE LIVES BY HIS OWN STANDARDS, NOT YOURS OR ANY-ONE ELSE'S.
AT LEAST I GOT OUT BEFORE HE GOT BORED. THAT'S WHEN HE GETS REALLY MEAN.
IS SHE TRYING TO WARN ME TO LEAVE HIM BEFORE HE TIRES OF ME?
HE MERELY TREATS THEM LIKE FOOD HE'S HAD HIS FILL OF.
WHEN HE DOES THAT, I FIGURE HE'S EARNING HIS PLACE IN HELL.

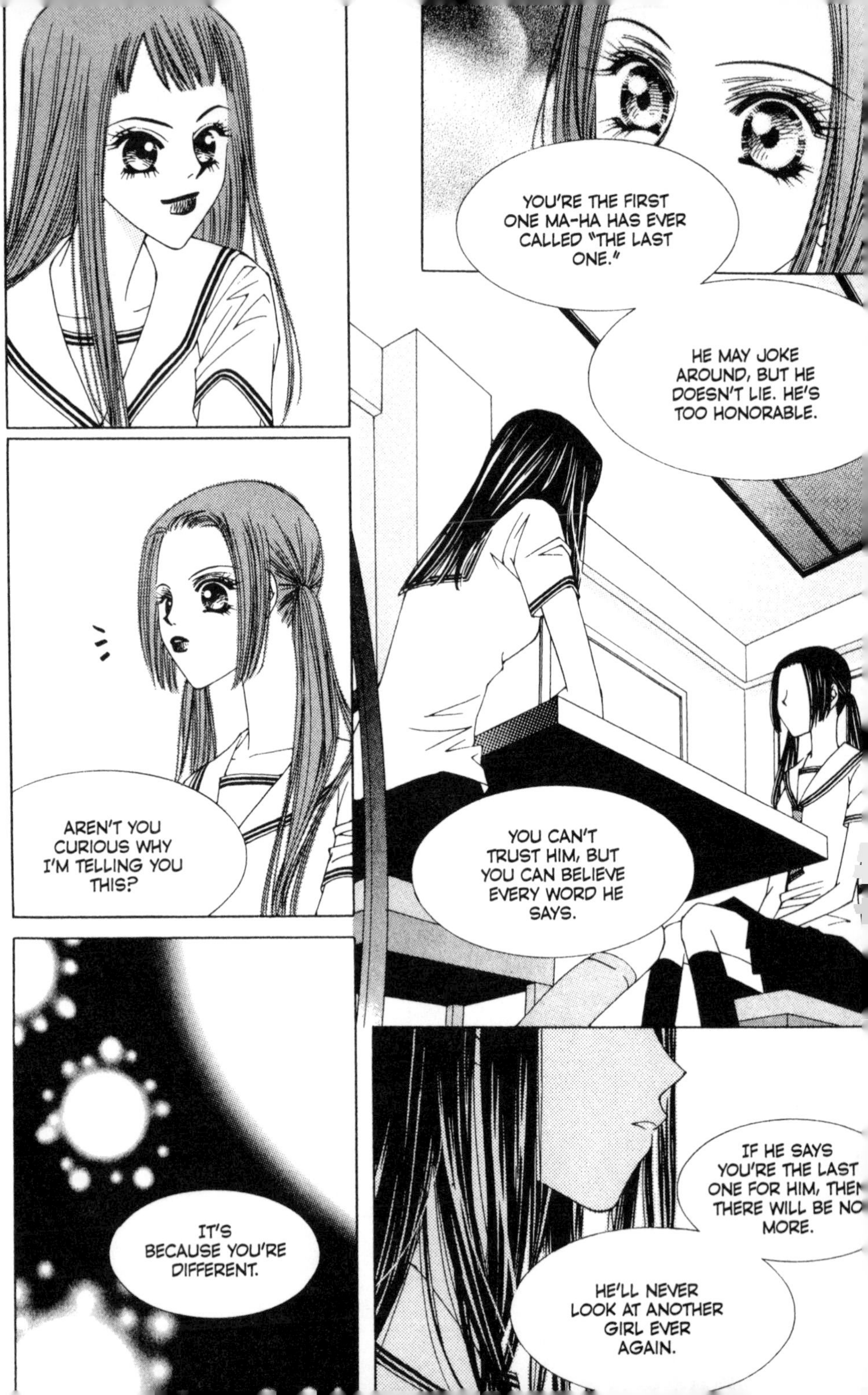

AREN'T YOU CURIOUS WHY I'M TELLING YOU THIS?
IT'S BECAUSE YOU'RE DIFFERENT.
YOU'RE THE FIRST ONE MA-HA HAS EVER CALLED "THE LAST ONE."
HE MAY JOKE AROUND, BUT HE DOESN'T LIE. HE'S TOO HONORABLE.
YOU CAN'T TRUST HIM, BUT YOU CAN BELIEVE EVERY WORD HE SAYS.
IF HE SAYS YOU'RE THE LAST ONE FOR HIM, THEN THERE WILL BE NO MORE.
HE'LL NEVER LOOK AT ANOTHER GIRL EVER AGAIN.

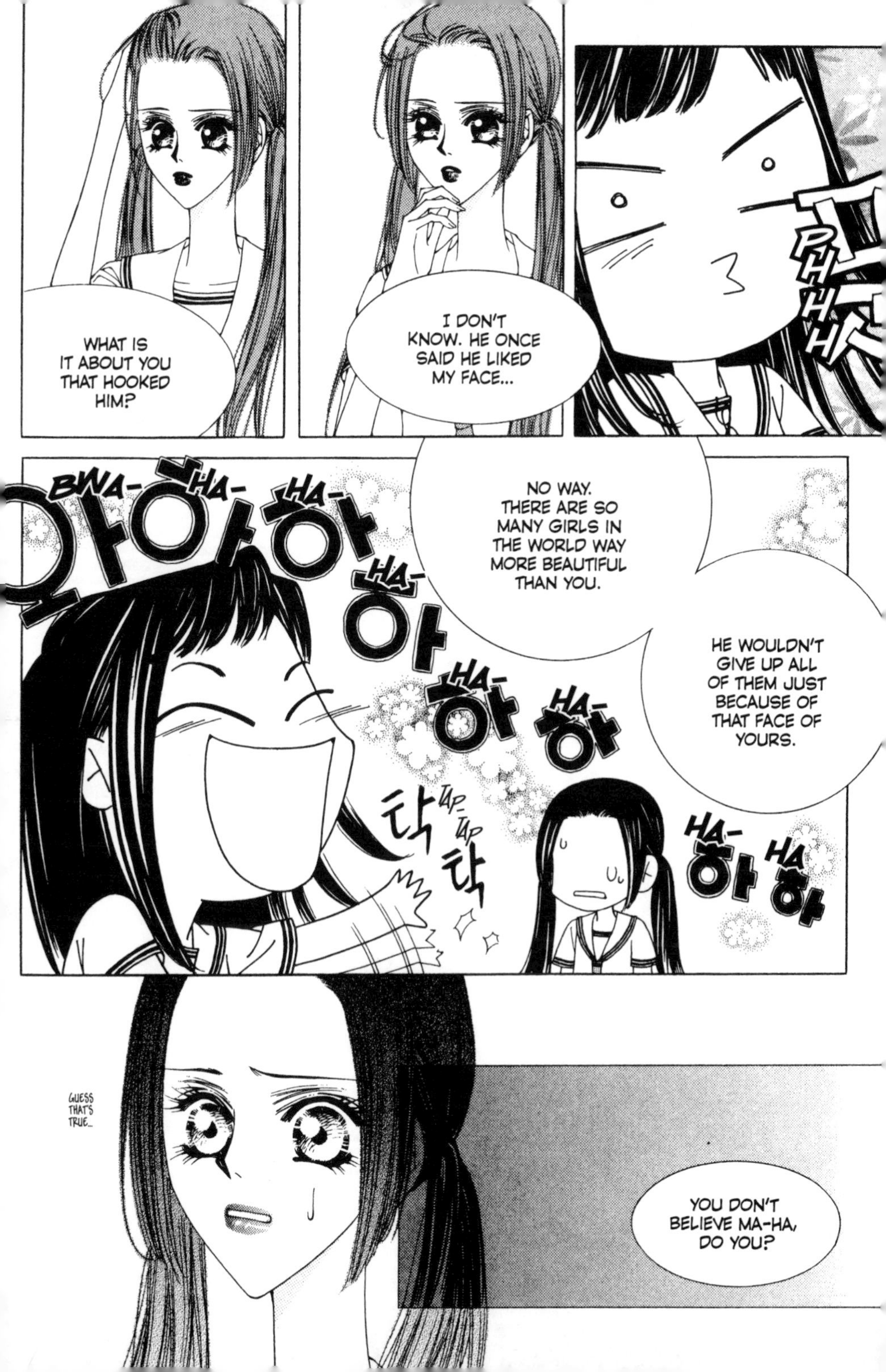
WHAT IS IT ABOUT YOU THAT HOOKED HIM?
I DON'T KNOW. HE ONCE SAID HE LIKED MY FACE...
PHHHH
BWA-HA-HA-HA-HA-HA-
NO WAY. THERE ARE SO MANY GIRLS IN THE WORLD WAY MORE BEAUTIFUL THAN YOU.
HE WOULDN'T GIVE UP ALL OF THEM JUST BECAUSE OF THAT FACE OF YOURS.
TAP-TAP
HA-HA
GUESS THAT'S TRUE...
YOU DON'T BELIEVE MA-HA, DO YOU?

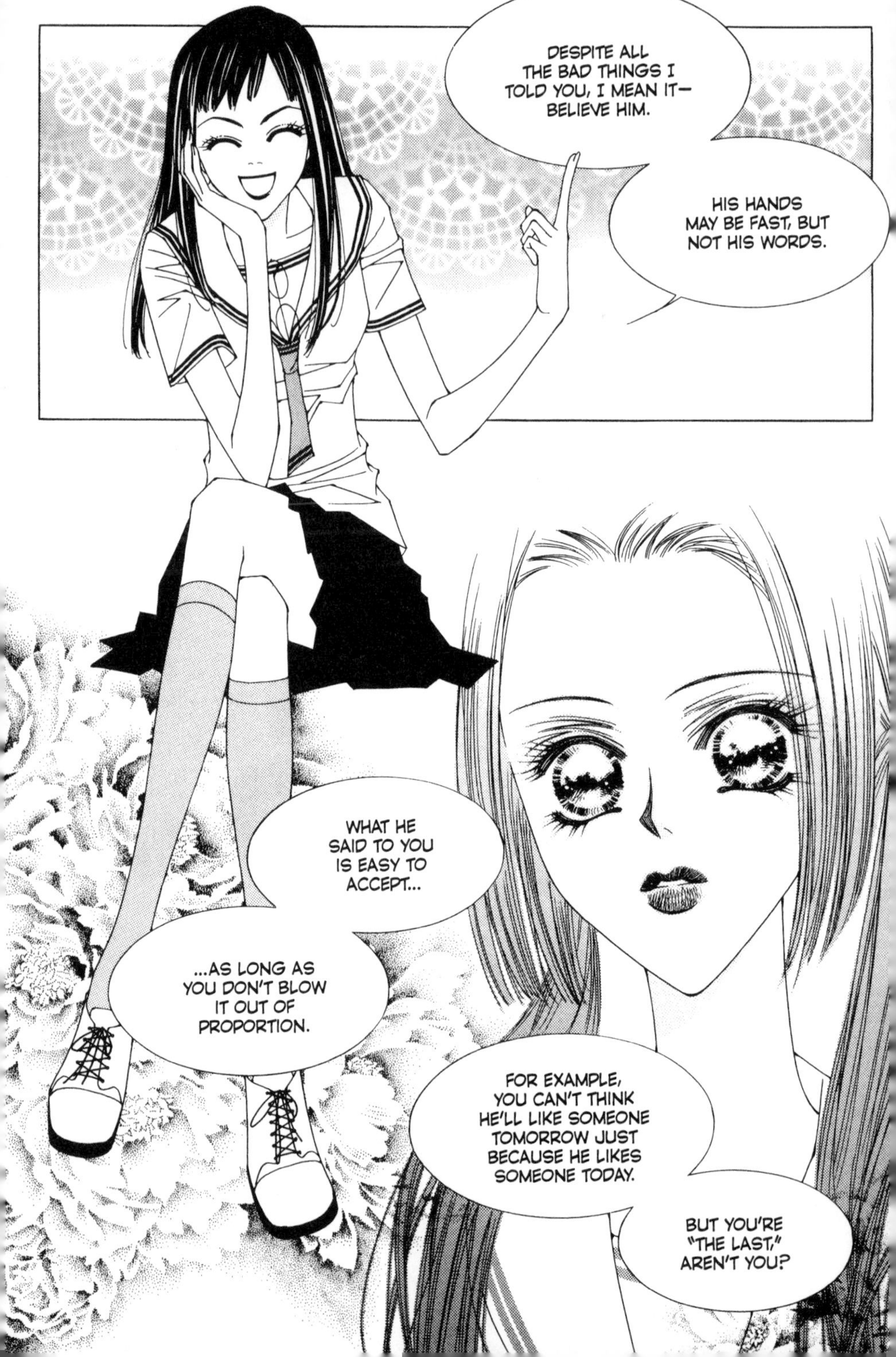
DESPITE ALL THE BAD THINGS I TOLD YOU, I MEAN IT—BELIEVE HIM.
HIS HANDS MAY BE FAST, BUT NOT HIS WORDS.
WHAT HE SAID TO YOU IS EASY TO ACCEPT...
...AS LONG AS YOU DON'T BLOW IT OUT OF PROPORTION.
FOR EXAMPLE, YOU CAN'T THINK HE'LL LIKE SOMEONE TOMORROW JUST BECAUSE HE LIKES SOMEONE TODAY.
BUT YOU'RE "THE LAST," AREN'T YOU?

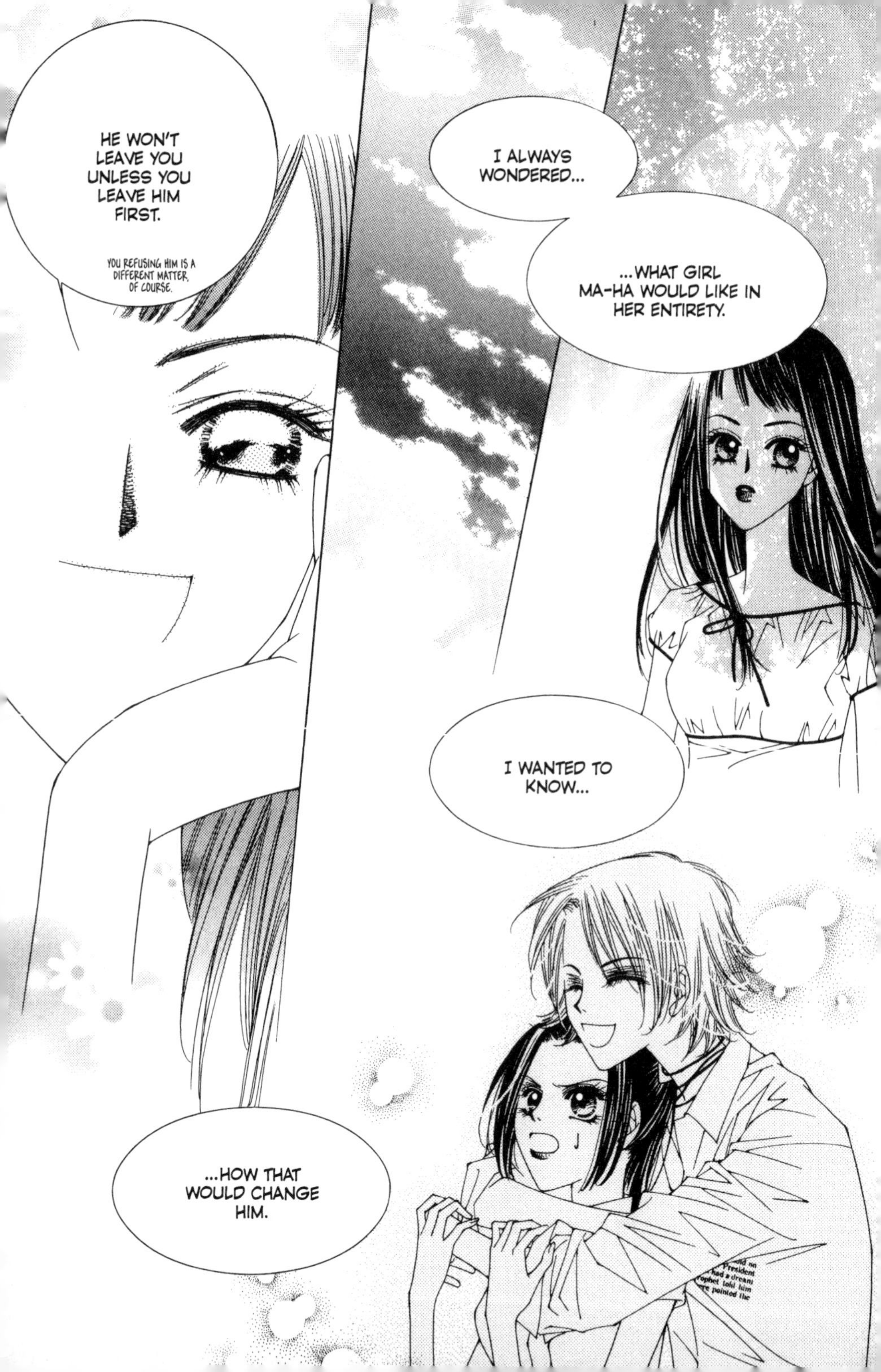
HE WON'T LEAVE YOU UNLESS YOU LEAVE HIM FIRST.
YOU REFUSING HIM IS A DIFFERENT MATTER, OF COURSE.
I ALWAYS WONDERED...
...WHAT GIRL MA-HA WOULD LIKE IN HER ENTIRETY.
I WANTED TO KNOW...
...HOW THAT WOULD CHANGE HIM.

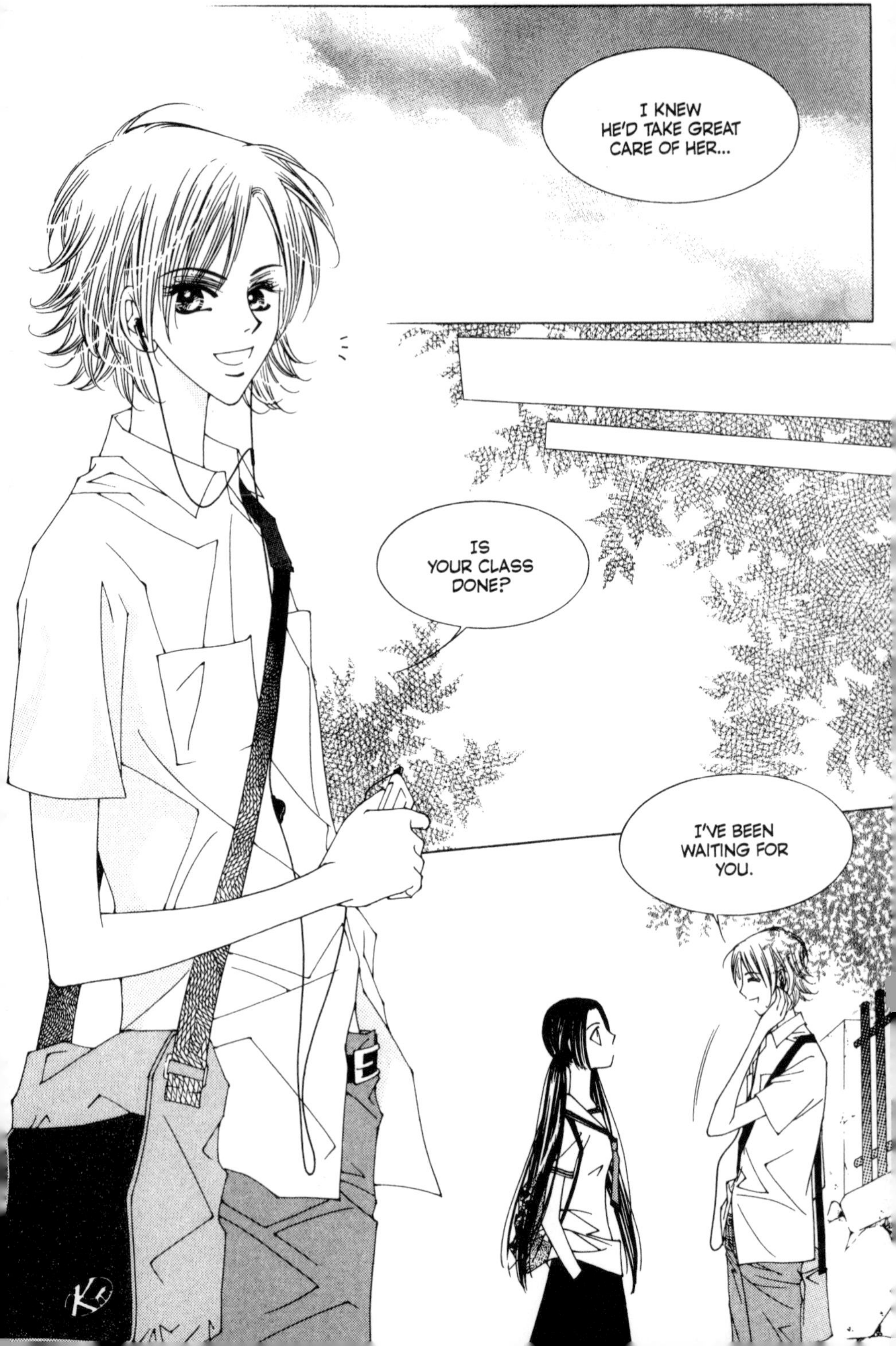
I KNEW HE'D TAKE GREAT CARE OF HER...
IS YOUR CLASS DONE?
I'VE BEEN WAITING FOR YOU.

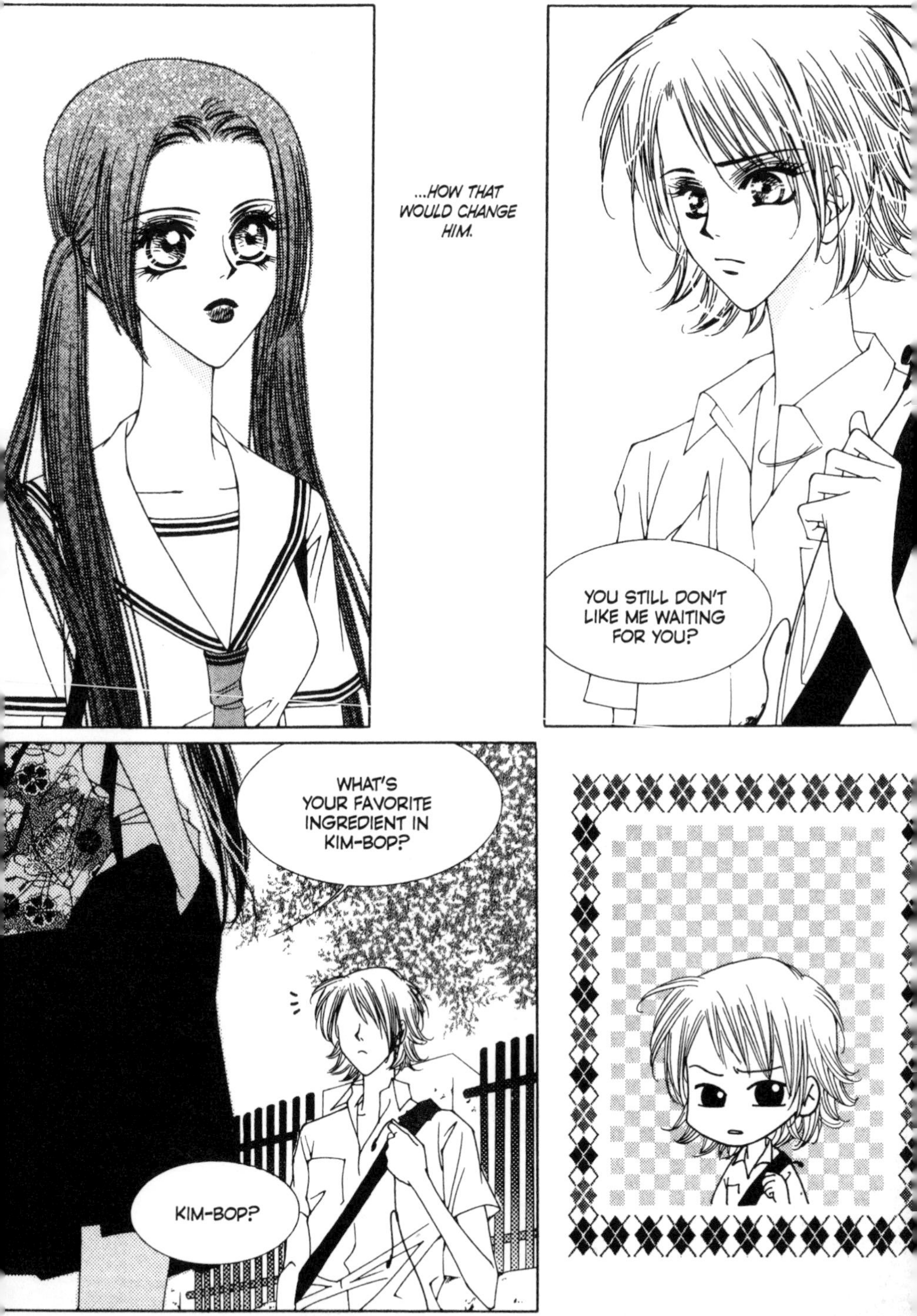
...HOW THAT WOULD CHANGE HIM.
YOU STILL DON'T LIKE ME WAITING FOR YOU?
WHAT'S YOUR FAVORITE INGREDIENT IN KIM-BOP?
KIM-BOP?

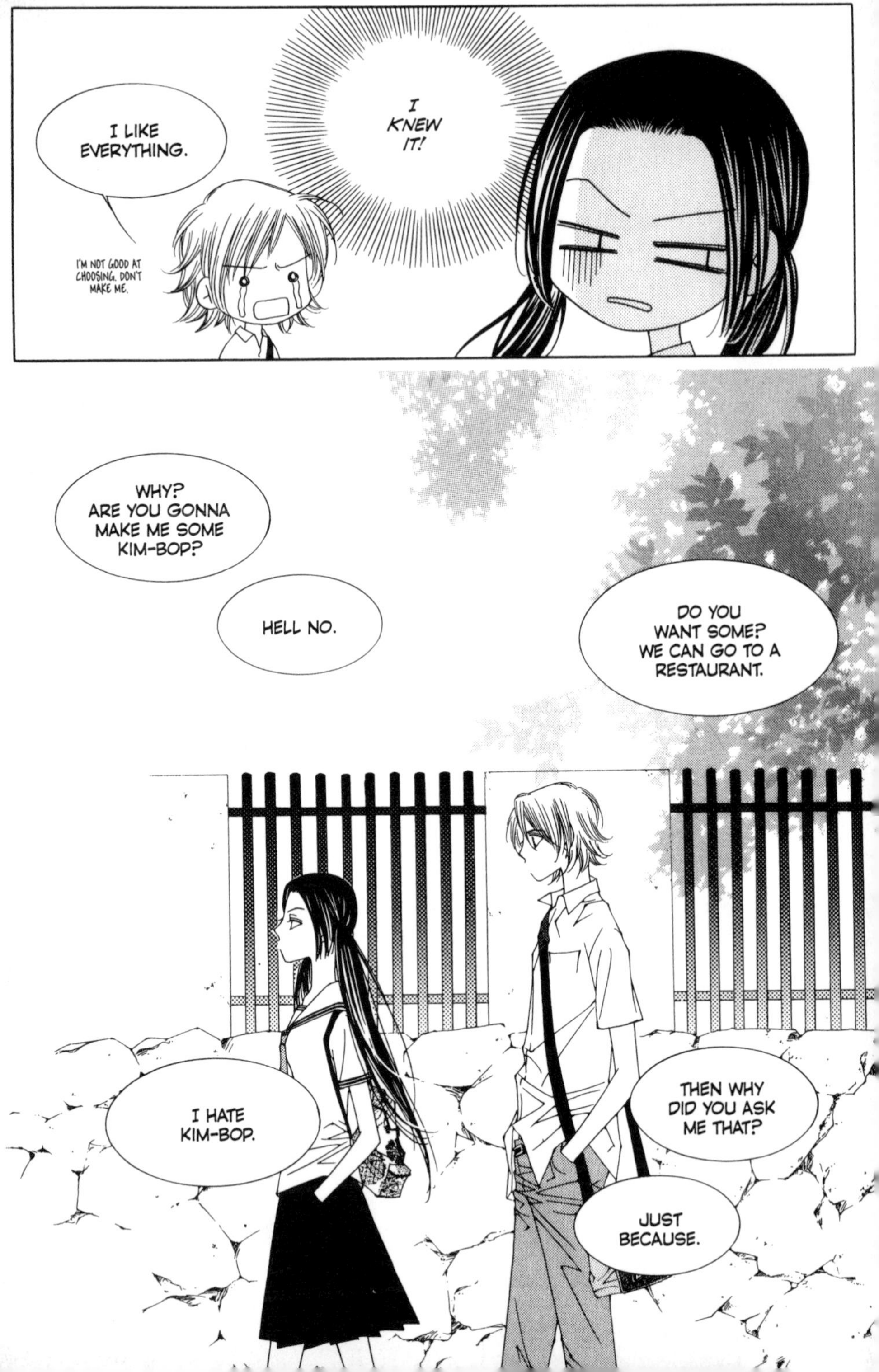
I LIKE EVERYTHING.
I'M NOT GOOD AT CHOOSING. DON'T MAKE ME.
I KNEW IT!
WHY? ARE YOU GONNA MAKE ME SOME KIM-BOP?
HELL NO.
DO YOU WANT SOME? WE CAN GO TO A RESTAURANT.
I HATE KIM-BOP.
THEN WHY DID YOU ASK ME THAT?
JUST BECAUSE.

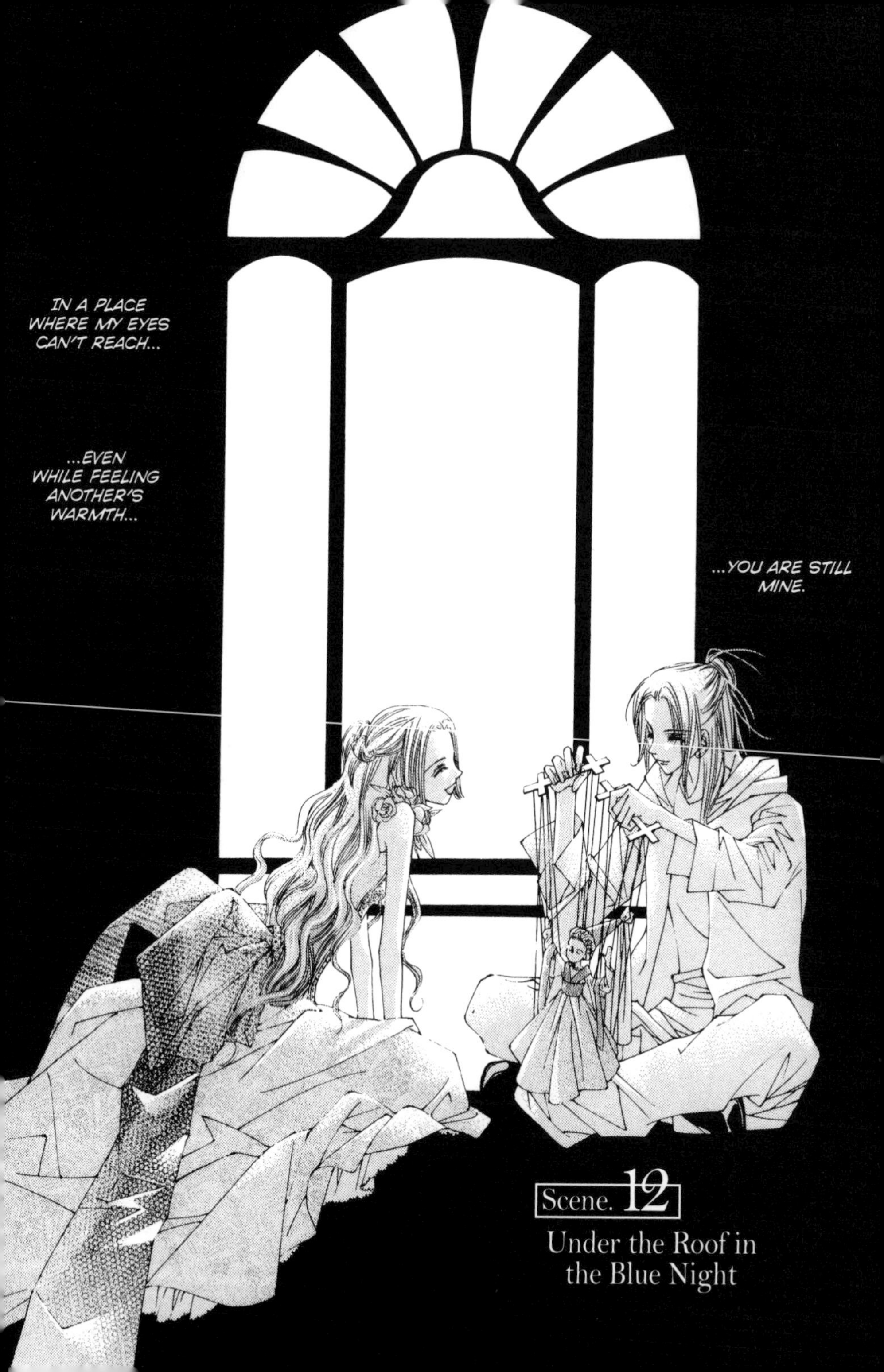
IN A PLACE WHERE MY EYES CAN'T REACH...
...EVEN WHILE FEELING ANOTHER'S WARMTH...
...YOU ARE STILL MINE.
Scene. 12
Under the Roof in the Blue Night

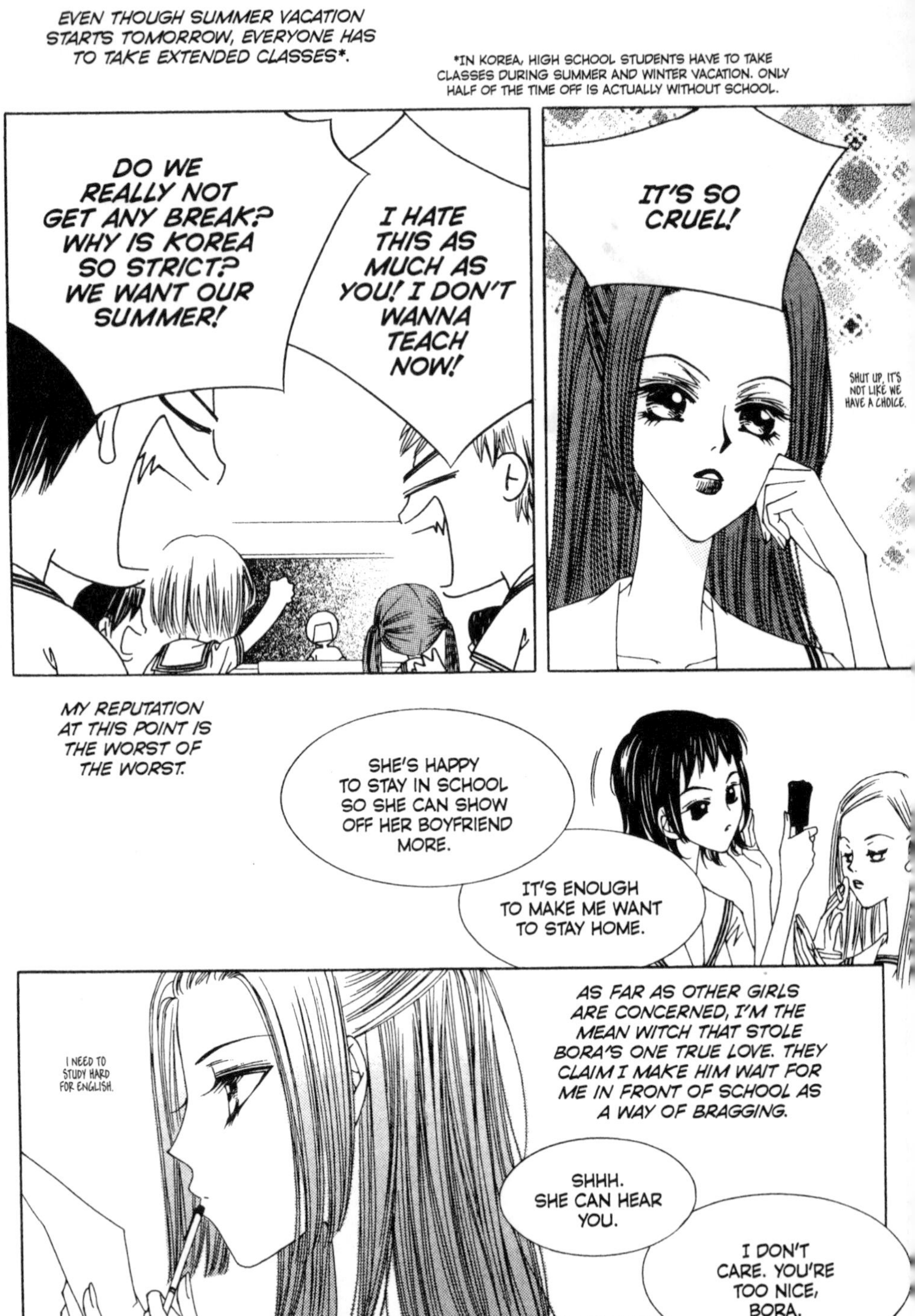
EVEN THOUGH SUMMER VACATION STARTS TOMORROW, EVERYONE HAS TO TAKE EXTENDED CLASSES*.
*IN KOREA, HIGH SCHOOL STUDENTS HAVE TO TAKE CLASSES DURING SUMMER AND WINTER VACATION. ONLY HALF OF THE TIME OFF IS ACTUALLY WITHOUT SCHOOL.
DO WE REALLY NOT GET ANY BREAK? WHY IS KOREA SO STRICT? WE WANT OUR SUMMER!
I HATE THIS AS MUCH AS YOU! I DON'T WANNA TEACH NOW!
IT'S SO CRUEL!
SHUT UP, IT'S NOT LIKE WE HAVE A CHOICE.
MY REPUTATION AT THIS POINT IS THE WORST OF THE WORST.
SHE'S HAPPY TO STAY IN SCHOOL SO SHE CAN SHOW OFF HER BOYFRIEND MORE.
IT'S ENOUGH TO MAKE ME WANT TO STAY HOME.
I NEED TO STUDY HARD FOR ENGLISH.
AS FAR AS OTHER GIRLS ARE CONCERNED, I'M THE MEAN WITCH THAT STOLE BORA'S ONE TRUE LOVE. THEY CLAIM I MAKE HIM WAIT FOR ME IN FRONT OF SCHOOL AS A WAY OF BRAGGING.
SHHH. SHE CAN HEAR YOU.
I DON'T CARE. YOU'RE TOO NICE, BORA.

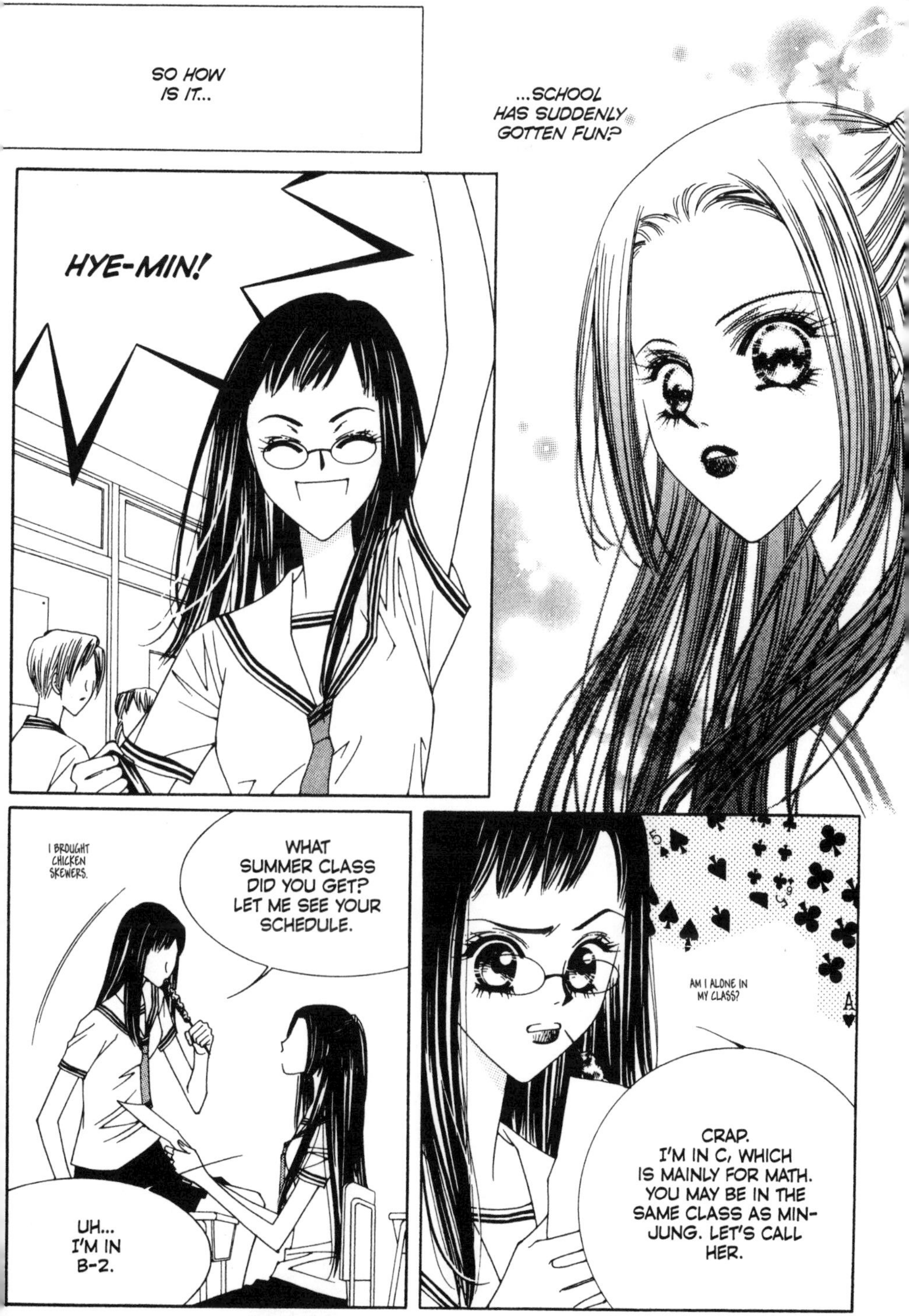
SO HOW IS IT...
...SCHOOL HAS SUDDENLY GOTTEN FUN?
HYE-MIN!
I BROUGHT CHICKEN SKEWERS.
WHAT SUMMER CLASS DID YOU GET? LET ME SEE YOUR SCHEDULE.
UH... I'M IN B-2.
AM I ALONE IN MY CLASS?
CRAP. I'M IN C, WHICH IS MAINLY FOR MATH. YOU MAY BE IN THE SAME CLASS AS MIN-JUNG. LET'S CALL HER.

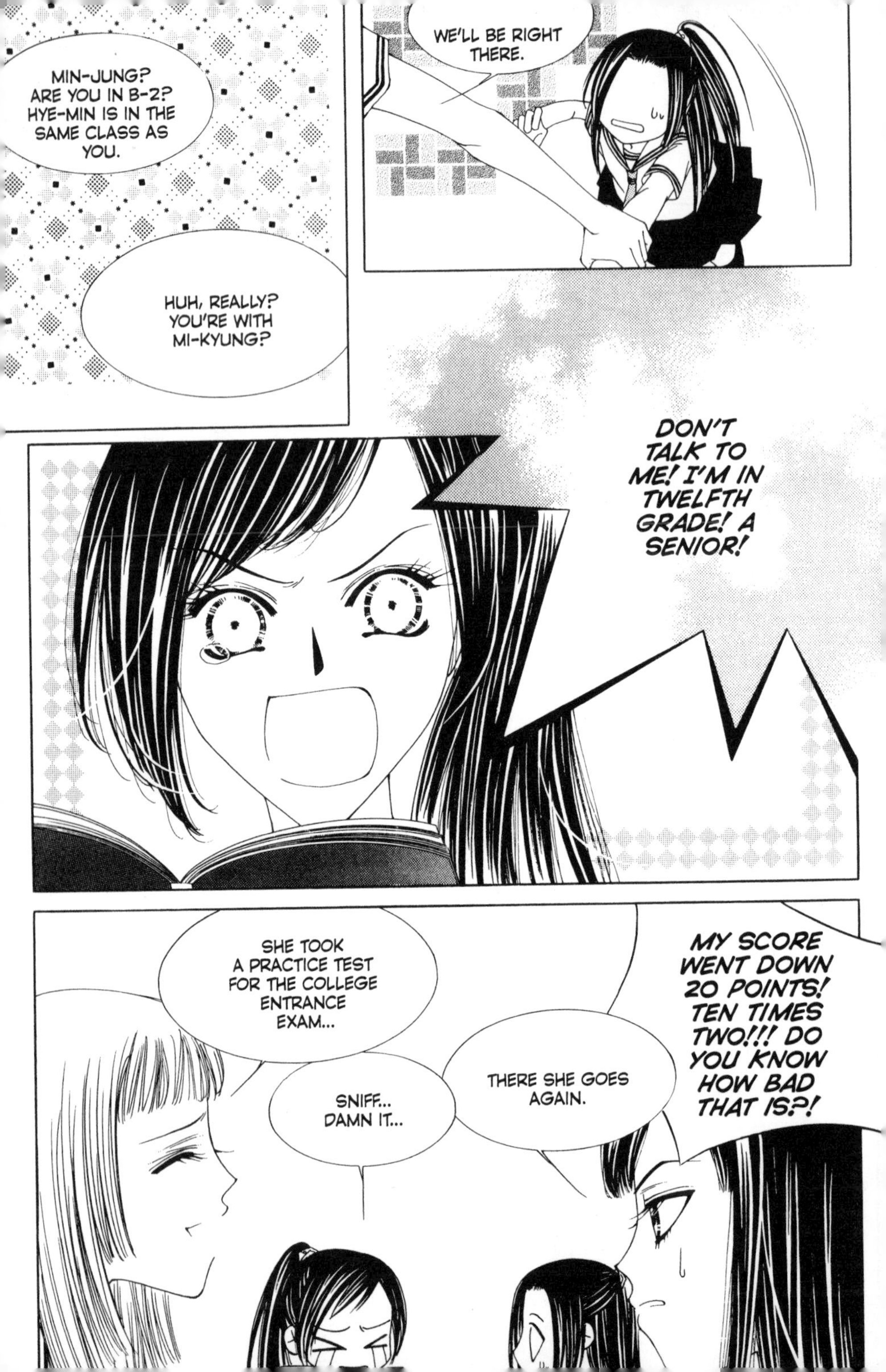
MIN-JUNG? ARE YOU IN B-2? HYE-MIN IS IN THE SAME CLASS AS YOU.
HUH, REALLY? YOU'RE WITH MI-KYUNG?
WE'LL BE RIGHT THERE.
DON'T TALK TO ME! I'M IN TWELFTH GRADE! A SENIOR!
SHE TOOK A PRACTICE TEST FOR THE COLLEGE ENTRANCE EXAM...
SNIFF... DAMN IT...
THERE SHE GOES AGAIN.
MY SCORE WENT DOWN 20 POINTS! TEN TIMES TWO!!! DO YOU KNOW HOW BAD THAT IS?!

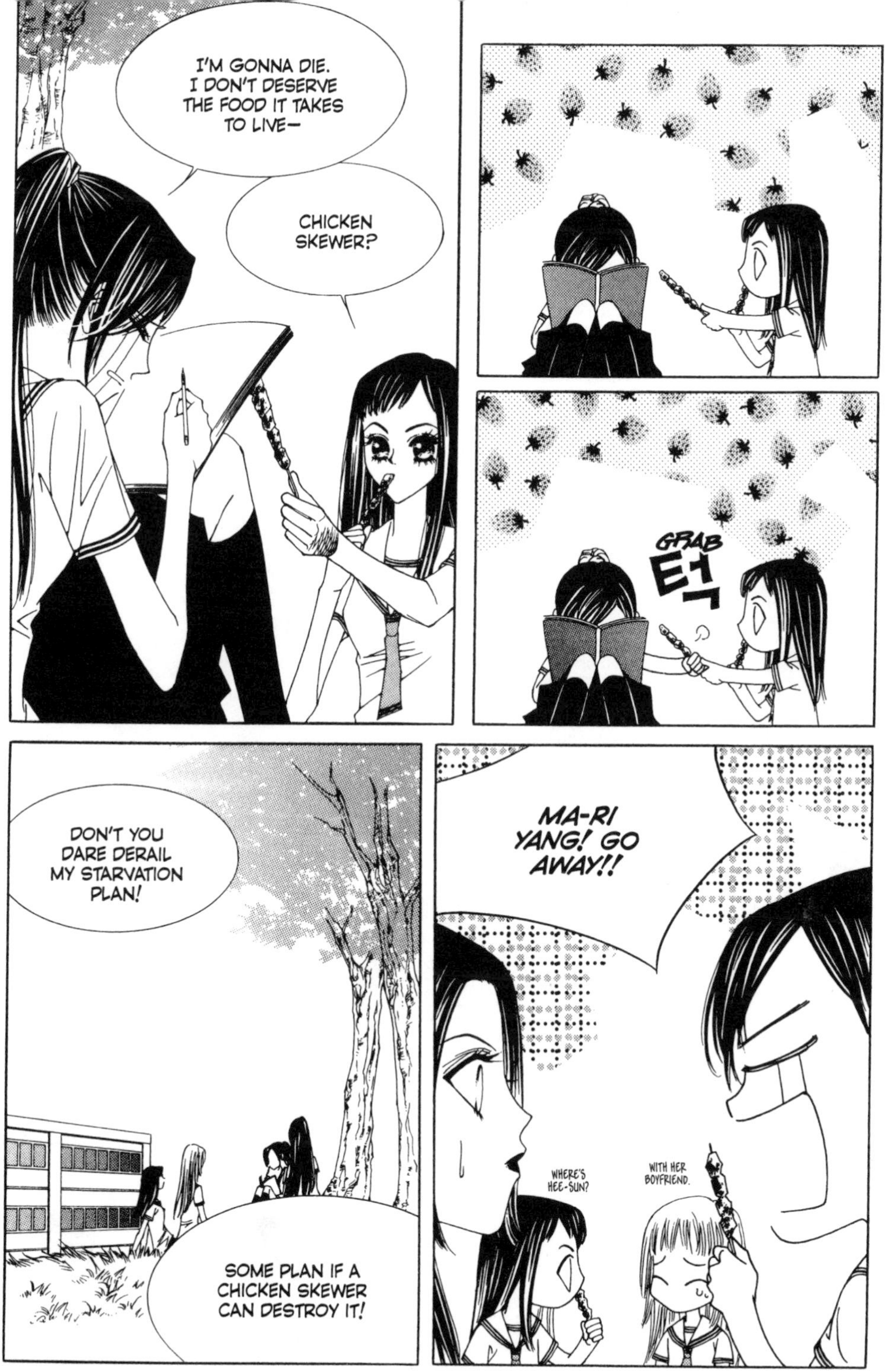
I'M GONNA DIE. I DON'T DESERVE THE FOOD IT TAKES TO LIVE—
CHICKEN SKEWER?
GRAB
DON'T YOU DARE DERAIL MY STARVATION PLAN!
SOME PLAN IF A CHICKEN SKEWER CAN DESTROY IT!
MA-RI YANG! GO AWAY!!
WHERE'S HEE-SUN?
WITH HER BOYFRIEND.

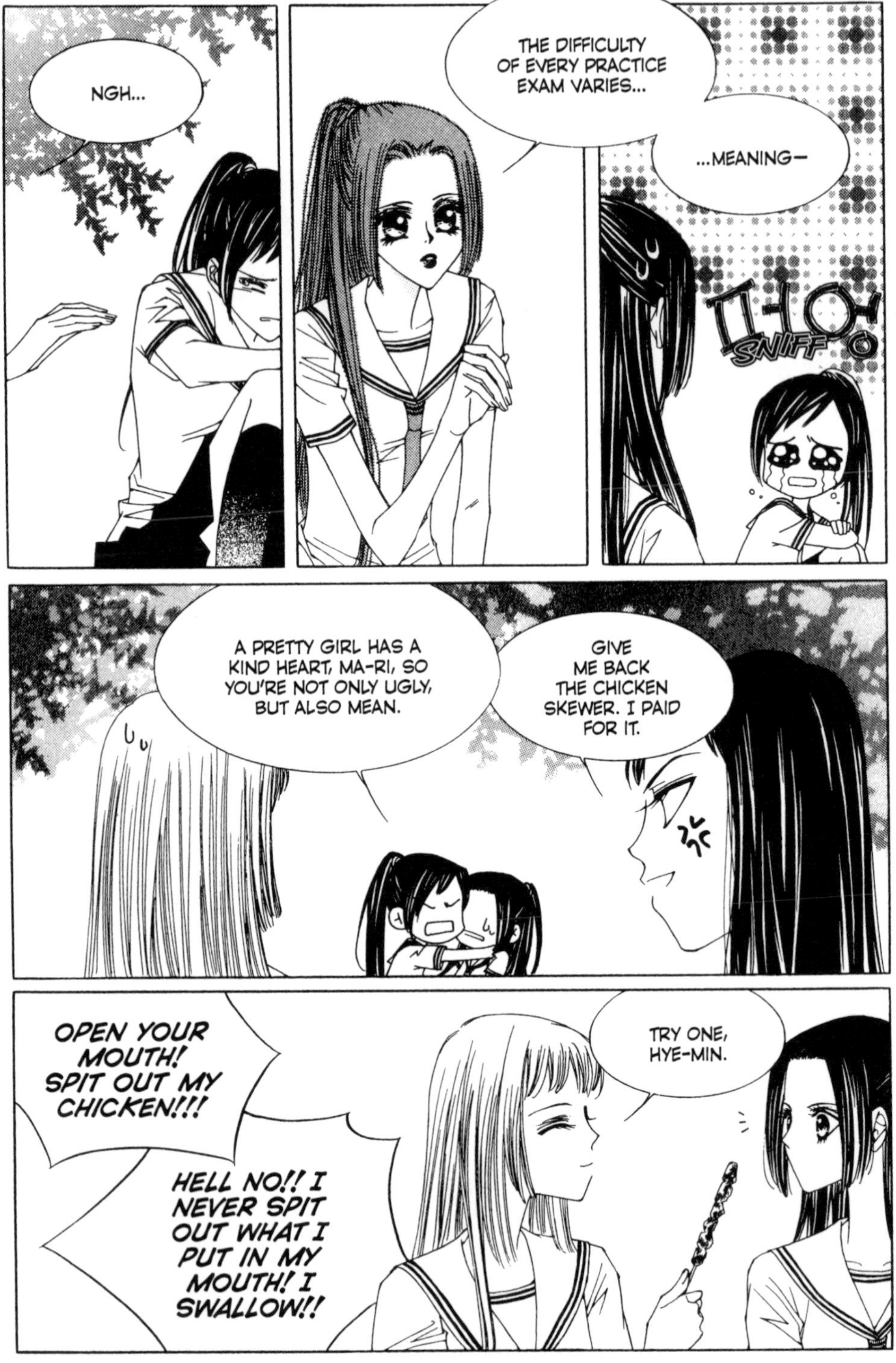

NGH...
THE DIFFICULTY OF EVERY PRACTICE EXAM VARIES...
...MEANING—
SNIFF
A PRETTY GIRL HAS A KIND HEART, MA-RI, SO YOU'RE NOT ONLY UGLY, BUT ALSO MEAN.
GIVE ME BACK THE CHICKEN SKEWER. I PAID FOR IT.
OPEN YOUR MOUTH! SPIT OUT MY CHICKEN!!!
HELL NO!! I NEVER SPIT OUT WHAT I PUT IN MY MOUTH! I SWALLOW!!
TRY ONE, HYE-MIN.

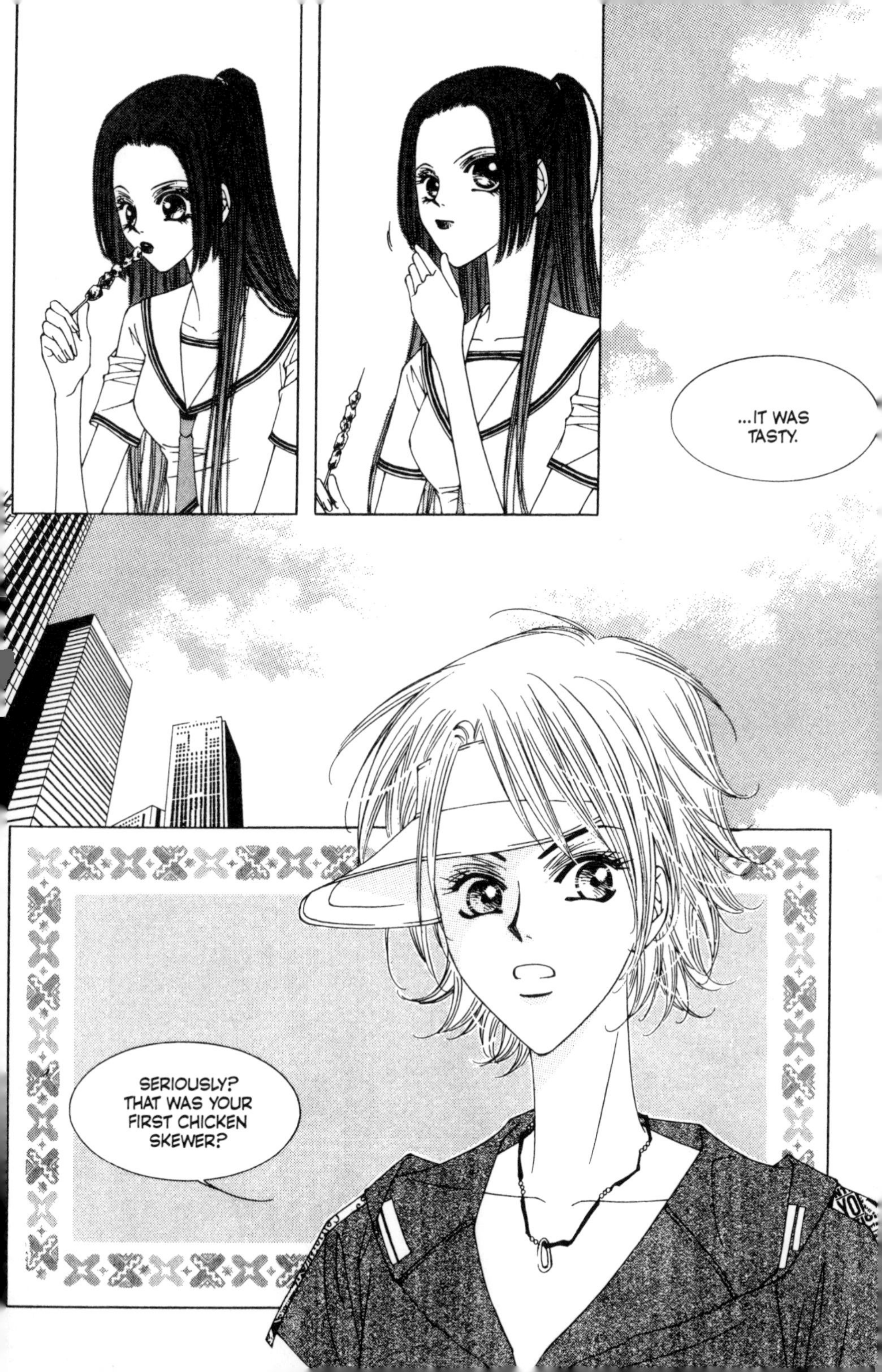
...IT WAS TASTY.
SERIOUSLY? THAT WAS YOUR FIRST CHICKEN SKEWER?

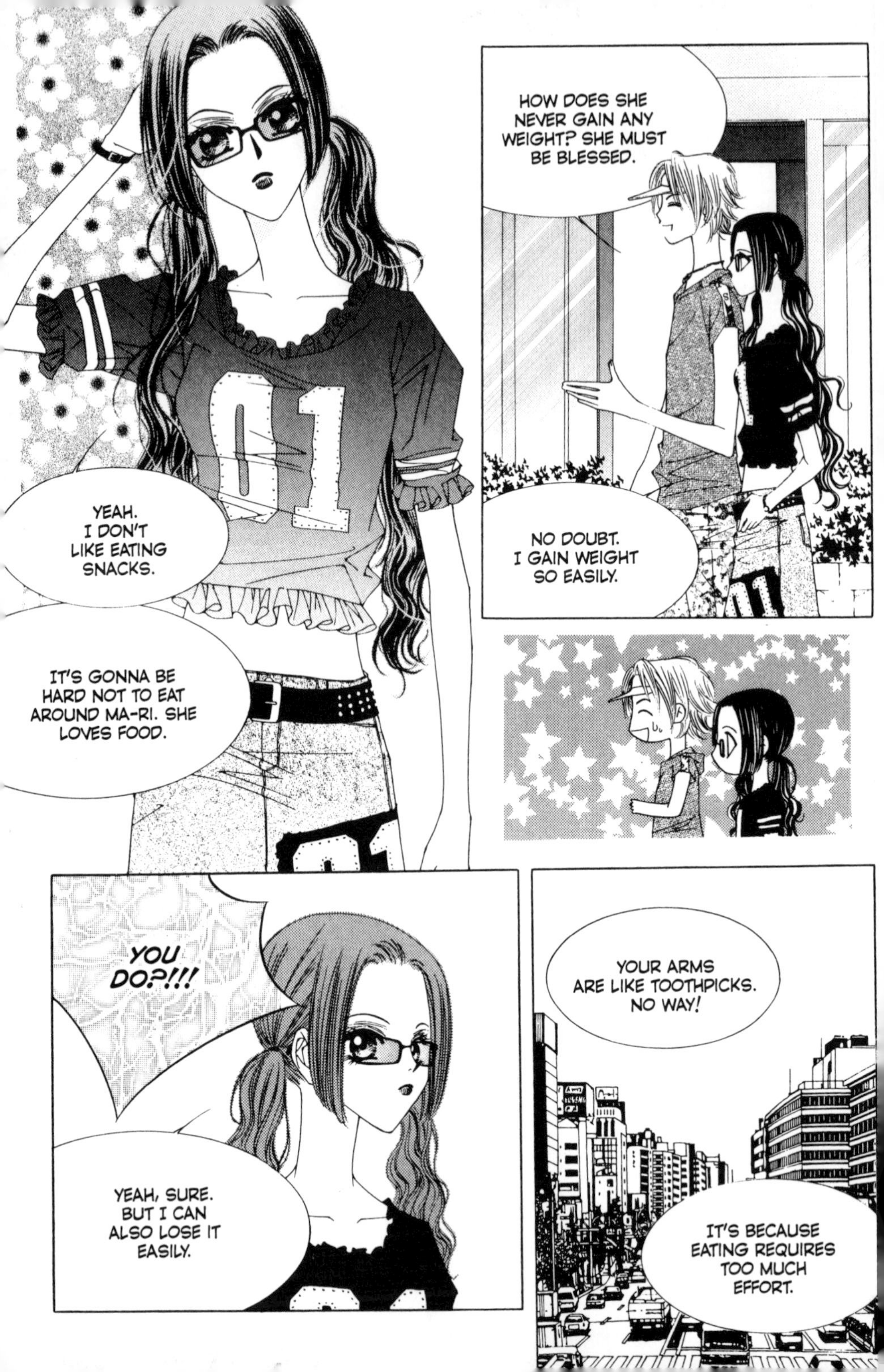
YEAH. I DON'T LIKE EATING SNACKS.
IT'S GONNA BE HARD NOT TO EAT AROUND MA-RI. SHE LOVES FOOD.
HOW DOES SHE NEVER GAIN ANY WEIGHT? SHE MUST BE BLESSED.
NO DOUBT. I GAIN WEIGHT SO EASILY.
YOU DO?!!!
YEAH, SURE. BUT I CAN ALSO LOSE IT EASILY.
YOUR ARMS ARE LIKE TOOTHPICKS. NO WAY!
IT'S BECAUSE EATING REQUIRES TOO MUCH EFFORT.

DID YOU HAVE BREAKFAST?

AN APPLE...

...AND WATER...

WATER?

WHAT ABOUT LUNCH?

HOW ARE YOU EVEN WALKING RIGHT NOW?

THAT CHICKEN SKEWER.

I'M NOT HUNGRY.

YOU'RE SO STARVED, YOU'VE LAPPED YOUR OWN HUNGER. IT'S BACKWARDS!

COUNT

Casting in the Sov
only to highlight
e says, ience. her interes
ating once again the
out if they can use
elicopter."
"-cost French Puma,
strictly ma claims
es; we knows.
we cannot fin
with innovative twists, his clothes s
e design. With a reputation for witty
wear, she's largely responsible for r
nd her otten
ost forgotten art and she is intrigu
an Muir, Betty Jacks
e has produced individual ranges
See into her new sh

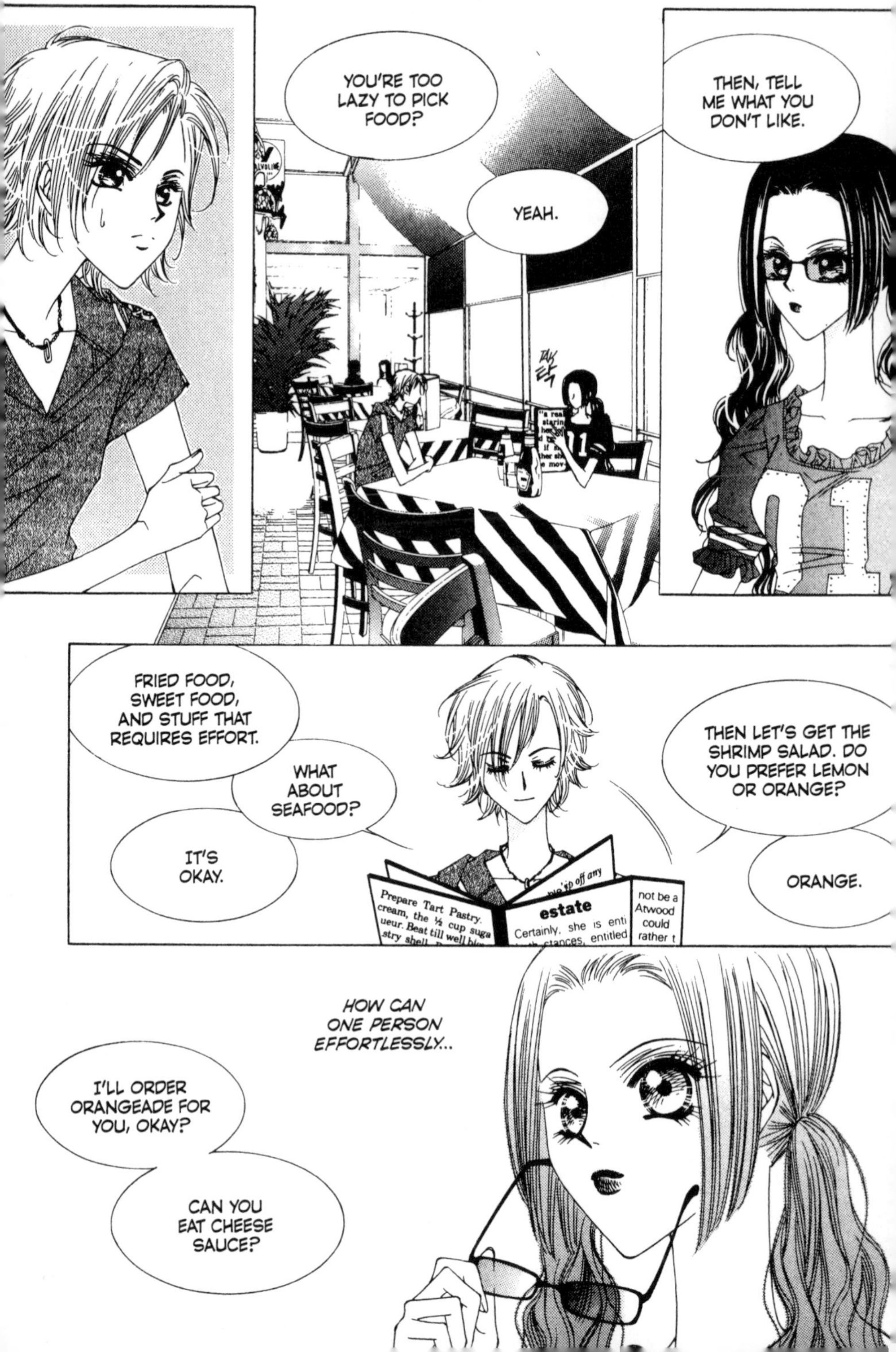

YOU'RE TOO LAZY TO PICK FOOD?
YEAH.
THEN, TELL ME WHAT YOU DON'T LIKE.
FRIED FOOD, SWEET FOOD, AND STUFF THAT REQUIRES EFFORT.
WHAT ABOUT SEAFOOD?
IT'S OKAY.
THEN LET'S GET THE SHRIMP SALAD. DO YOU PREFER LEMON OR ORANGE?
ORANGE.
HOW CAN ONE PERSON EFFORTLESSLY...
I'LL ORDER ORANGEADE FOR YOU, OKAY?
CAN YOU EAT CHEESE SAUCE?

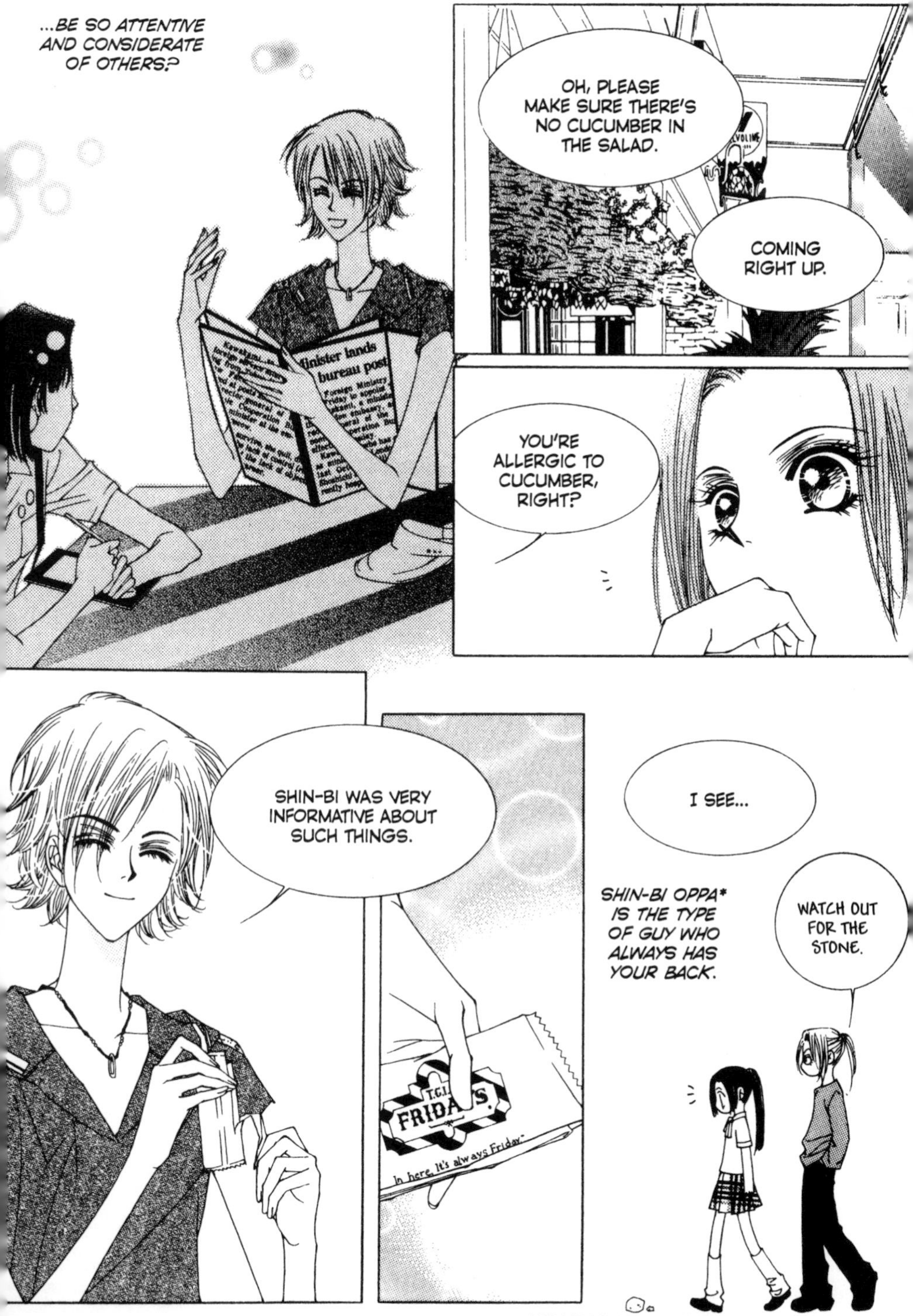
...BE SO ATTENTIVE AND CONSIDERATE OF OTHERS?
Minister lands bureau post
OH, PLEASE MAKE SURE THERE'S NO CUCUMBER IN THE SALAD.
COMING RIGHT UP.
YOU'RE ALLERGIC TO CUCUMBER, RIGHT?
SHIN-BI WAS VERY INFORMATIVE ABOUT SUCH THINGS.
In here, It's always Friday.
I SEE...
SHIN-BI OPPA* IS THE TYPE OF GUY WHO ALWAYS HAS YOUR BACK.
WATCH OUT FOR THE STONE.

*TERM KOREAN GIRLS USE FOR OLDER BOYS. LITERALLY MEANS "OLDER BROTHER."

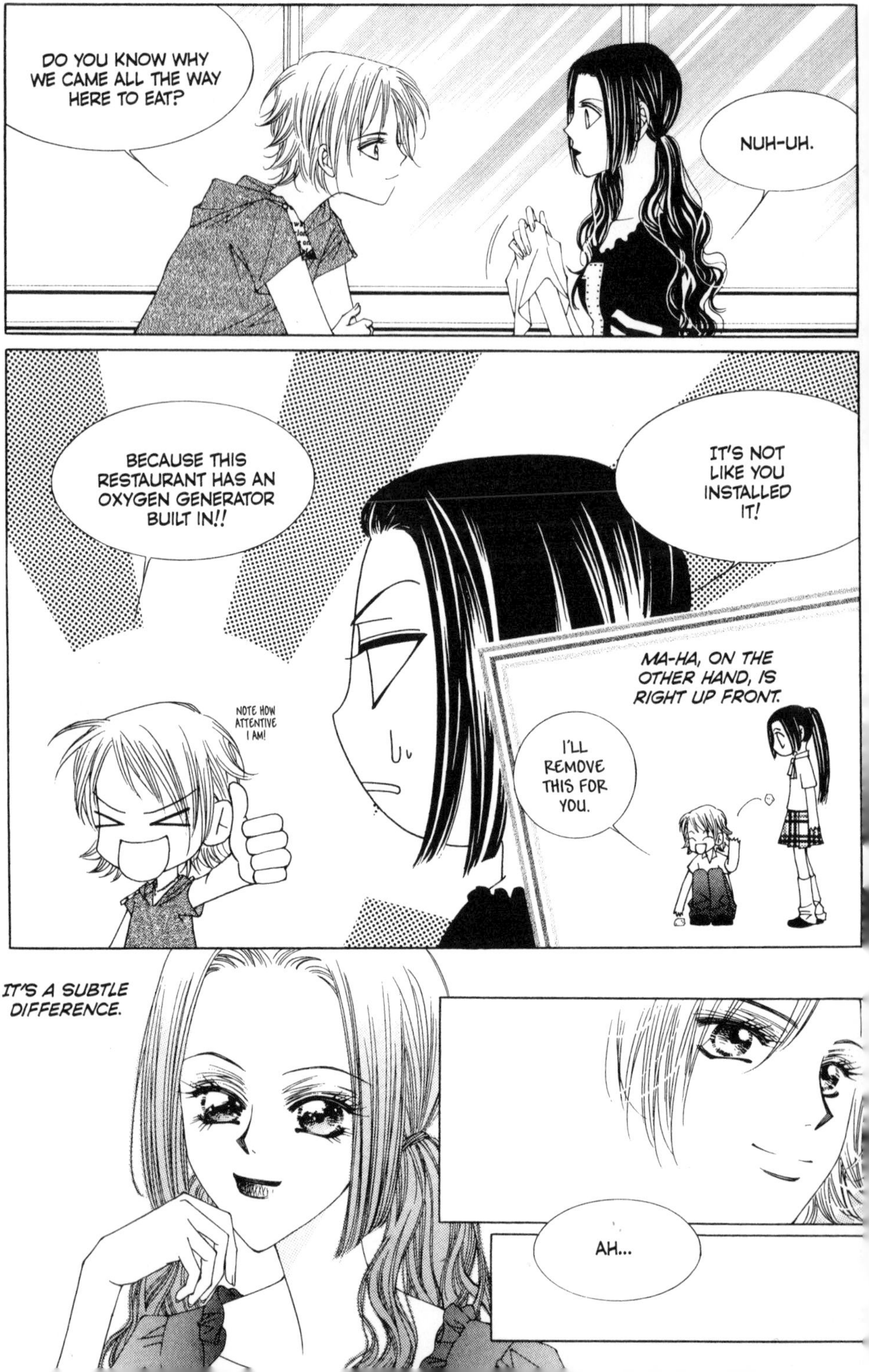
DO YOU KNOW WHY WE CAME ALL THE WAY HERE TO EAT?
NUH-UH.
BECAUSE THIS RESTAURANT HAS AN OXYGEN GENERATOR BUILT IN!!
NOTE HOW ATTENTIVE I AM!
IT'S NOT LIKE YOU INSTALLED IT!
MA-HA, ON THE OTHER HAND, IS RIGHT UP FRONT.
I'LL REMOVE THIS FOR YOU.
IT'S A SUBTLE DIFFERENCE.
AH...

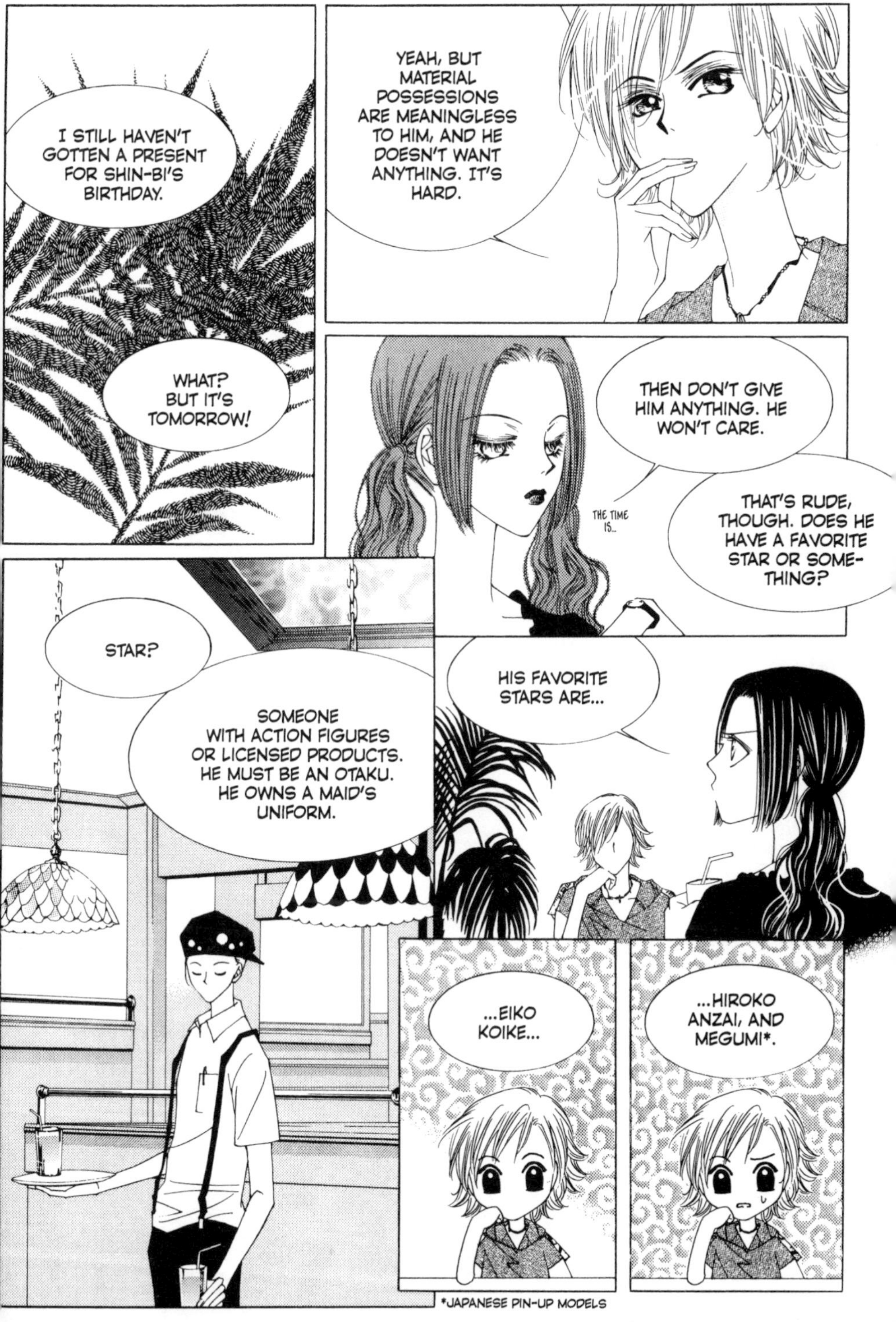
I STILL HAVEN'T GOTTEN A PRESENT FOR SHIN-BI'S BIRTHDAY.
WHAT? BUT IT'S TOMORROW!
YEAH, BUT MATERIAL POSSESSIONS ARE MEANINGLESS TO HIM, AND HE DOESN'T WANT ANYTHING. IT'S HARD.
THEN DON'T GIVE HIM ANYTHING. HE WON'T CARE.
THE TIME IS...
THAT'S RUDE, THOUGH. DOES HE HAVE A FAVORITE STAR OR SOME-THING?
STAR?
SOMEONE WITH ACTION FIGURES OR LICENSED PRODUCTS. HE MUST BE AN OTAKU. HE OWNS A MAID'S UNIFORM.
HIS FAVORITE STARS ARE...
...EIKO KOIKE...
...HIROKO ANZAI, AND MEGUMI*.
*JAPANESE PIN-UP MODELS

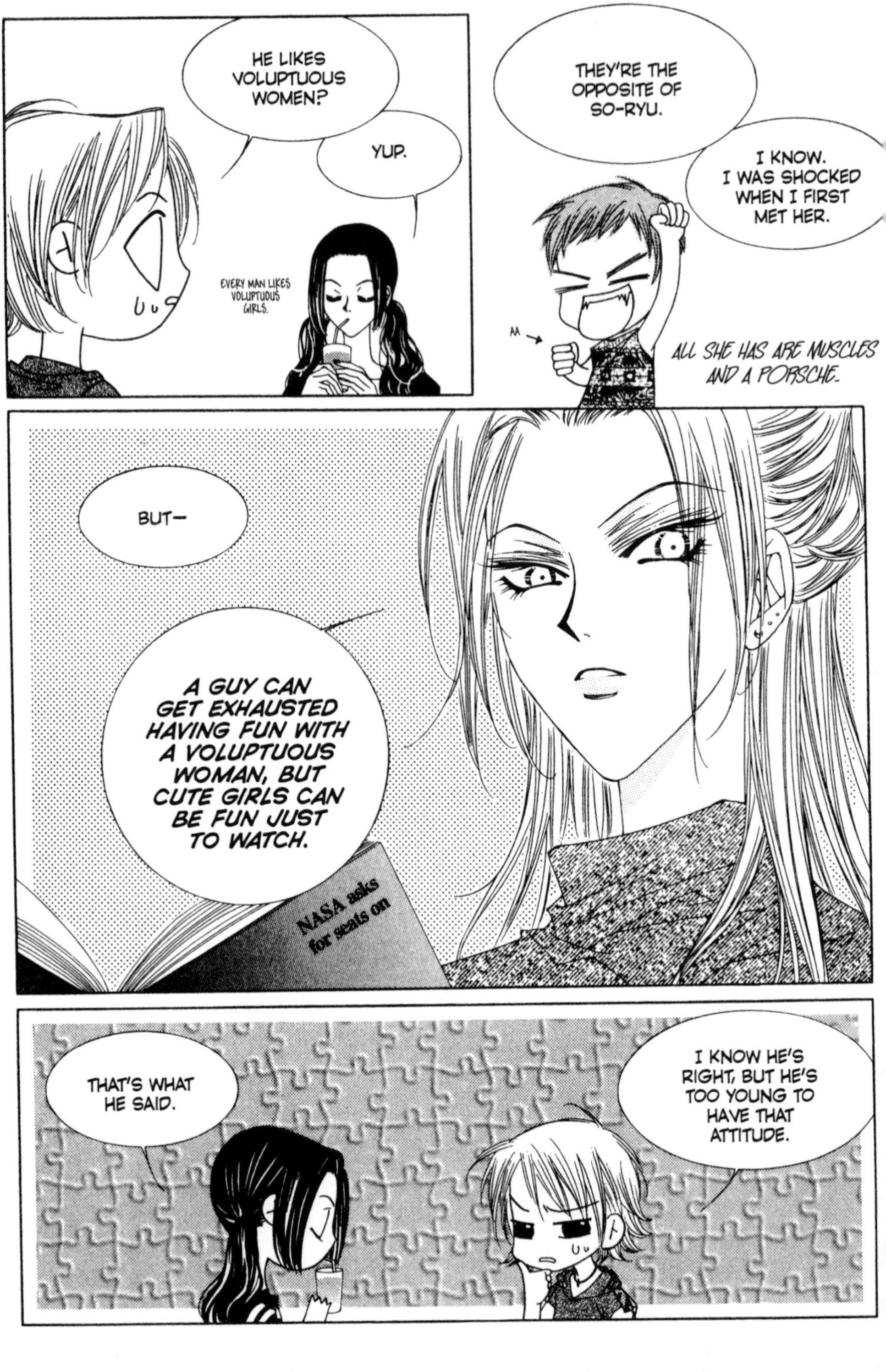
HE LIKES VOLUPTUOUS WOMEN?
YUP.
EVERY MAN LIKES VOLUPTUOUS GIRLS.
THEY'RE THE OPPOSITE OF SO-RYU.
I KNOW. I WAS SHOCKED WHEN I FIRST MET HER.
AA
ALL SHE HAS ARE MUSCLES AND A PORSCHE.
BUT—
A GUY CAN GET EXHAUSTED HAVING FUN WITH A VOLUPTUOUS WOMAN, BUT CUTE GIRLS CAN BE FUN JUST TO WATCH.
NASA asks for seats on
THAT'S WHAT HE SAID.
I KNOW HE'S RIGHT, BUT HE'S TOO YOUNG TO HAVE THAT ATTITUDE.

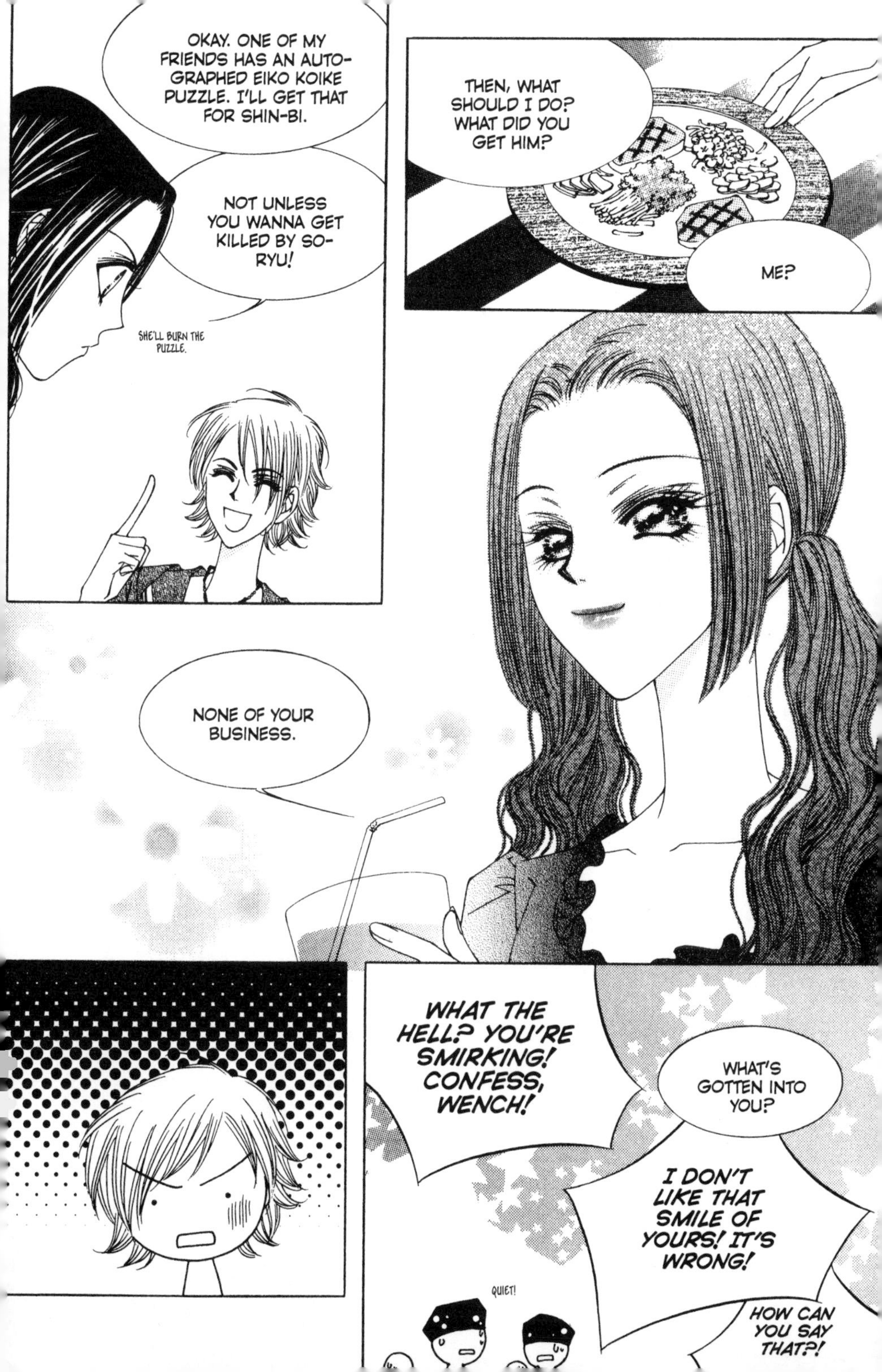
OKAY. ONE OF MY FRIENDS HAS AN AUTO-GRAPHED EIKO KOIKE PUZZLE. I'LL GET THAT FOR SHIN-BI.
NOT UNLESS YOU WANNA GET KILLED BY SO-RYU!
SHE'LL BURN THE PUZZLE.
THEN, WHAT SHOULD I DO? WHAT DID YOU GET HIM?
ME?
NONE OF YOUR BUSINESS.
WHAT THE HELL? YOU'RE SMIRKING! CONFESS, WENCH!
WHAT'S GOTTEN INTO YOU?
I DON'T LIKE THAT SMILE OF YOURS! IT'S WRONG!
QUIET!
HOW CAN YOU SAY THAT?!

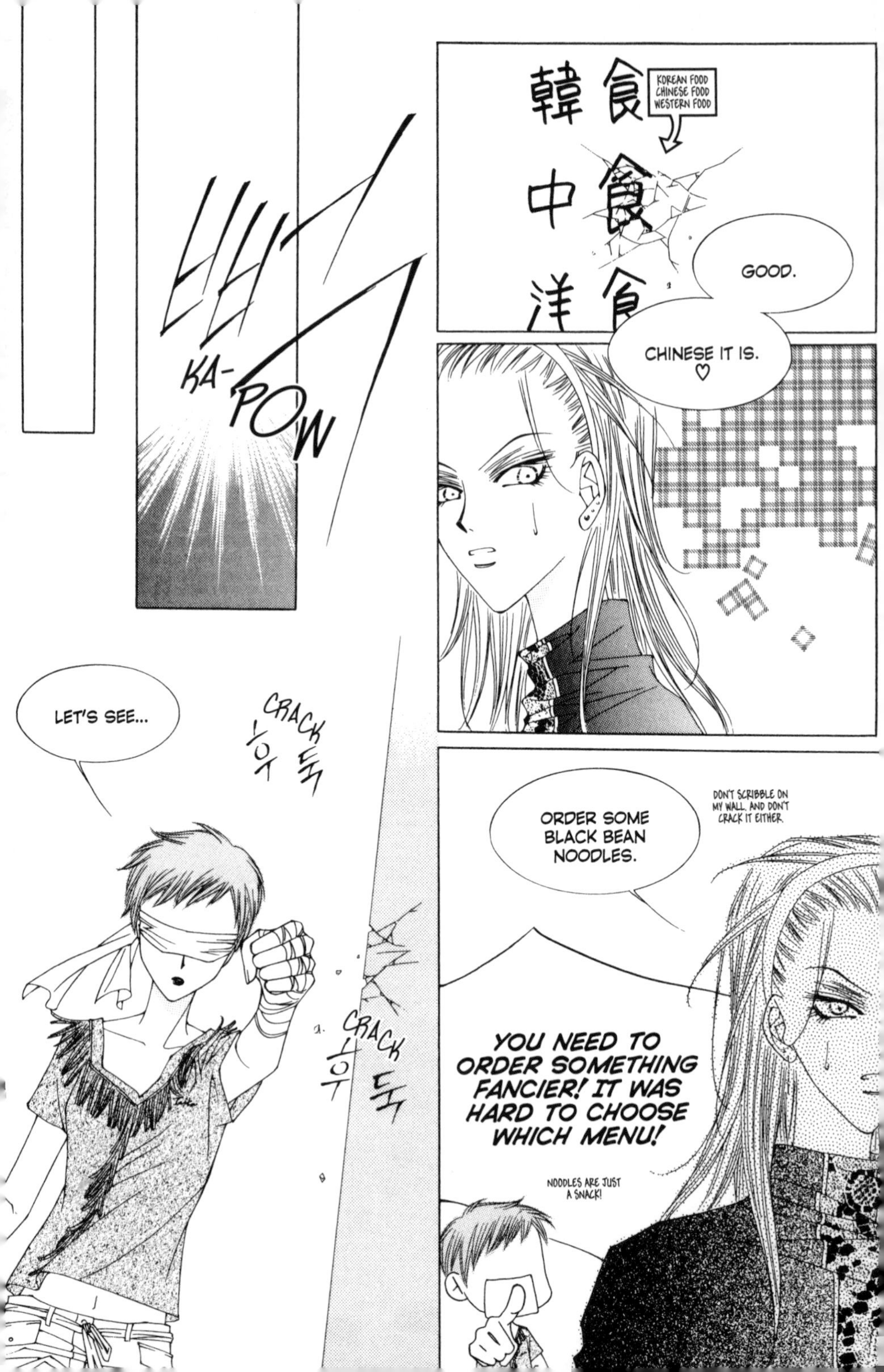
KA-POW
韓食
中食
洋食
KOREAN FOOD CHINESE FOOD WESTERN FOOD
GOOD.
CHINESE IT IS. ♡
LET'S SEE...
CRACK
CRACK
ORDER SOME BLACK BEAN NOODLES.
DON'T SCRIBBLE ON MY WALL, AND DON'T CRACK IT EITHER.
YOU NEED TO ORDER SOMETHING FANCIER! IT WAS HARD TO CHOOSE WHICH MENU!
NOODLES ARE JUST A SNACK!

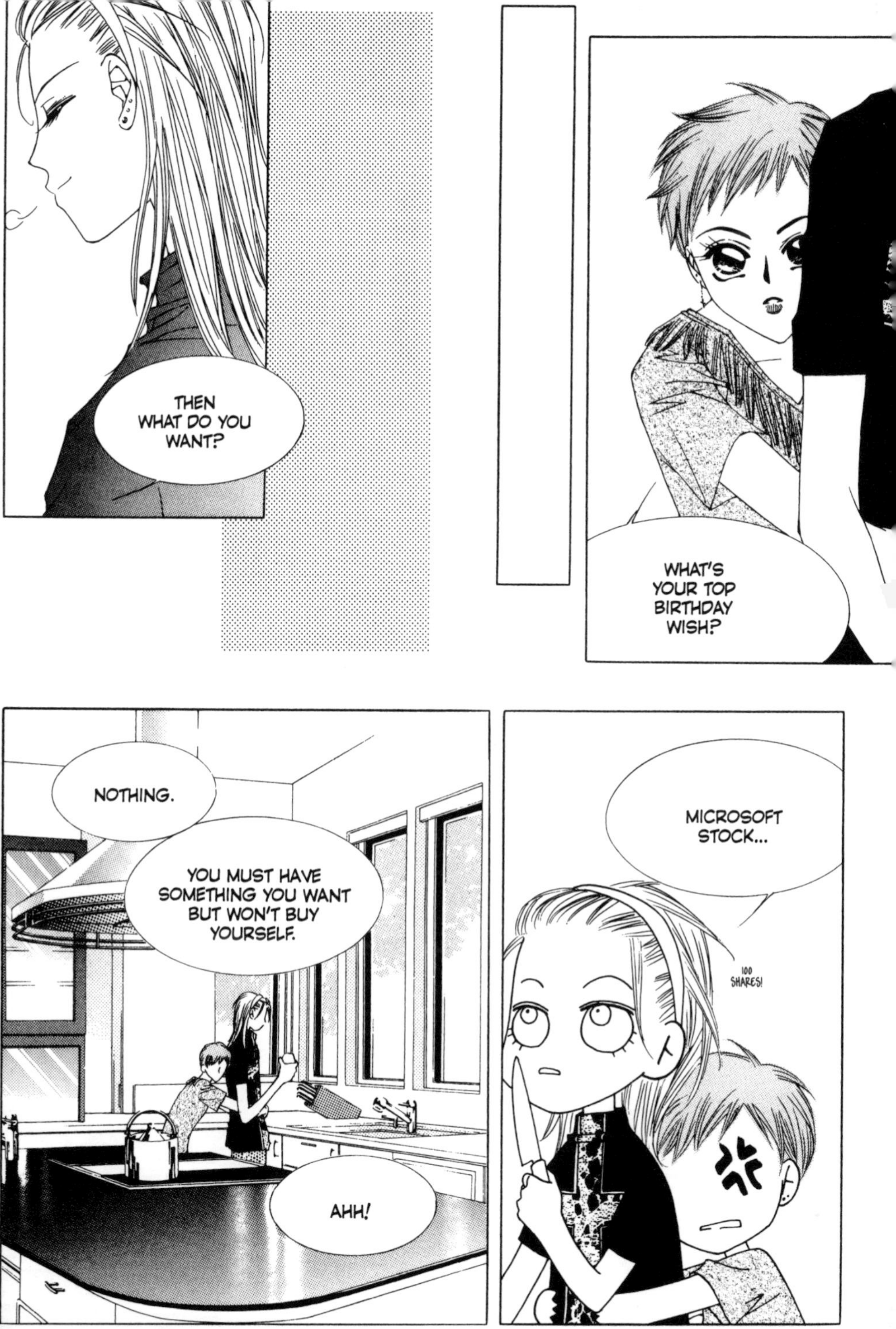
THEN WHAT DO YOU WANT?
WHAT'S YOUR TOP BIRTHDAY WISH?
NOTHING.
YOU MUST HAVE SOMETHING YOU WANT BUT WON'T BUY YOURSELF.
AHH!
MICROSOFT STOCK...
100 SHARES!

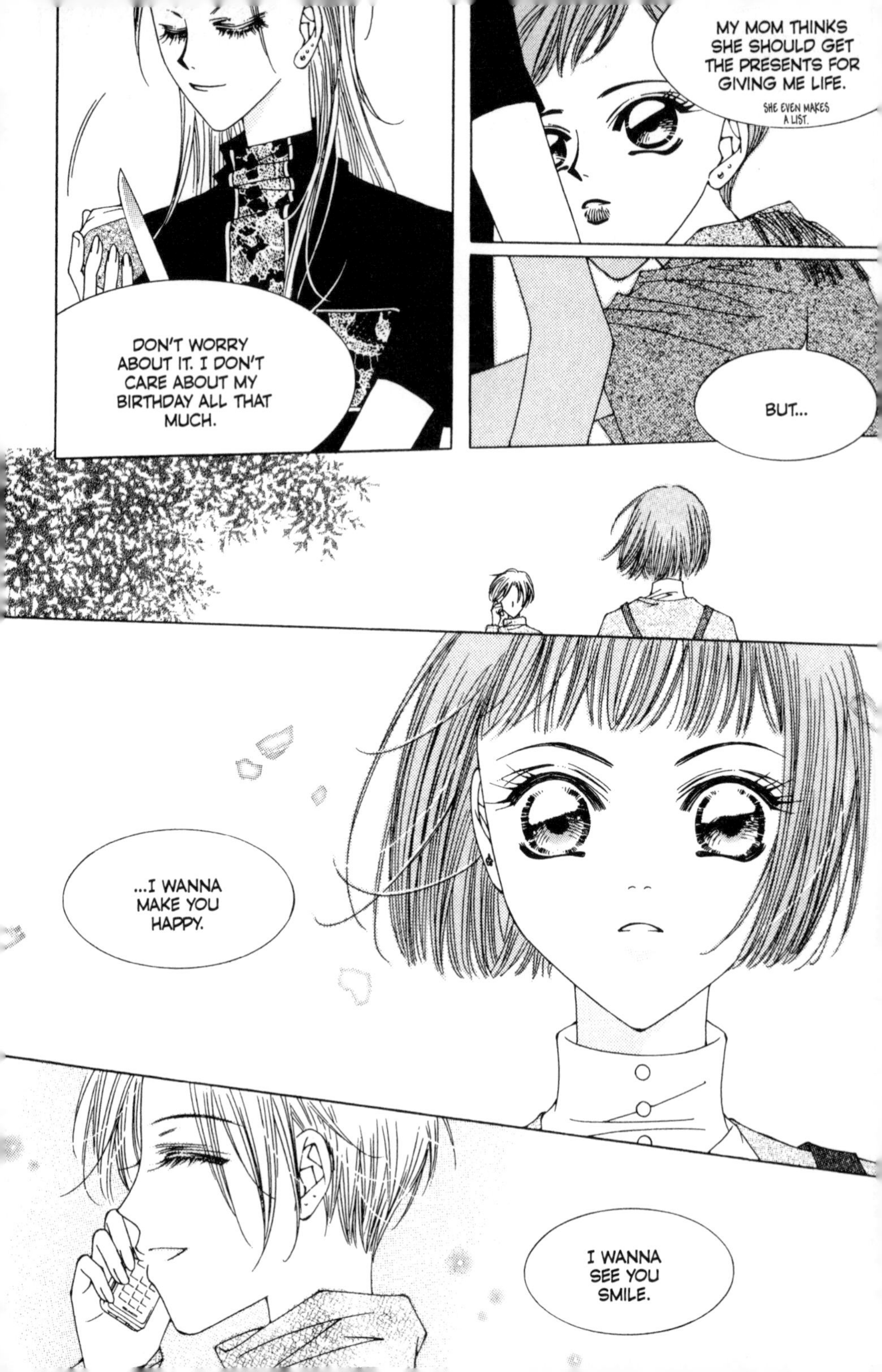
DON'T WORRY ABOUT IT. I DON'T CARE ABOUT MY BIRTHDAY ALL THAT MUCH.
MY MOM THINKS SHE SHOULD GET THE PRESENTS FOR GIVING ME LIFE.
SHE EVEN MAKES A LIST.
BUT...
...I WANNA MAKE YOU HAPPY.
I WANNA SEE YOU SMILE.

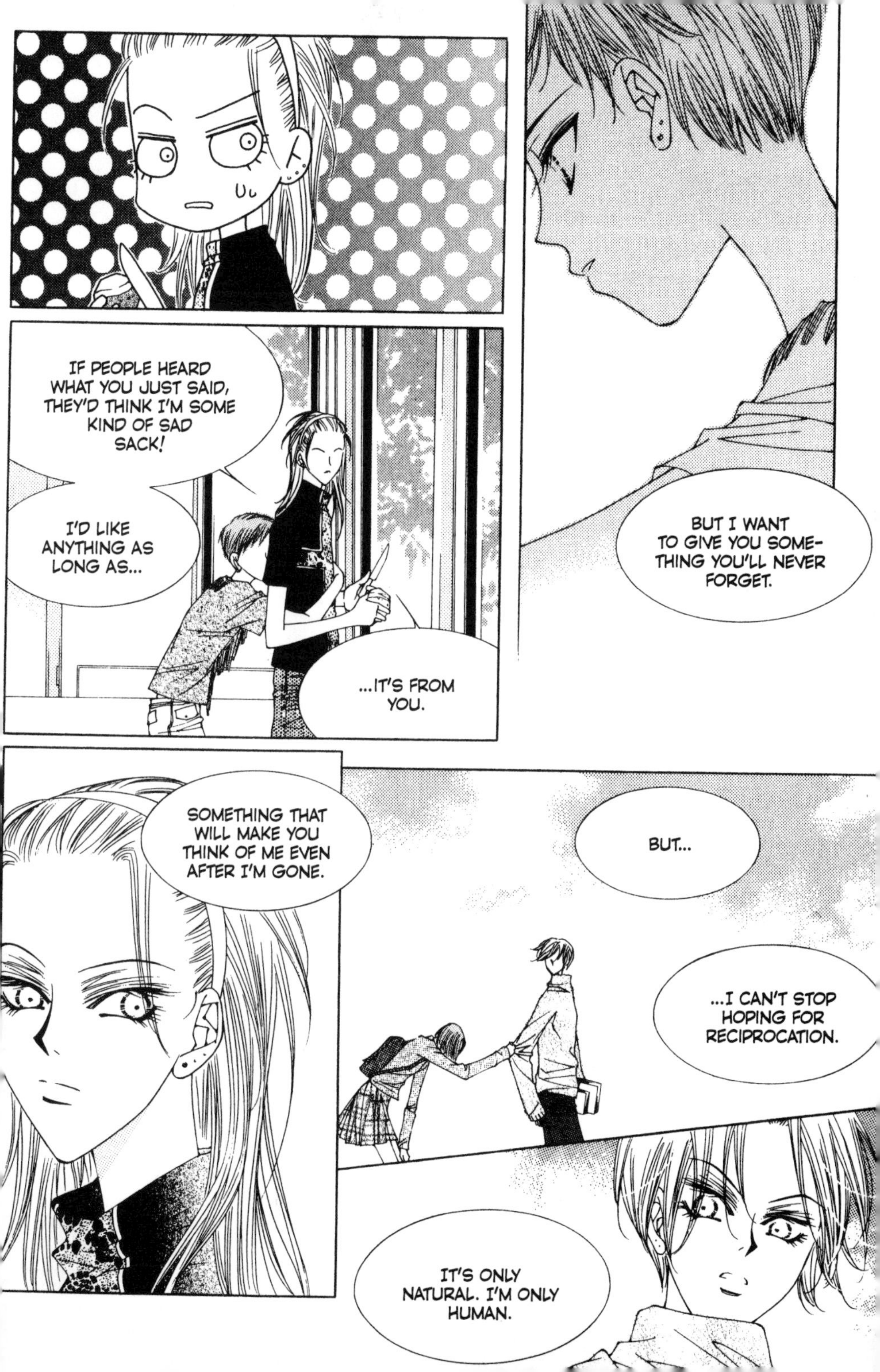
IF PEOPLE HEARD WHAT YOU JUST SAID, THEY'D THINK I'M SOME KIND OF SAD SACK!
I'D LIKE ANYTHING AS LONG AS...
...IT'S FROM YOU.
BUT I WANT TO GIVE YOU SOME-THING YOU'LL NEVER FORGET.
SOMETHING THAT WILL MAKE YOU THINK OF ME EVEN AFTER I'M GONE.
BUT...
...I CAN'T STOP HOPING FOR RECIPROCATION.
IT'S ONLY NATURAL. I'M ONLY HUMAN.

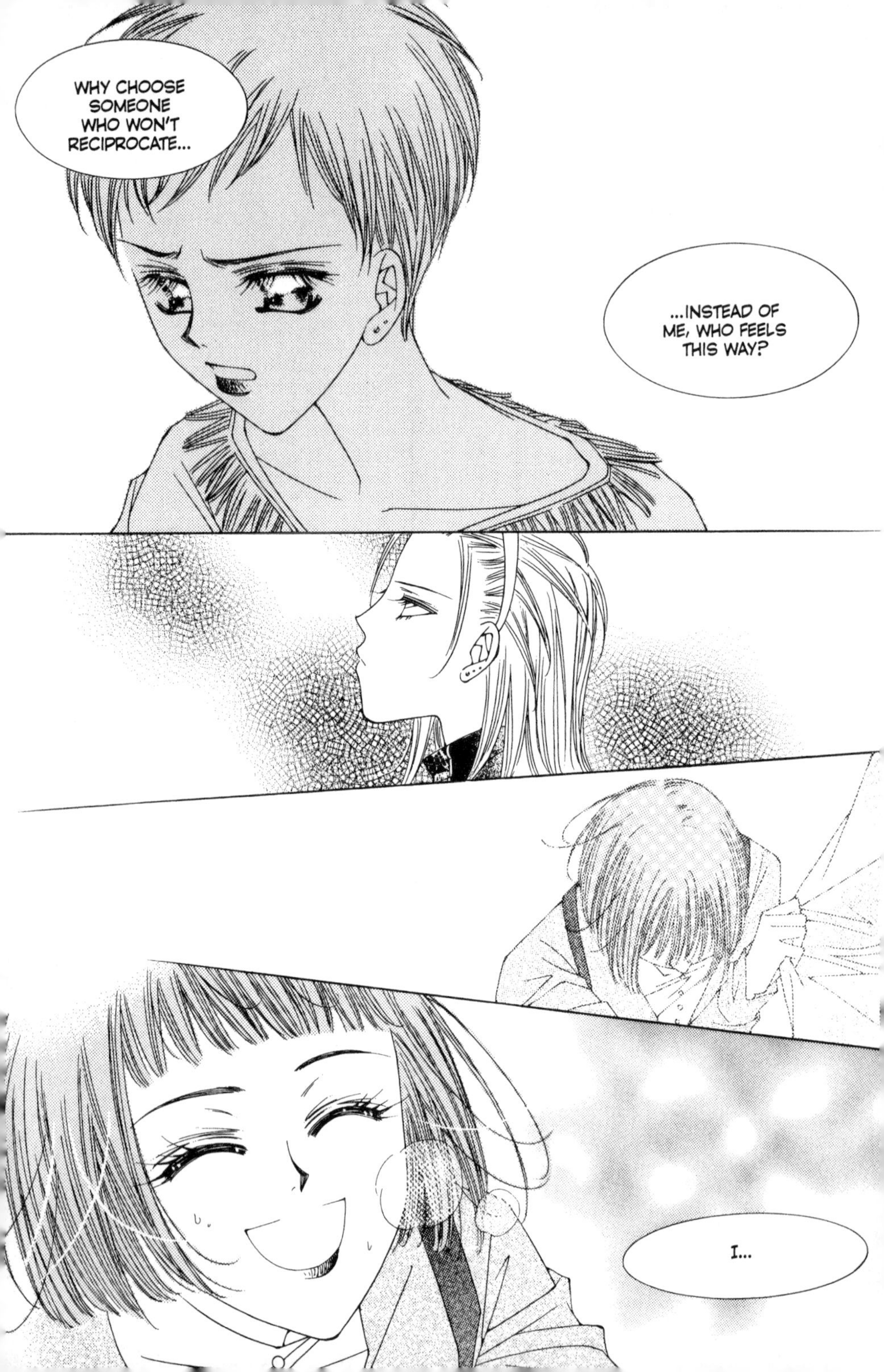
WHY CHOOSE SOMEONE WHO WON'T RECIPROCATE...
...INSTEAD OF ME, WHO FEELS THIS WAY?
I...

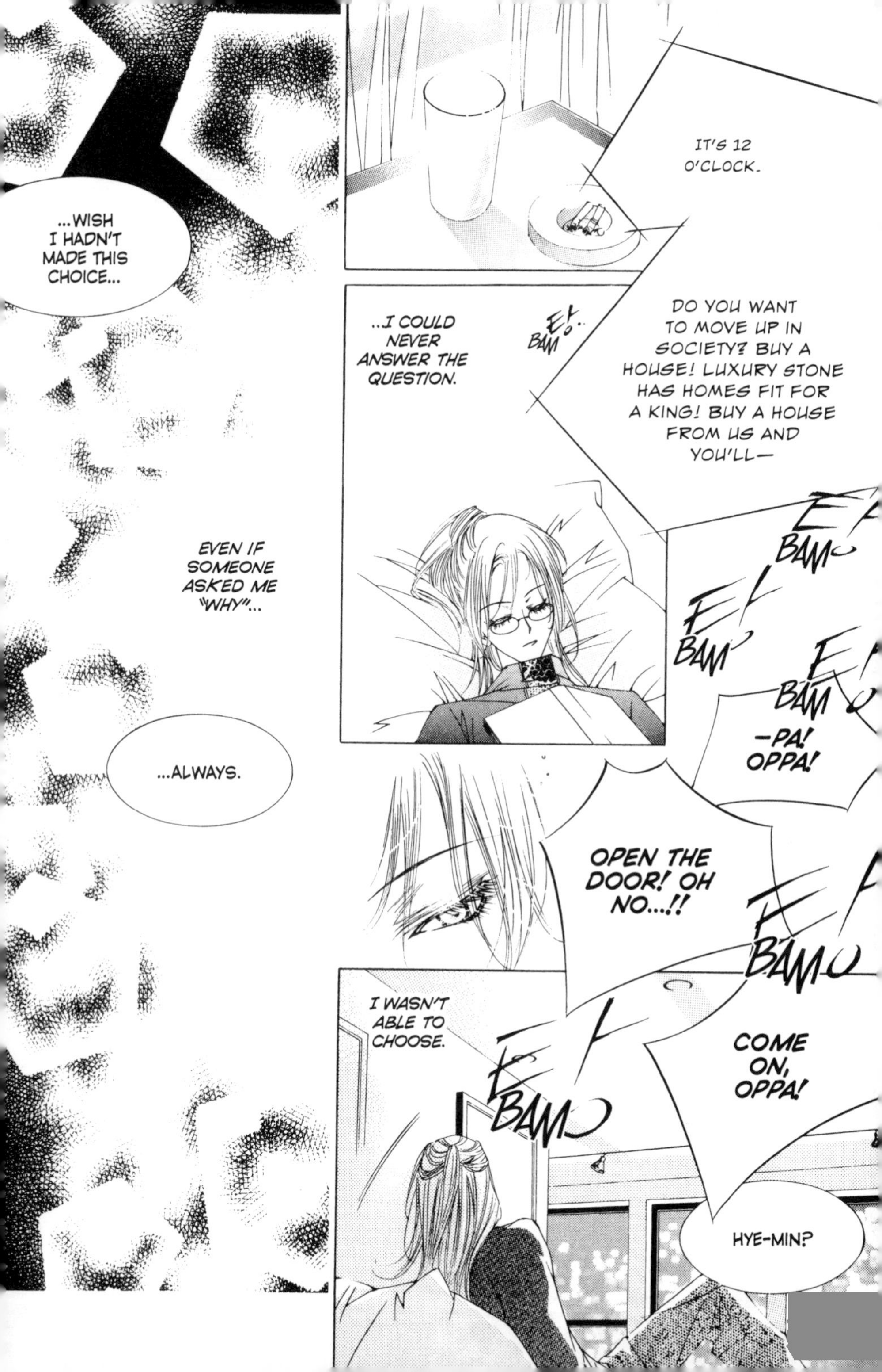
...WISH I HADN'T MADE THIS CHOICE...
EVEN IF SOMEONE ASKED ME "WHY"...
...ALWAYS.
IT'S 12 O'CLOCK.
...I COULD NEVER ANSWER THE QUESTION.
BAM
DO YOU WANT TO MOVE UP IN SOCIETY? BUY A HOUSE! LUXURY STONE HAS HOMES FIT FOR A KING! BUY A HOUSE FROM US AND YOU'LL—
BAM
BAM
BAM
-PA! OPPA!
OPEN THE DOOR! OH NO...!!
BAM
I WASN'T ABLE TO CHOOSE.
BAM
COME ON, OPPA!
HYE-MIN?

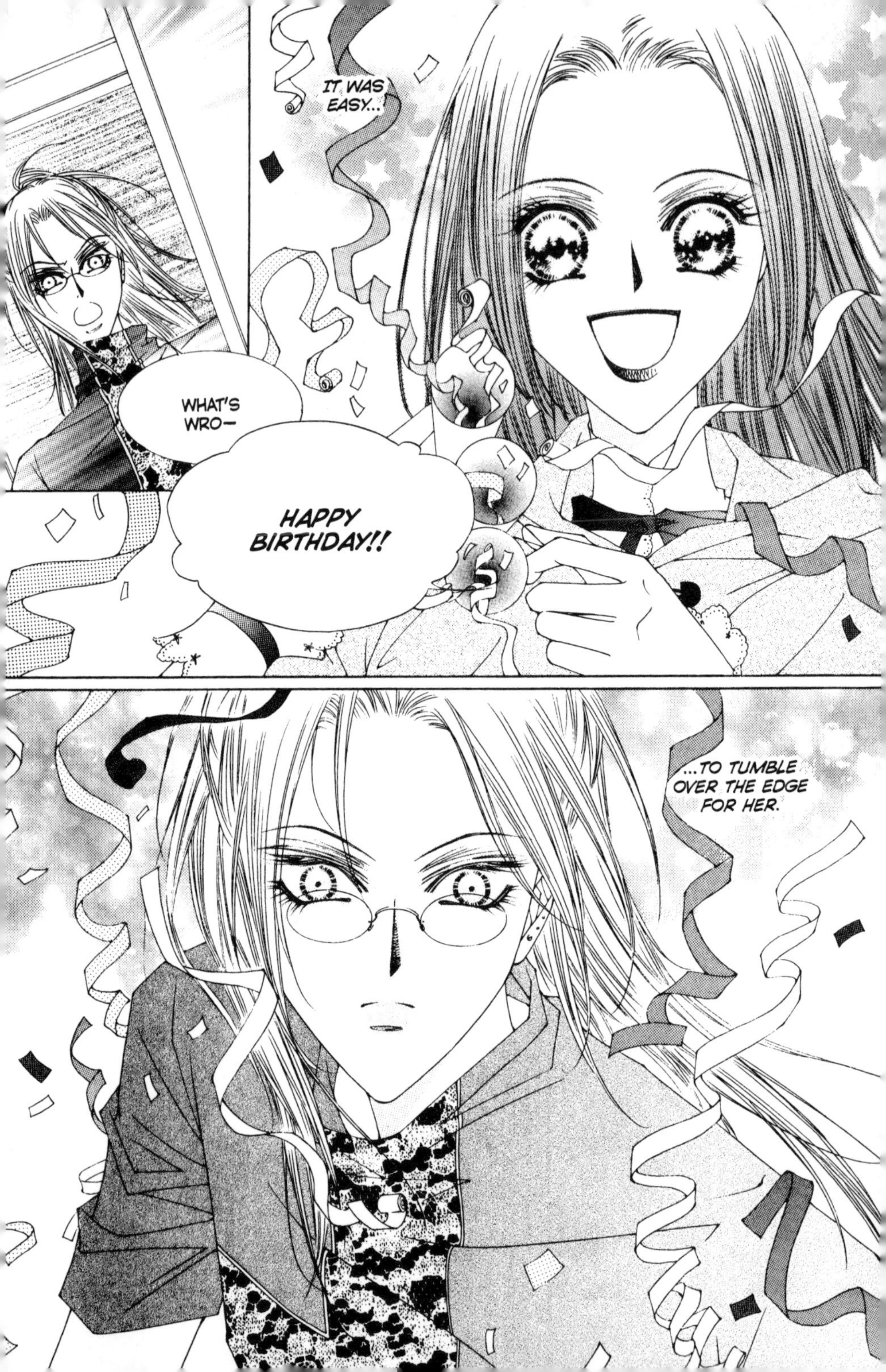
IT WAS EASY...
WHAT'S WRO—
HAPPY BIRTHDAY!!
...TO TUMBLE OVER THE EDGE FOR HER.

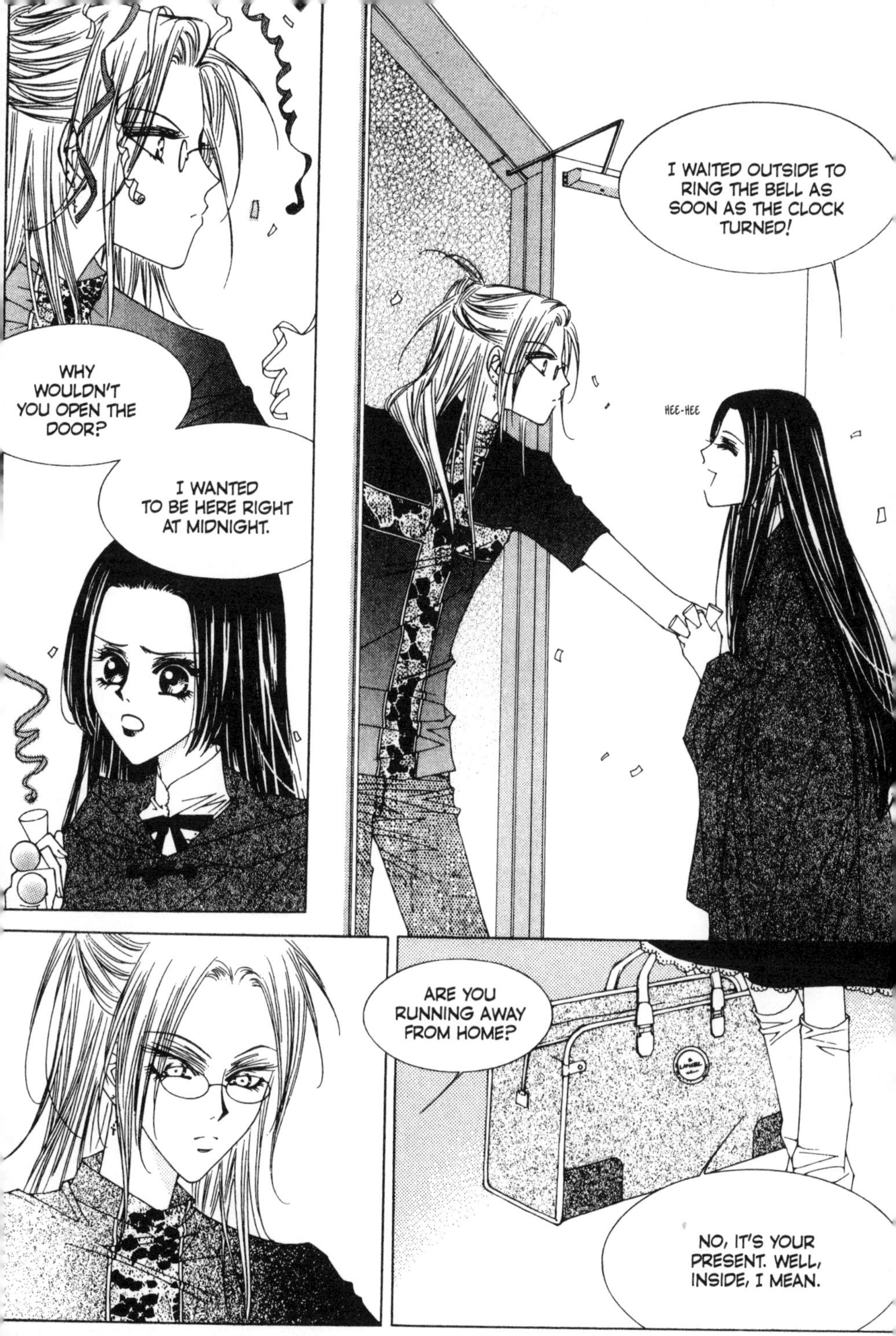
WHY WOULDN'T YOU OPEN THE DOOR?
I WANTED TO BE HERE RIGHT AT MIDNIGHT.
I WAITED OUTSIDE TO RING THE BELL AS SOON AS THE CLOCK TURNED!
HEE-HEE
ARE YOU RUNNING AWAY FROM HOME?
NO, IT'S YOUR PRESENT. WELL, INSIDE, I MEAN.

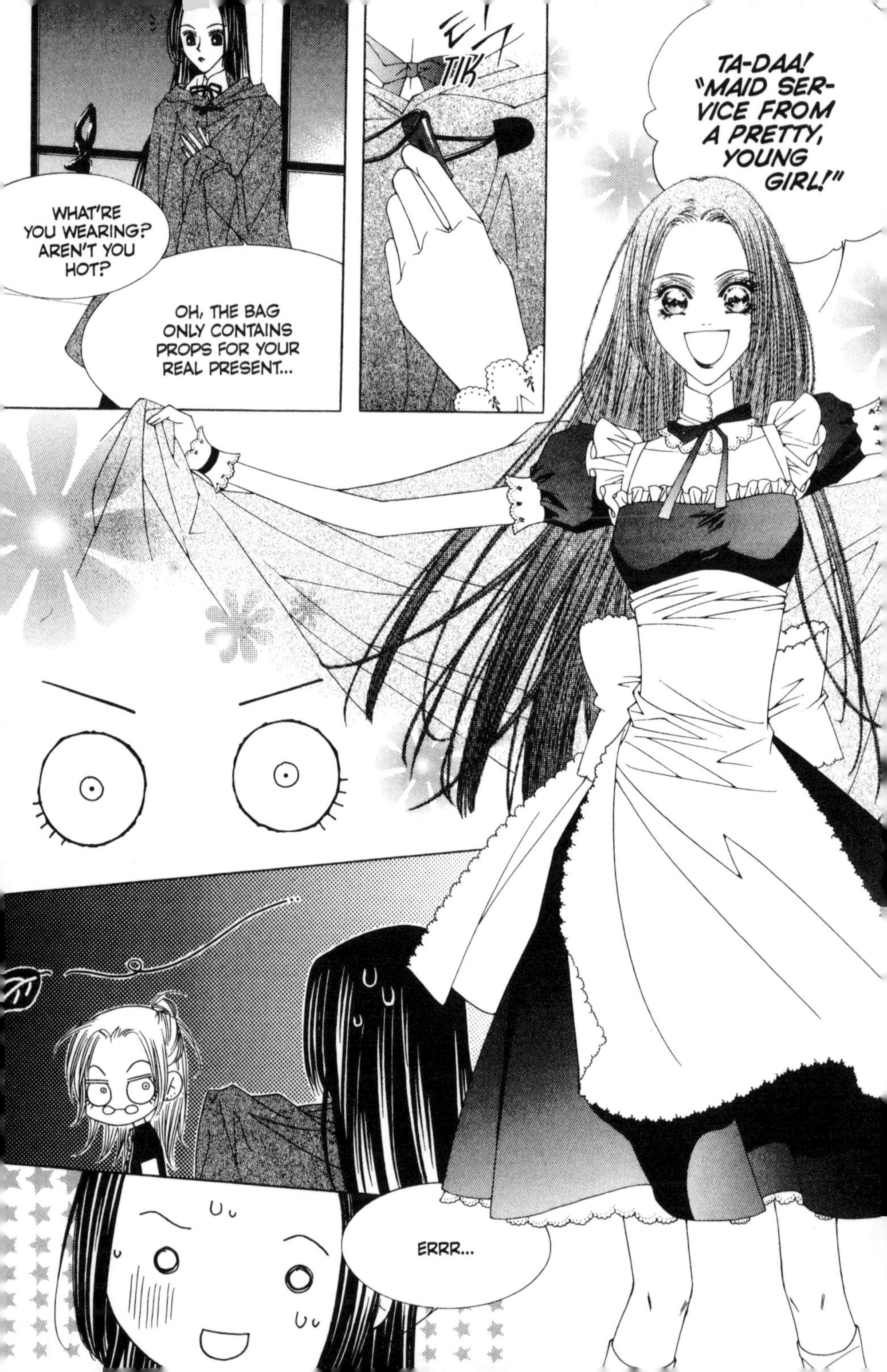
WHAT'RE YOU WEARING? AREN'T YOU HOT?
OH, THE BAG ONLY CONTAINS PROPS FOR YOUR REAL PRESENT...
TIK
TA-DAA! "MAID SER-VICE FROM A PRETTY, YOUNG GIRL!"
ERRR...

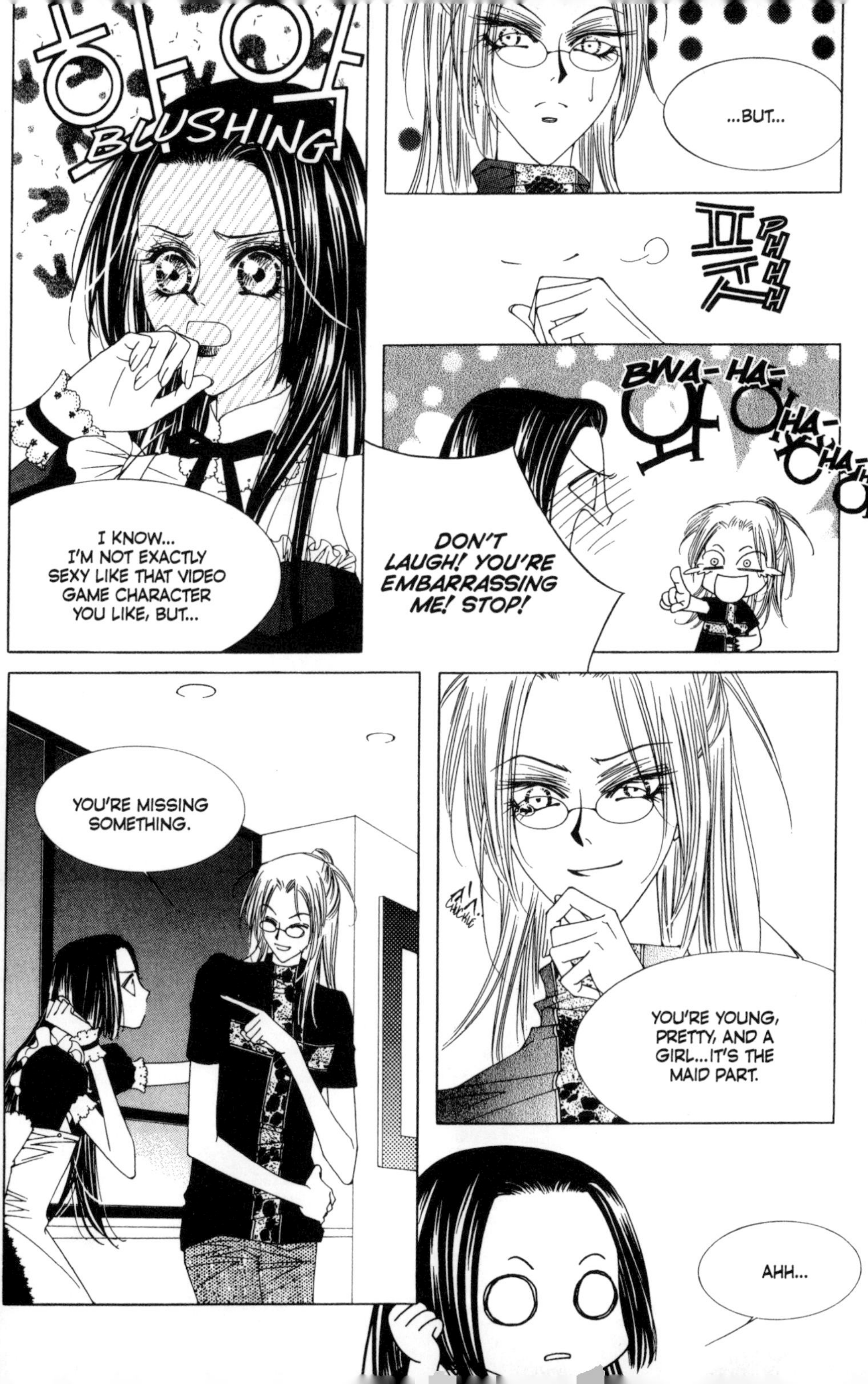
BLUSHING
I KNOW... I'M NOT EXACTLY SEXY LIKE THAT VIDEO GAME CHARACTER YOU LIKE, BUT...
...BUT...
PHHHH
BWA-HA-HA-HA-HA
DON'T LAUGH! YOU'RE EMBARRASSING ME! STOP!
YOU'RE MISSING SOMETHING.
CHUCKLE
YOU'RE YOUNG, PRETTY, AND A GIRL...IT'S THE MAID PART.
AHH...

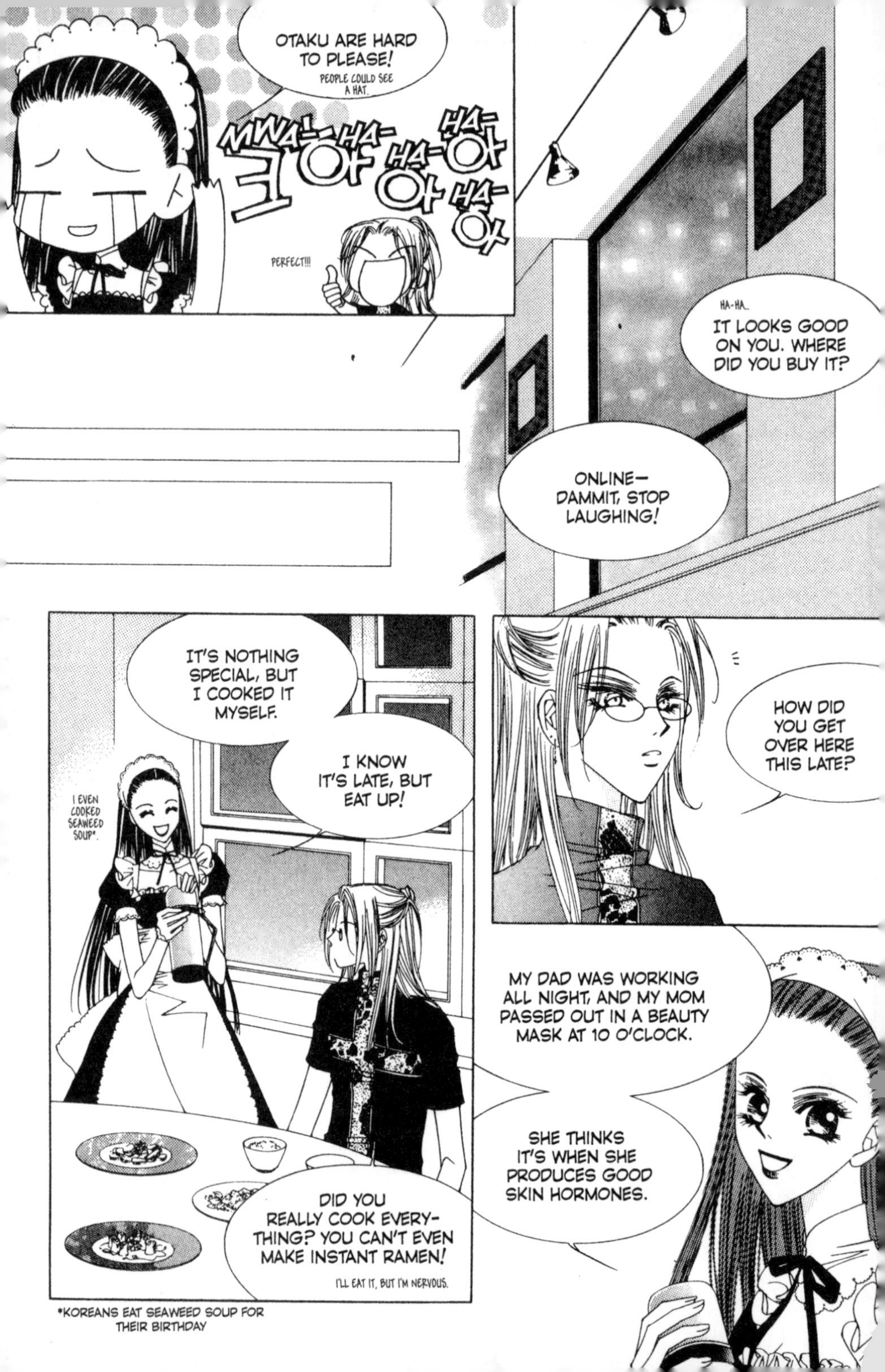
OTAKU ARE HARD TO PLEASE!
PEOPLE COULD SEE A HAT.
MWA-HA- HA- HA- HA-
PERFECT!!!
HA-HA..
IT LOOKS GOOD ON YOU. WHERE DID YOU BUY IT?
ONLINE—DAMMIT, STOP LAUGHING!
IT'S NOTHING SPECIAL, BUT I COOKED IT MYSELF.
I KNOW IT'S LATE, BUT EAT UP!
I EVEN COOKED SEAWEED SOUP*.
DID YOU REALLY COOK EVERY-THING? YOU CAN'T EVEN MAKE INSTANT RAMEN!
I'LL EAT IT, BUT I'M NERVOUS.
HOW DID YOU GET OVER HERE THIS LATE?
MY DAD WAS WORKING ALL NIGHT, AND MY MOM PASSED OUT IN A BEAUTY MASK AT 10 O'CLOCK.
SHE THINKS IT'S WHEN SHE PRODUCES GOOD SKIN HORMONES.

*KOREANS EAT SEAWEED SOUP FOR THEIR BIRTHDAY

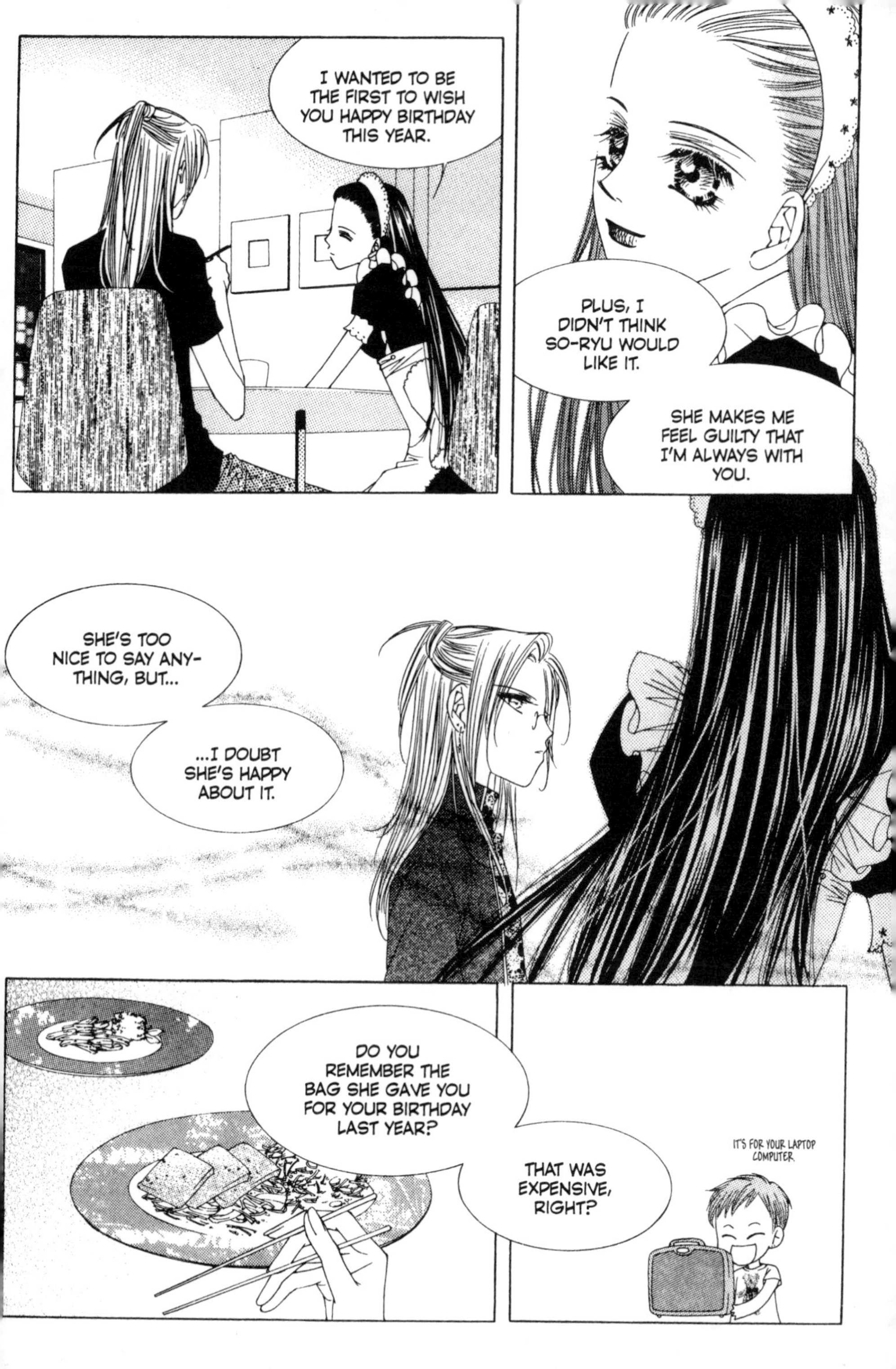
I WANTED TO BE THE FIRST TO WISH YOU HAPPY BIRTHDAY THIS YEAR.
PLUS, I DIDN'T THINK SO-RYU WOULD LIKE IT.
SHE MAKES ME FEEL GUILTY THAT I'M ALWAYS WITH YOU.
SHE'S TOO NICE TO SAY ANY-THING, BUT...
...I DOUBT SHE'S HAPPY ABOUT IT.
DO YOU REMEMBER THE BAG SHE GAVE YOU FOR YOUR BIRTHDAY LAST YEAR?
THAT WAS EXPENSIVE, RIGHT?
IT'S FOR YOUR LAPTOP COMPUTER.

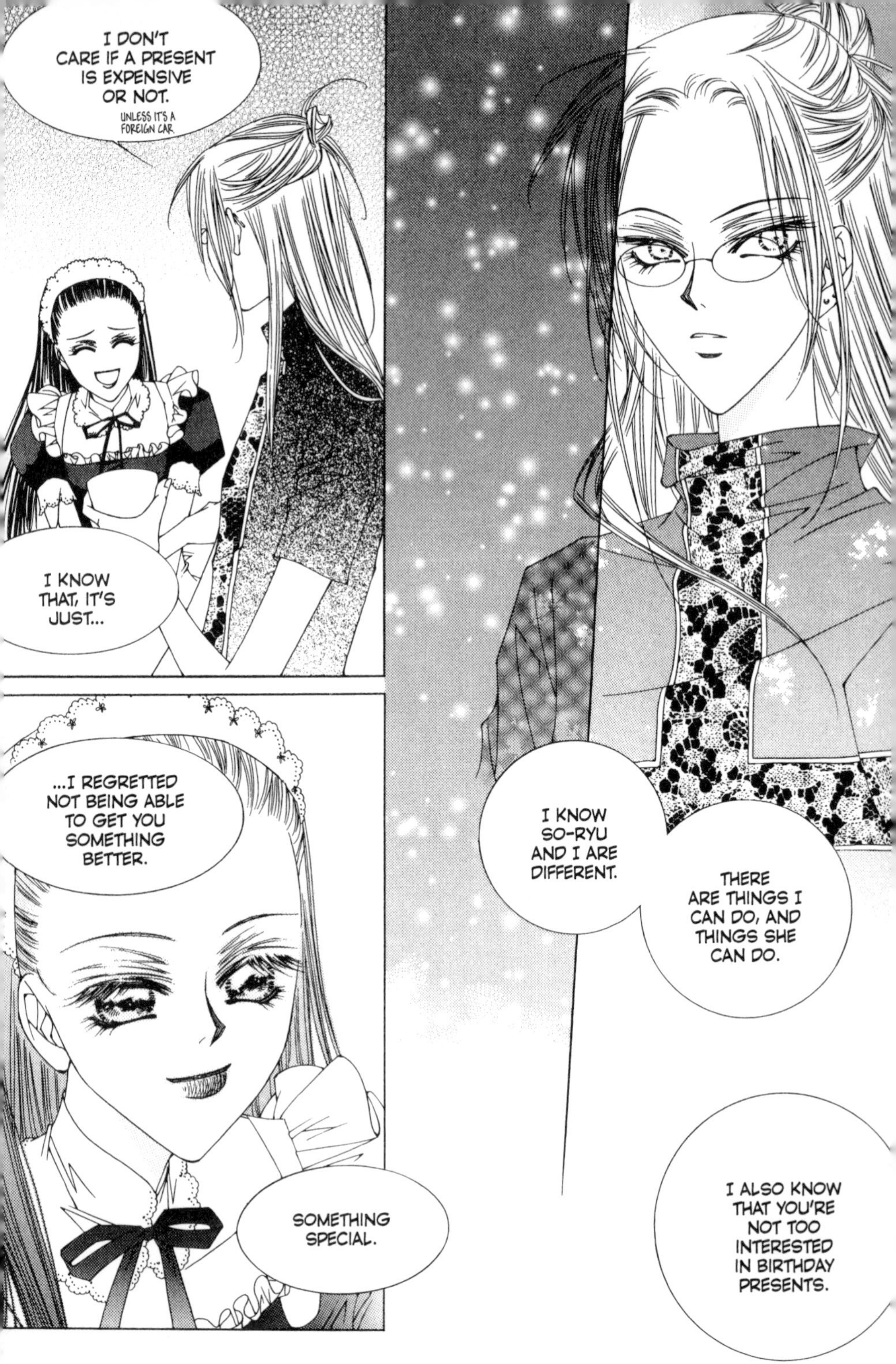
I DON'T CARE IF A PRESENT IS EXPENSIVE OR NOT.
UNLESS IT'S A FOREIGN CAR.
I KNOW THAT, IT'S JUST...
...I REGRETTED NOT BEING ABLE TO GET YOU SOMETHING BETTER.
SOMETHING SPECIAL.
I KNOW SO-RYU AND I ARE DIFFERENT.
THERE ARE THINGS I CAN DO, AND THINGS SHE CAN DO.
I ALSO KNOW THAT YOU'RE NOT TOO INTERESTED IN BIRTHDAY PRESENTS.

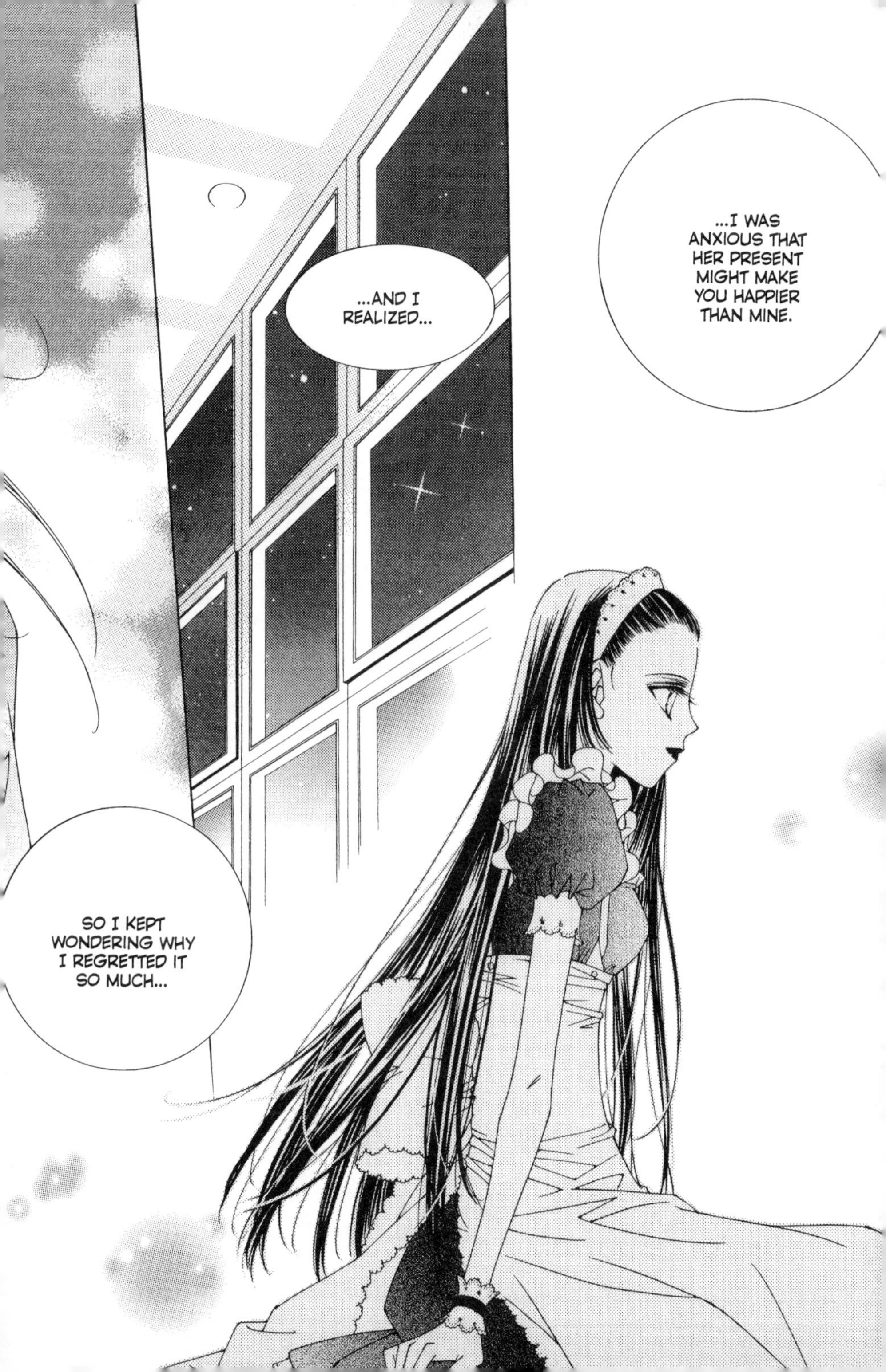
SO I KEPT WONDERING WHY I REGRETTED IT SO MUCH...
...AND I REALIZED...
...I WAS ANXIOUS THAT HER PRESENT MIGHT MAKE YOU HAPPIER THAN MINE.

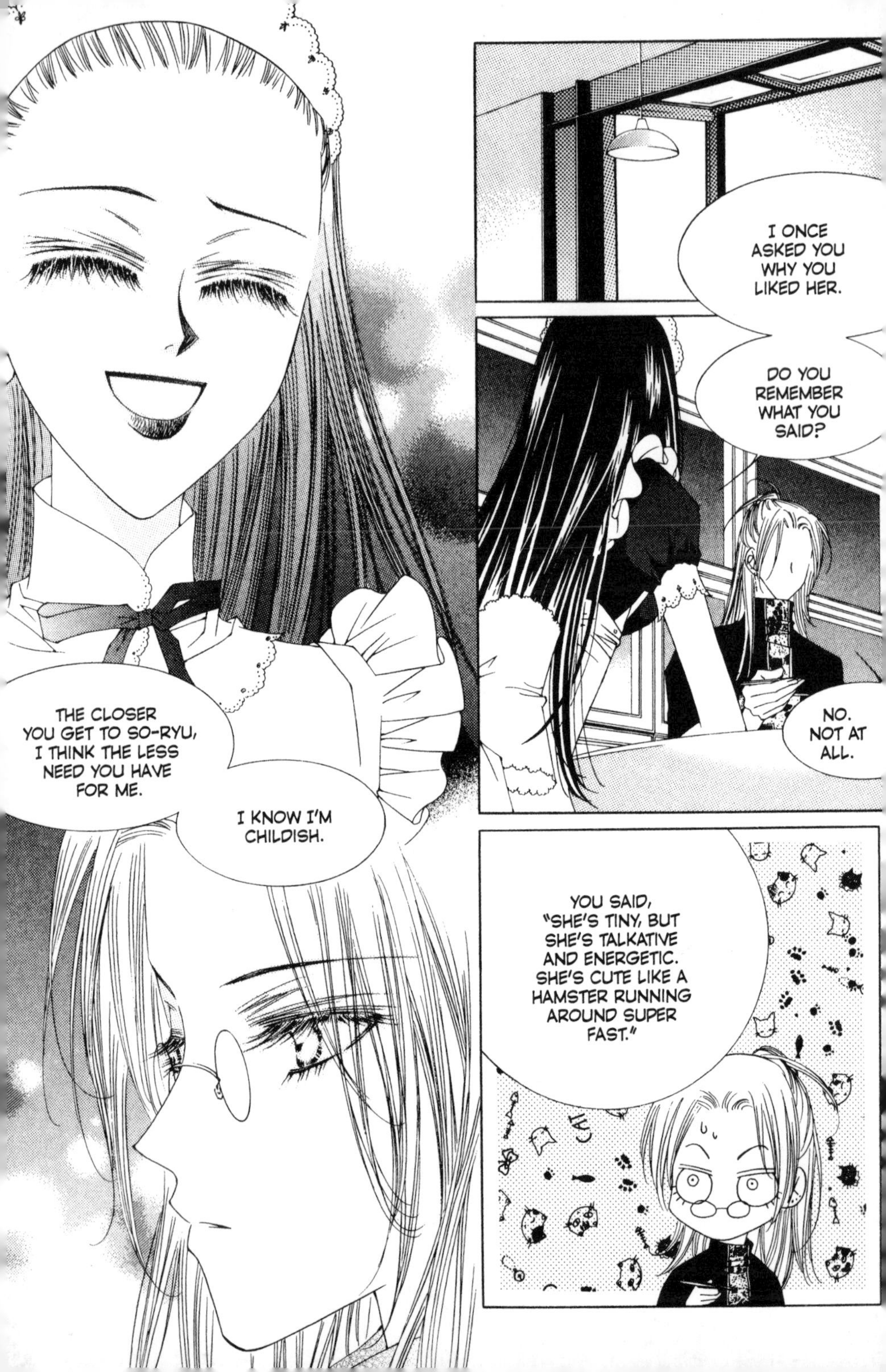
I ONCE ASKED YOU WHY YOU LIKED HER.
DO YOU REMEMBER WHAT YOU SAID?
NO. NOT AT ALL.
YOU SAID, "SHE'S TINY, BUT SHE'S TALKATIVE AND ENERGETIC. SHE'S CUTE LIKE A HAMSTER RUNNING AROUND SUPER FAST."
CAT
THE CLOSER YOU GET TO SO-RYU, I THINK THE LESS NEED YOU HAVE FOR ME.
I KNOW I'M CHILDISH.

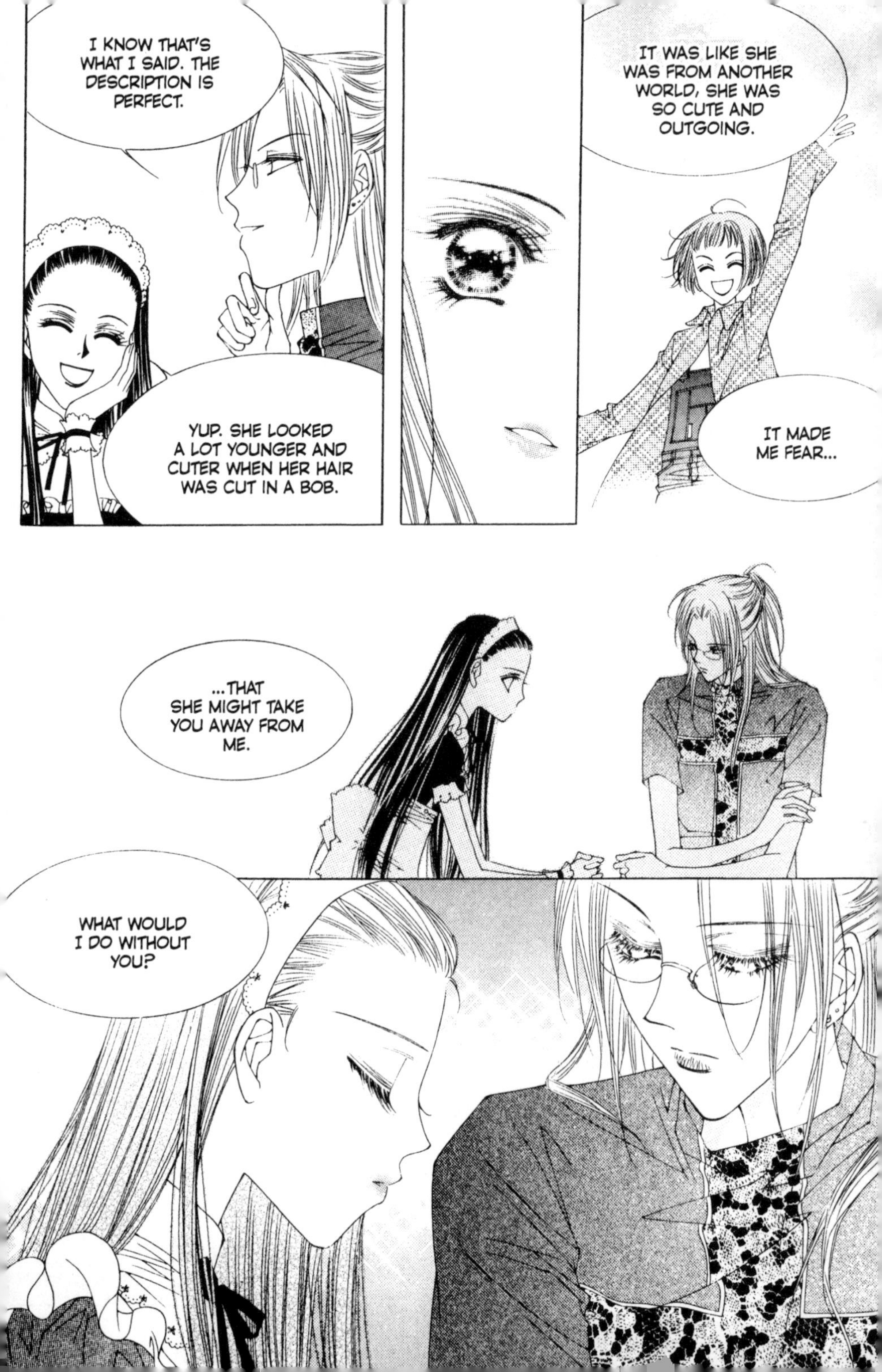
I KNOW THAT'S WHAT I SAID. THE DESCRIPTION IS PERFECT.
YUP. SHE LOOKED A LOT YOUNGER AND CUTER WHEN HER HAIR WAS CUT IN A BOB.
IT WAS LIKE SHE WAS FROM ANOTHER WORLD, SHE WAS SO CUTE AND OUTGOING.
IT MADE ME FEAR...
...THAT SHE MIGHT TAKE YOU AWAY FROM ME.
WHAT WOULD I DO WITHOUT YOU?

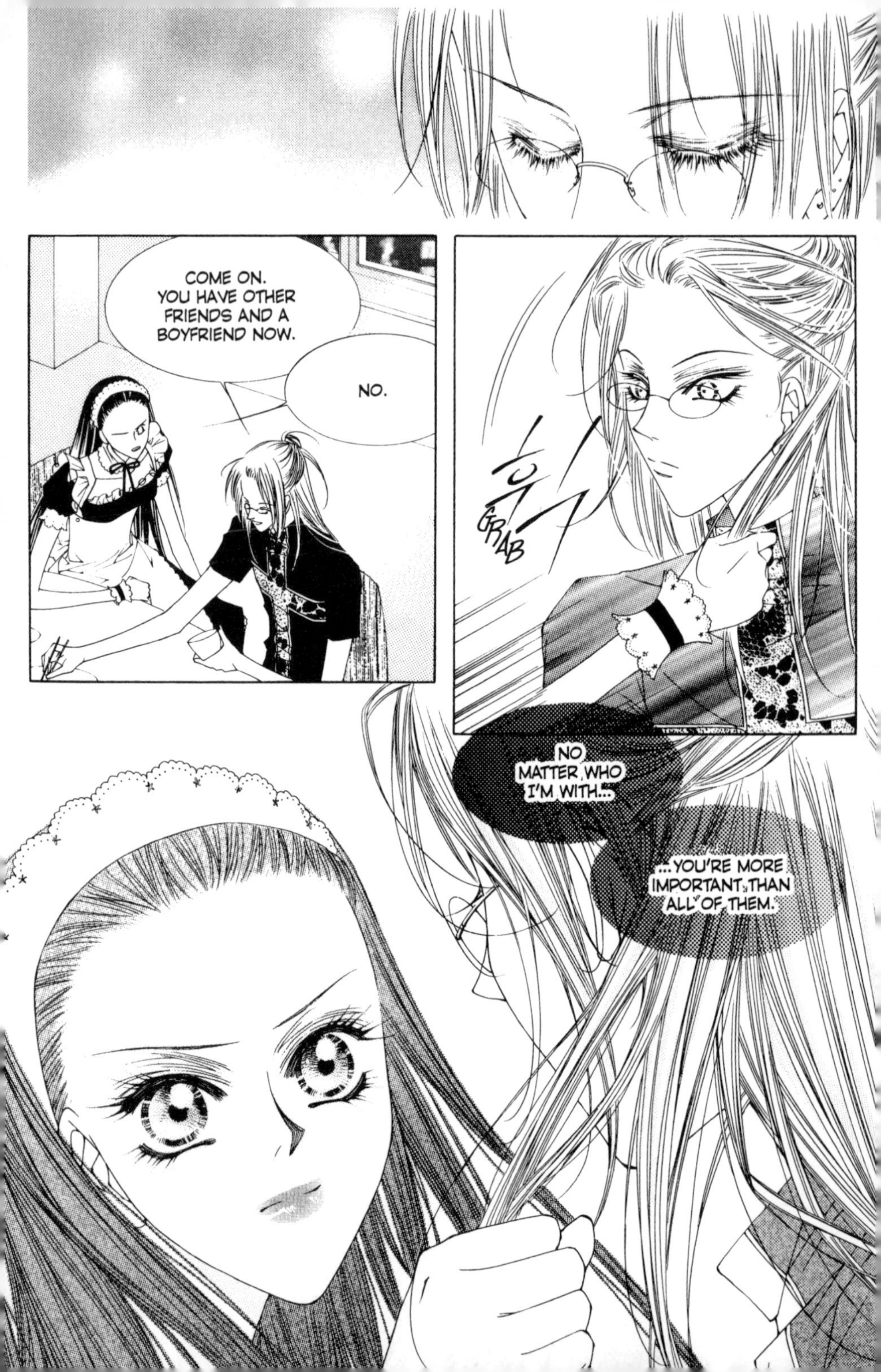
COME ON. YOU HAVE OTHER FRIENDS AND A BOYFRIEND NOW.
NO.
GRAB
NO MATTER WHO I'M WITH...
...YOU'RE MORE IMPORTANT THAN ALL OF THEM.

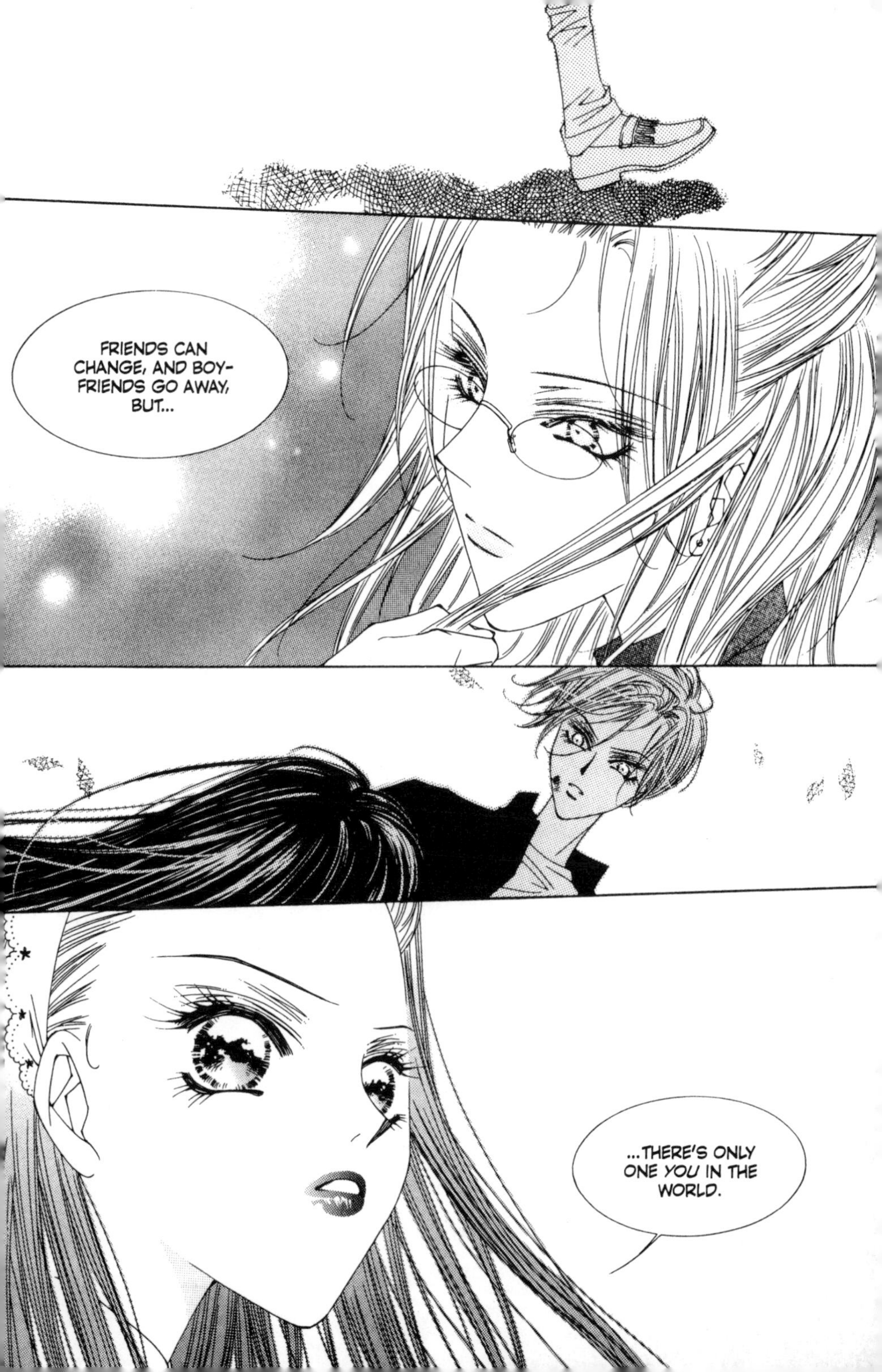
FRIENDS CAN CHANGE, AND BOY-FRIENDS GO AWAY, BUT...
...THERE'S ONLY ONE *YOU* IN THE WORLD.

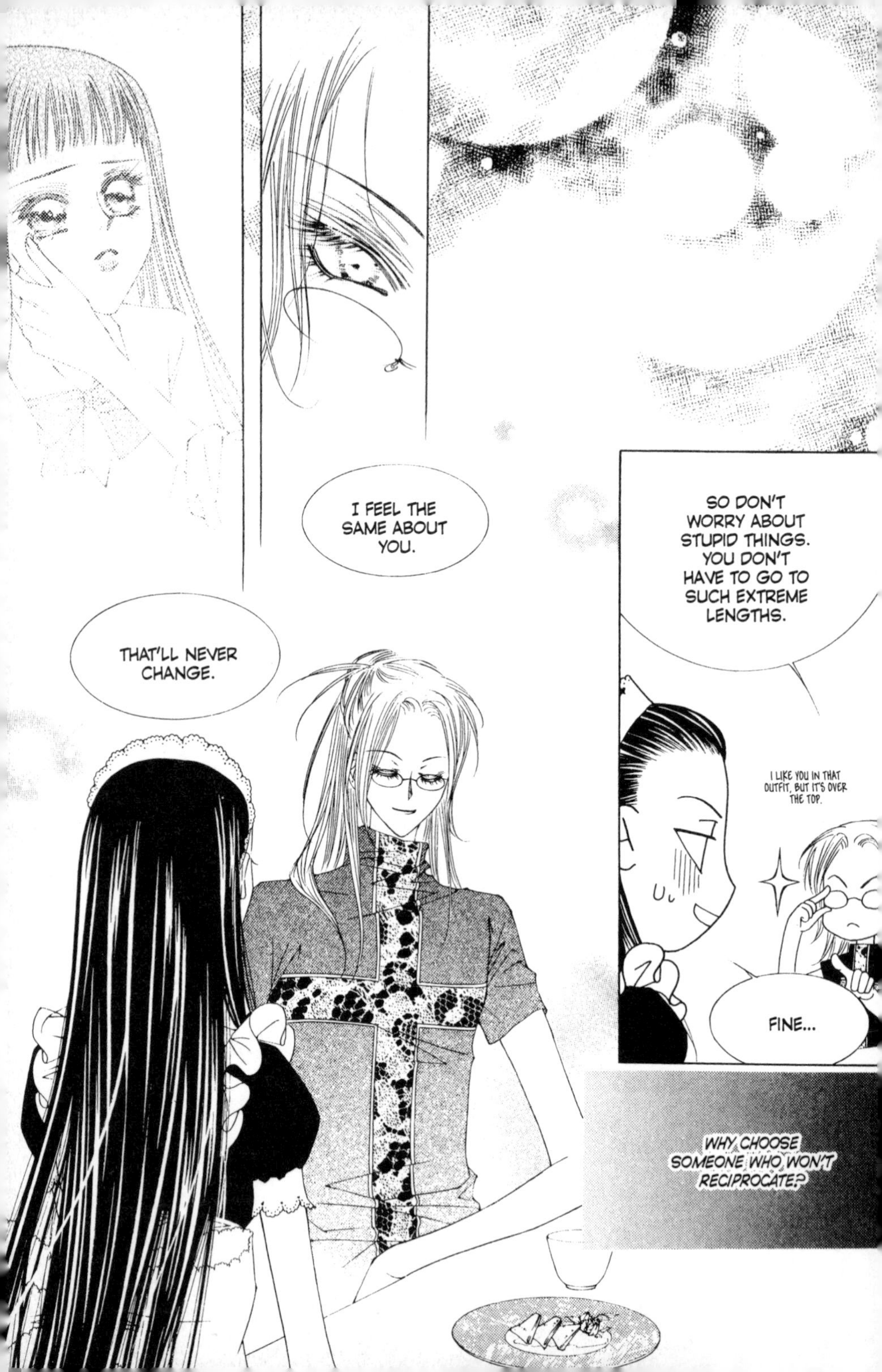
I FEEL THE SAME ABOUT YOU.
THAT'LL NEVER CHANGE.
SO DON'T WORRY ABOUT STUPID THINGS. YOU DON'T HAVE TO GO TO SUCH EXTREME LENGTHS.
I LIKE YOU IN THAT OUTFIT, BUT IT'S OVER THE TOP.
FINE...
WHY CHOOSE SOMEONE WHO WON'T RECIPROCATE?

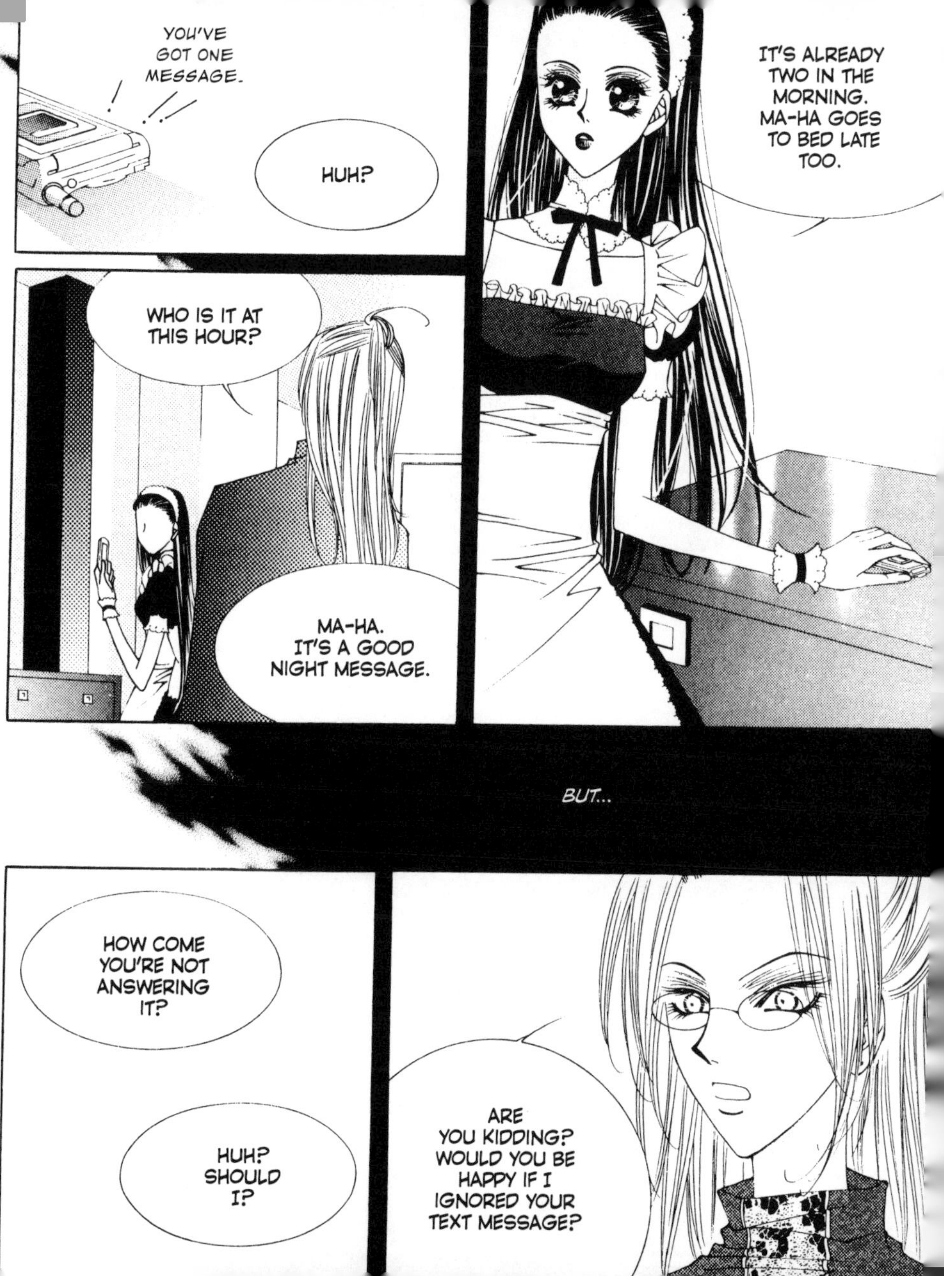
YOU'VE GOT ONE MESSAGE.
HUH?
WHO IS IT AT THIS HOUR?
MA-HA. IT'S A GOOD NIGHT MESSAGE.
IT'S ALREADY TWO IN THE MORNING. MA-HA GOES TO BED LATE TOO.
BUT...
HOW COME YOU'RE NOT ANSWERING IT?
HUH? SHOULD I?
ARE YOU KIDDING? WOULD YOU BE HAPPY IF I IGNORED YOUR TEXT MESSAGE?

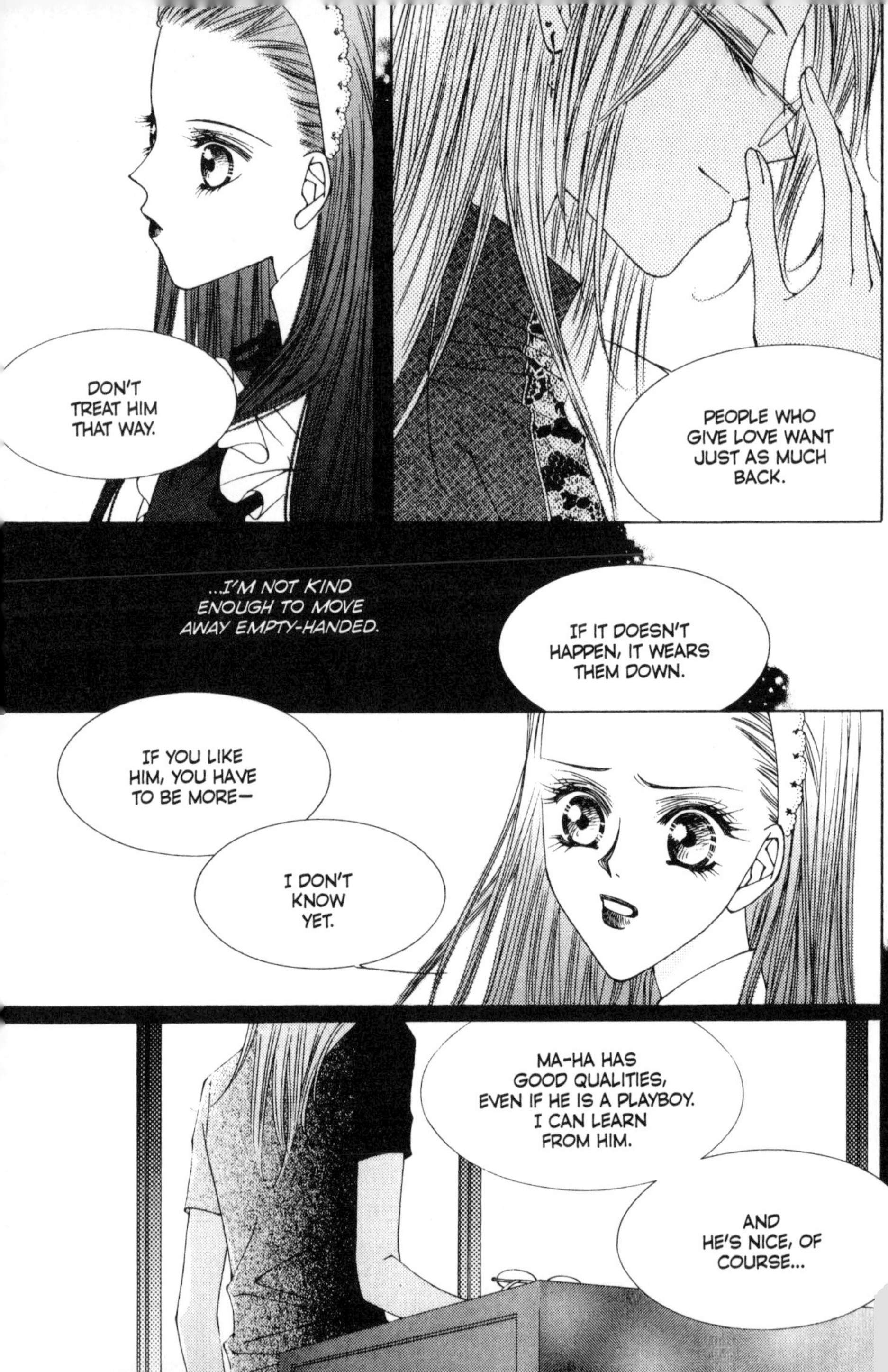
DON'T TREAT HIM THAT WAY.
PEOPLE WHO GIVE LOVE WANT JUST AS MUCH BACK.
...I'M NOT KIND ENOUGH TO MOVE AWAY EMPTY-HANDED.
IF IT DOESN'T HAPPEN, IT WEARS THEM DOWN.
IF YOU LIKE HIM, YOU HAVE TO BE MORE—
I DON'T KNOW YET.
MA-HA HAS GOOD QUALITIES, EVEN IF HE IS A PLAYBOY. I CAN LEARN FROM HIM.
AND HE'S NICE, OF COURSE...

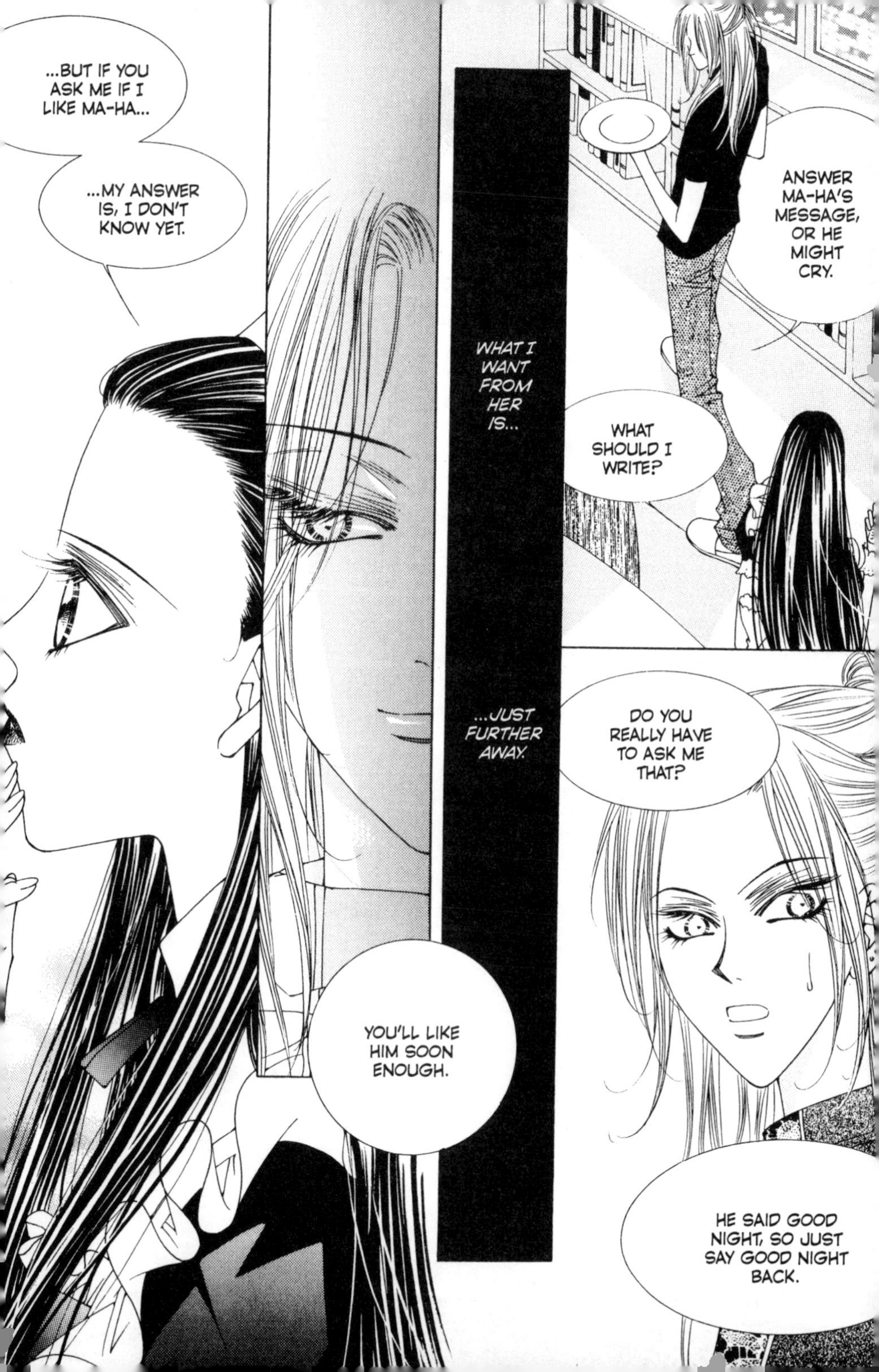
...BUT IF YOU ASK ME IF I LIKE MA-HA...
...MY ANSWER IS, I DON'T KNOW YET.
YOU'LL LIKE HIM SOON ENOUGH.
WHAT I WANT FROM HER IS...
...JUST FURTHER AWAY.
ANSWER MA-HA'S MESSAGE, OR HE MIGHT CRY.
WHAT SHOULD I WRITE?
DO YOU REALLY HAVE TO ASK ME THAT?
HE SAID GOOD NIGHT, SO JUST SAY GOOD NIGHT BACK.

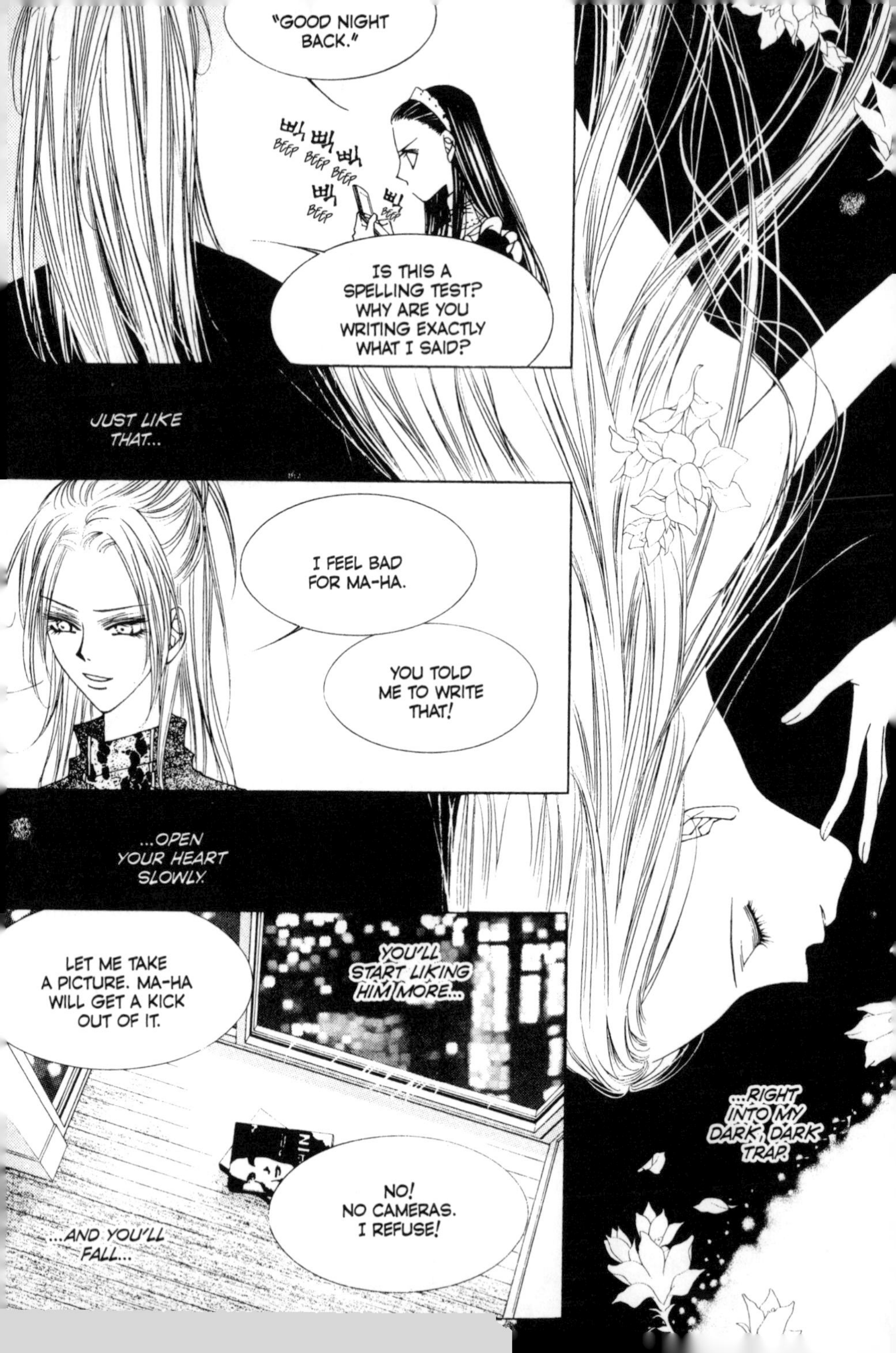
"GOOD NIGHT BACK."
삑 BEEP
삑 BEEP
삑 BEEP
삑 BEEP
삑 BEEP
IS THIS A SPELLING TEST? WHY ARE YOU WRITING EXACTLY WHAT I SAID?
JUST LIKE THAT...
I FEEL BAD FOR MA-HA.
YOU TOLD ME TO WRITE THAT!
...OPEN YOUR HEART SLOWLY.
LET ME TAKE A PICTURE. MA-HA WILL GET A KICK OUT OF IT.
YOU'LL START LIKING HIM MORE...
...AND YOU'LL FALL...
NO! NO CAMERAS. I REFUSE!
...RIGHT INTO MY DARK, DARK TRAP.

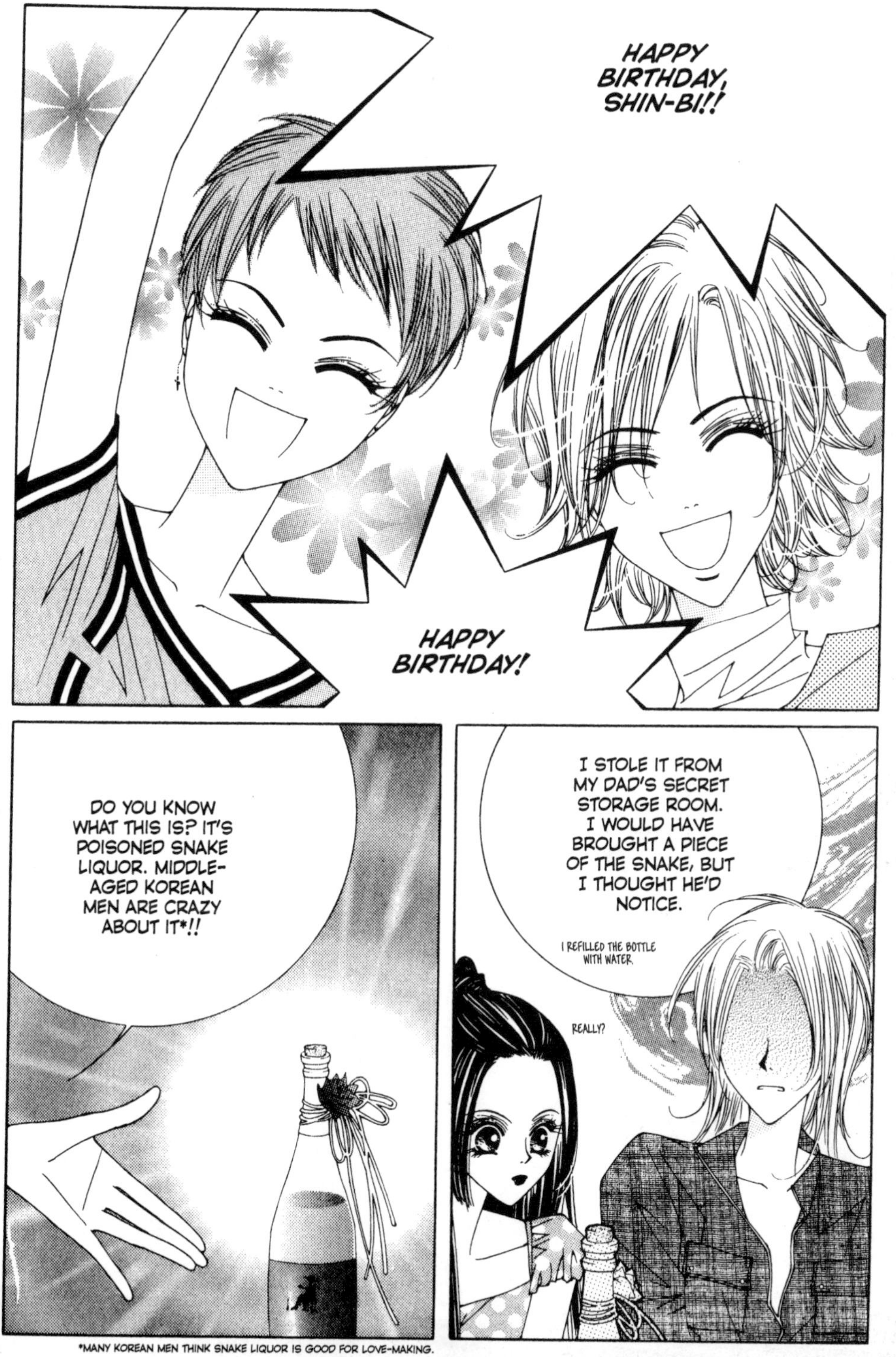
HAPPY BIRTHDAY, SHIN-BI!!
HAPPY BIRTHDAY!
DO YOU KNOW WHAT THIS IS? IT'S POISONED SNAKE LIQUOR. MIDDLE-AGED KOREAN MEN ARE CRAZY ABOUT IT*!!
I STOLE IT FROM MY DAD'S SECRET STORAGE ROOM. I WOULD HAVE BROUGHT A PIECE OF THE SNAKE, BUT I THOUGHT HE'D NOTICE.
I REFILLED THE BOTTLE WITH WATER.
REALLY?

*MANY KOREAN MEN THINK SNAKE LIQUOR IS GOOD FOR LOVE-MAKING.

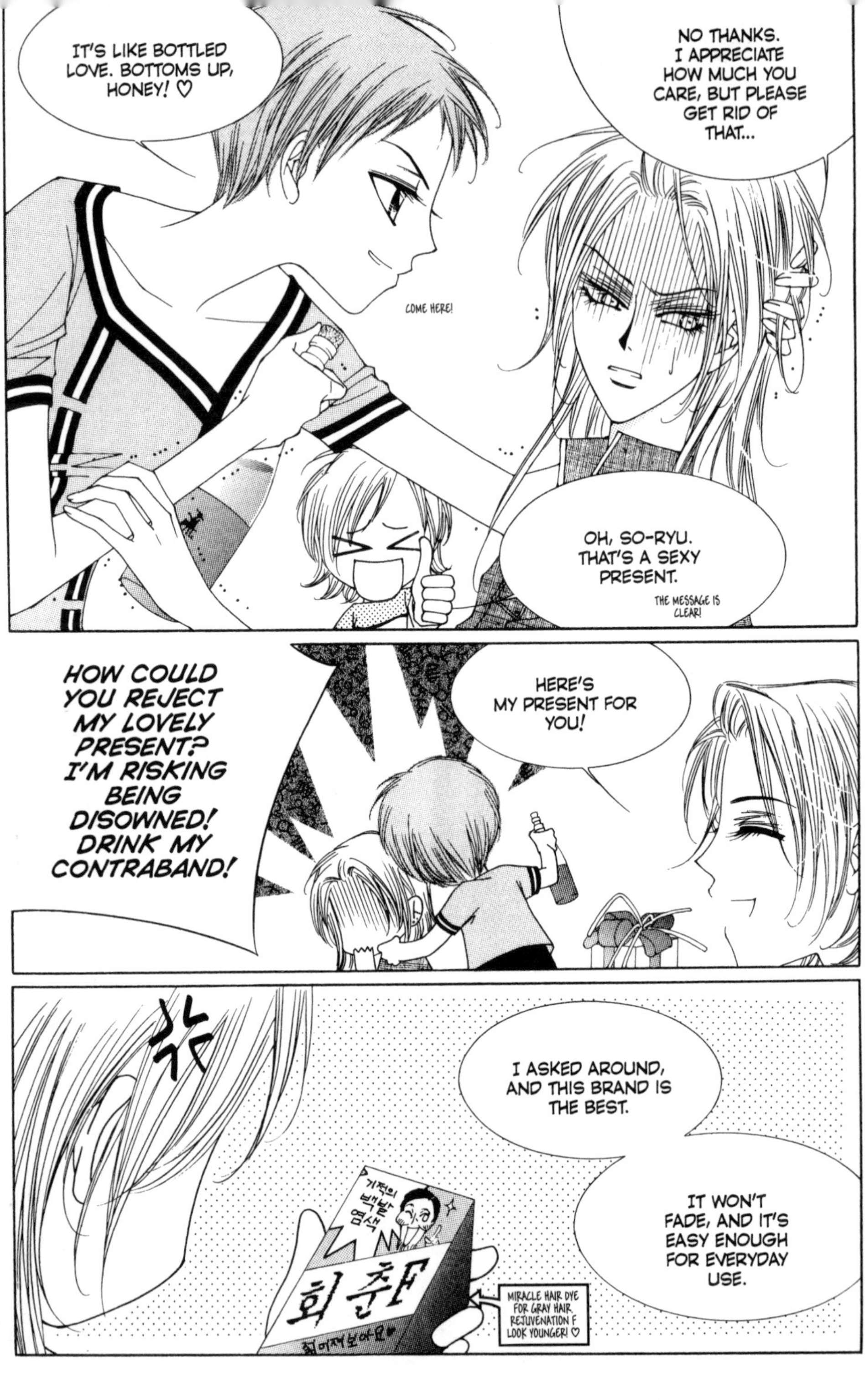
IT'S LIKE BOTTLED LOVE. BOTTOMS UP, HONEY! ♡
NO THANKS. I APPRECIATE HOW MUCH YOU CARE, BUT PLEASE GET RID OF THAT...
COME HERE!
OH, SO-RYU. THAT'S A SEXY PRESENT.
THE MESSAGE IS CLEAR!
HOW COULD YOU REJECT MY LOVELY PRESENT? I'M RISKING BEING DISOWNED! DRINK MY CONTRABAND!
HERE'S MY PRESENT FOR YOU!
I ASKED AROUND, AND THIS BRAND IS THE BEST.
기적의 백발 염색
회춘F
MIRACLE HAIR DYE FOR GRAY HAIR REJUVENATION F LOOK YOUNGER! ♡
IT WON'T FADE, AND IT'S EASY ENOUGH FOR EVERYDAY USE.

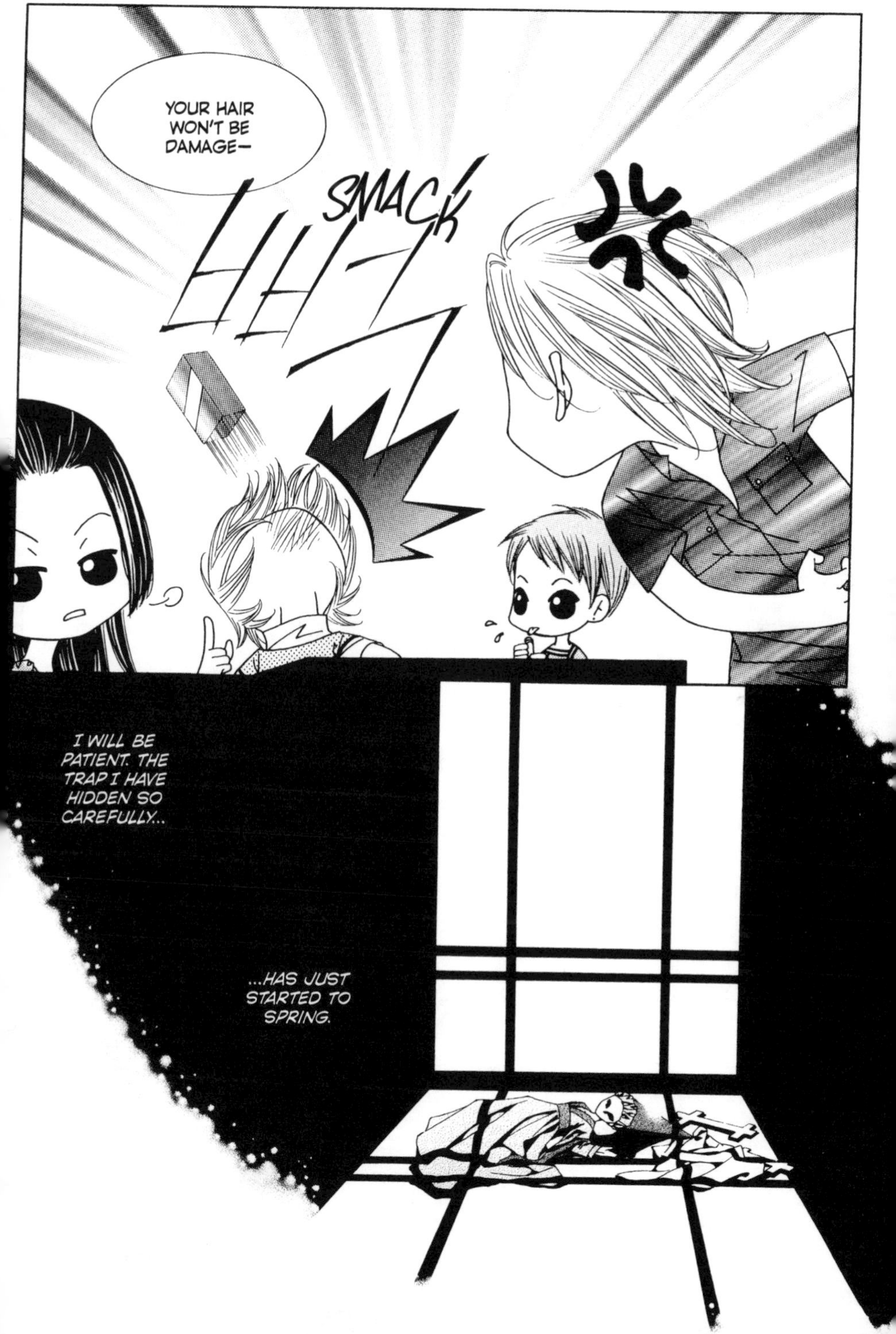
YOUR HAIR WON'T BE DAMAGE—
SMACK!
I WILL BE PATIENT. THE TRAP I HAVE HIDDEN SO CAREFULLY...
...HAS JUST STARTED TO SPRING.

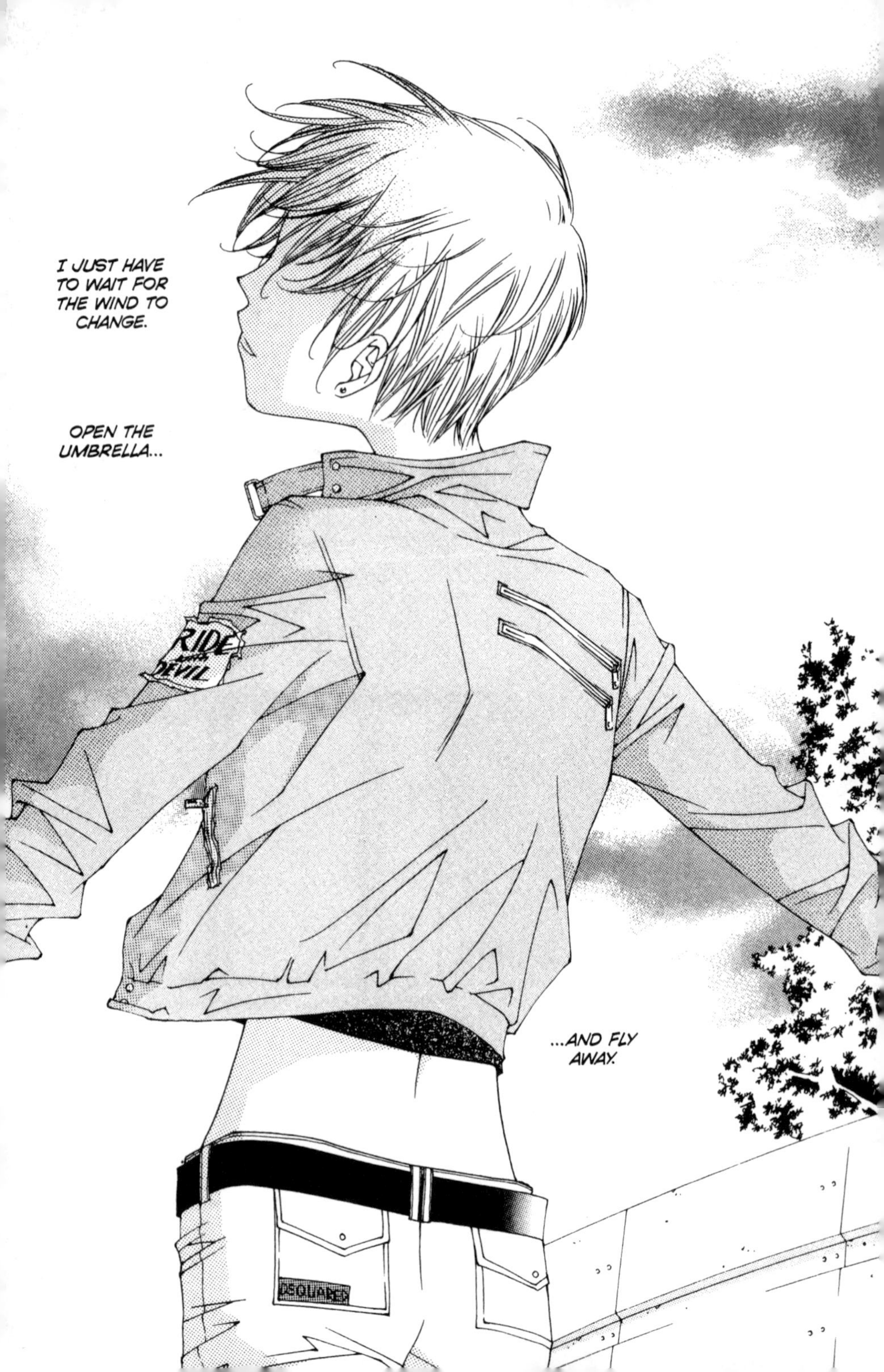
I JUST HAVE TO WAIT FOR THE WIND TO CHANGE.
OPEN THE UMBRELLA...
...AND FLY AWAY.

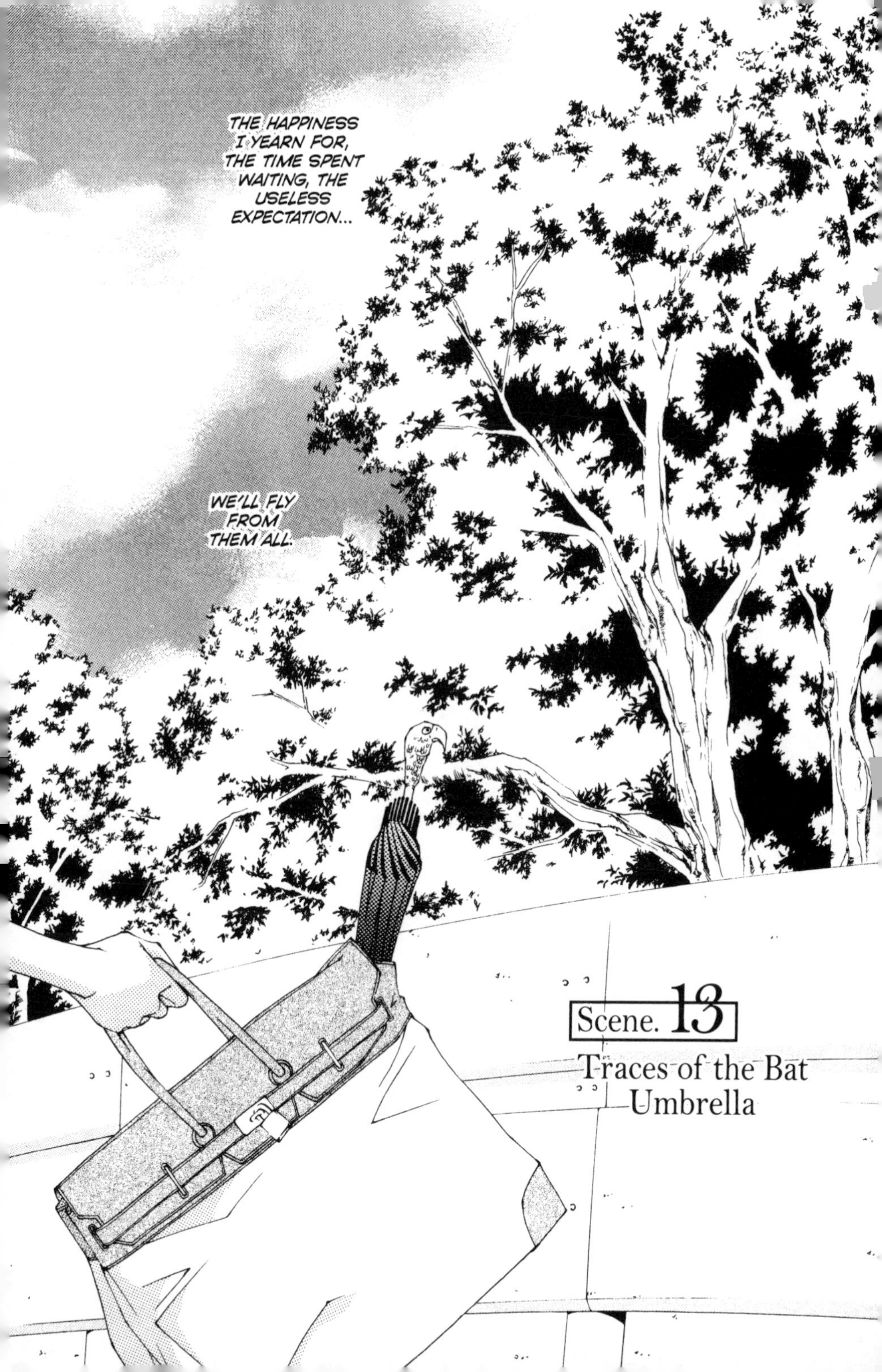
THE HAPPINESS I YEARN FOR, THE TIME SPENT WAITING, THE USELESS EXPECTATION...
WE'LL FLY FROM THEM ALL.
Scene. 13
Traces of the Bat Umbrella

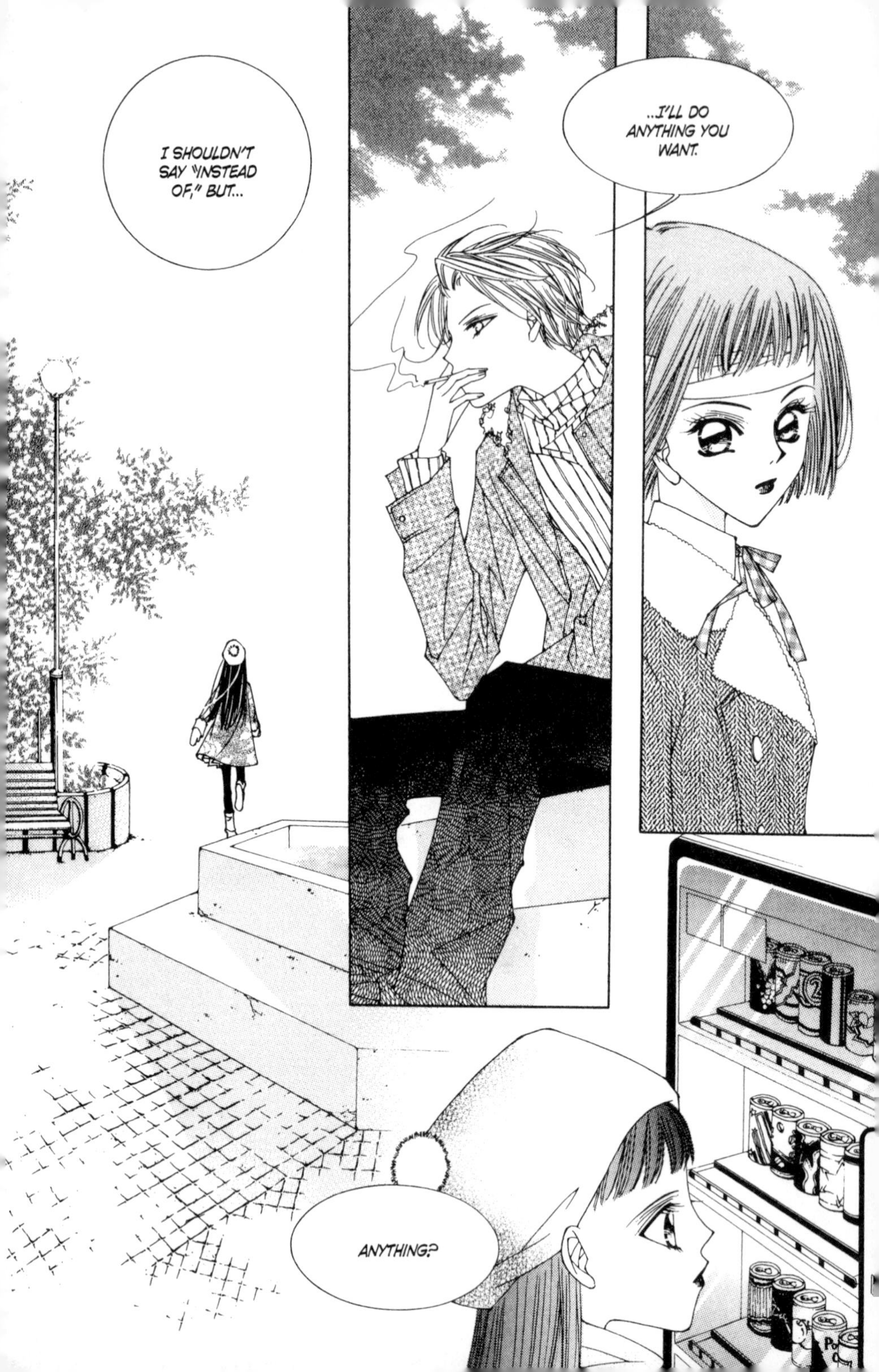
I SHOULDN'T SAY "INSTEAD OF," BUT...
...I'LL DO ANYTHING YOU WANT.
ANYTHING?

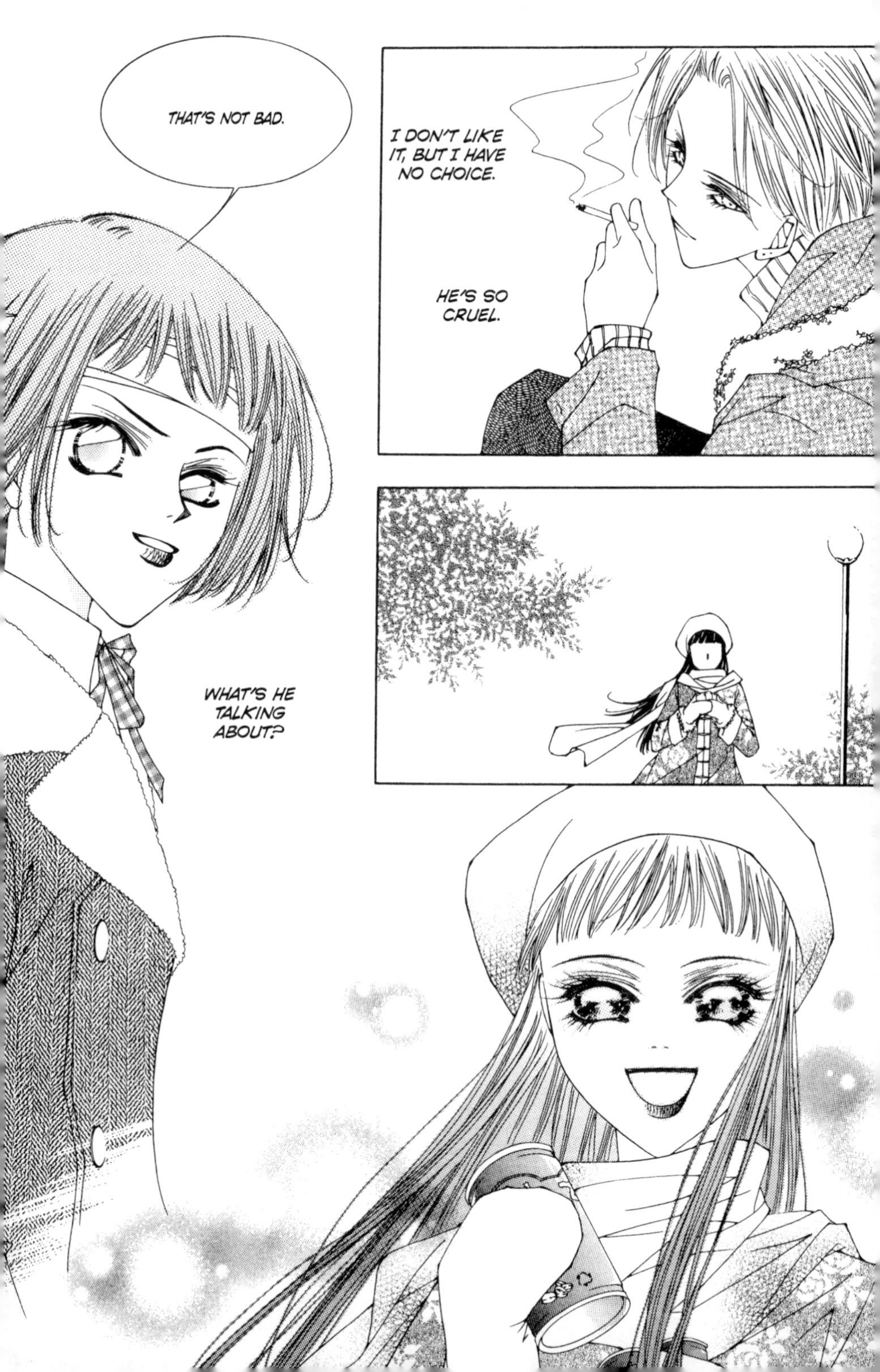
THAT'S NOT BAD.
WHAT'S HE TALKING ABOUT?
I DON'T LIKE IT, BUT I HAVE NO CHOICE.
HE'S SO CRUEL.

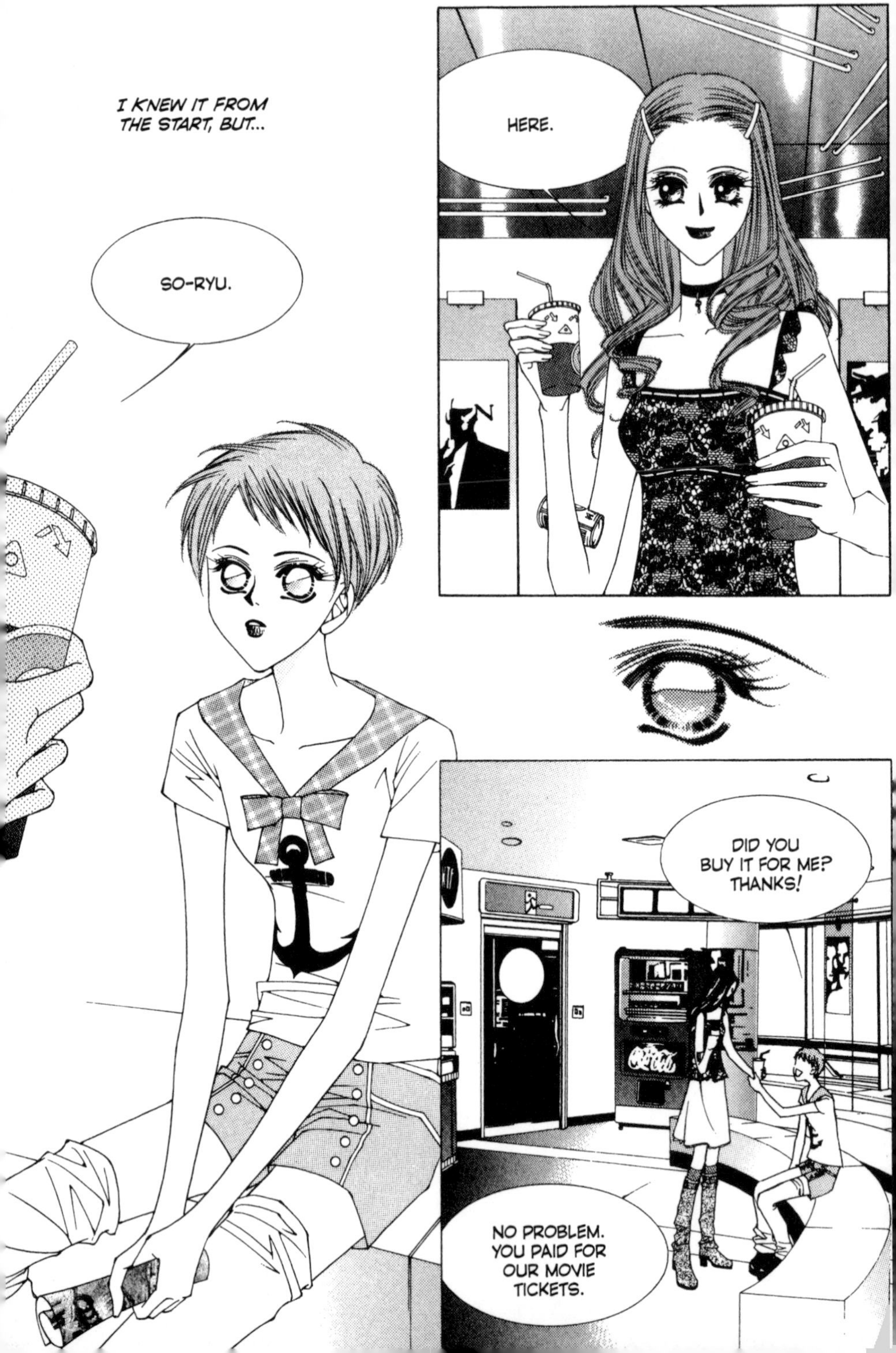
I KNEW IT FROM THE START, BUT...
SO-RYU.
HERE.
DID YOU BUY IT FOR ME? THANKS!
NO PROBLEM. YOU PAID FOR OUR MOVIE TICKETS.

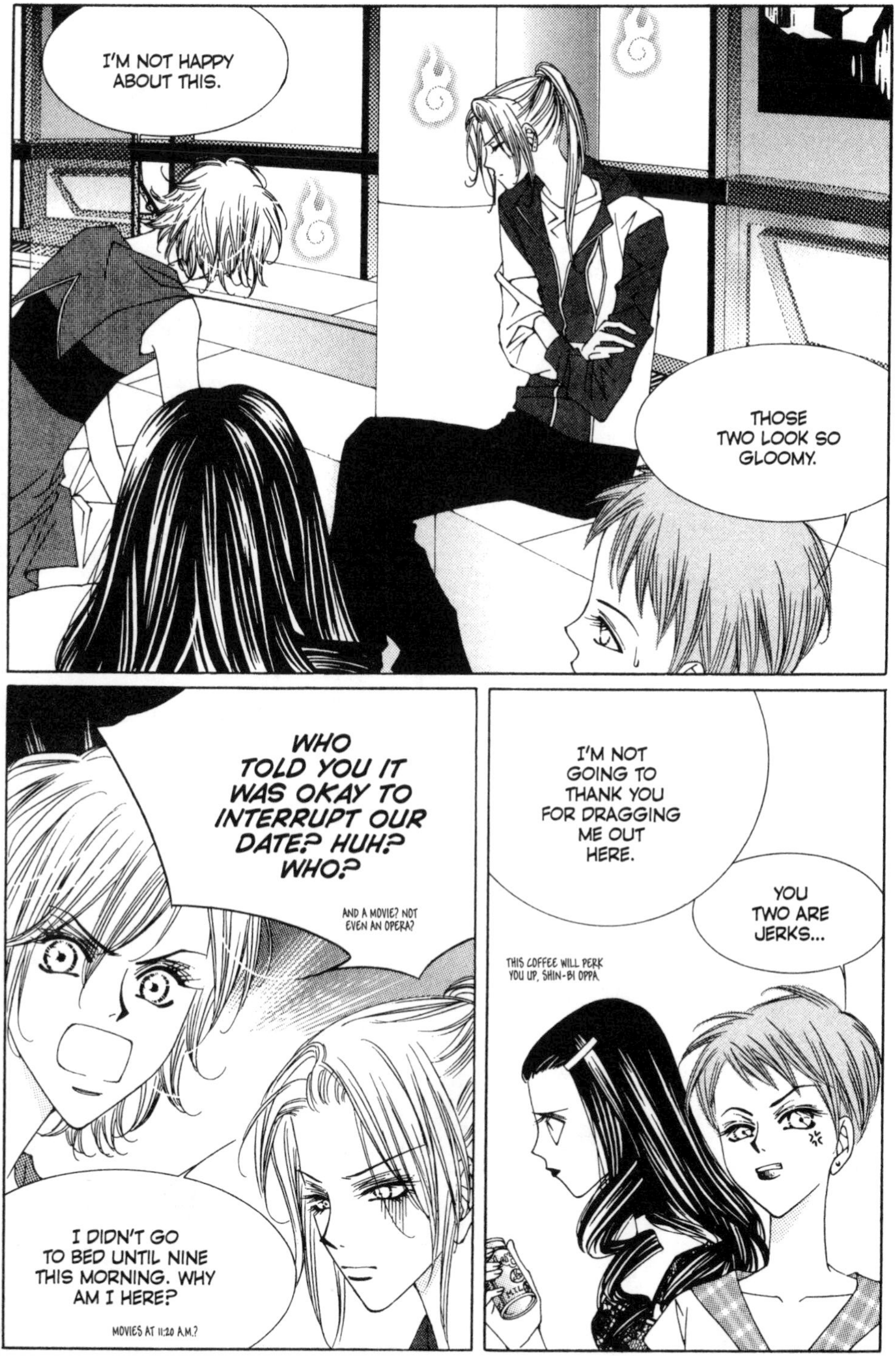
I'M NOT HAPPY ABOUT THIS.
THOSE TWO LOOK SO GLOOMY.
WHO TOLD YOU IT WAS OKAY TO INTERRUPT OUR DATE? HUH? WHO?
AND A MOVIE? NOT EVEN AN OPERA?
I DIDN'T GO TO BED UNTIL NINE THIS MORNING. WHY AM I HERE?
MOVIES AT 11:20 A.M.?
I'M NOT GOING TO THANK YOU FOR DRAGGING ME OUT HERE.
YOU TWO ARE JERKS...
THIS COFFEE WILL PERK YOU UP, SHIN-BI OPPA.

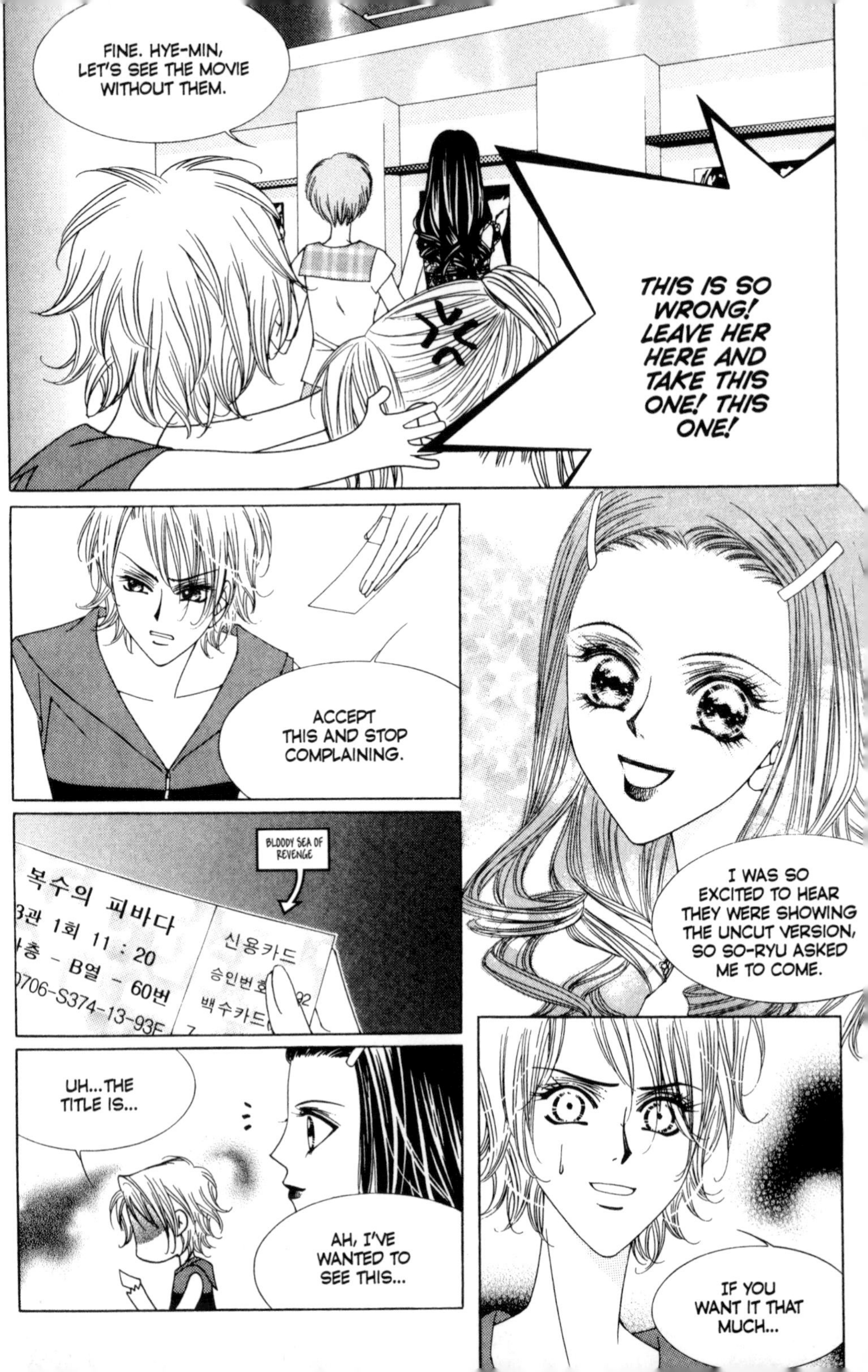
FINE. HYE-MIN, LET'S SEE THE MOVIE WITHOUT THEM.
THIS IS SO WRONG! LEAVE HER HERE AND TAKE THIS ONE! THIS ONE!
ACCEPT THIS AND STOP COMPLAINING.
BLOODY SEA OF REVENGE
복수의 피바다
1회 11 : 20
B열 - 60번
신용카드
UH...THE TITLE IS...
AH, I'VE WANTED TO SEE THIS...
I WAS SO EXCITED TO HEAR THEY WERE SHOWING THE UNCUT VERSION, SO SO-RYU ASKED ME TO COME.
IF YOU WANT IT THAT MUCH...

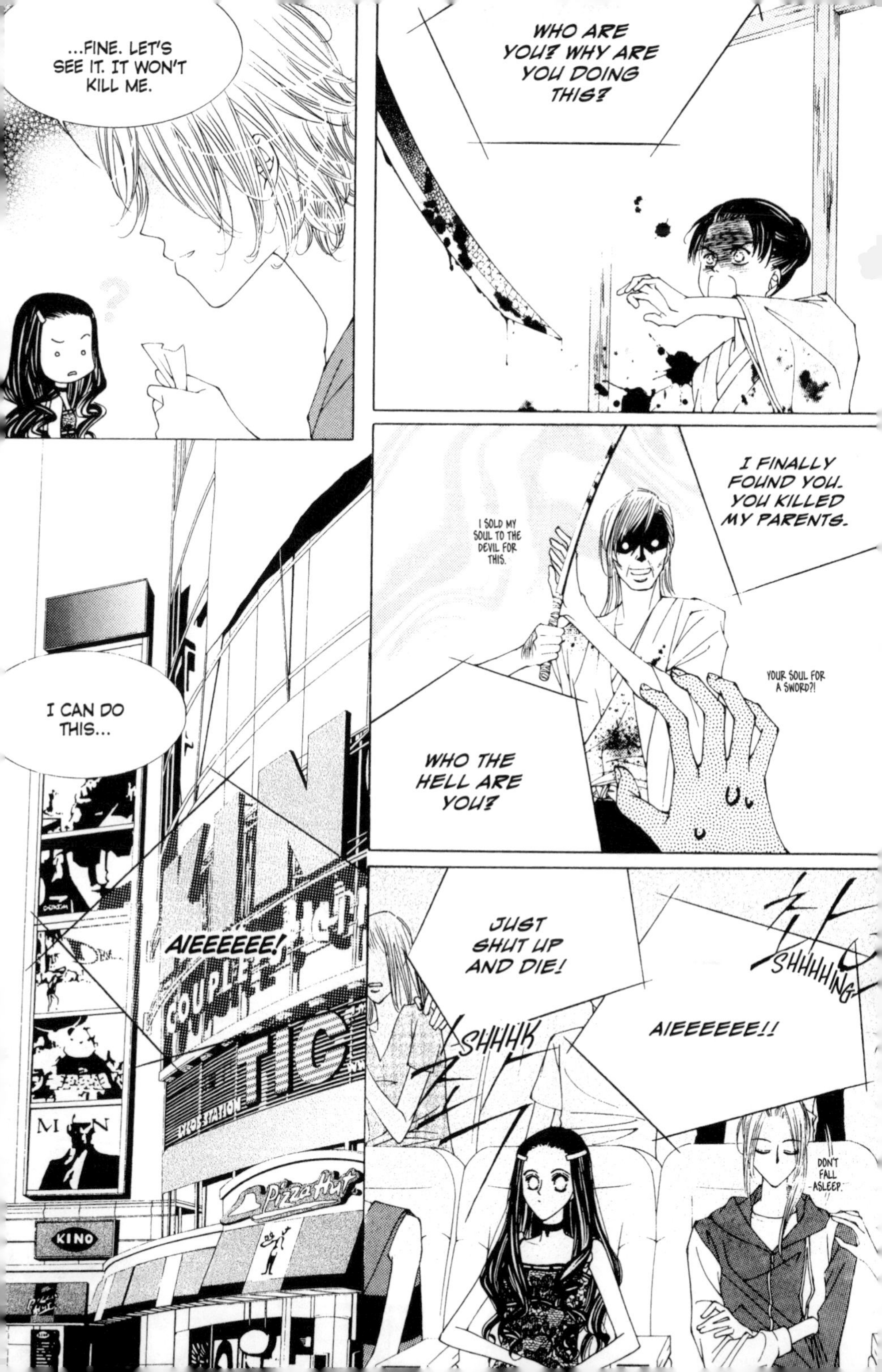
...FINE. LET'S SEE IT. IT WON'T KILL ME.
WHO ARE YOU? WHY ARE YOU DOING THIS?
I CAN DO THIS...
AIEEEEEE!
Pizza Hut
KINO
I FINALLY FOUND YOU. YOU KILLED MY PARENTS.
I SOLD MY SOUL TO THE DEVIL FOR THIS.
YOUR SOUL FOR A SWORD?!
WHO THE HELL ARE YOU?
JUST SHUT UP AND DIE!
SHHHHING
SHHHK
AIEEEEEE!!
DON'T FALL ASLEEP.

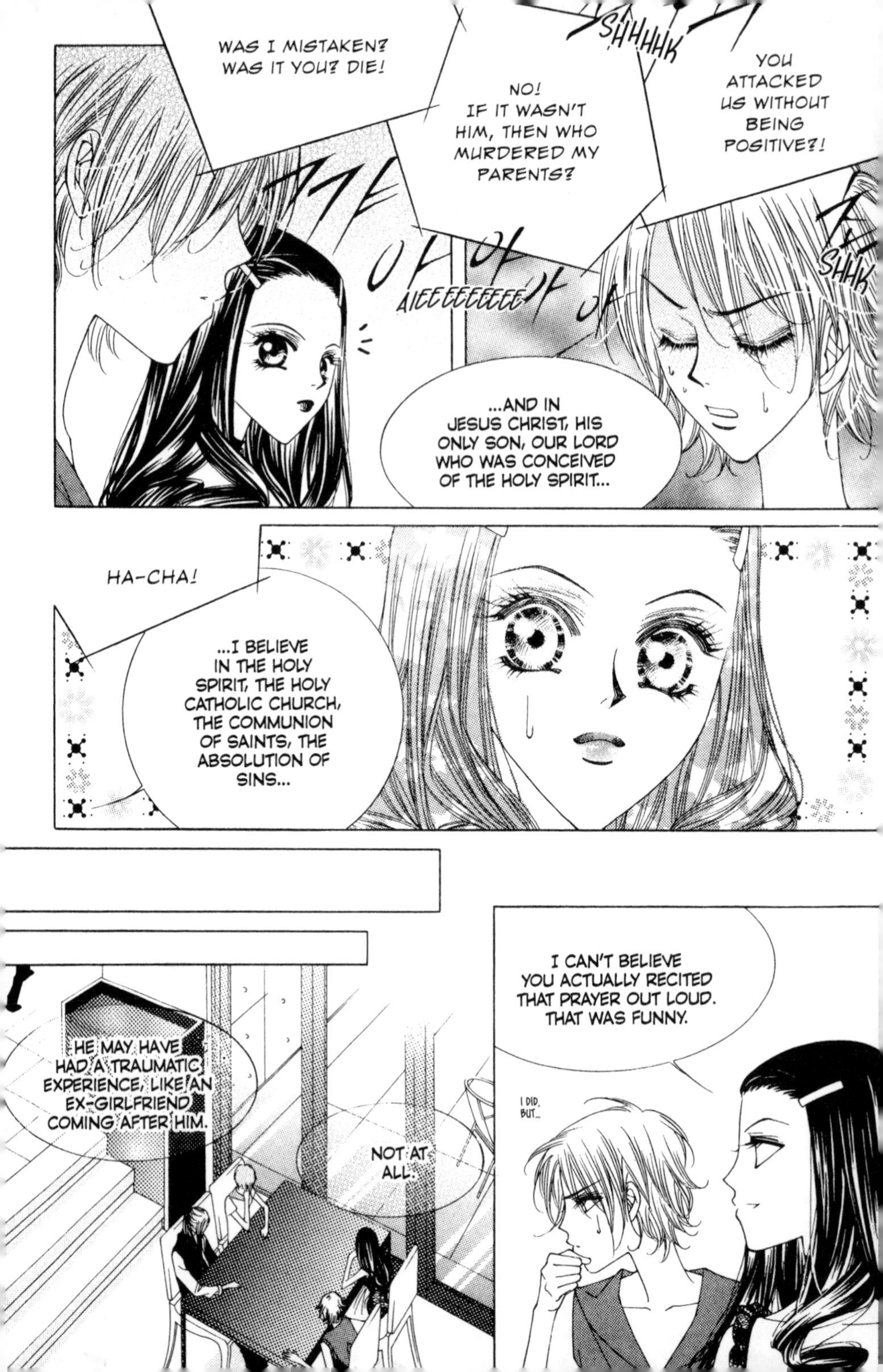
WAS I MISTAKEN? WAS IT YOU? DIE!
NO! IF IT WASN'T HIM, THEN WHO MURDERED MY PARENTS?
SHHHHK
YOU ATTACKED US WITHOUT BEING POSITIVE?!
AIEEEEEEEEE
SHHK
...AND IN JESUS CHRIST, HIS ONLY SON, OUR LORD WHO WAS CONCEIVED OF THE HOLY SPIRIT...
HA-CHA!
...I BELIEVE IN THE HOLY SPIRIT, THE HOLY CATHOLIC CHURCH, THE COMMUNION OF SAINTS, THE ABSOLUTION OF SINS...
HE MAY HAVE HAD A TRAUMATIC EXPERIENCE, LIKE AN EX-GIRLFRIEND COMING AFTER HIM.
NOT AT ALL.
I CAN'T BELIEVE YOU ACTUALLY RECITED THAT PRAYER OUT LOUD. THAT WAS FUNNY.
I DID, BUT...

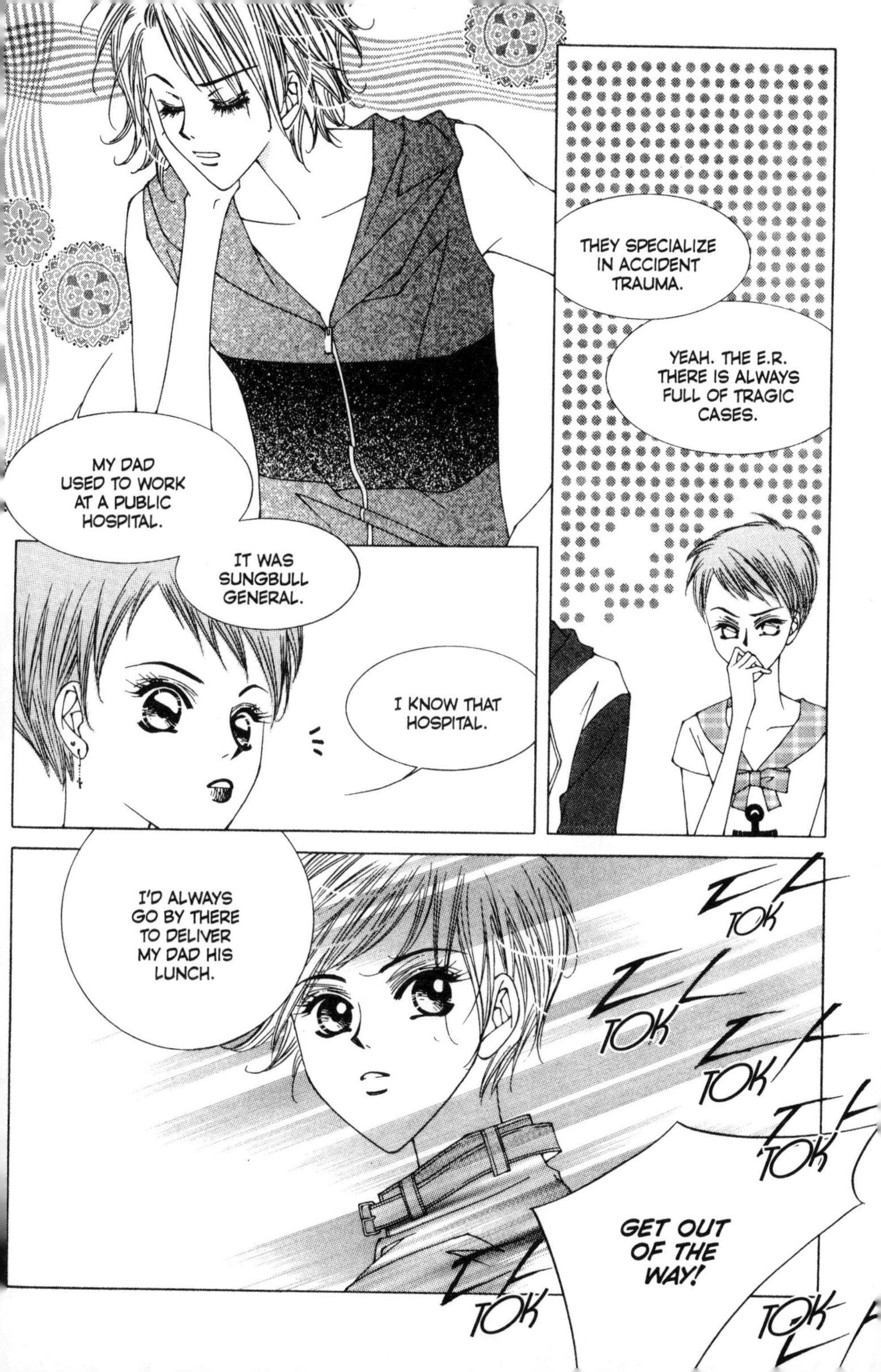
MY DAD USED TO WORK AT A PUBLIC HOSPITAL.
IT WAS SUNGBULL GENERAL.
I KNOW THAT HOSPITAL.
THEY SPECIALIZE IN ACCIDENT TRAUMA.
YEAH. THE E.R. THERE IS ALWAYS FULL OF TRAGIC CASES.
I'D ALWAYS GO BY THERE TO DELIVER MY DAD HIS LUNCH.
TOK
TOK
TOK
TOK
GET OUT OF THE WAY!
TOK
TOK

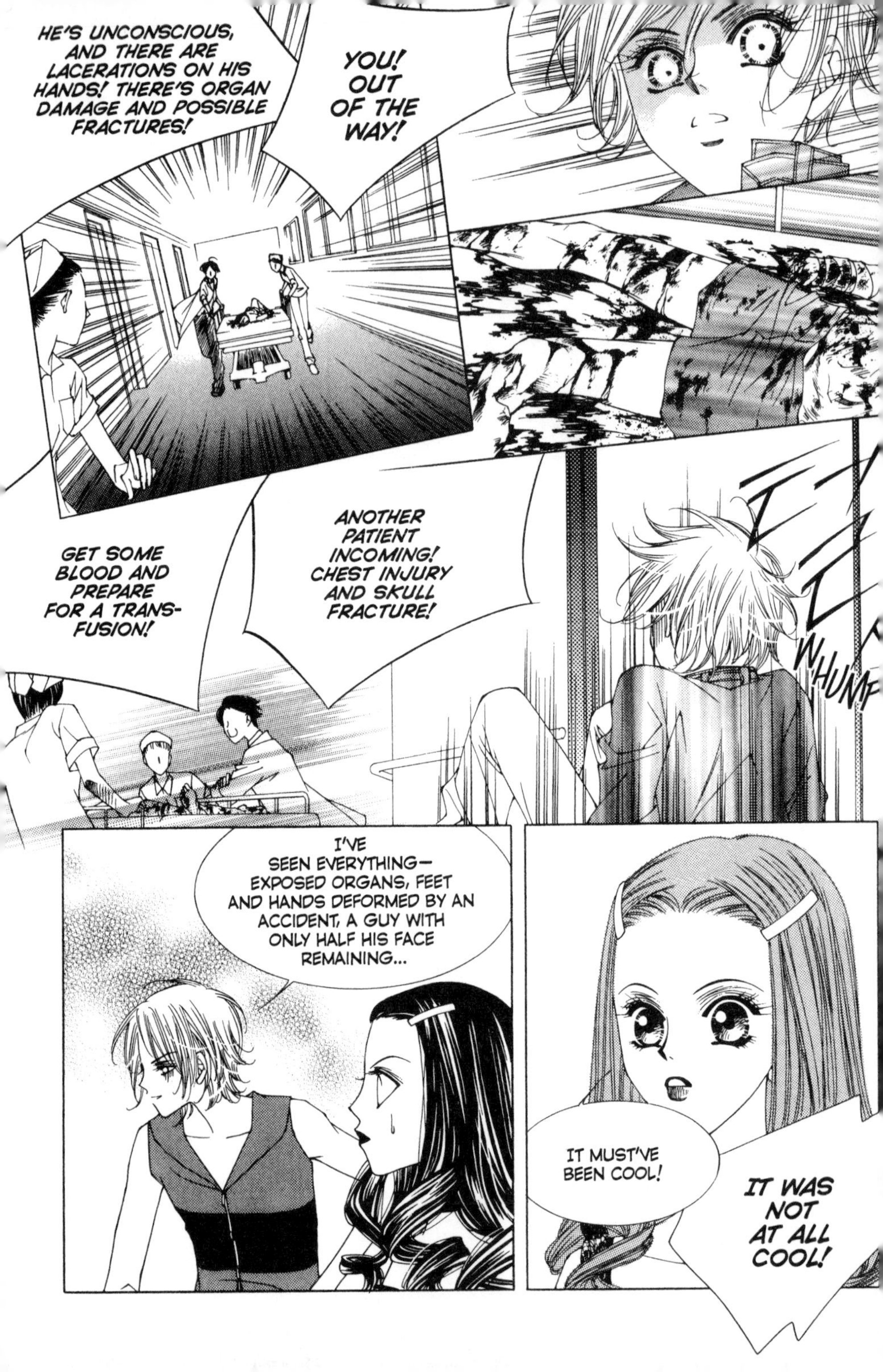
HE'S UNCONSCIOUS, AND THERE ARE LACERATIONS ON HIS HANDS! THERE'S ORGAN DAMAGE AND POSSIBLE FRACTURES!
YOU! OUT OF THE WAY!
GET SOME BLOOD AND PREPARE FOR A TRANS-FUSION!
ANOTHER PATIENT INCOMING! CHEST INJURY AND SKULL FRACTURE!
I'VE SEEN EVERYTHING— EXPOSED ORGANS, FEET AND HANDS DEFORMED BY AN ACCIDENT, A GUY WITH ONLY HALF HIS FACE REMAINING...
IT MUST'VE BEEN COOL!
IT WAS NOT AT ALL COOL!

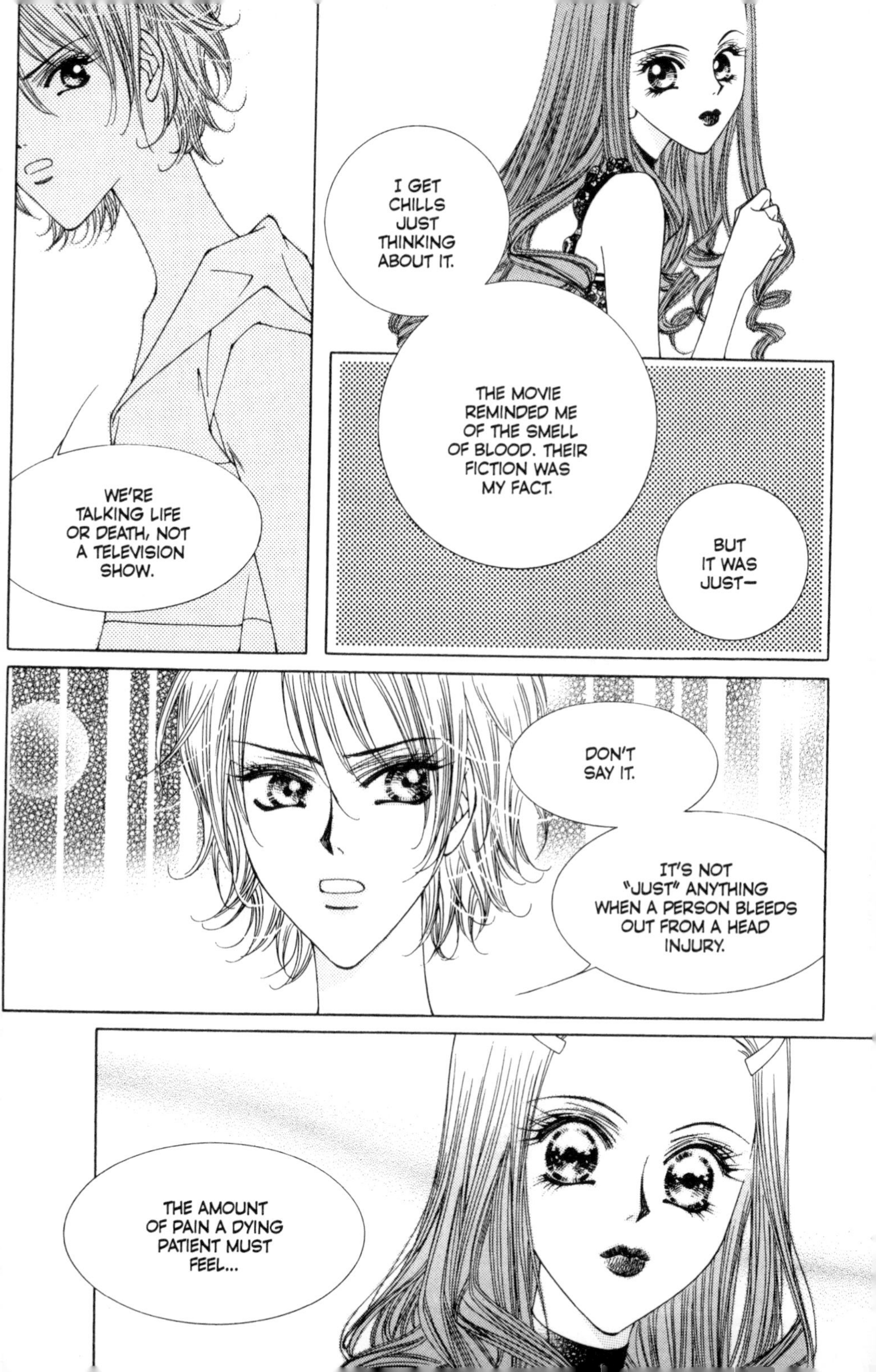
WE'RE TALKING LIFE OR DEATH, NOT A TELEVISION SHOW.
I GET CHILLS JUST THINKING ABOUT IT.
THE MOVIE REMINDED ME OF THE SMELL OF BLOOD. THEIR FICTION WAS MY FACT.
BUT IT WAS JUST—
DON'T SAY IT.
IT'S NOT "JUST" ANYTHING WHEN A PERSON BLEEDS OUT FROM A HEAD INJURY.
THE AMOUNT OF PAIN A DYING PATIENT MUST FEEL...

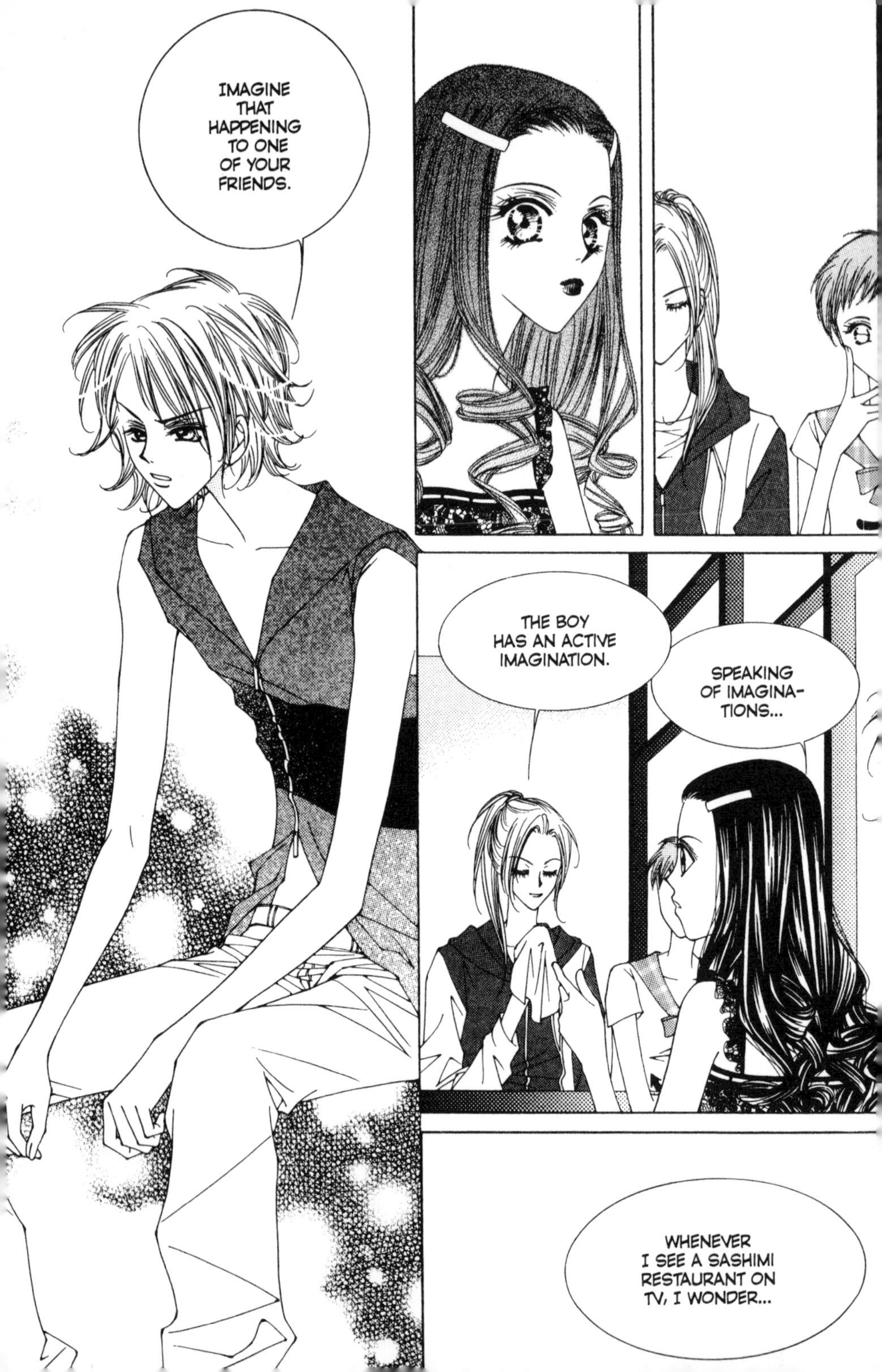
IMAGINE THAT HAPPENING TO ONE OF YOUR FRIENDS.
THE BOY HAS AN ACTIVE IMAGINATION.
SPEAKING OF IMAGINA-TIONS...
WHENEVER I SEE A SASHIMI RESTAURANT ON TV, I WONDER...

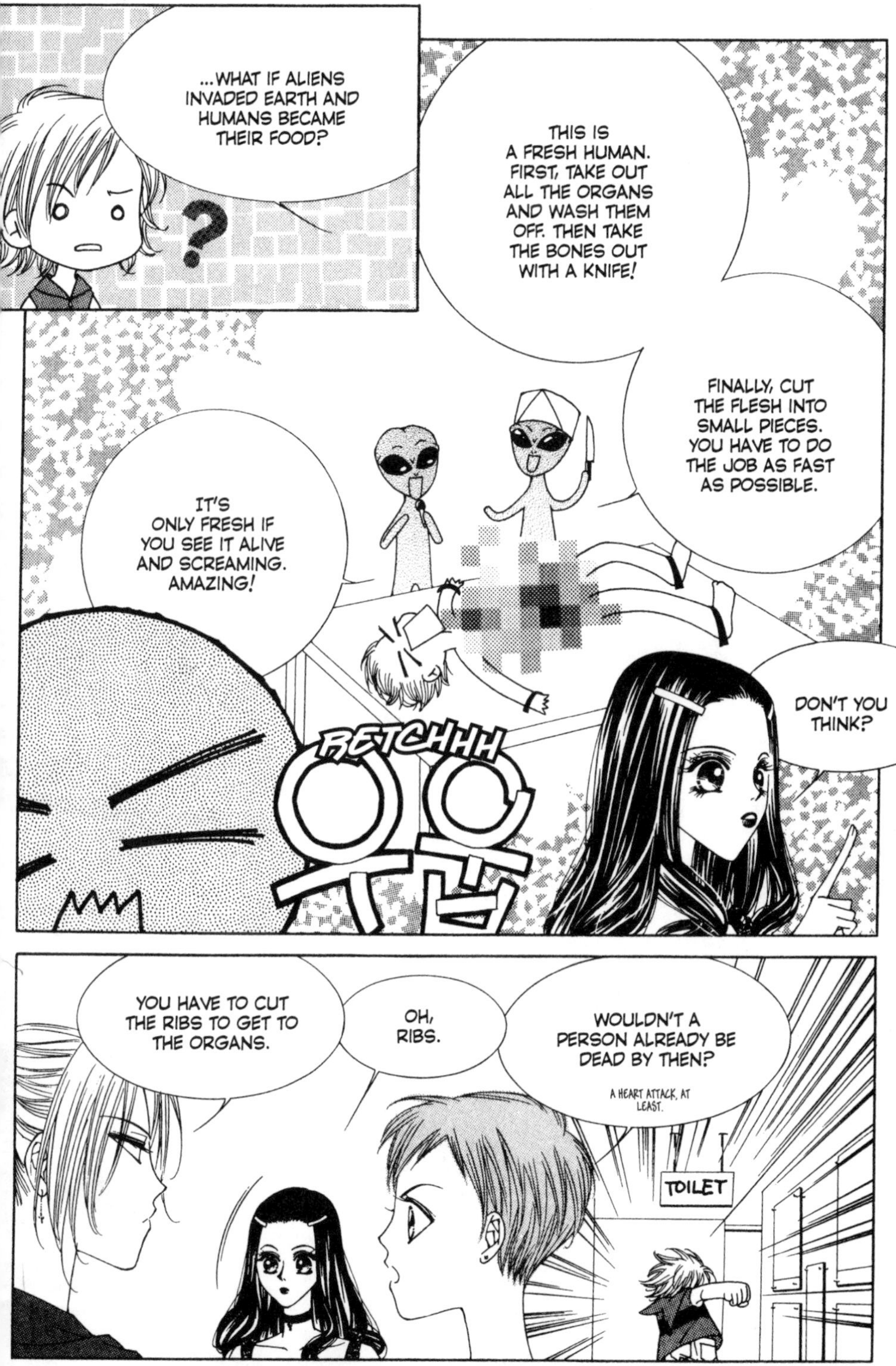
...WHAT IF ALIENS INVADED EARTH AND HUMANS BECAME THEIR FOOD?
THIS IS A FRESH HUMAN. FIRST, TAKE OUT ALL THE ORGANS AND WASH THEM OFF. THEN TAKE THE BONES OUT WITH A KNIFE!
FINALLY, CUT THE FLESH INTO SMALL PIECES. YOU HAVE TO DO THE JOB AS FAST AS POSSIBLE.
IT'S ONLY FRESH IF YOU SEE IT ALIVE AND SCREAMING. AMAZING!
RETCHHH
DON'T YOU THINK?
YOU HAVE TO CUT THE RIBS TO GET TO THE ORGANS.
OH, RIBS.
WOULDN'T A PERSON ALREADY BE DEAD BY THEN?
A HEART ATTACK, AT LEAST.
TOILET

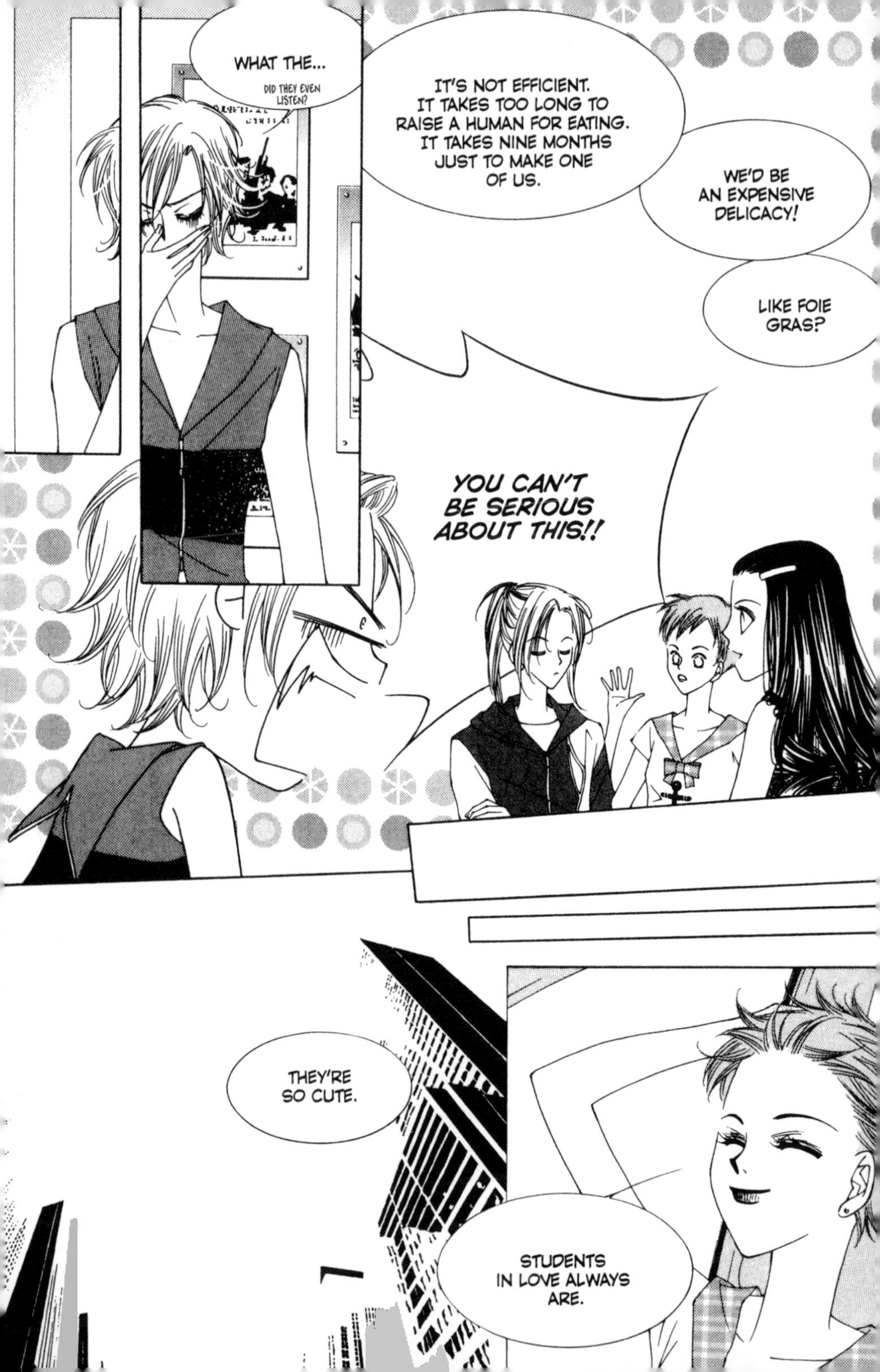
WHAT THE...
DID THEY EVEN LISTEN?
IT'S NOT EFFICIENT. IT TAKES TOO LONG TO RAISE A HUMAN FOR EATING. IT TAKES NINE MONTHS JUST TO MAKE ONE OF US.
WE'D BE AN EXPENSIVE DELICACY!
LIKE FOIE GRAS?
YOU CAN'T BE SERIOUS ABOUT THIS!!
THEY'RE SO CUTE.
STUDENTS IN LOVE ALWAYS ARE.

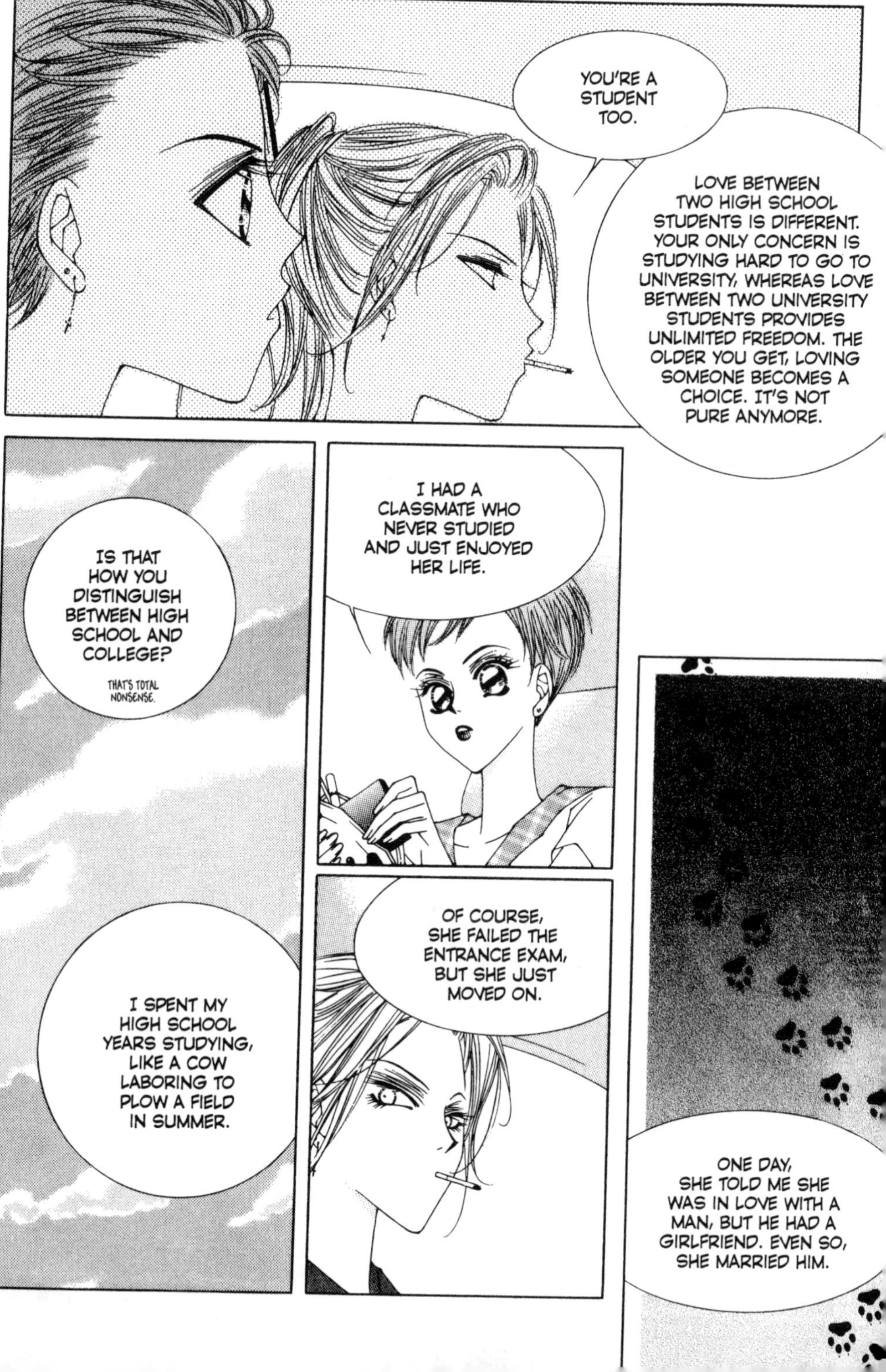
YOU'RE A STUDENT TOO.
LOVE BETWEEN TWO HIGH SCHOOL STUDENTS IS DIFFERENT. YOUR ONLY CONCERN IS STUDYING HARD TO GO TO UNIVERSITY, WHEREAS LOVE BETWEEN TWO UNIVERSITY STUDENTS PROVIDES UNLIMITED FREEDOM. THE OLDER YOU GET, LOVING SOMEONE BECOMES A CHOICE. IT'S NOT PURE ANYMORE.
IS THAT HOW YOU DISTINGUISH BETWEEN HIGH SCHOOL AND COLLEGE?
THAT'S TOTAL NONSENSE.
I SPENT MY HIGH SCHOOL YEARS STUDYING, LIKE A COW LABORING TO PLOW A FIELD IN SUMMER.
I HAD A CLASSMATE WHO NEVER STUDIED AND JUST ENJOYED HER LIFE.
OF COURSE, SHE FAILED THE ENTRANCE EXAM, BUT SHE JUST MOVED ON.
ONE DAY, SHE TOLD ME SHE WAS IN LOVE WITH A MAN, BUT HE HAD A GIRLFRIEND. EVEN SO, SHE MARRIED HIM.

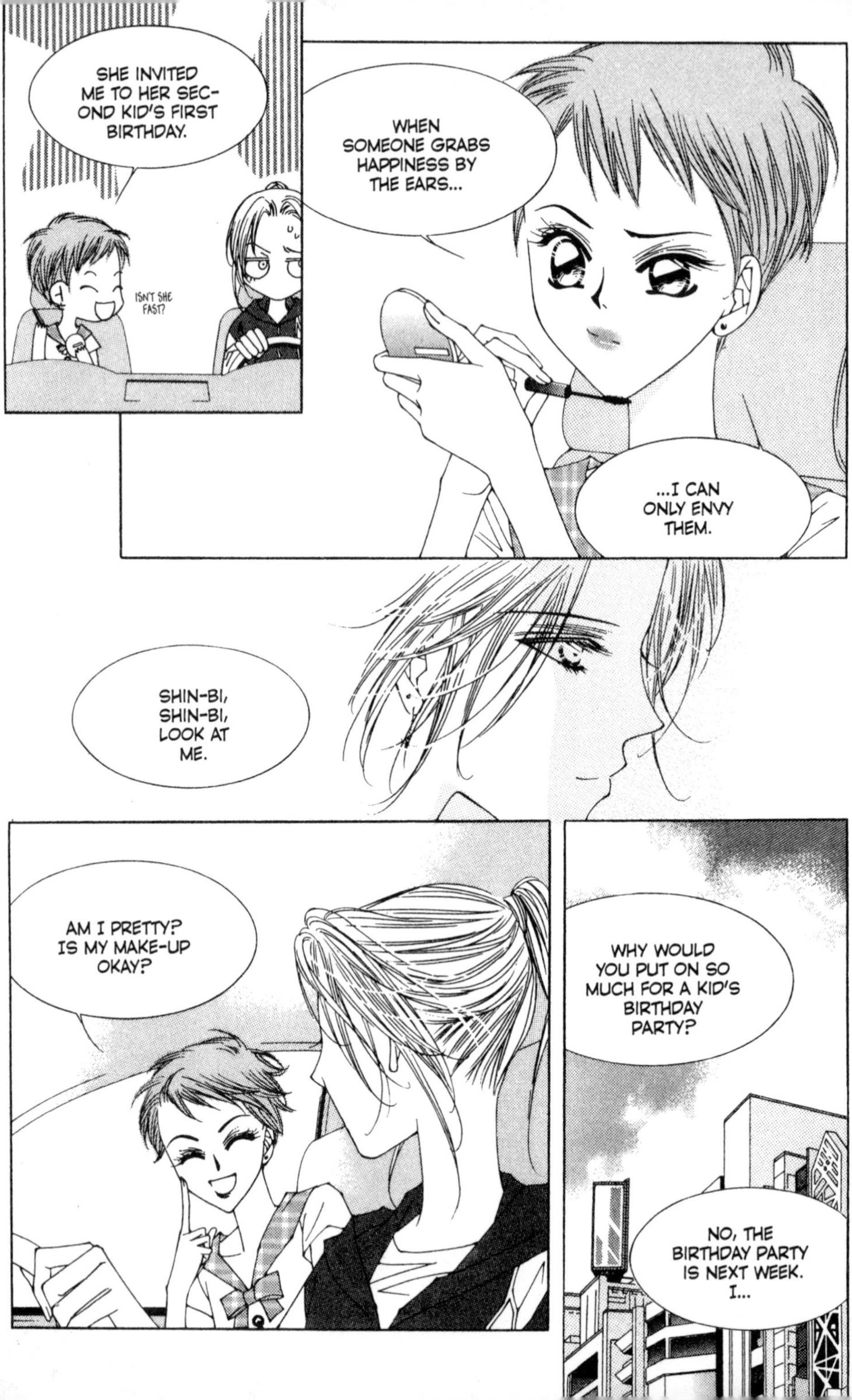
SHE INVITED ME TO HER SEC-OND KID'S FIRST BIRTHDAY.
ISN'T SHE FAST?
WHEN SOMEONE GRABS HAPPINESS BY THE EARS...
...I CAN ONLY ENVY THEM.
SHIN-BI, SHIN-BI, LOOK AT ME.
AM I PRETTY? IS MY MAKE-UP OKAY?
WHY WOULD YOU PUT ON SO MUCH FOR A KID'S BIRTHDAY PARTY?
NO, THE BIRTHDAY PARTY IS NEXT WEEK. I...

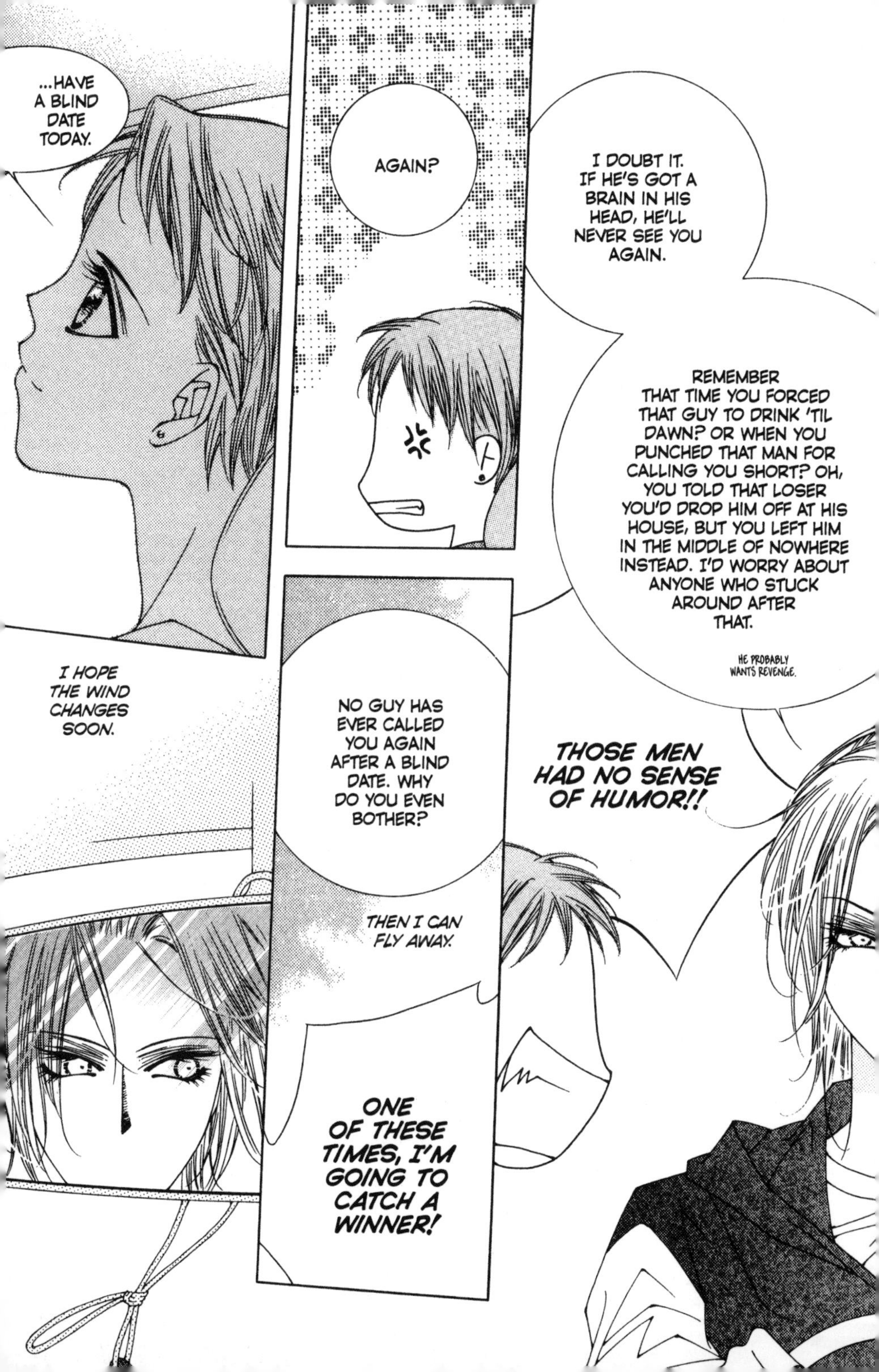
...HAVE A BLIND DATE TODAY.
AGAIN?
I DOUBT IT. IF HE'S GOT A BRAIN IN HIS HEAD, HE'LL NEVER SEE YOU AGAIN.
REMEMBER THAT TIME YOU FORCED THAT GUY TO DRINK 'TIL DAWN? OR WHEN YOU PUNCHED THAT MAN FOR CALLING YOU SHORT? OH, YOU TOLD THAT LOSER YOU'D DROP HIM OFF AT HIS HOUSE, BUT YOU LEFT HIM IN THE MIDDLE OF NOWHERE INSTEAD. I'D WORRY ABOUT ANYONE WHO STUCK AROUND AFTER THAT.
HE PROBABLY WANTS REVENGE.
I HOPE THE WIND CHANGES SOON.
THEN I CAN FLY AWAY.
NO GUY HAS EVER CALLED YOU AGAIN AFTER A BLIND DATE. WHY DO YOU EVEN BOTHER?
ONE OF THESE TIMES, I'M GOING TO CATCH A WINNER!
THOSE MEN HAD NO SENSE OF HUMOR!!

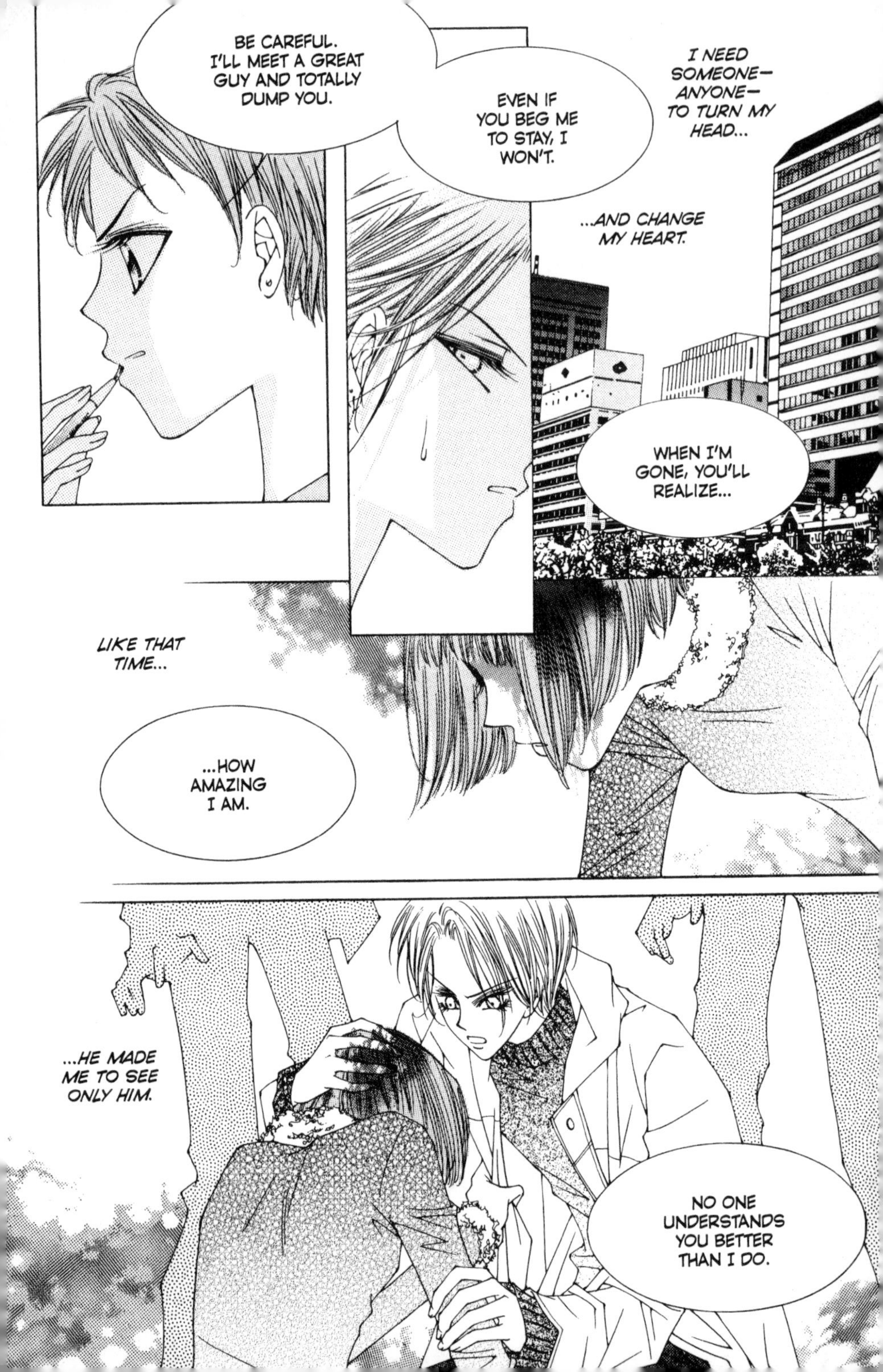
BE CAREFUL. I'LL MEET A GREAT GUY AND TOTALLY DUMP YOU.
EVEN IF YOU BEG ME TO STAY, I WON'T.
I NEED SOMEONE—ANYONE—TO TURN MY HEAD...
...AND CHANGE MY HEART.
WHEN I'M GONE, YOU'LL REALIZE...
LIKE THAT TIME...
...HOW AMAZING I AM.
...HE MADE ME TO SEE ONLY HIM.
NO ONE UNDERSTANDS YOU BETTER THAN I DO.

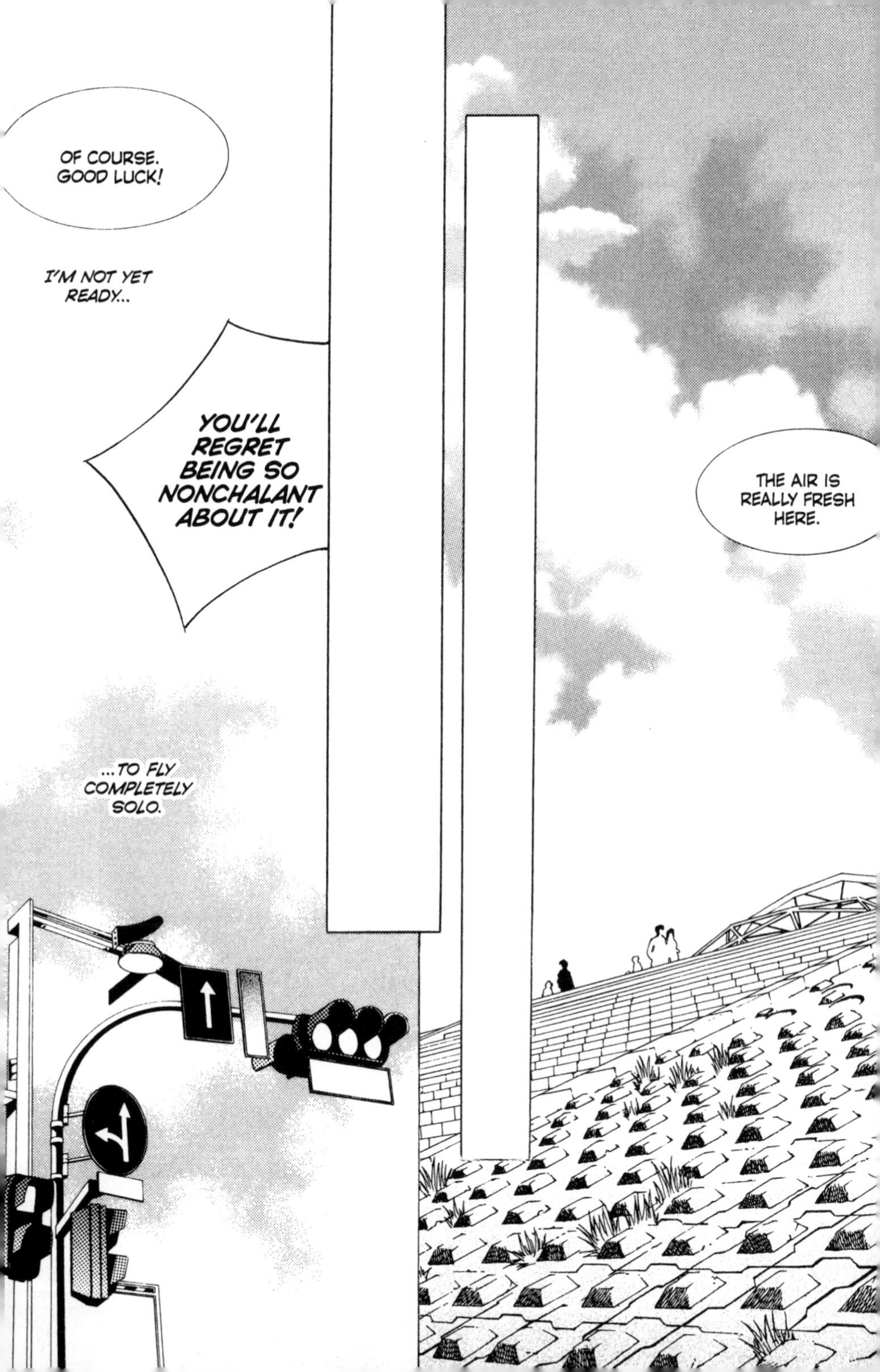
OF COURSE. GOOD LUCK!
I'M NOT YET READY...
YOU'LL REGRET BEING SO NONCHALANT ABOUT IT!
...TO FLY COMPLETELY SOLO.
THE AIR IS REALLY FRESH HERE.

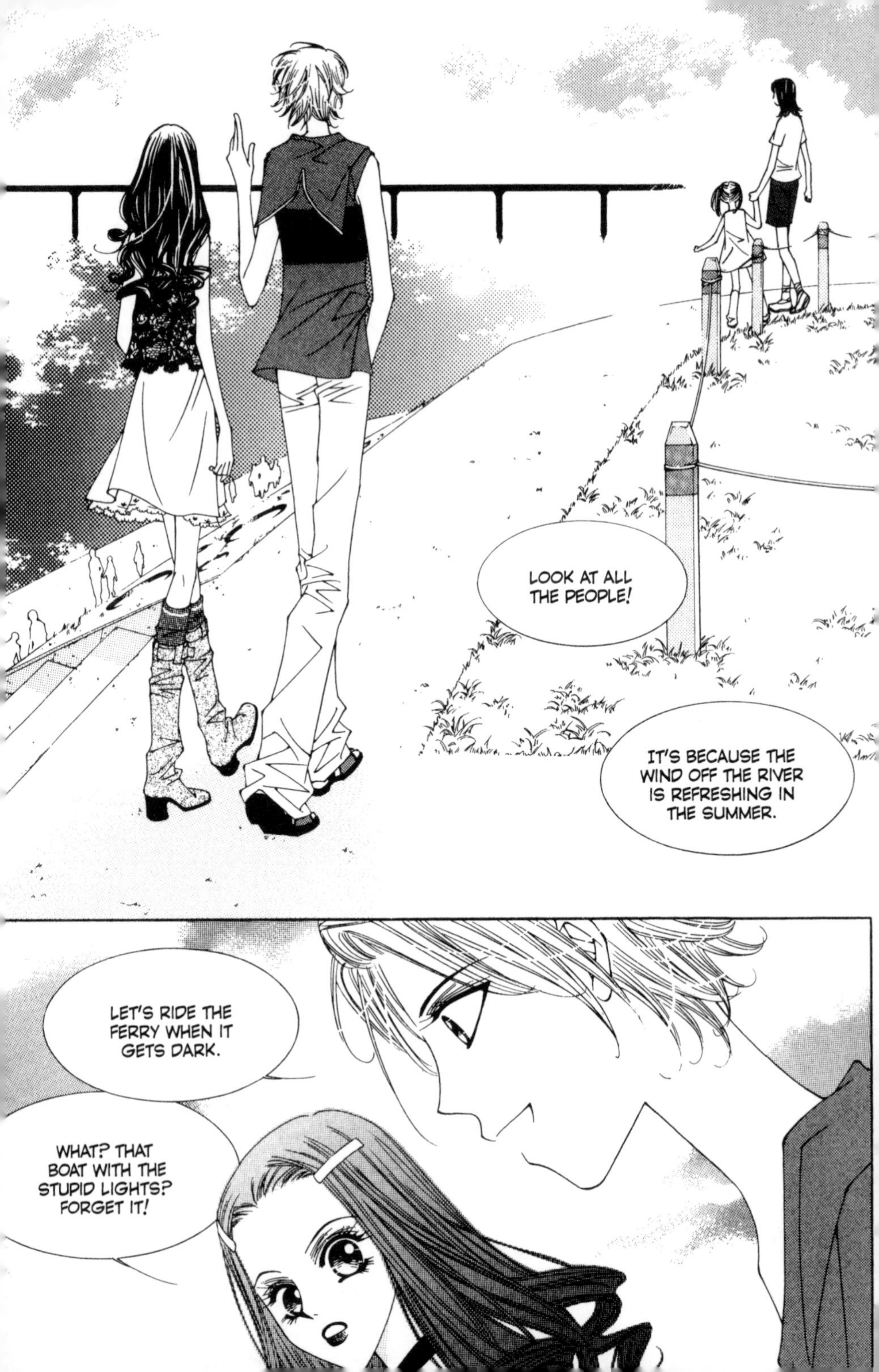
LOOK AT ALL THE PEOPLE!
IT'S BECAUSE THE WIND OFF THE RIVER IS REFRESHING IN THE SUMMER.
LET'S RIDE THE FERRY WHEN IT GETS DARK.
WHAT? THAT BOAT WITH THE STUPID LIGHTS? FORGET IT!

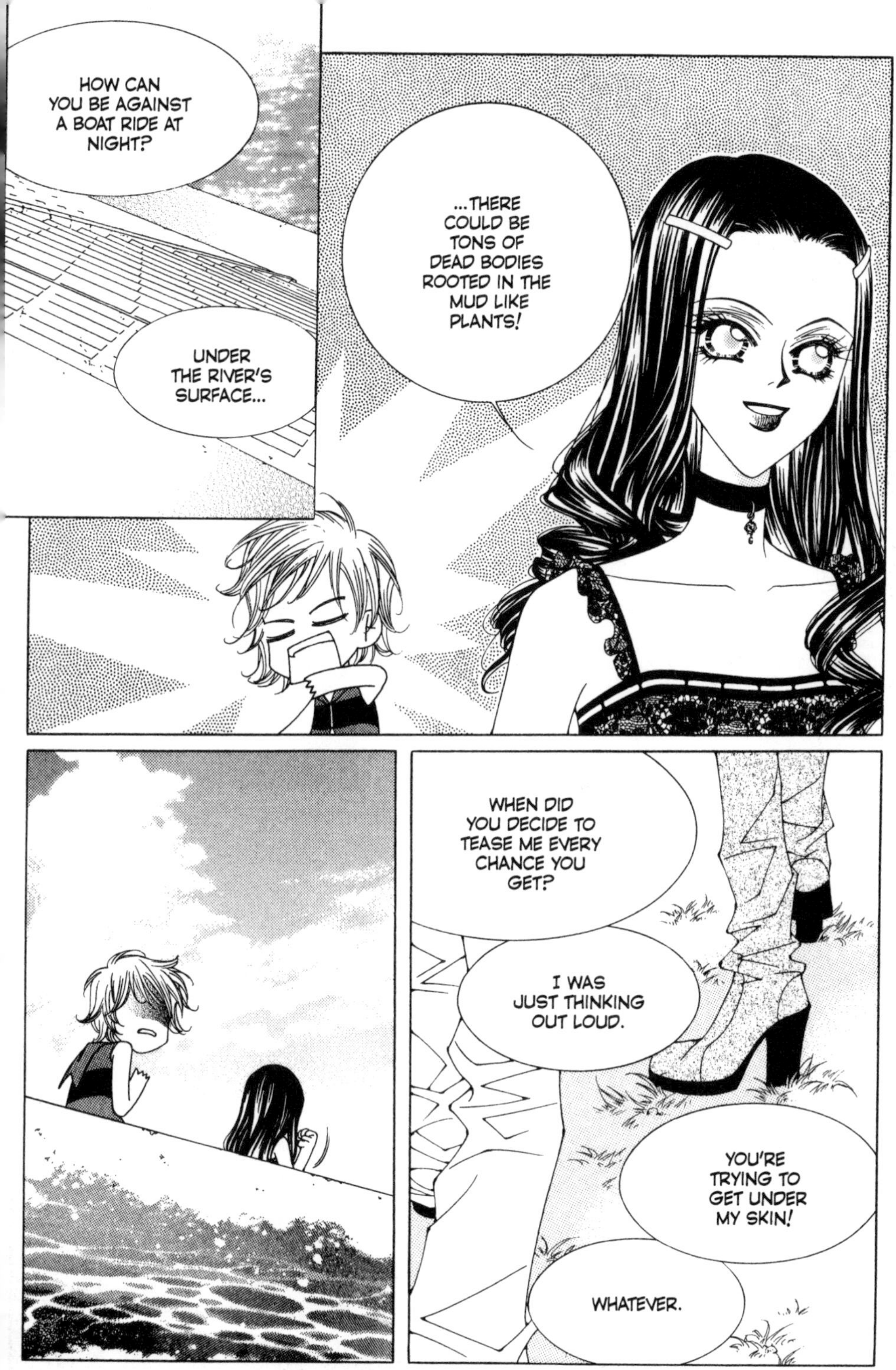
HOW CAN YOU BE AGAINST A BOAT RIDE AT NIGHT?
UNDER THE RIVER'S SURFACE...
...THERE COULD BE TONS OF DEAD BODIES ROOTED IN THE MUD LIKE PLANTS!
WHEN DID YOU DECIDE TO TEASE ME EVERY CHANCE YOU GET?
I WAS JUST THINKING OUT LOUD.
YOU'RE TRYING TO GET UNDER MY SKIN!
WHATEVER.

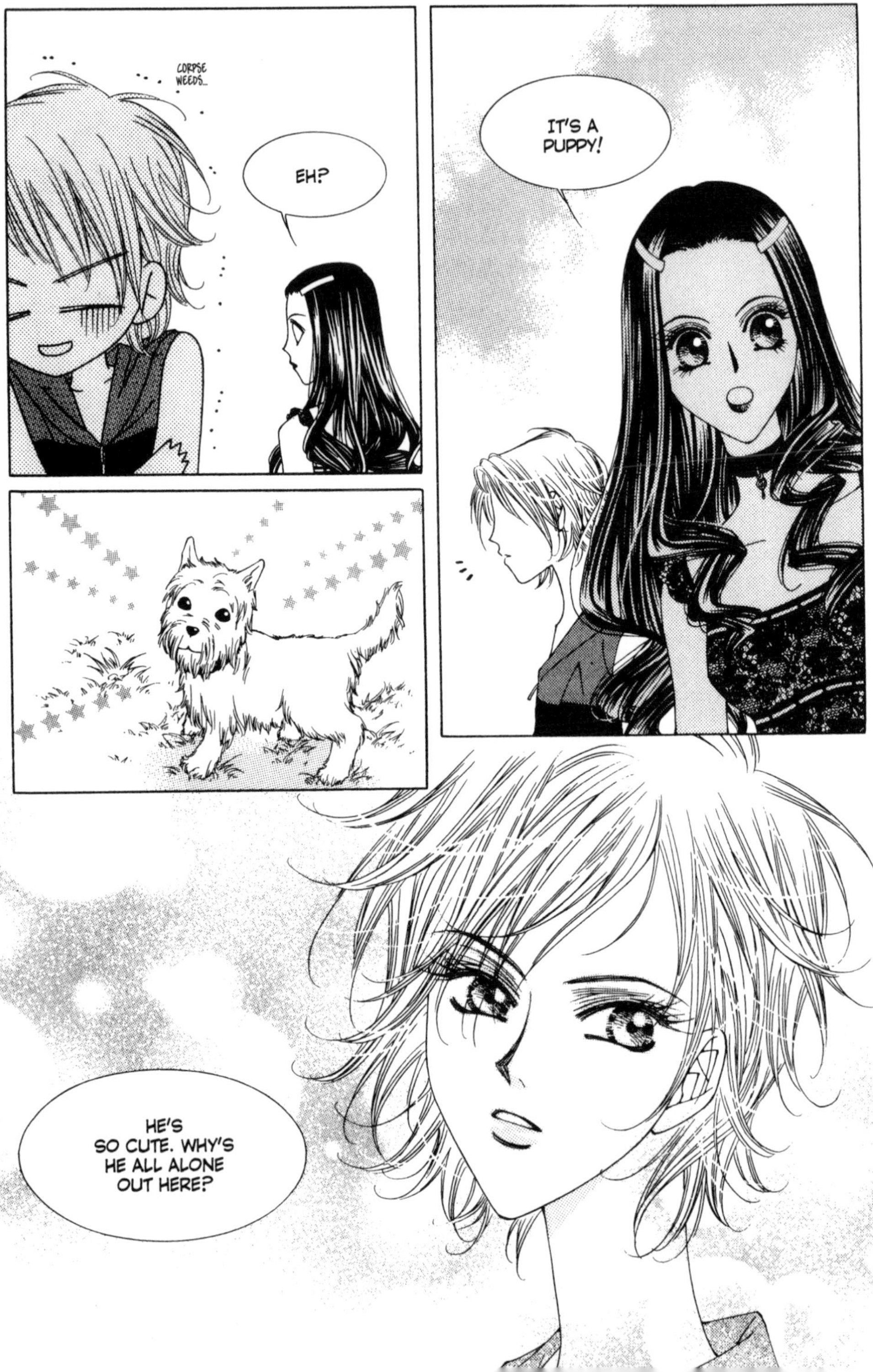
CORPSE WEEDS...
EH?
IT'S A PUPPY!
HE'S SO CUTE. WHY'S HE ALL ALONE OUT HERE?

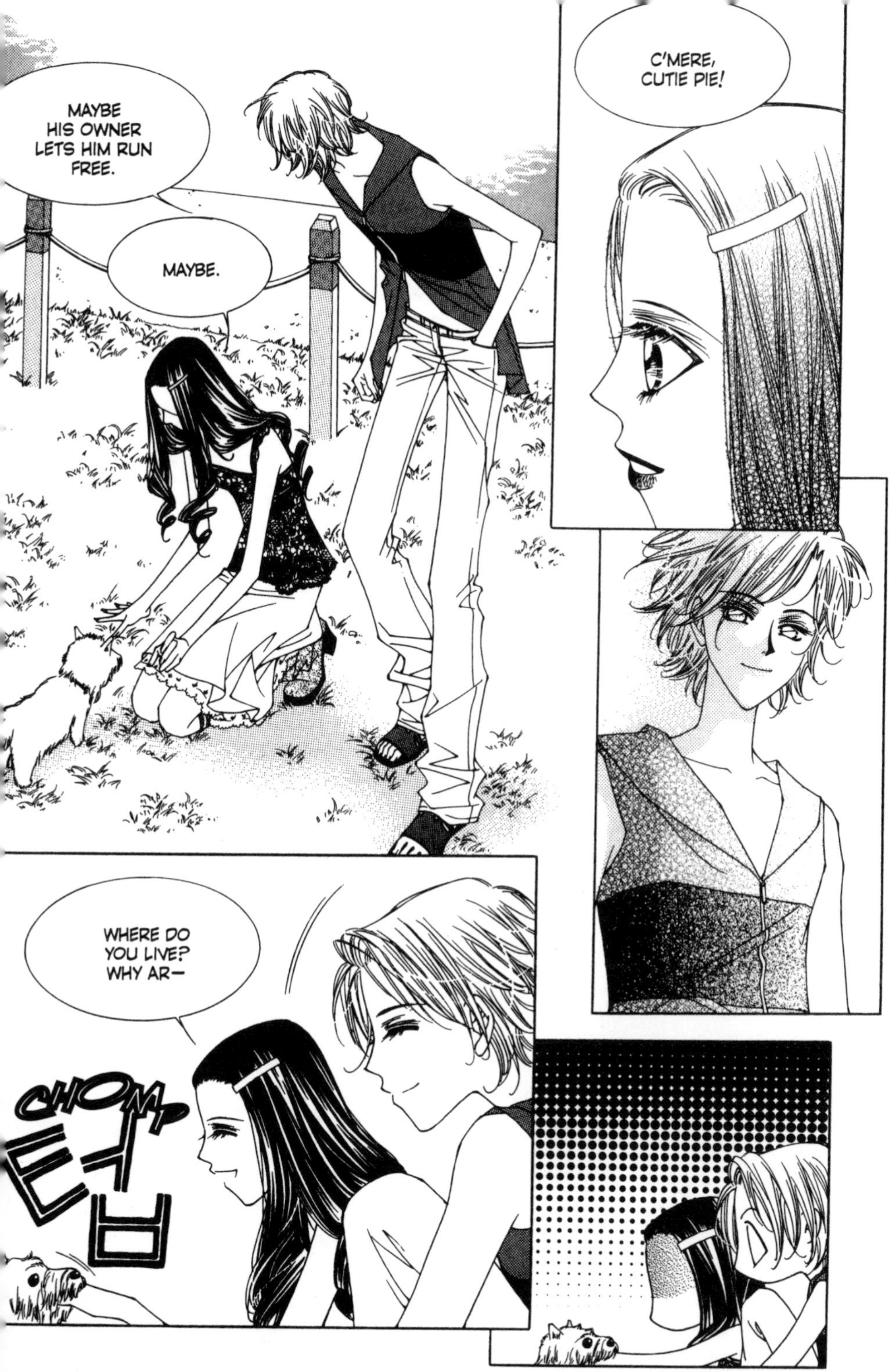
MAYBE HIS OWNER LETS HIM RUN FREE.
MAYBE.
C'MERE, CUTIE PIE!
WHERE DO YOU LIVE? WHY AR—
CHOMP

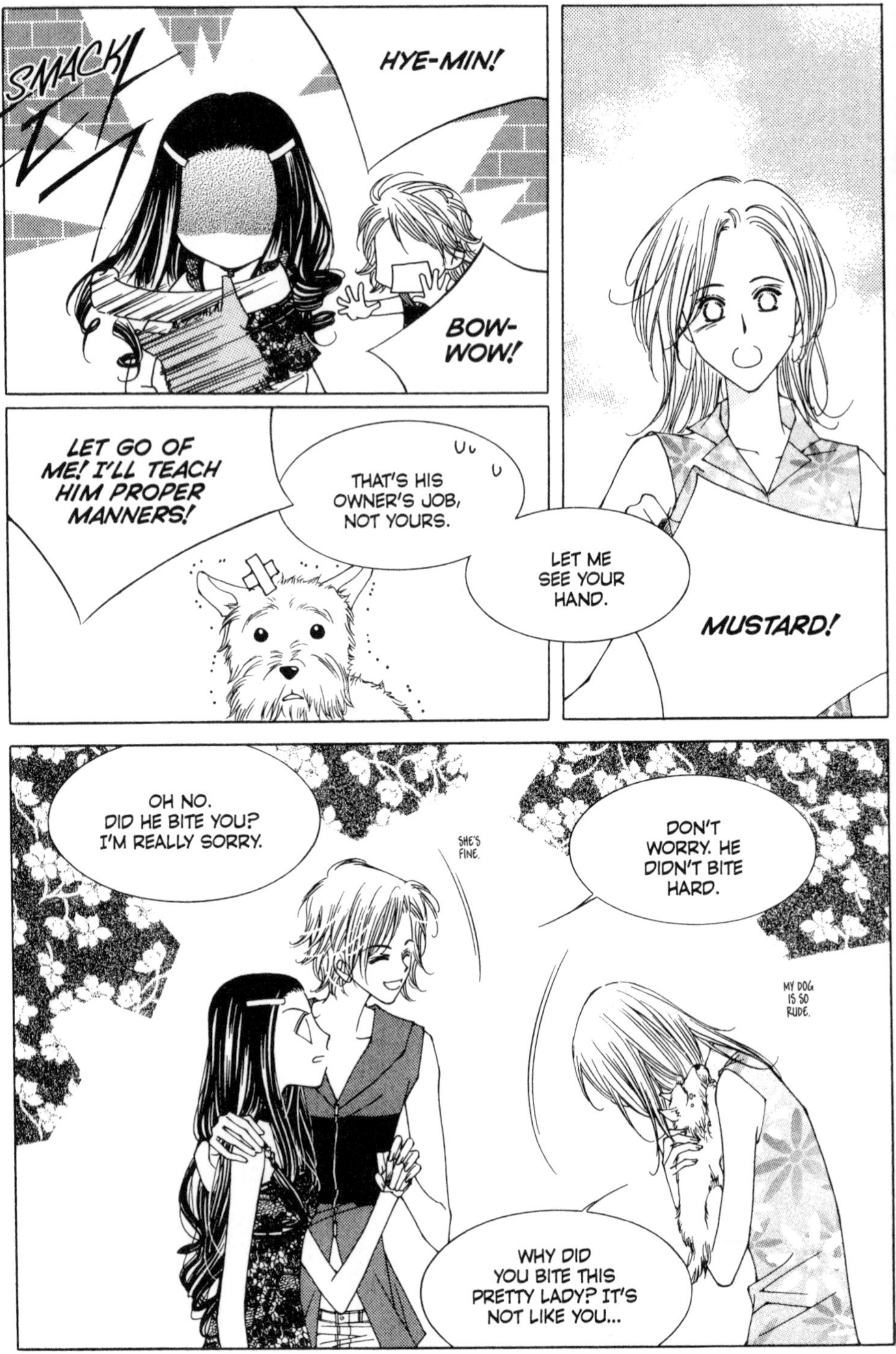
SMACK!
HYE-MIN!
BOW-WOW!
LET GO OF ME! I'LL TEACH HIM PROPER MANNERS!
THAT'S HIS OWNER'S JOB, NOT YOURS.
LET ME SEE YOUR HAND.
MUSTARD!
OH NO. DID HE BITE YOU? I'M REALLY SORRY.
SHE'S FINE.
DON'T WORRY. HE DIDN'T BITE HARD.
MY DOG IS SO RUDE.
WHY DID YOU BITE THIS PRETTY LADY? IT'S NOT LIKE YOU...

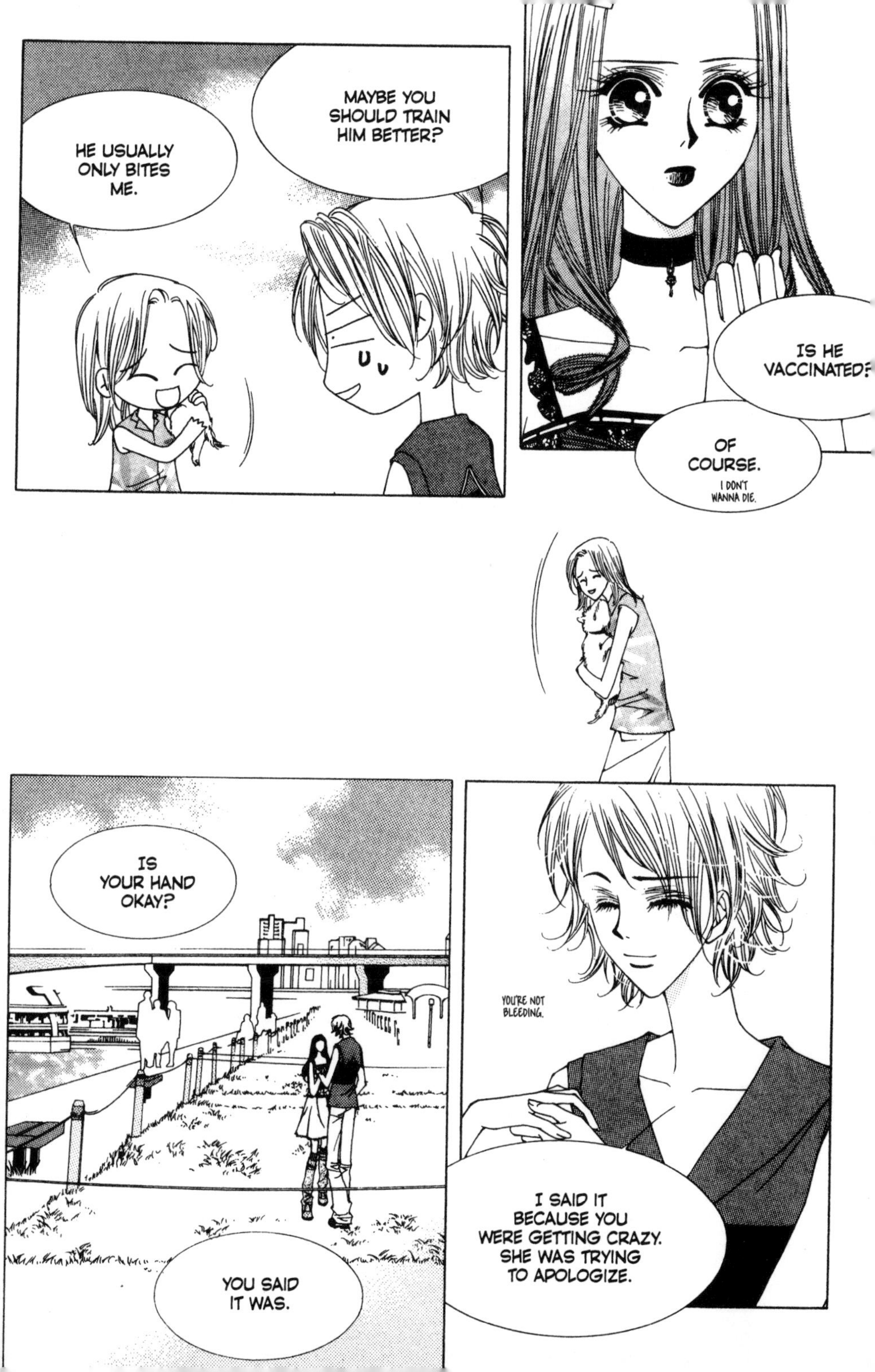
HE USUALLY ONLY BITES ME.
MAYBE YOU SHOULD TRAIN HIM BETTER?
IS HE VACCINATED?
OF COURSE.
I DON'T WANNA DIE.
IS YOUR HAND OKAY?
YOU SAID IT WAS.
YOU'RE NOT BLEEDING.
I SAID IT BECAUSE YOU WERE GETTING CRAZY. SHE WAS TRYING TO APOLOGIZE.

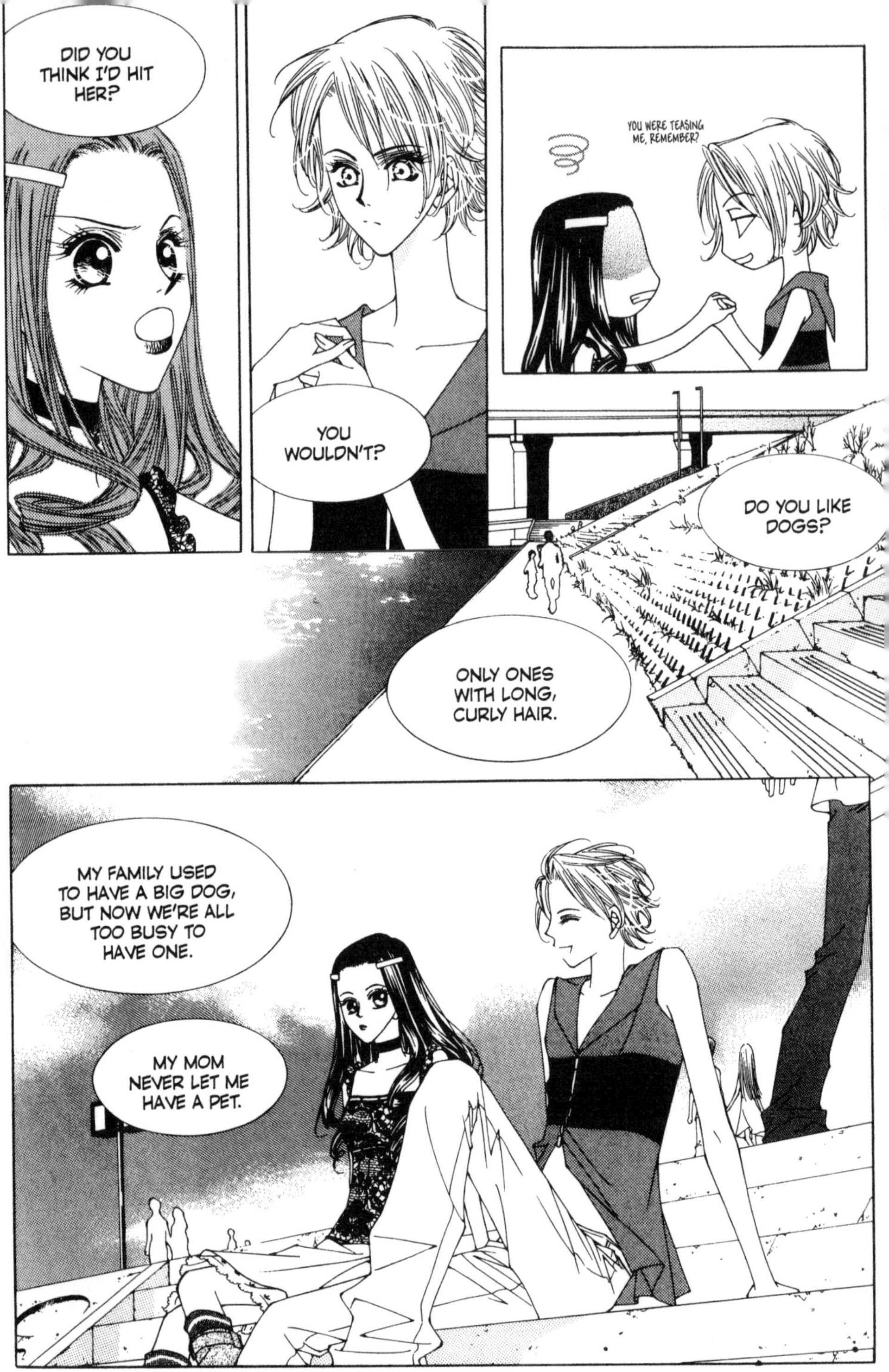
DID YOU THINK I'D HIT HER?
YOU WOULDN'T?
YOU WERE TEASING ME, REMEMBER?
DO YOU LIKE DOGS?
ONLY ONES WITH LONG, CURLY HAIR.
MY FAMILY USED TO HAVE A BIG DOG, BUT NOW WE'RE ALL TOO BUSY TO HAVE ONE.
MY MOM NEVER LET ME HAVE A PET.

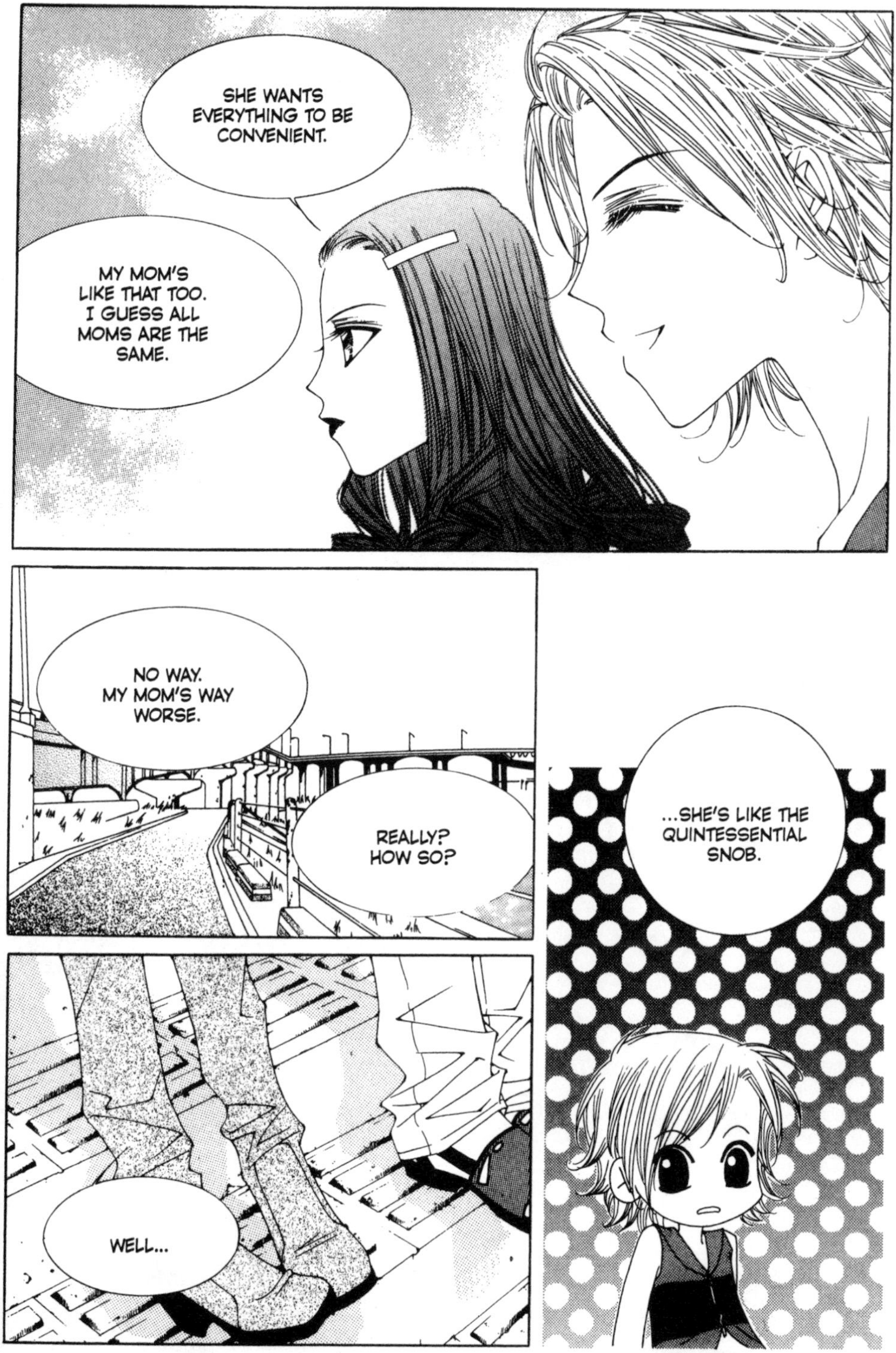
SHE WANTS EVERYTHING TO BE CONVENIENT.
MY MOM'S LIKE THAT TOO. I GUESS ALL MOMS ARE THE SAME.
NO WAY. MY MOM'S WAY WORSE.
REALLY? HOW SO?
WELL...
...SHE'S LIKE THE QUINTESSENTIAL SNOB.

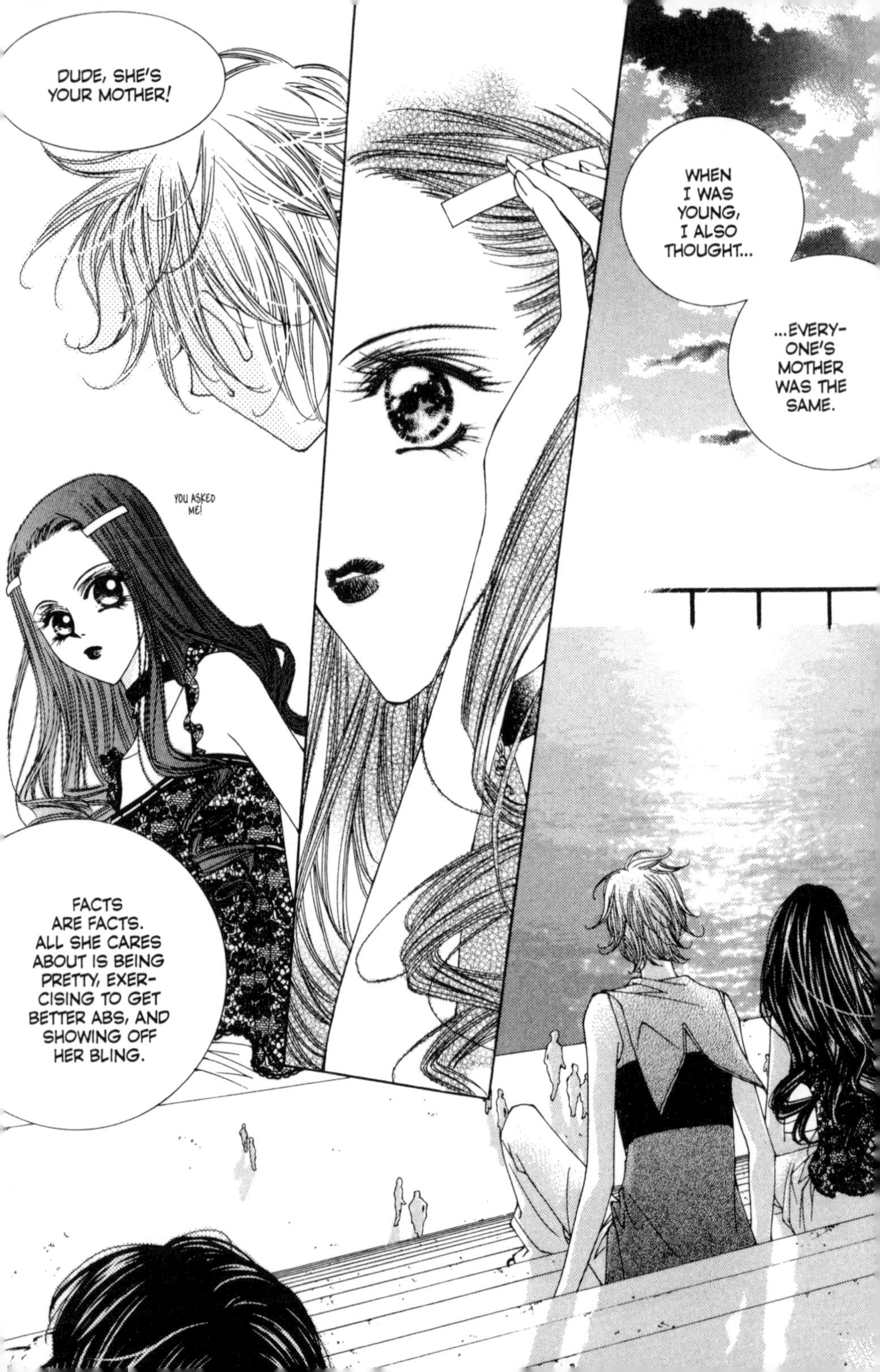
DUDE, SHE'S YOUR MOTHER!
WHEN I WAS YOUNG, I ALSO THOUGHT...
...EVERY-ONE'S MOTHER WAS THE SAME.
YOU ASKED ME!
FACTS ARE FACTS. ALL SHE CARES ABOUT IS BEING PRETTY, EXER-CISING TO GET BETTER ABS, AND SHOWING OFF HER BLING.

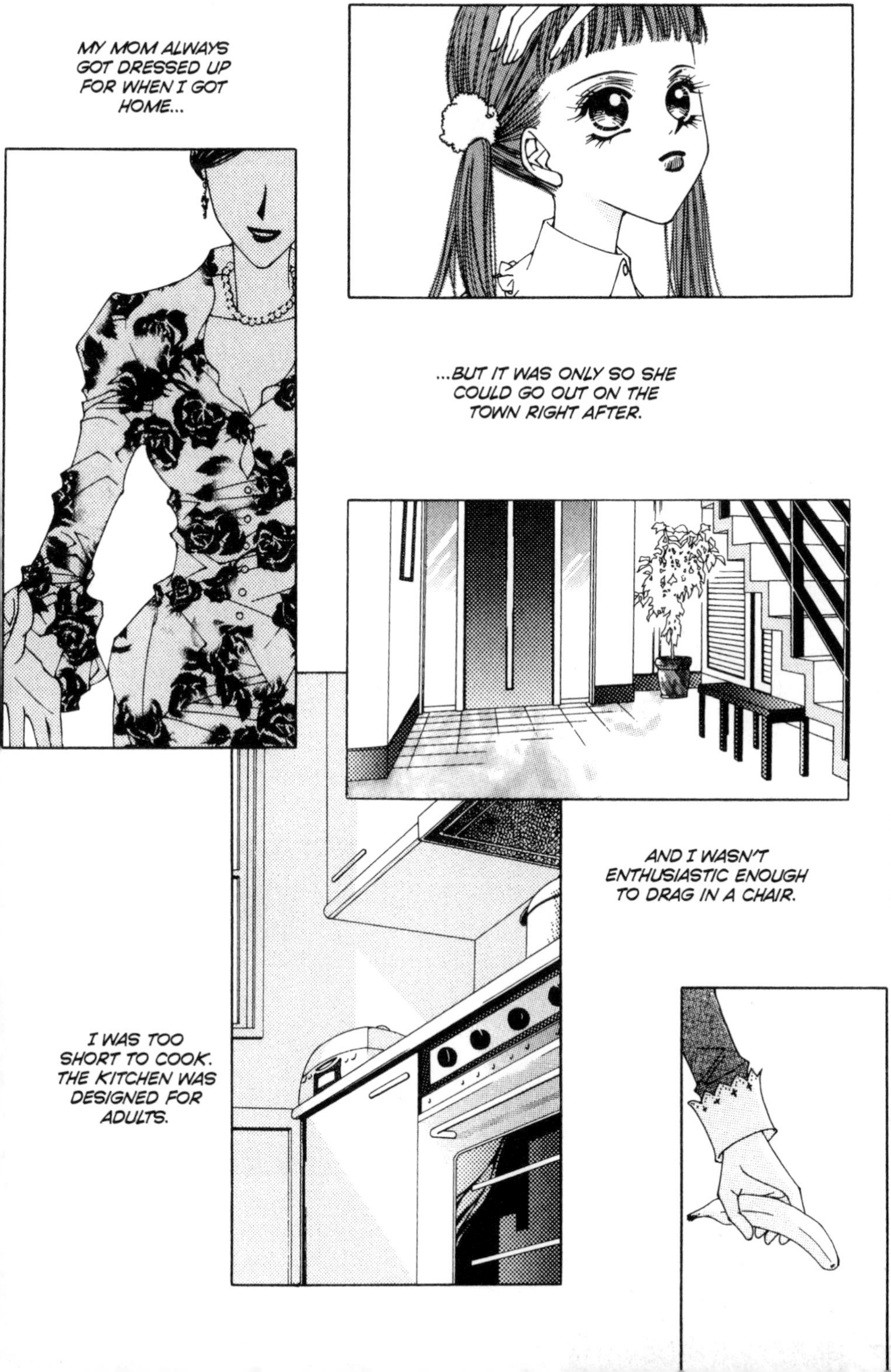
MY MOM ALWAYS GOT DRESSED UP FOR WHEN I GOT HOME...
...BUT IT WAS ONLY SO SHE COULD GO OUT ON THE TOWN RIGHT AFTER.
I WAS TOO SHORT TO COOK. THE KITCHEN WAS DESIGNED FOR ADULTS.
AND I WASN'T ENTHUSIASTIC ENOUGH TO DRAG IN A CHAIR.

SHE NEVER MISSED A PARENT-TEACHER NIGHT AT SCHOOL.

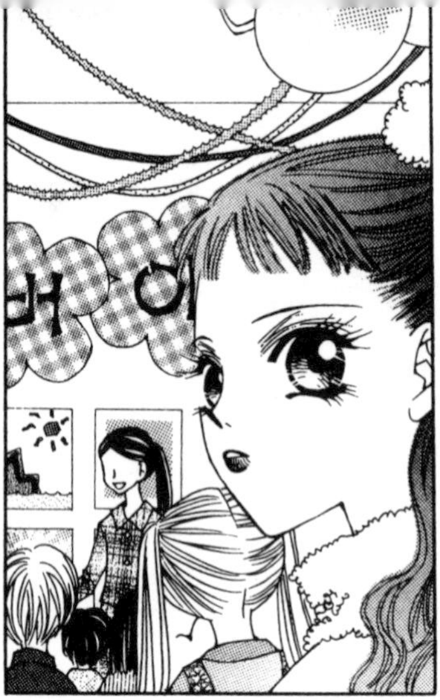

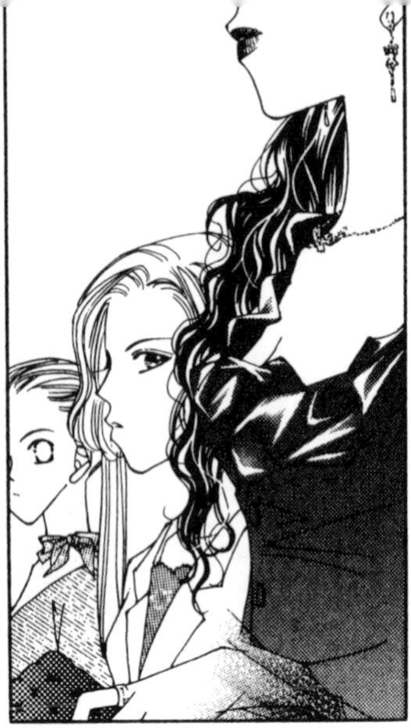

BUT IT WASN'T FOR ME, IT WAS TO MODEL HER FANCY CLOTHES FOR THE OTHER PARENTS.

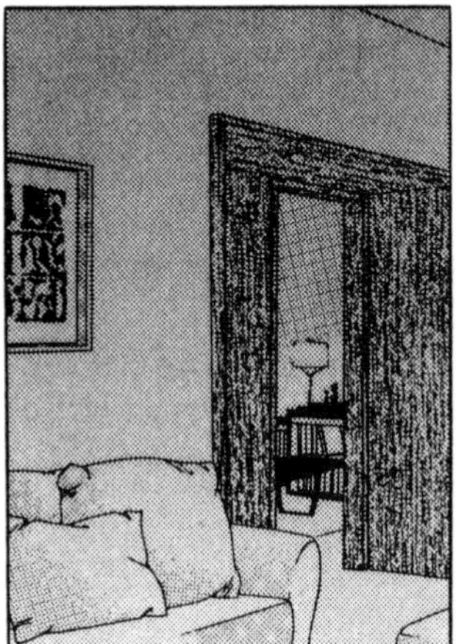

MY DAD HAD TO WORK HARD TO SATISFY MOTHER'S VANITY...

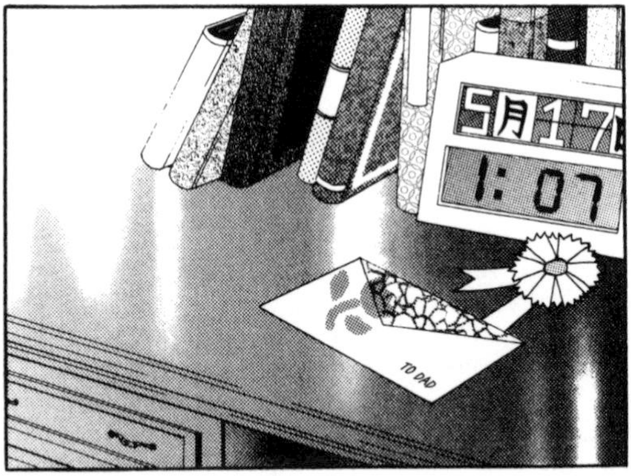
5月17
1:07
TO DAD

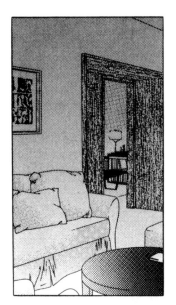

...WHICH MEANT HE HAD NO TIME FOR ME. I WASN'T UPSET. I FELT BAD FOR HIM.

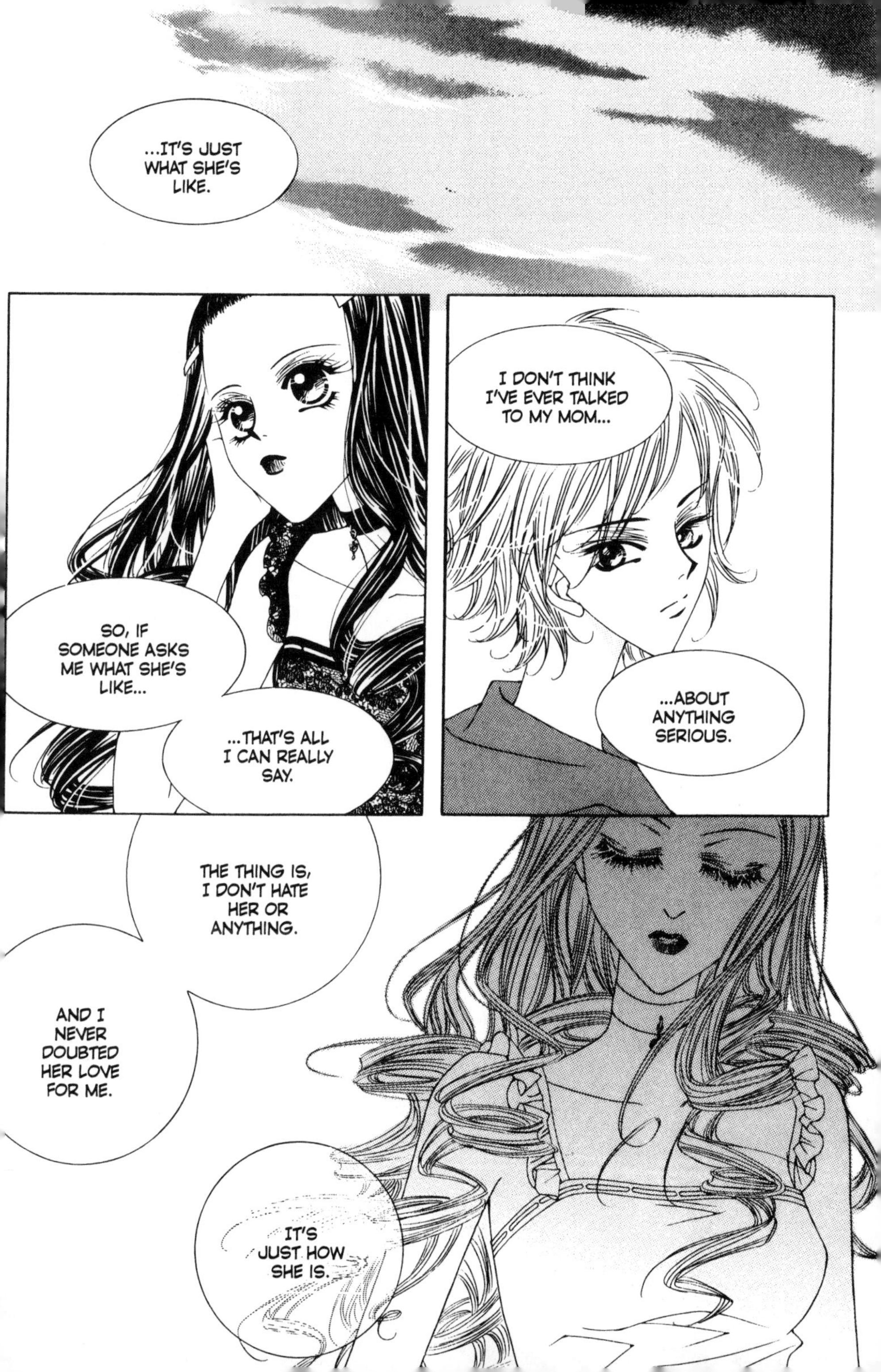
...IT'S JUST WHAT SHE'S LIKE.
SO, IF SOMEONE ASKS ME WHAT SHE'S LIKE...
...THAT'S ALL I CAN REALLY SAY.
I DON'T THINK I'VE EVER TALKED TO MY MOM...
...ABOUT ANYTHING SERIOUS.
THE THING IS, I DON'T HATE HER OR ANYTHING.
AND I NEVER DOUBTED HER LOVE FOR ME.
IT'S JUST HOW SHE IS.

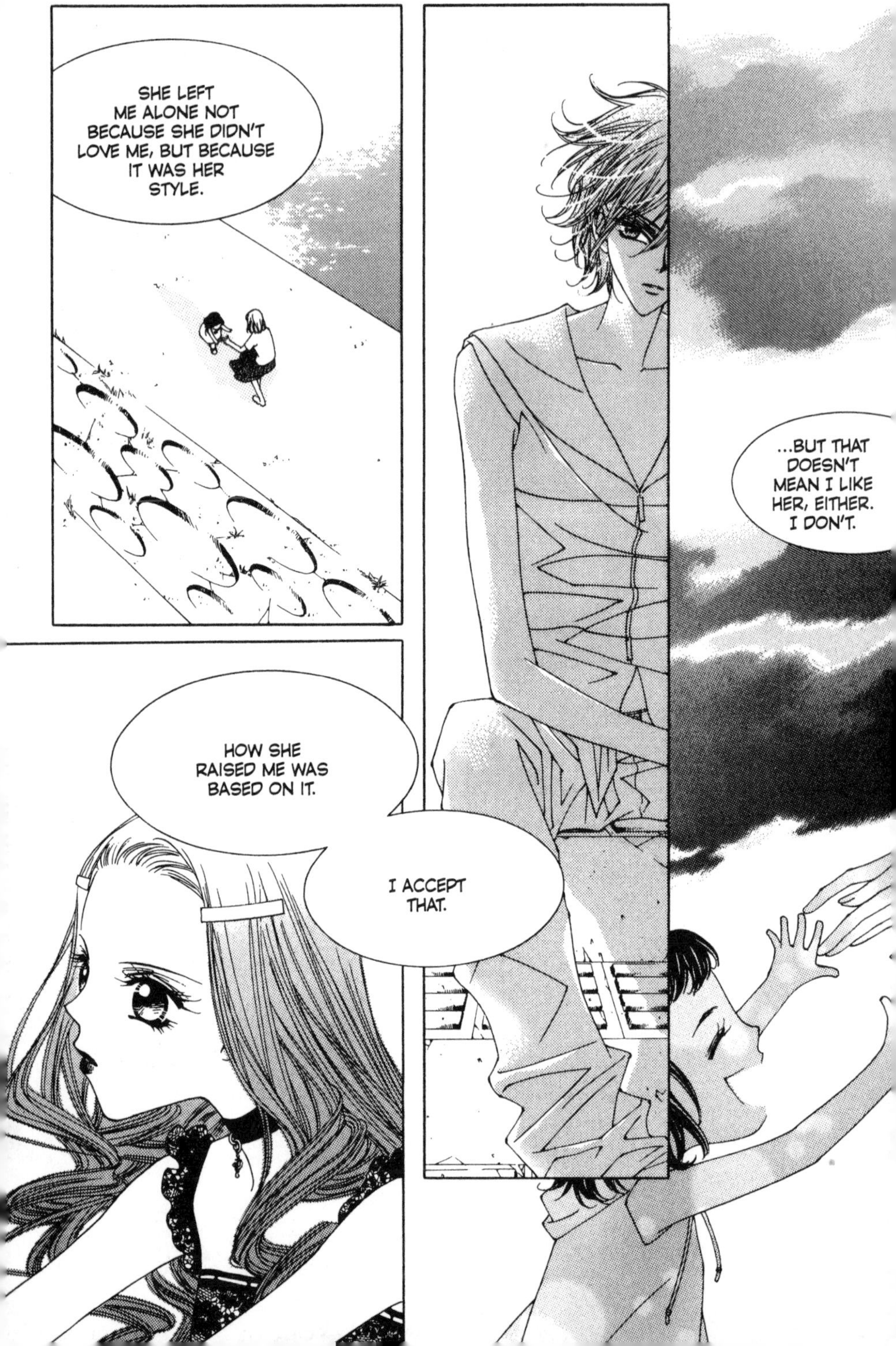
SHE LEFT ME ALONE NOT BECAUSE SHE DIDN'T LOVE ME, BUT BECAUSE IT WAS HER STYLE.
...BUT THAT DOESN'T MEAN I LIKE HER, EITHER. I DON'T.
HOW SHE RAISED ME WAS BASED ON IT.
I ACCEPT THAT.

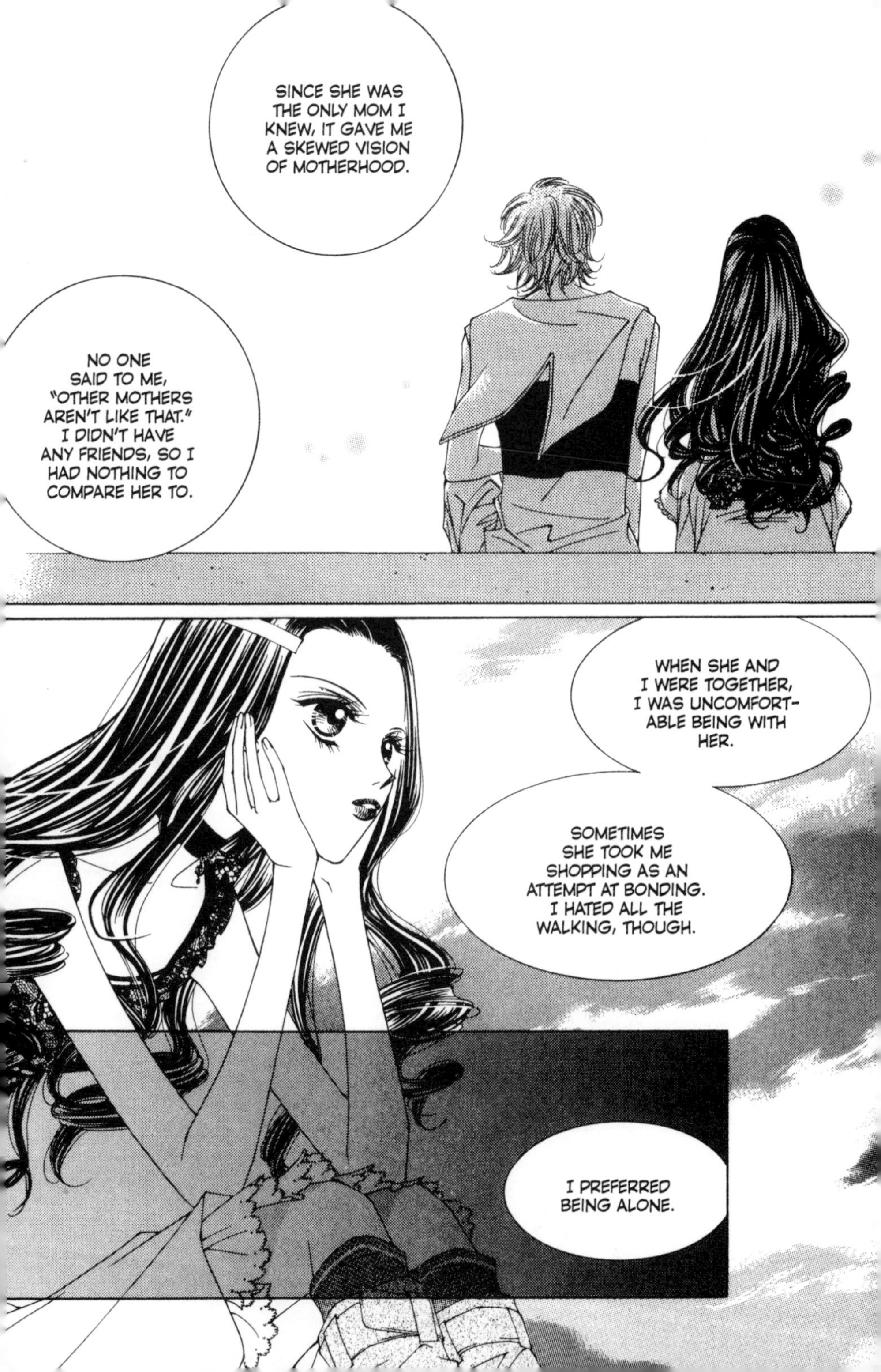
SINCE SHE WAS THE ONLY MOM I KNEW, IT GAVE ME A SKEWED VISION OF MOTHERHOOD.
NO ONE SAID TO ME, "OTHER MOTHERS AREN'T LIKE THAT." I DIDN'T HAVE ANY FRIENDS, SO I HAD NOTHING TO COMPARE HER TO.
WHEN SHE AND I WERE TOGETHER, I WAS UNCOMFORT-ABLE BEING WITH HER.
SOMETIMES SHE TOOK ME SHOPPING AS AN ATTEMPT AT BONDING. I HATED ALL THE WALKING, THOUGH.
I PREFERRED BEING ALONE.

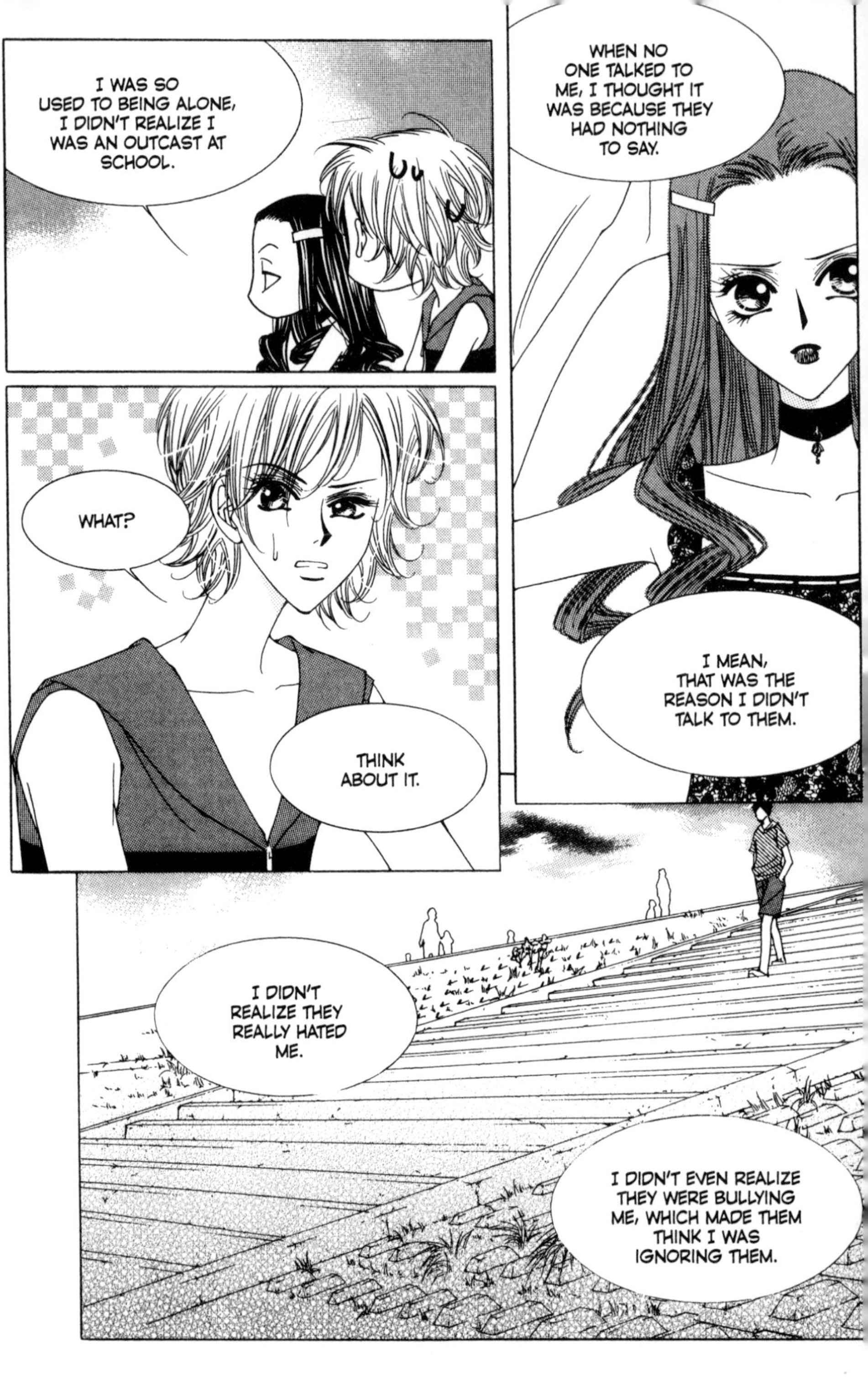
I WAS SO USED TO BEING ALONE, I DIDN'T REALIZE I WAS AN OUTCAST AT SCHOOL.
WHAT?
THINK ABOUT IT.
WHEN NO ONE TALKED TO ME, I THOUGHT IT WAS BECAUSE THEY HAD NOTHING TO SAY.
I MEAN, THAT WAS THE REASON I DIDN'T TALK TO THEM.
I DIDN'T REALIZE THEY REALLY HATED ME.
I DIDN'T EVEN REALIZE THEY WERE BULLYING ME, WHICH MADE THEM THINK I WAS IGNORING THEM.

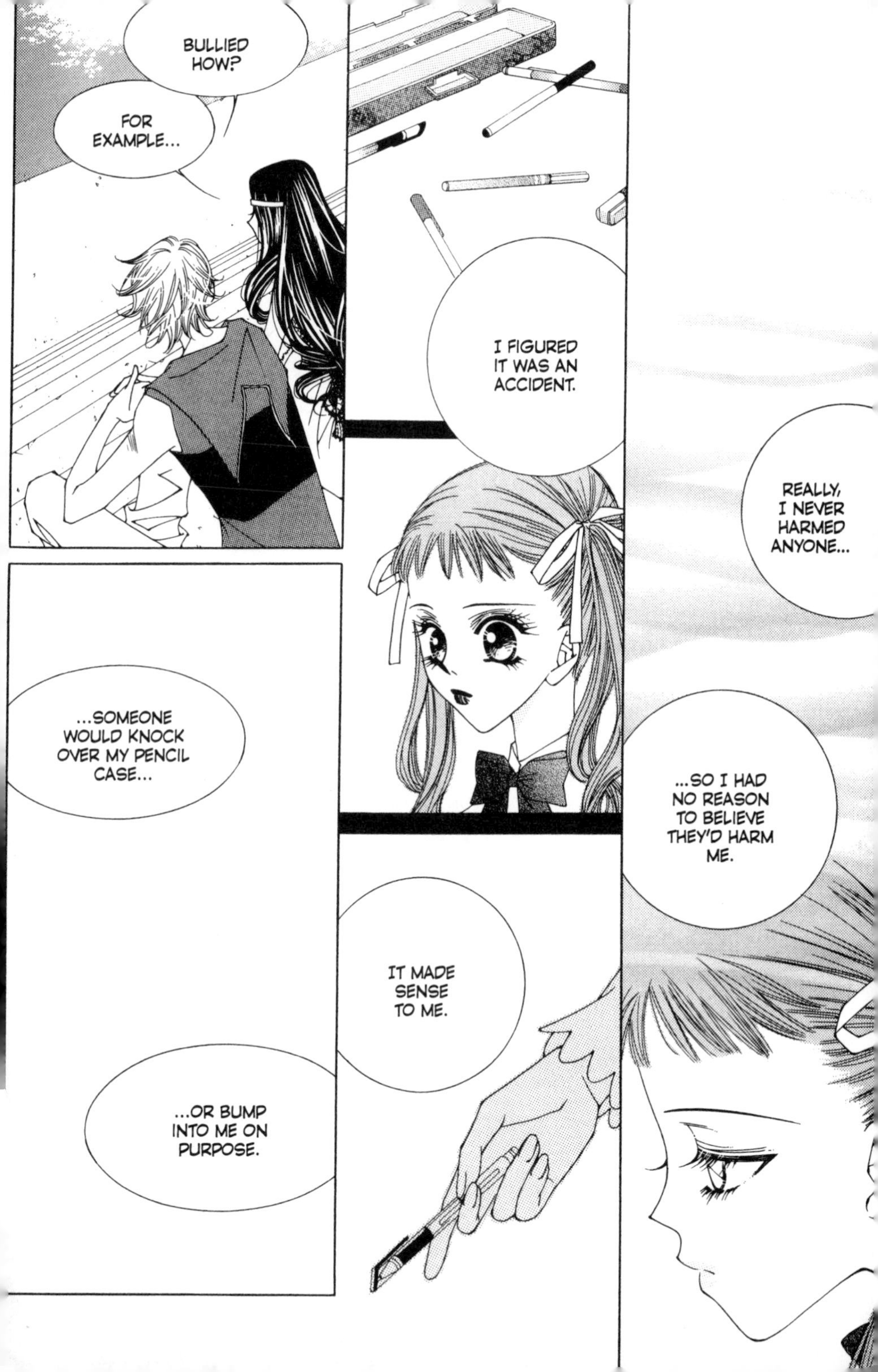
BULLIED HOW?
FOR EXAMPLE...
...SOMEONE WOULD KNOCK OVER MY PENCIL CASE...
...OR BUMP INTO ME ON PURPOSE.
I FIGURED IT WAS AN ACCIDENT.
IT MADE SENSE TO ME.
REALLY, I NEVER HARMED ANYONE...
...SO I HAD NO REASON TO BELIEVE THEY'D HARM ME.

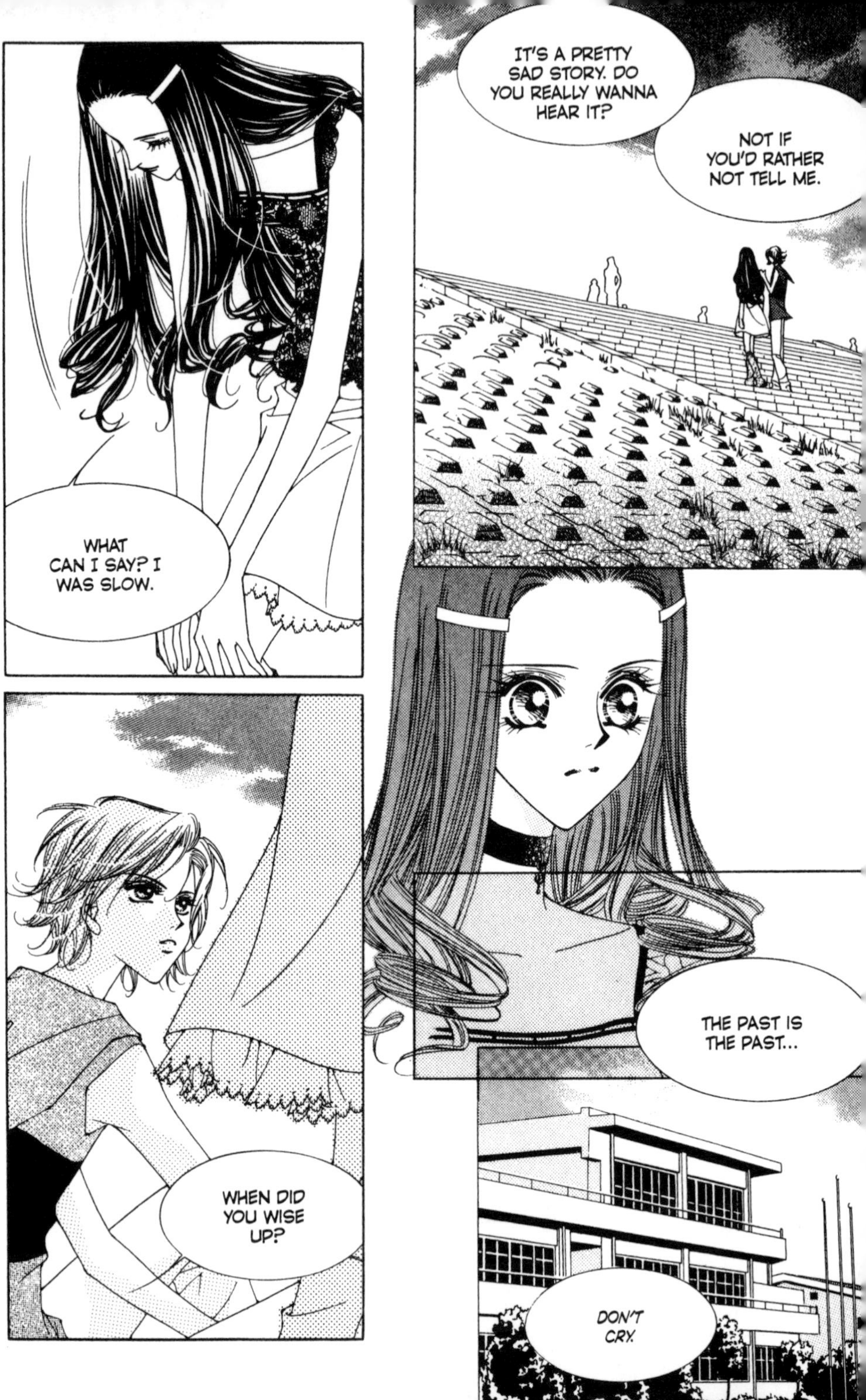
WHAT CAN I SAY? I WAS SLOW.
IT'S A PRETTY SAD STORY. DO YOU REALLY WANNA HEAR IT?
NOT IF YOU'D RATHER NOT TELL ME.
WHEN DID YOU WISE UP?
THE PAST IS THE PAST...
DON'T CRY.

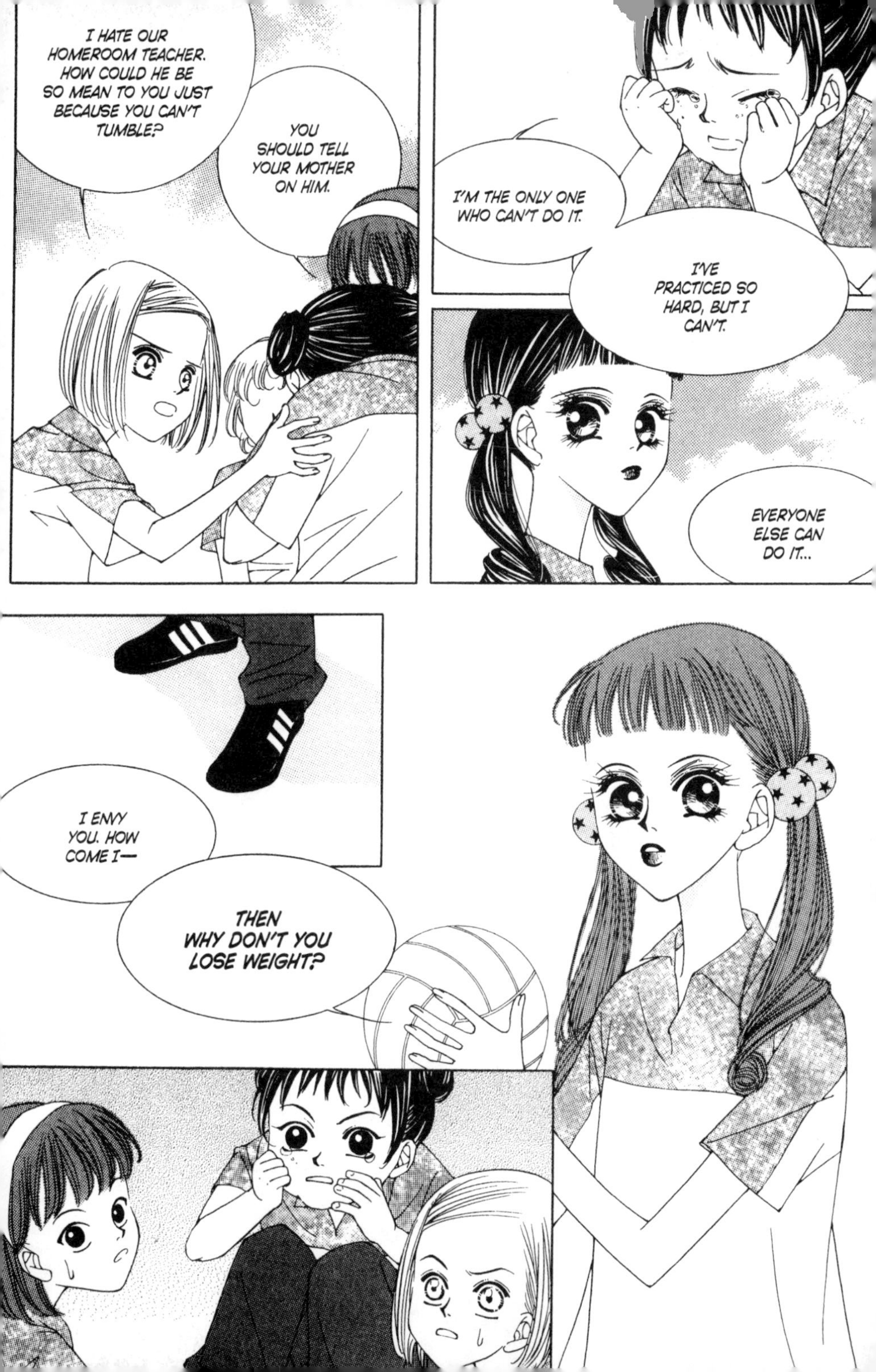
I HATE OUR HOMEROOM TEACHER. HOW COULD HE BE SO MEAN TO YOU JUST BECAUSE YOU CAN'T TUMBLE?
YOU SHOULD TELL YOUR MOTHER ON HIM.
I'M THE ONLY ONE WHO CAN'T DO IT.
I'VE PRACTICED SO HARD, BUT I CAN'T.
EVERYONE ELSE CAN DO IT...
I ENVY YOU. HOW COME I—
THEN WHY DON'T YOU LOSE WEIGHT?

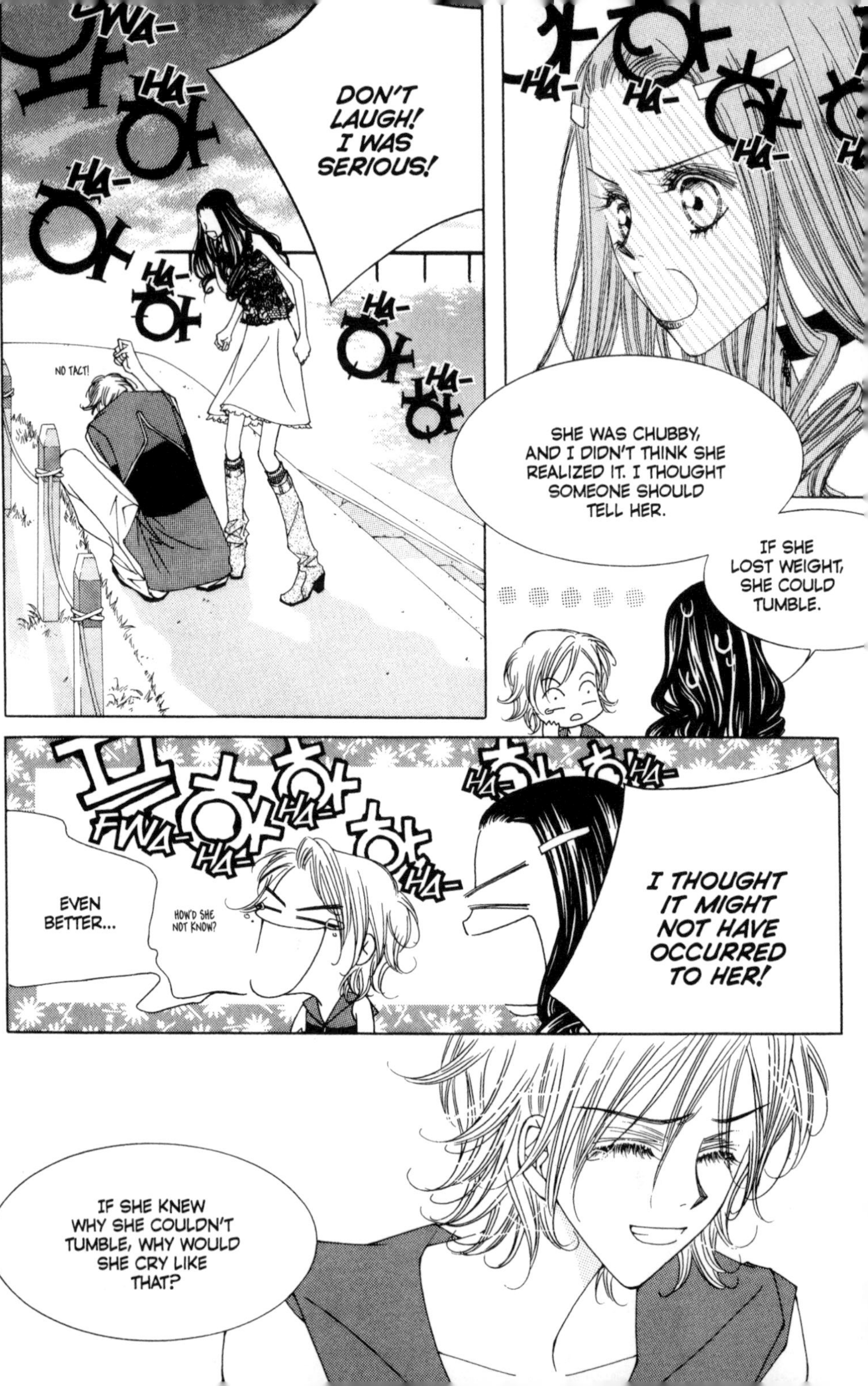
WA-
HA-
HA-
HA-
DON'T LAUGH! I WAS SERIOUS!
HA-
HA-
NO TACT!
-HA-
HA-
HA-
SHE WAS CHUBBY, AND I DIDN'T THINK SHE REALIZED IT. I THOUGHT SOMEONE SHOULD TELL HER.
IF SHE LOST WEIGHT, SHE COULD TUMBLE.
FWA-
HA-
HA-
HA-
HA-
HA-
EVEN BETTER...
HOW'D SHE NOT KNOW?
I THOUGHT IT MIGHT NOT HAVE OCCURRED TO HER!
IF SHE KNEW WHY SHE COULDN'T TUMBLE, WHY WOULD SHE CRY LIKE THAT?

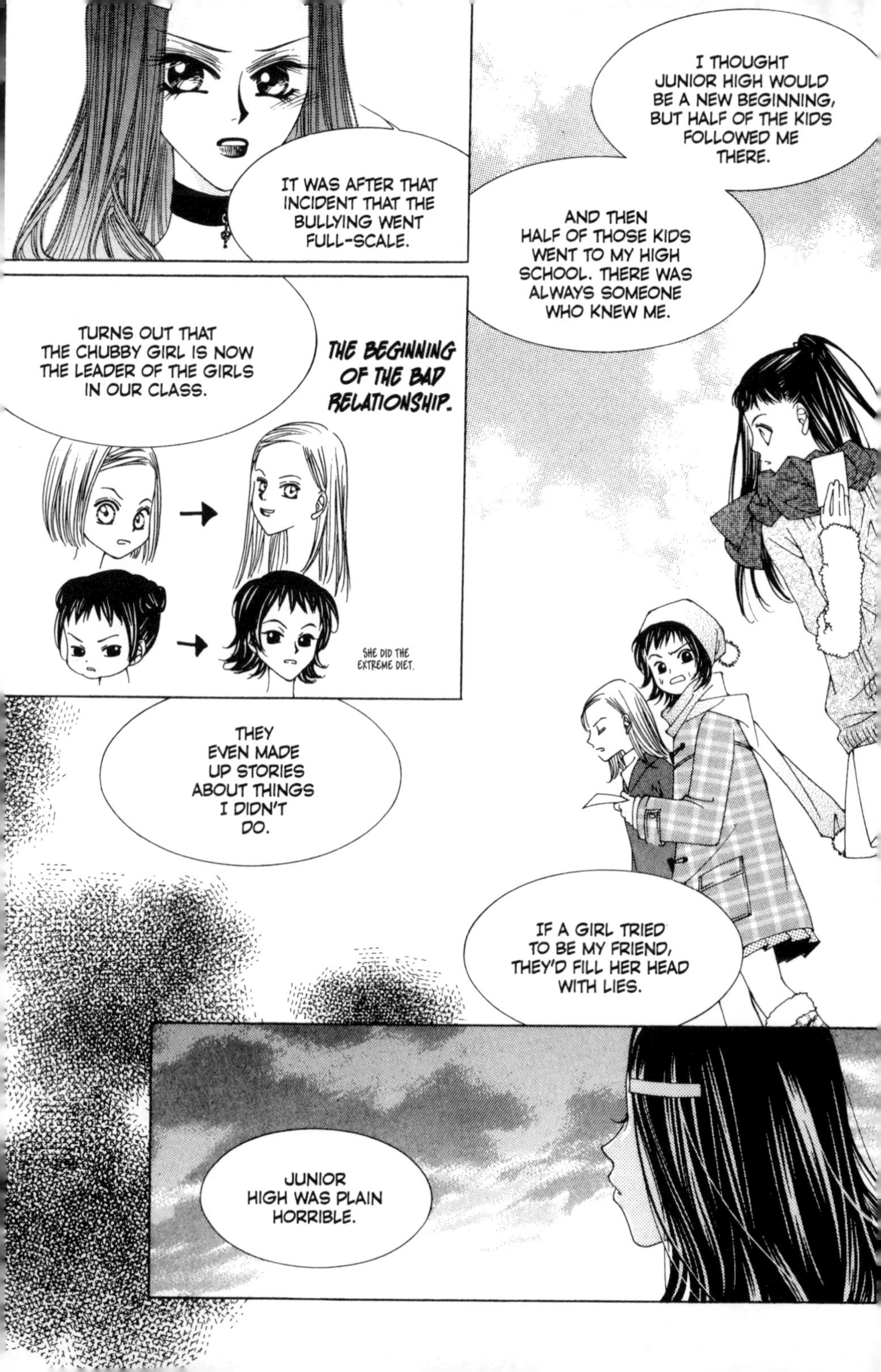
IT WAS AFTER THAT INCIDENT THAT THE BULLYING WENT FULL-SCALE.
TURNS OUT THAT THE CHUBBY GIRL IS NOW THE LEADER OF THE GIRLS IN OUR CLASS.
THE BEGINNING OF THE BAD RELATIONSHIP.
SHE DID THE EXTREME DIET.
I THOUGHT JUNIOR HIGH WOULD BE A NEW BEGINNING, BUT HALF OF THE KIDS FOLLOWED ME THERE.
AND THEN HALF OF THOSE KIDS WENT TO MY HIGH SCHOOL. THERE WAS ALWAYS SOMEONE WHO KNEW ME.
THEY EVEN MADE UP STORIES ABOUT THINGS I DIDN'T DO.
IF A GIRL TRIED TO BE MY FRIEND, THEY'D FILL HER HEAD WITH LIES.
JUNIOR HIGH WAS PLAIN HORRIBLE.

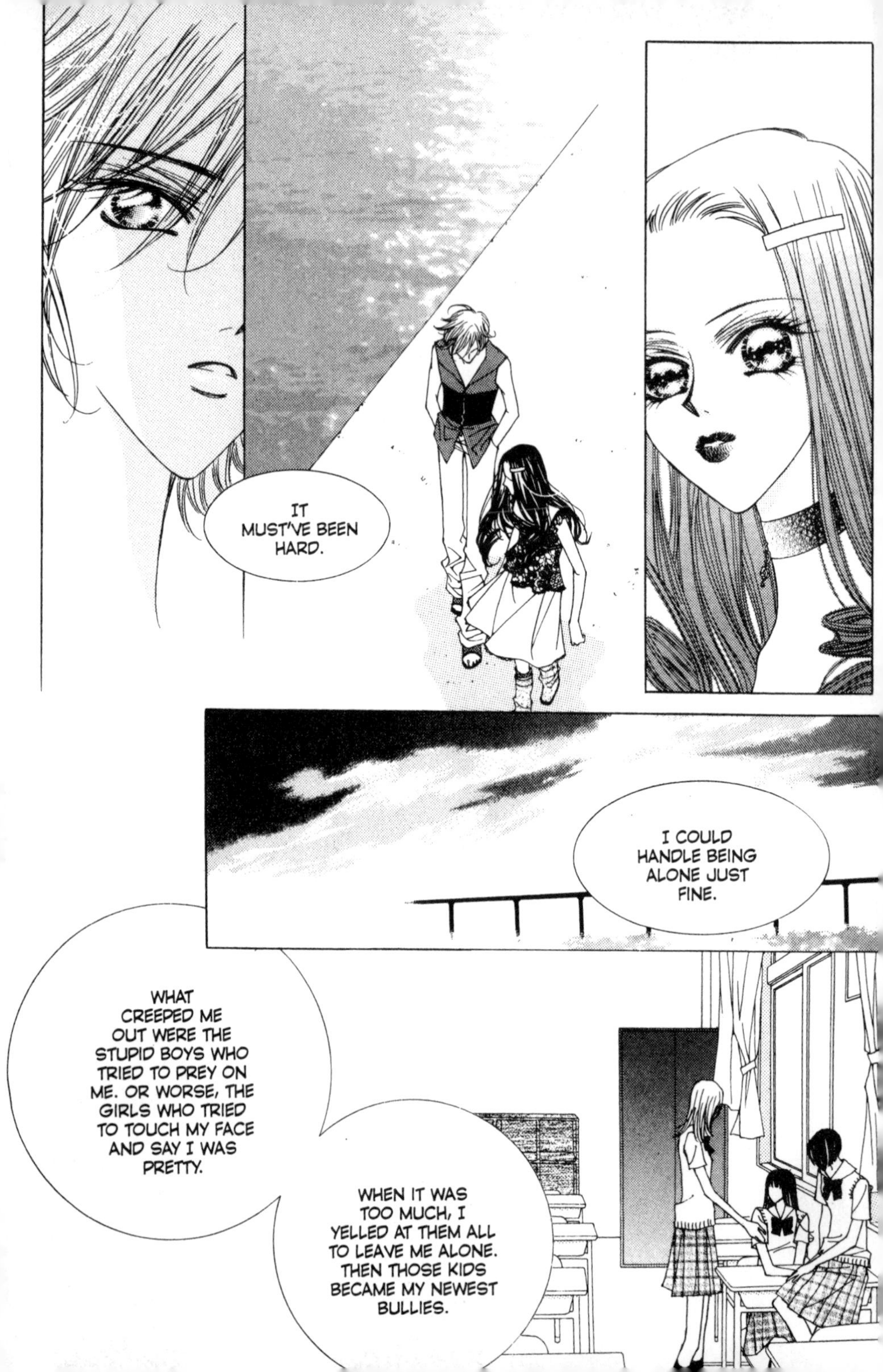
IT MUST'VE BEEN HARD.
I COULD HANDLE BEING ALONE JUST FINE.
WHAT CREEPED ME OUT WERE THE STUPID BOYS WHO TRIED TO PREY ON ME. OR WORSE, THE GIRLS WHO TRIED TO TOUCH MY FACE AND SAY I WAS PRETTY.
WHEN IT WAS TOO MUCH, I YELLED AT THEM ALL TO LEAVE ME ALONE. THEN THOSE KIDS BECAME MY NEWEST BULLIES.

PEOPLE HAVE BULLIED ME FOR SO LONG...

IT WAS ALMOST LIKE THEY SET ME UP.

...I SOMETIMES STARTED TO THINK I'D DONE SOMETHING WRONG.

BUT I COULDN'T FIGURE OUT WHAT I'D DONE.

I'M NOT AFRAID OF BEING ALONE.

THE SCARY THING WAS WHEN I STARTED DOUBTING MYSELF.

THAT'S WHEN THINGS GOT WORSE.

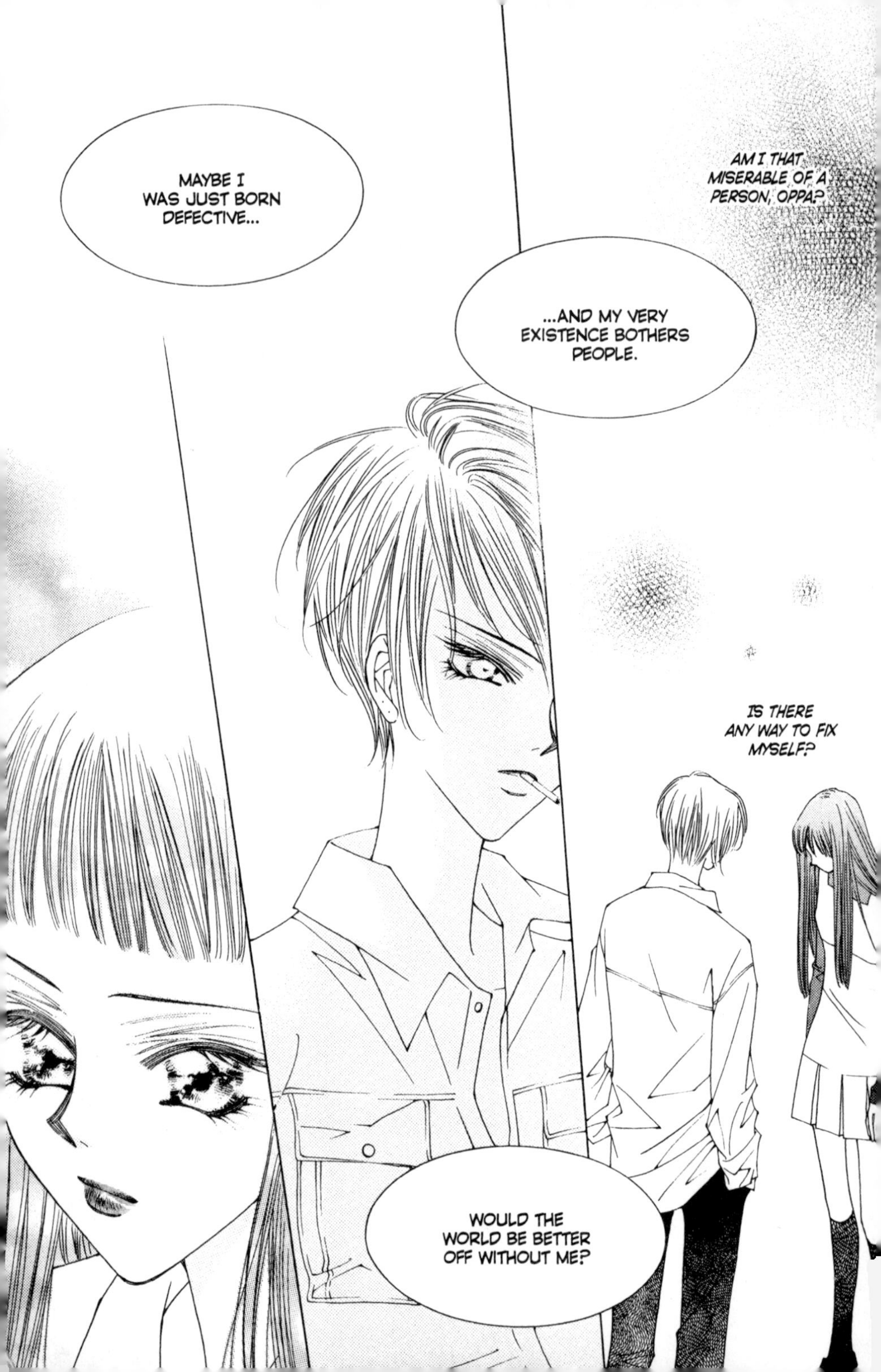
MAYBE I WAS JUST BORN DEFECTIVE...
...AND MY VERY EXISTENCE BOTHERS PEOPLE.
AM I THAT MISERABLE OF A PERSON, OPPA?
IS THERE ANY WAY TO FIX MYSELF?
WOULD THE WORLD BE BETTER OFF WITHOUT ME?

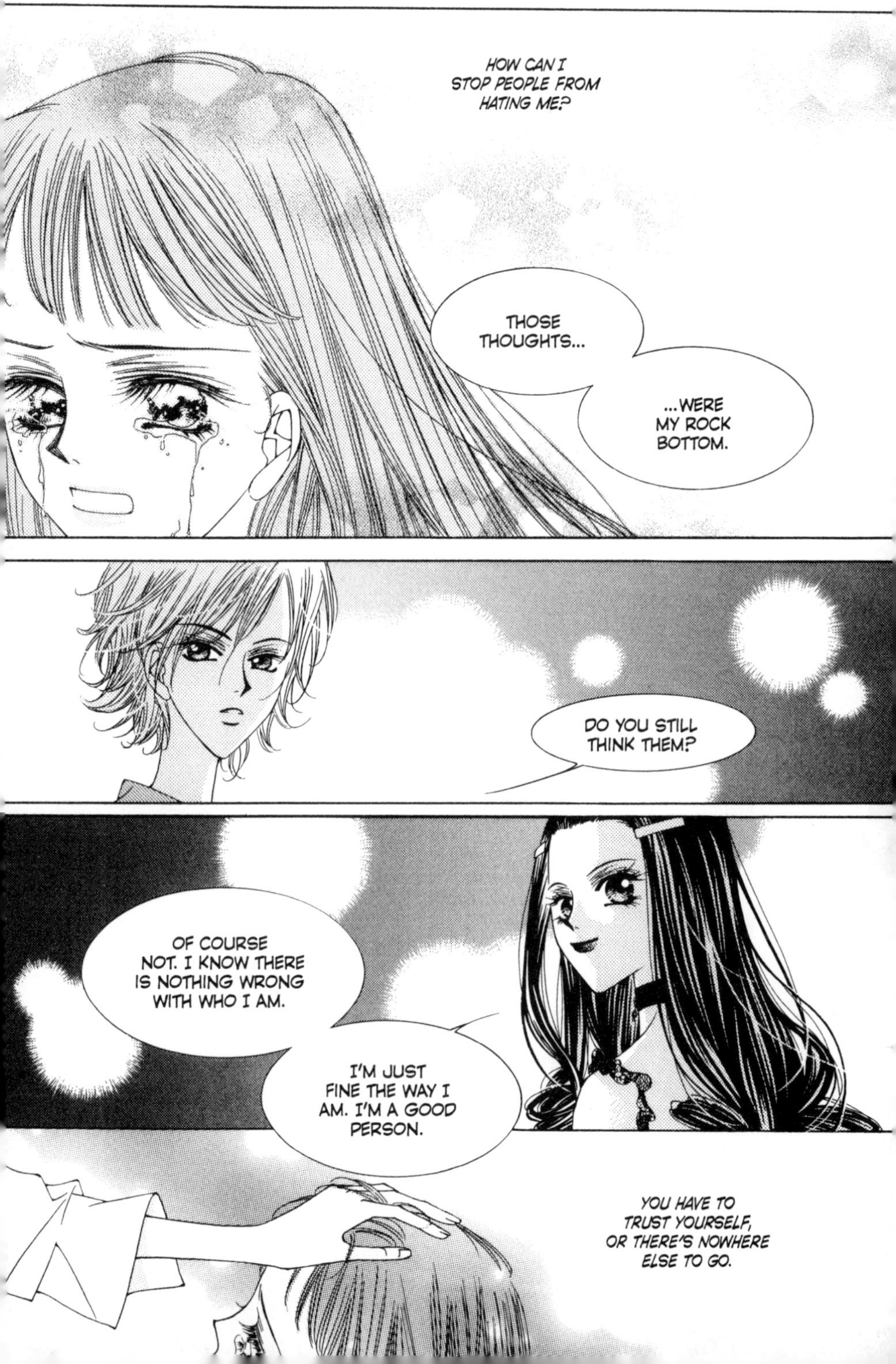
HOW CAN I STOP PEOPLE FROM HATING ME?
THOSE THOUGHTS...
...WERE MY ROCK BOTTOM.
DO YOU STILL THINK THEM?
OF COURSE NOT. I KNOW THERE IS NOTHING WRONG WITH WHO I AM.
I'M JUST FINE THE WAY I AM. I'M A GOOD PERSON.
YOU HAVE TO TRUST YOURSELF, OR THERE'S NOWHERE ELSE TO GO.

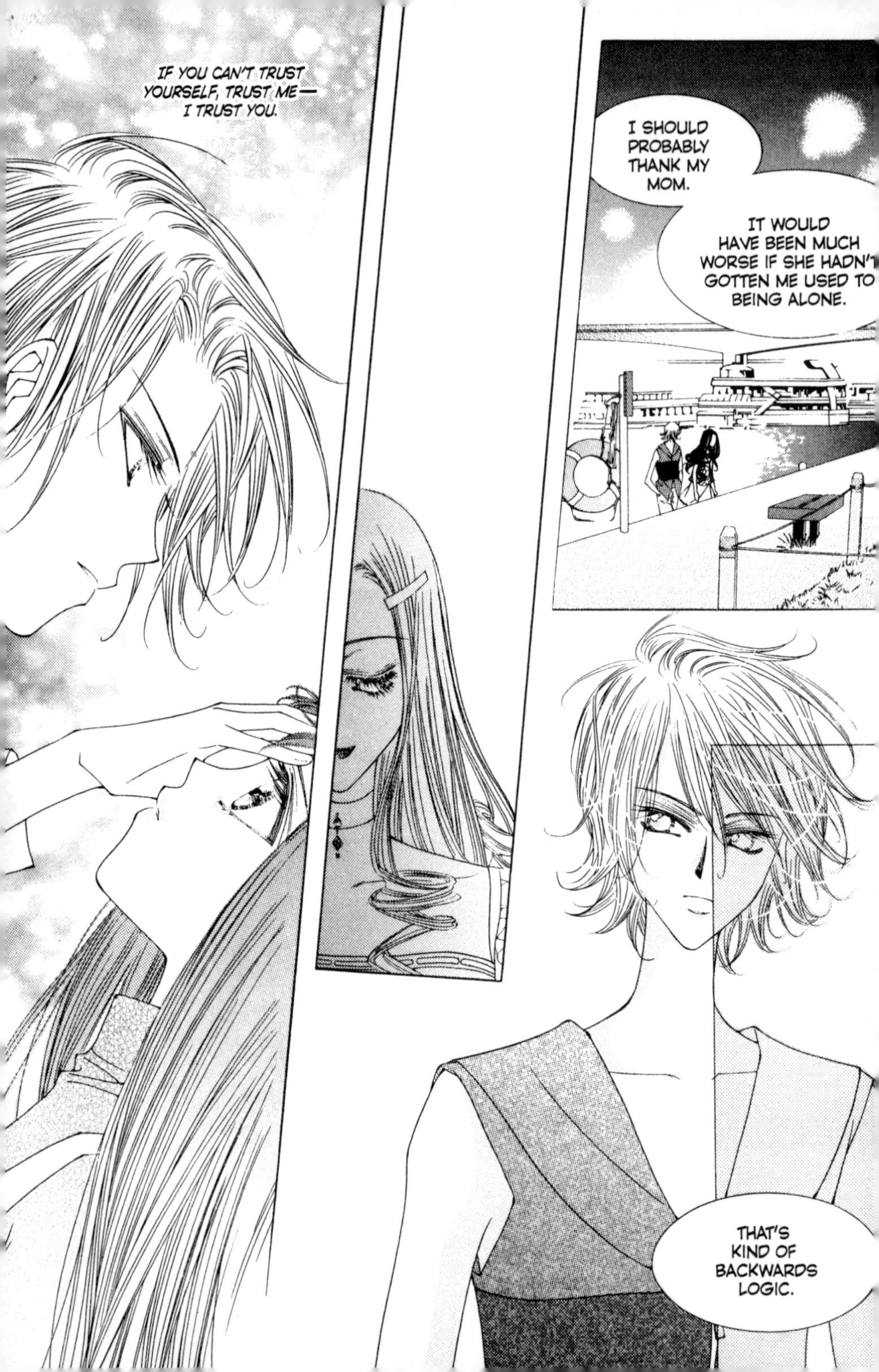
IF YOU CAN'T TRUST YOURSELF, TRUST ME— I TRUST YOU.
I SHOULD PROBABLY THANK MY MOM.
IT WOULD HAVE BEEN MUCH WORSE IF SHE HADN'T GOTTEN ME USED TO BEING ALONE.
THAT'S KIND OF BACKWARDS LOGIC.

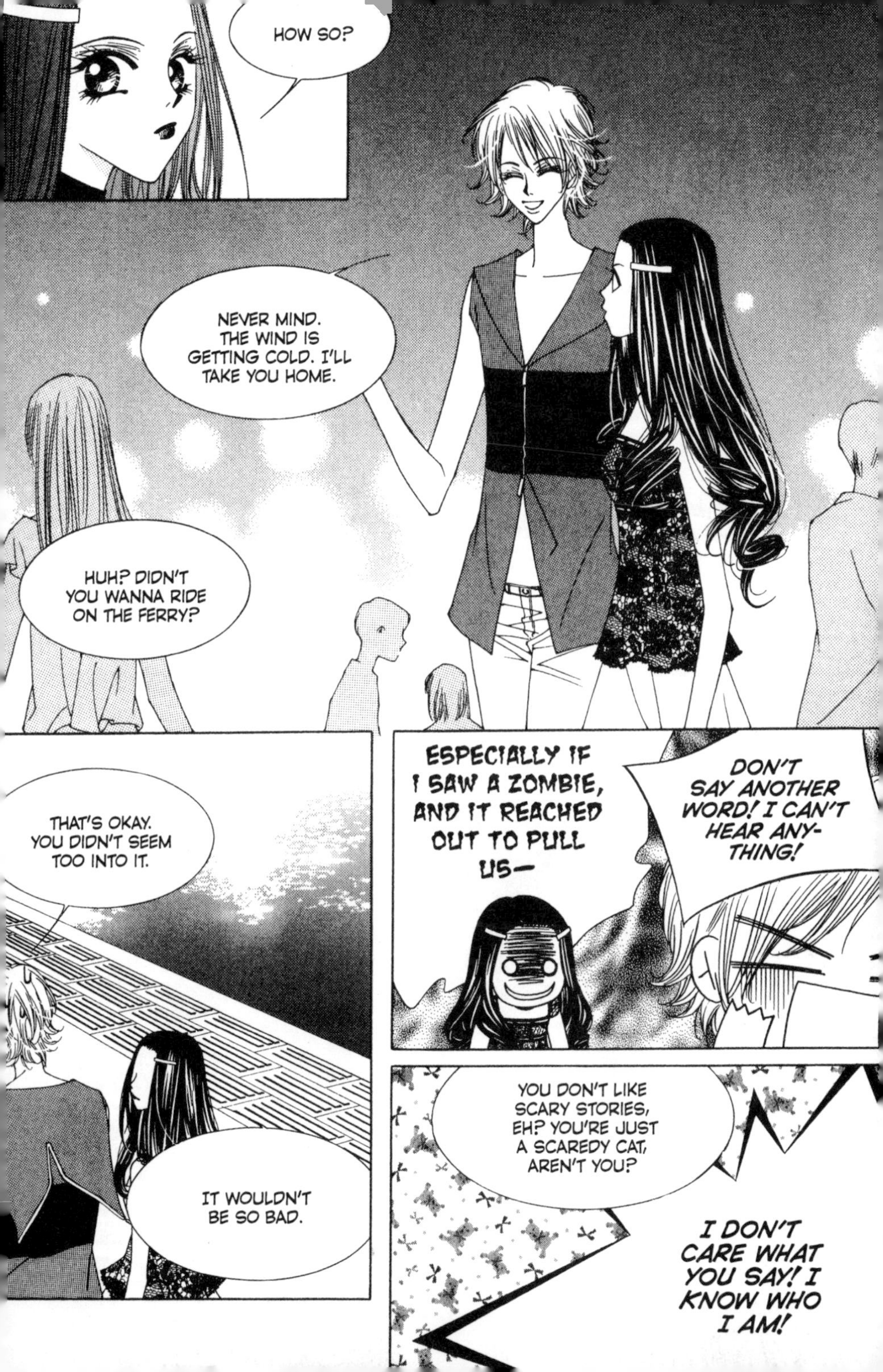
HOW SO?
NEVER MIND. THE WIND IS GETTING COLD. I'LL TAKE YOU HOME.
HUH? DIDN'T YOU WANNA RIDE ON THE FERRY?
THAT'S OKAY. YOU DIDN'T SEEM TOO INTO IT.
IT WOULDN'T BE SO BAD.
ESPECIALLY IF I SAW A ZOMBIE, AND IT REACHED OUT TO PULL US—
DON'T SAY ANOTHER WORD! I CAN'T HEAR ANY-THING!
YOU DON'T LIKE SCARY STORIES, EH? YOU'RE JUST A SCAREDY CAT, AREN'T YOU?
I DON'T CARE WHAT YOU SAY! I KNOW WHO I AM!

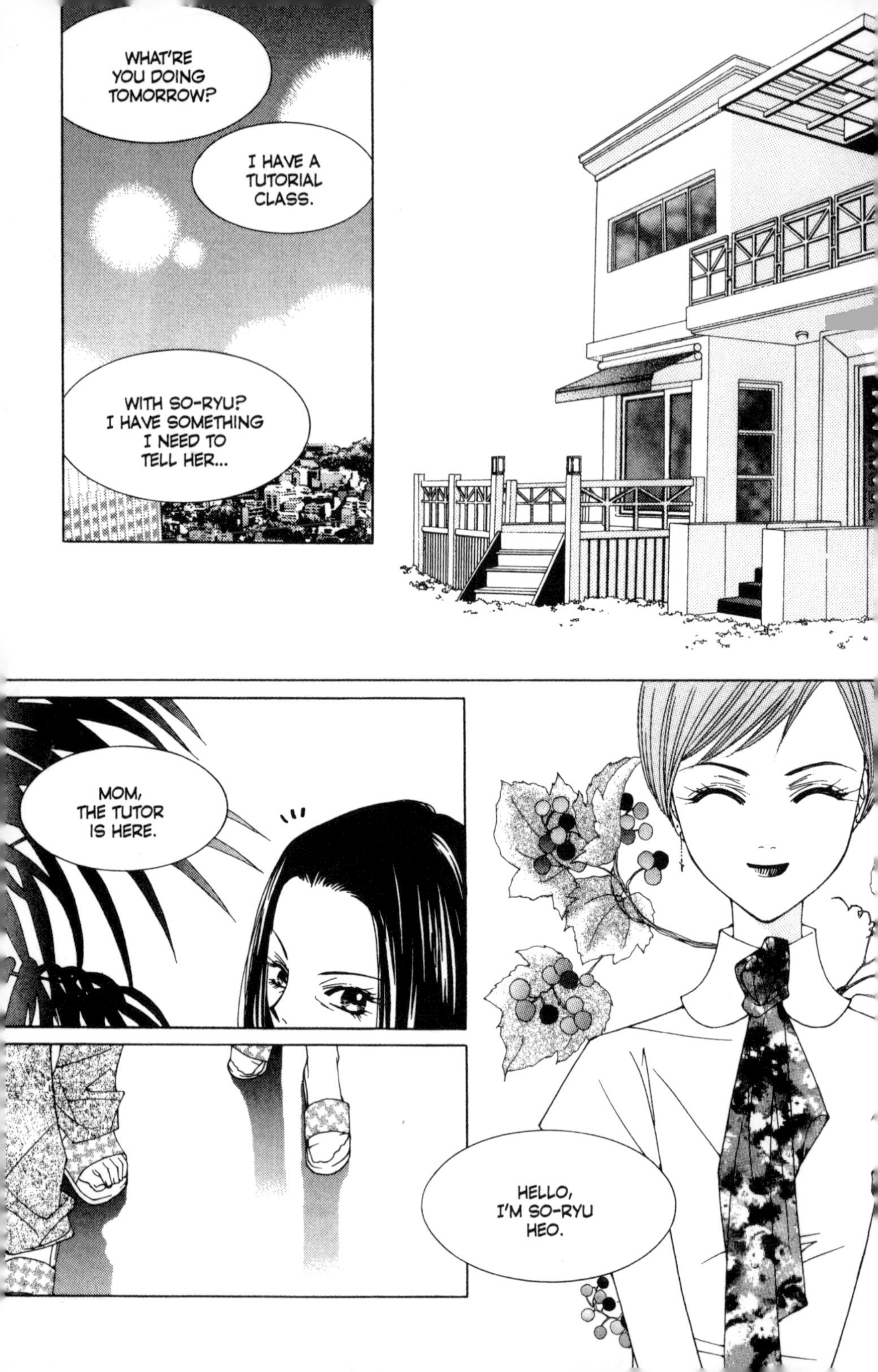
WHAT'RE YOU DOING TOMORROW?
I HAVE A TUTORIAL CLASS.
WITH SO-RYU? I HAVE SOMETHING I NEED TO TELL HER...
MOM, THE TUTOR IS HERE.
HELLO, I'M SO-RYU HEO.

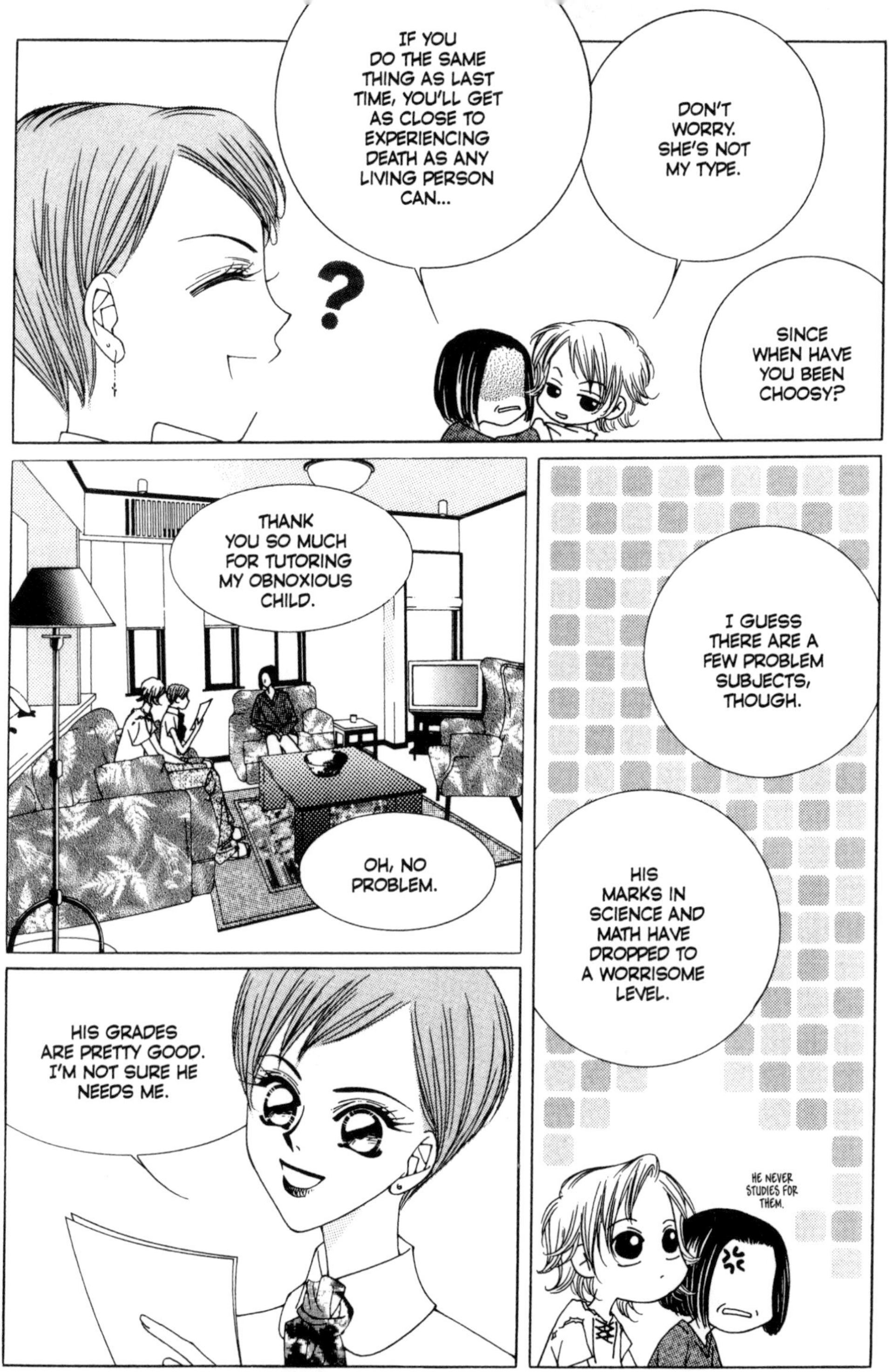
IF YOU DO THE SAME THING AS LAST TIME, YOU'LL GET AS CLOSE TO EXPERIENCING DEATH AS ANY LIVING PERSON CAN...
?
DON'T WORRY. SHE'S NOT MY TYPE.
SINCE WHEN HAVE YOU BEEN CHOOSY?
THANK YOU SO MUCH FOR TUTORING MY OBNOXIOUS CHILD.
OH, NO PROBLEM.
HIS GRADES ARE PRETTY GOOD. I'M NOT SURE HE NEEDS ME.
I GUESS THERE ARE A FEW PROBLEM SUBJECTS, THOUGH.
HIS MARKS IN SCIENCE AND MATH HAVE DROPPED TO A WORRISOME LEVEL.
HE NEVER STUDIES FOR THEM.

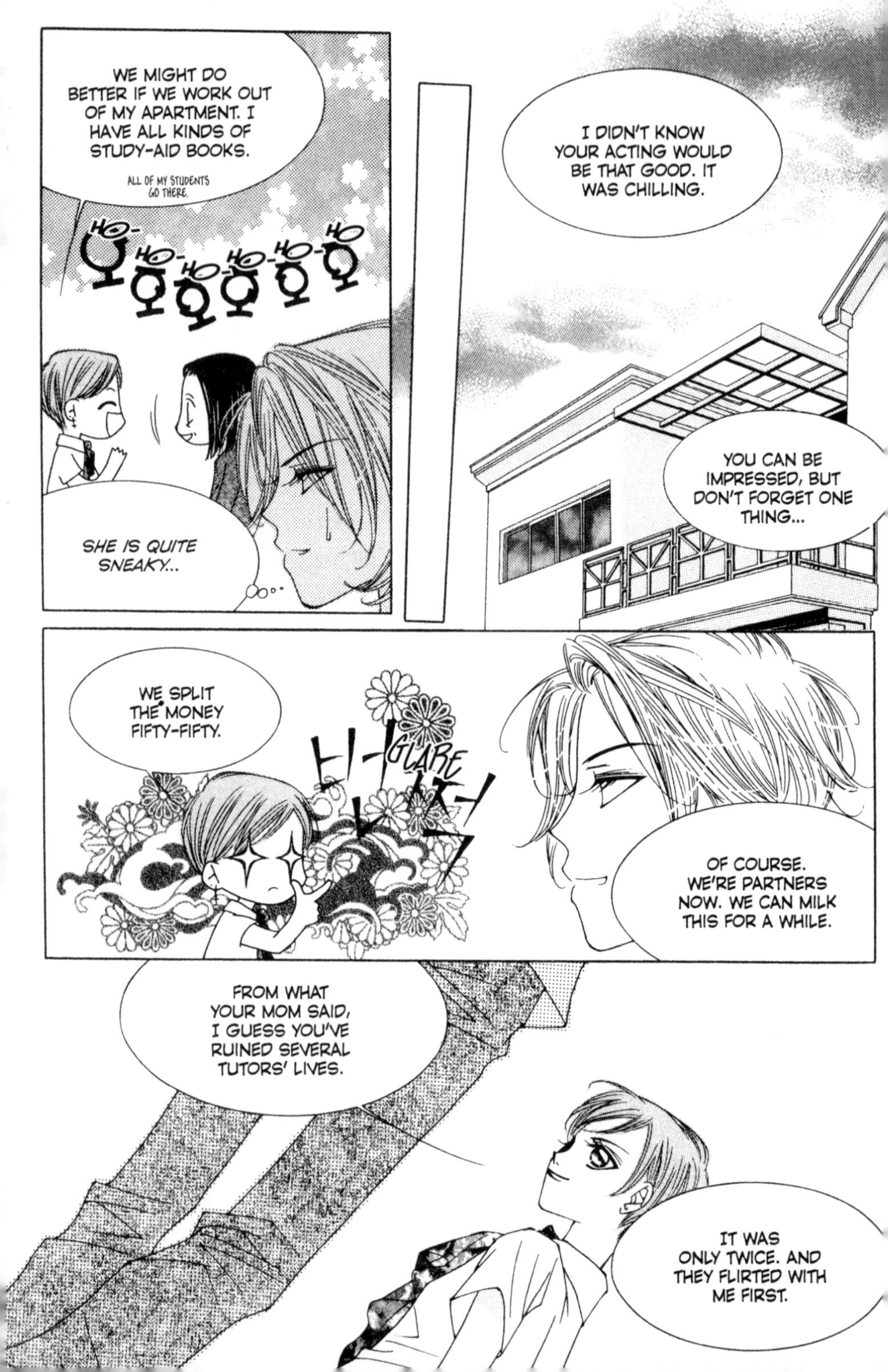
WE MIGHT DO BETTER IF WE WORK OUT OF MY APARTMENT. I HAVE ALL KINDS OF STUDY-AID BOOKS.
ALL OF MY STUDENTS GO THERE.
HO- HO- HO- HO- HO- HO-
SHE IS QUITE SNEAKY...
I DIDN'T KNOW YOUR ACTING WOULD BE THAT GOOD. IT WAS CHILLING.
YOU CAN BE IMPRESSED, BUT DON'T FORGET ONE THING...
WE SPLIT THE MONEY FIFTY-FIFTY.
GLARE
OF COURSE. WE'RE PARTNERS NOW. WE CAN MILK THIS FOR A WHILE.
FROM WHAT YOUR MOM SAID, I GUESS YOU'VE RUINED SEVERAL TUTORS' LIVES.
IT WAS ONLY TWICE. AND THEY FLIRTED WITH ME FIRST.

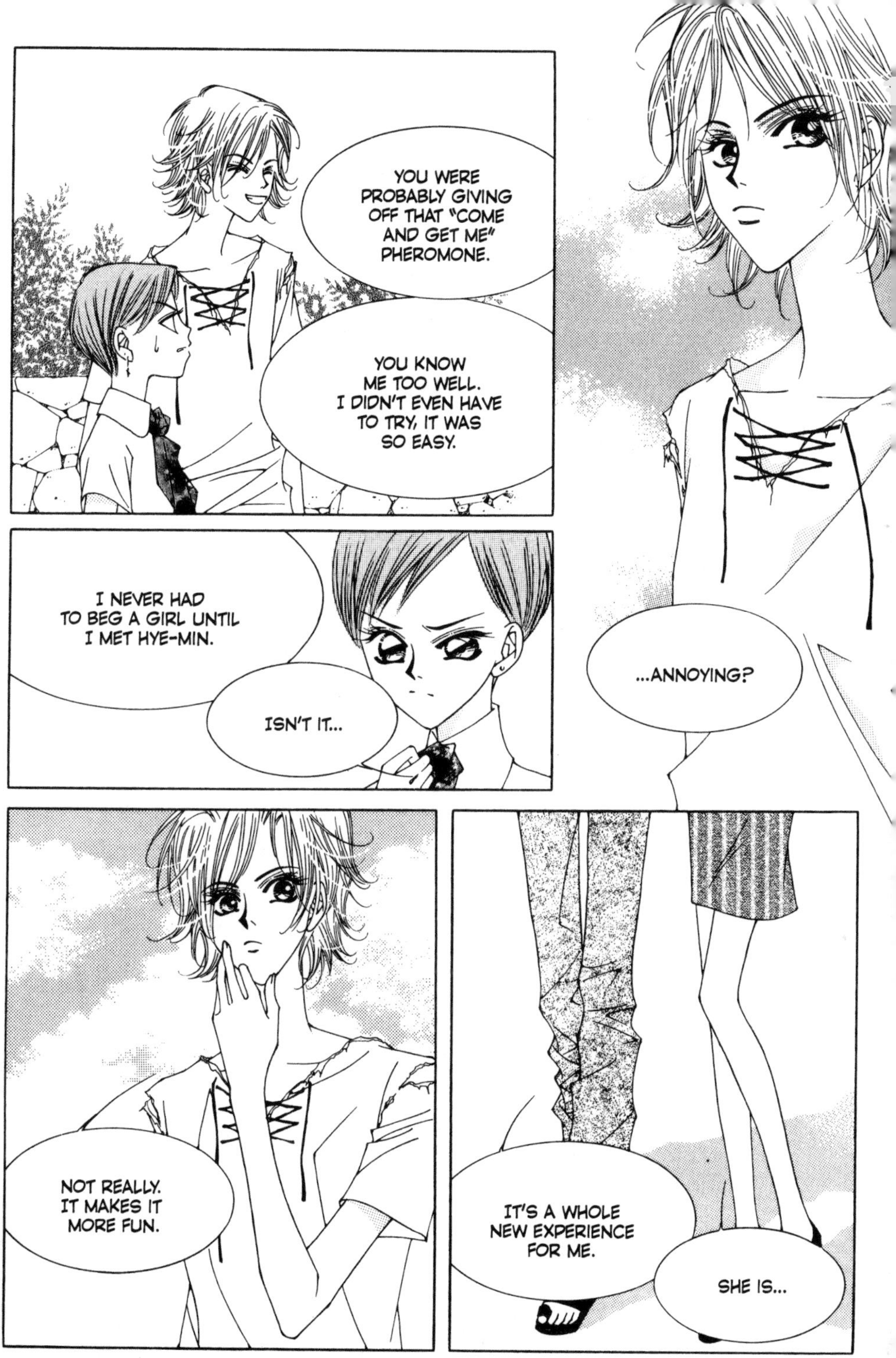
YOU WERE PROBABLY GIVING OFF THAT "COME AND GET ME" PHEROMONE.
YOU KNOW ME TOO WELL. I DIDN'T EVEN HAVE TO TRY, IT WAS SO EASY.
I NEVER HAD TO BEG A GIRL UNTIL I MET HYE-MIN.
ISN'T IT...
...ANNOYING?
NOT REALLY. IT MAKES IT MORE FUN.
IT'S A WHOLE NEW EXPERIENCE FOR ME.
SHE IS...

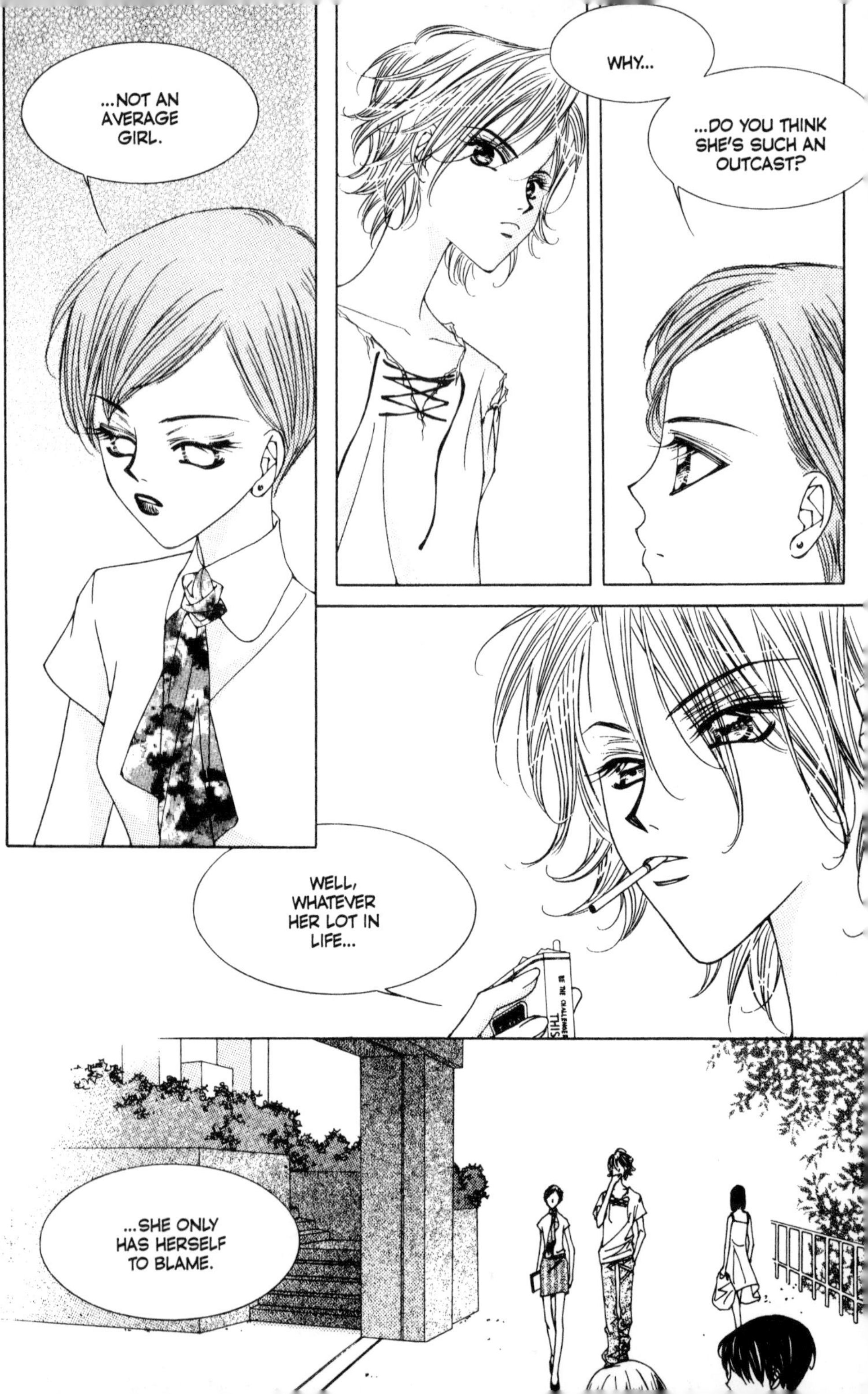
...NOT AN AVERAGE GIRL.
WHY...
...DO YOU THINK SHE'S SUCH AN OUTCAST?
WELL, WHATEVER HER LOT IN LIFE...
...SHE ONLY HAS HERSELF TO BLAME.

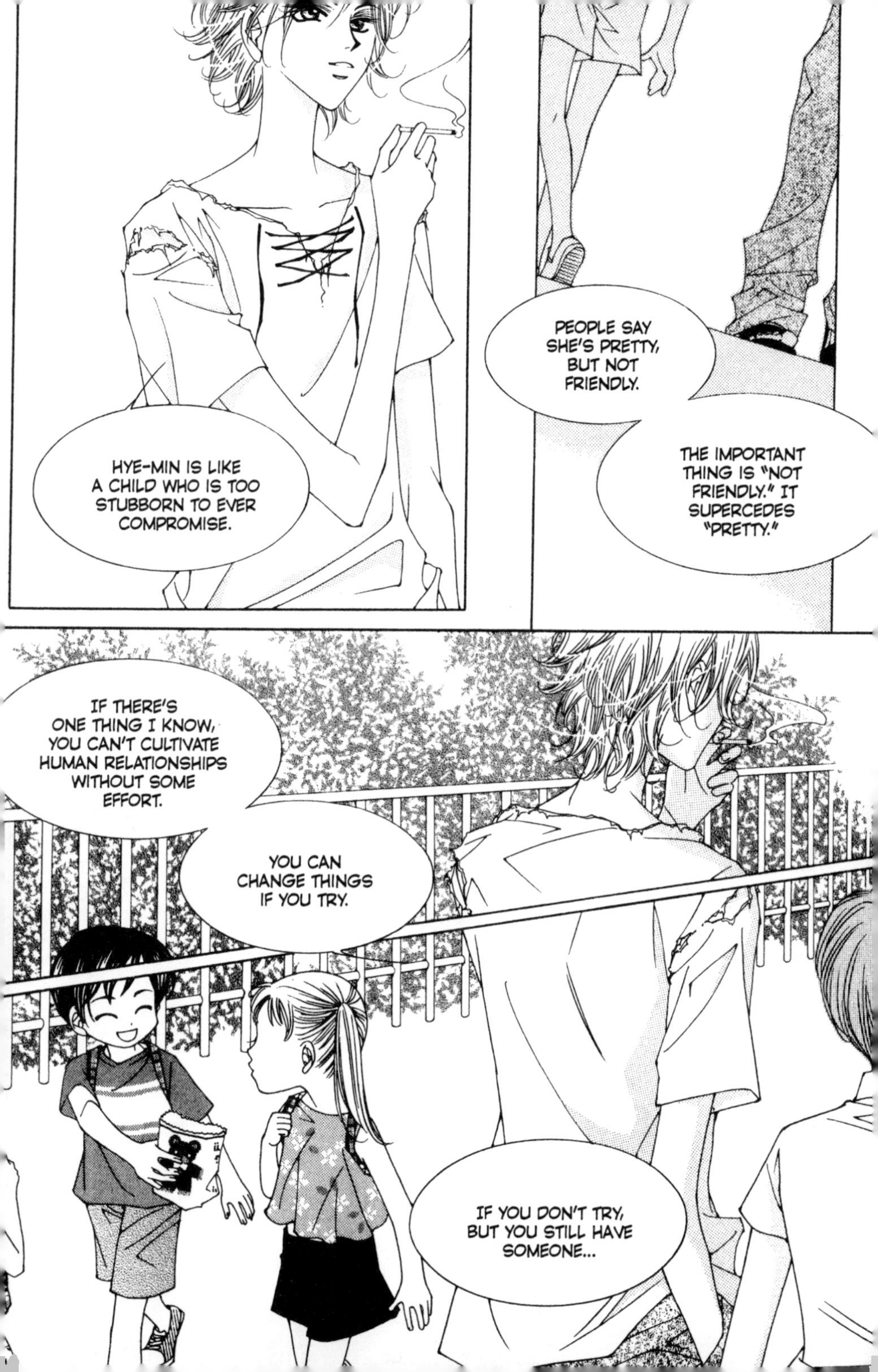
HYE-MIN IS LIKE A CHILD WHO IS TOO STUBBORN TO EVER COMPROMISE.
PEOPLE SAY SHE'S PRETTY, BUT NOT FRIENDLY.
THE IMPORTANT THING IS "NOT FRIENDLY." IT SUPERCEDES "PRETTY."
IF THERE'S ONE THING I KNOW, YOU CAN'T CULTIVATE HUMAN RELATIONSHIPS WITHOUT SOME EFFORT.
YOU CAN CHANGE THINGS IF YOU TRY.
IF YOU DON'T TRY, BUT YOU STILL HAVE SOMEONE...

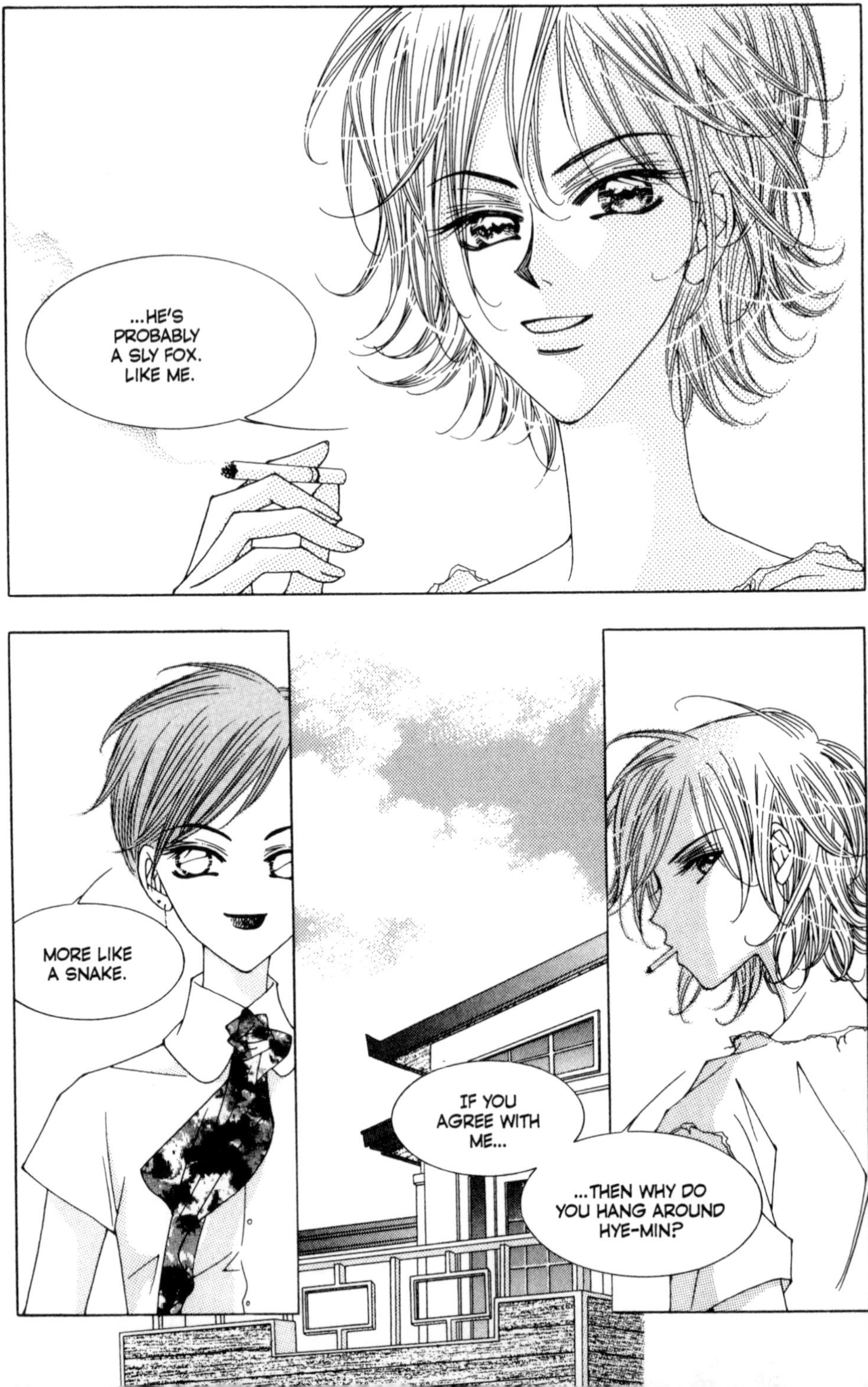
...HE'S PROBABLY A SLY FOX. LIKE ME.
MORE LIKE A SNAKE.
IF YOU AGREE WITH ME...
...THEN WHY DO YOU HANG AROUND HYE-MIN?

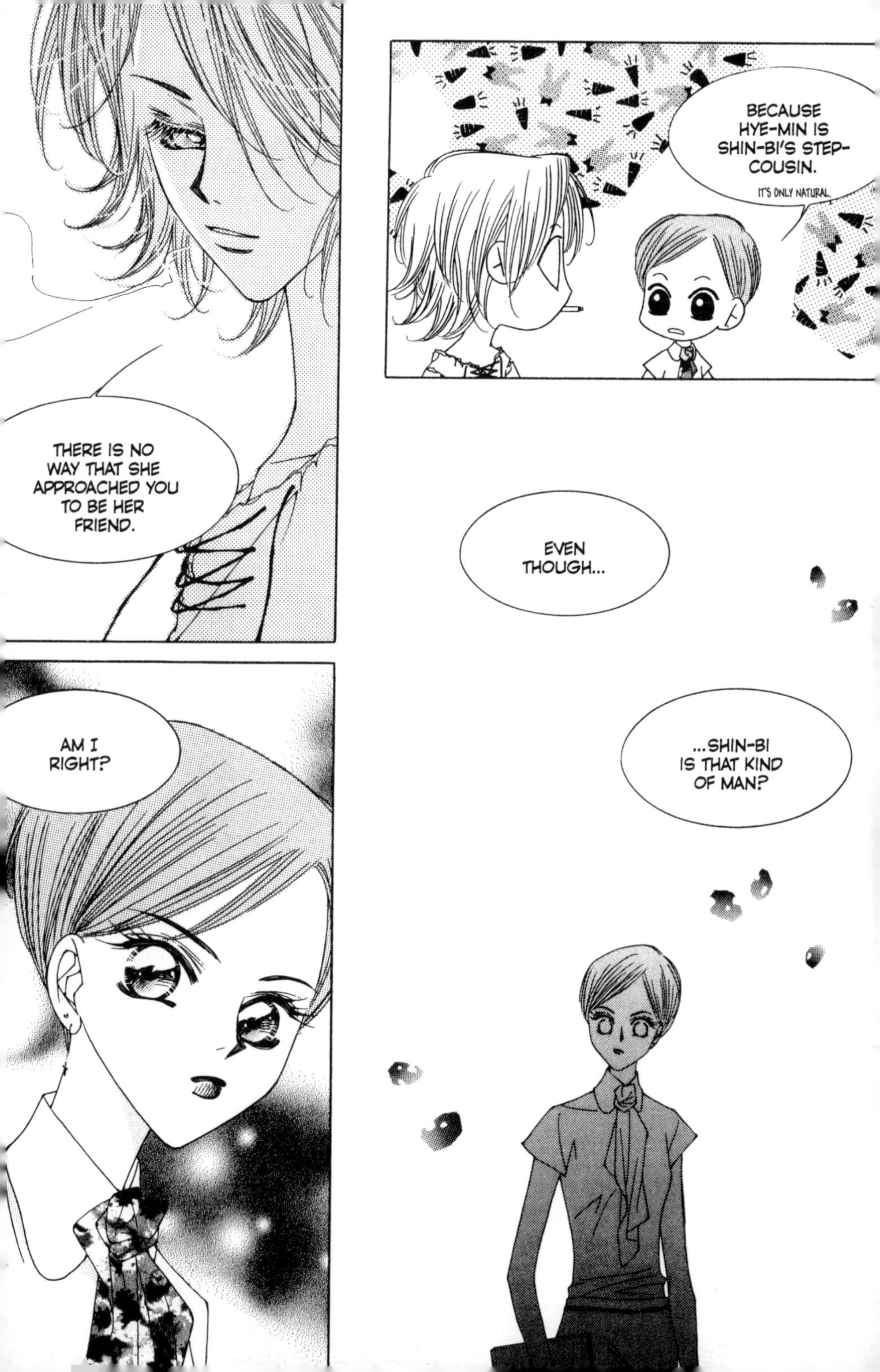
THERE IS NO WAY THAT SHE APPROACHED YOU TO BE HER FRIEND.
BECAUSE HYE-MIN IS SHIN-BI'S STEP-COUSIN.
IT'S ONLY NATURAL.
AM I RIGHT?
EVEN THOUGH...
...SHIN-BI IS THAT KIND OF MAN?

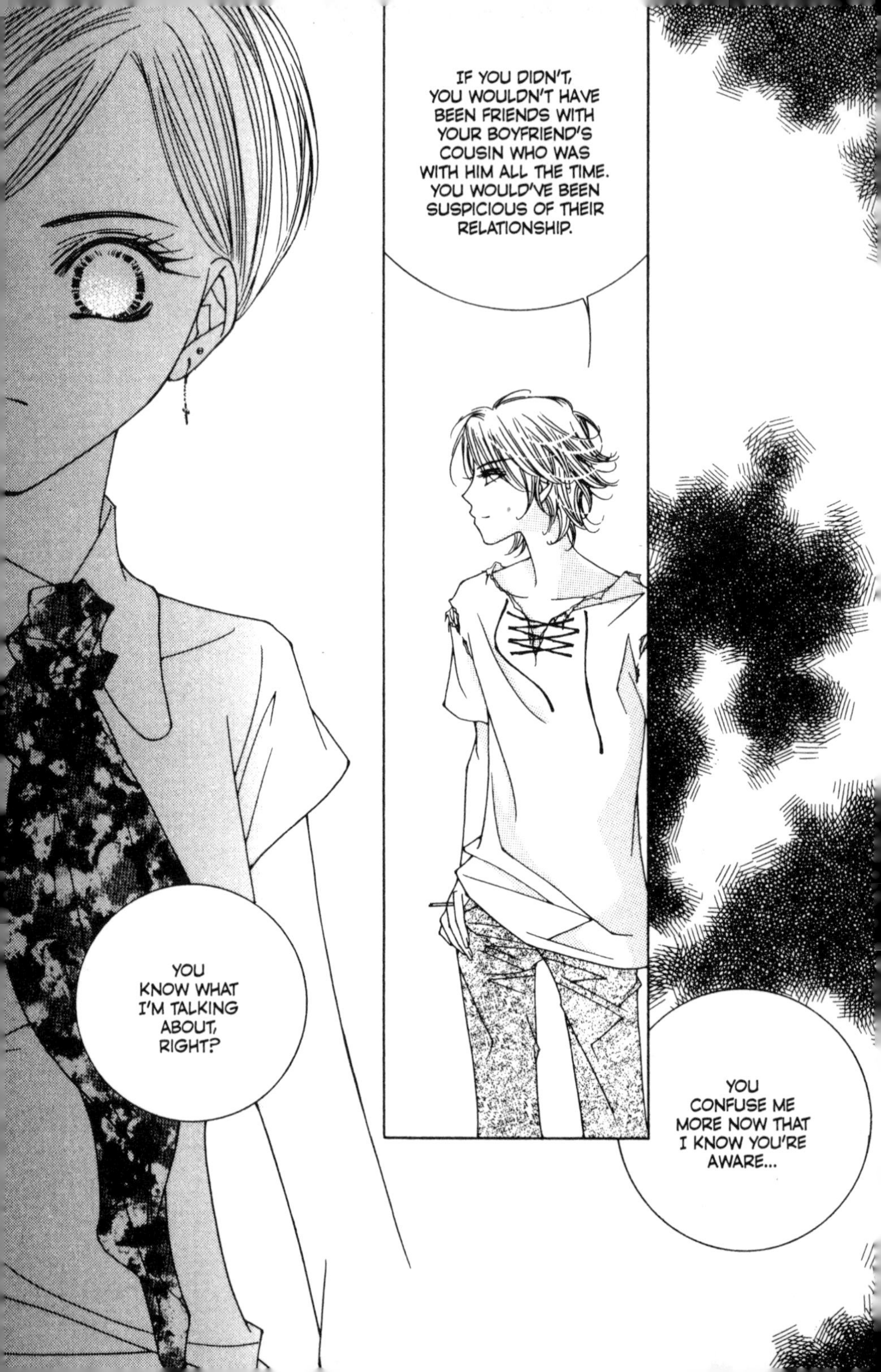
YOU KNOW WHAT I'M TALKING ABOUT, RIGHT?
IF YOU DIDN'T, YOU WOULDN'T HAVE BEEN FRIENDS WITH YOUR BOYFRIEND'S COUSIN WHO WAS WITH HIM ALL THE TIME. YOU WOULD'VE BEEN SUSPICIOUS OF THEIR RELATIONSHIP.
YOU CONFUSE ME MORE NOW THAT I KNOW YOU'RE AWARE...

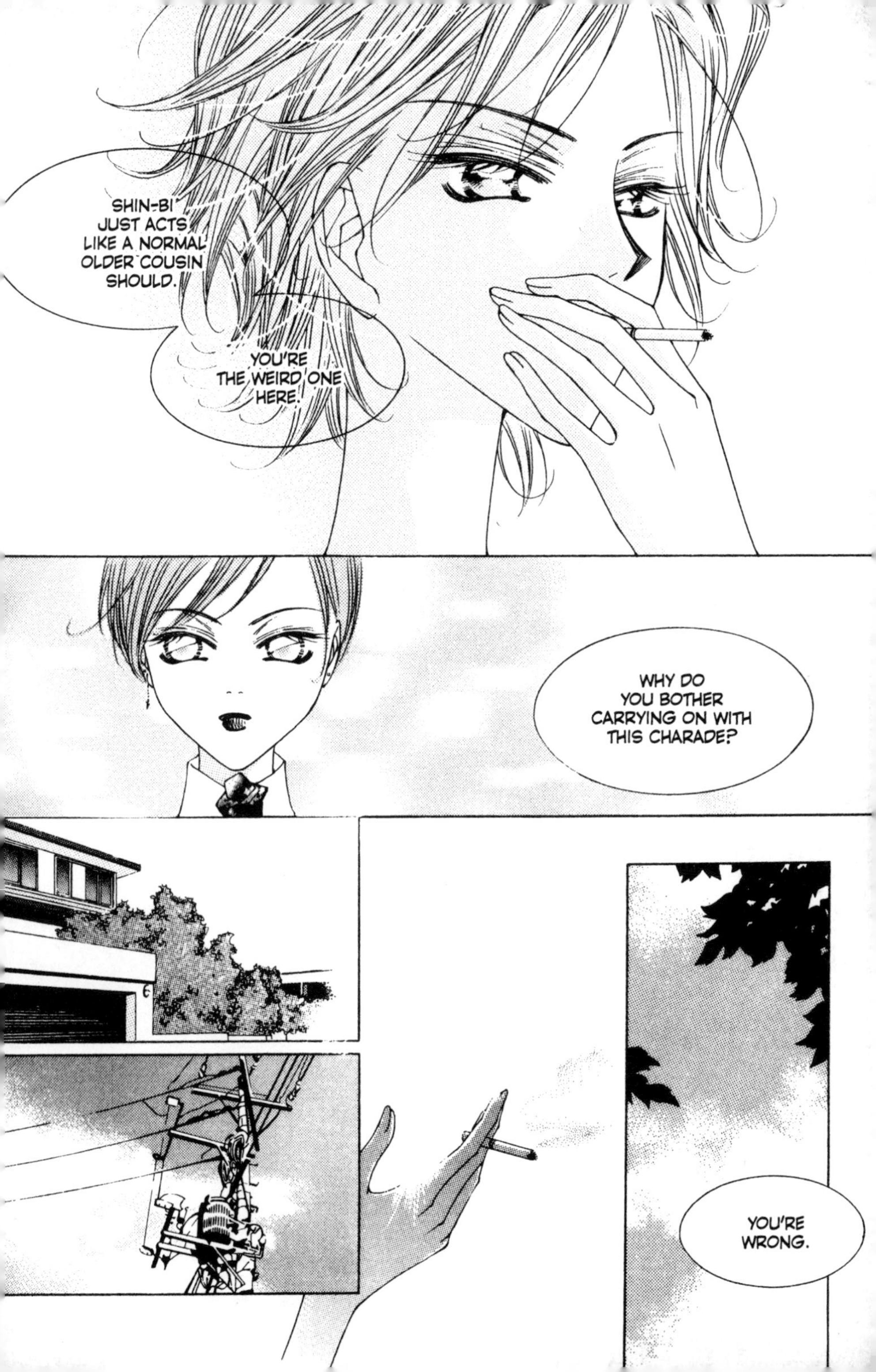
SHIN-BI JUST ACTS LIKE A NORMAL OLDER COUSIN SHOULD.
YOU'RE THE WEIRD ONE HERE.
WHY DO YOU BOTHER CARRYING ON WITH THIS CHARADE?
YOU'RE WRONG.

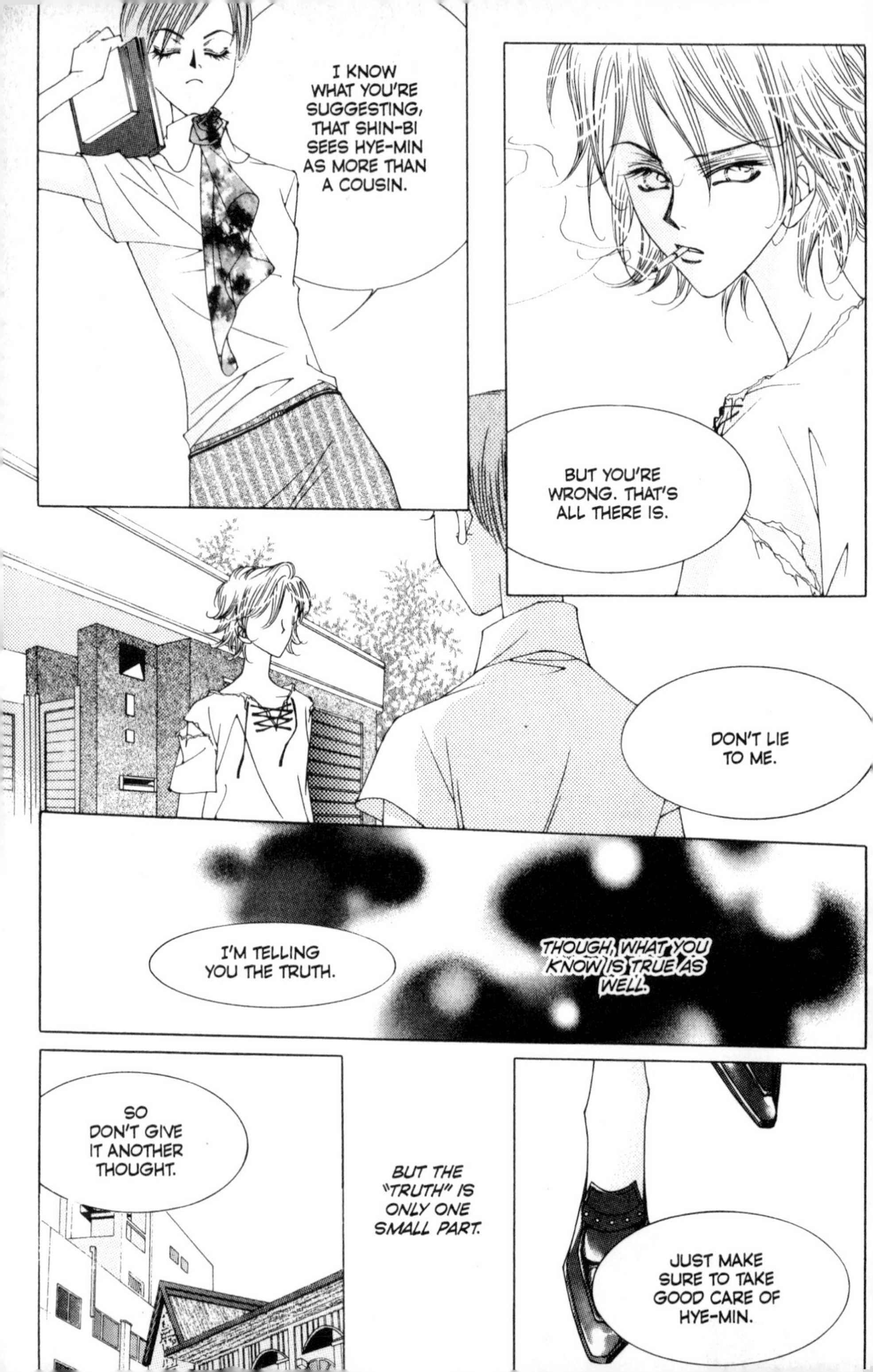
I KNOW WHAT YOU'RE SUGGESTING, THAT SHIN-BI SEES HYE-MIN AS MORE THAN A COUSIN.
BUT YOU'RE WRONG. THAT'S ALL THERE IS.
DON'T LIE TO ME.
I'M TELLING YOU THE TRUTH.
THOUGH, WHAT YOU KNOW IS TRUE AS WELL.
SO DON'T GIVE IT ANOTHER THOUGHT.
BUT THE "TRUTH" IS ONLY ONE SMALL PART.
JUST MAKE SURE TO TAKE GOOD CARE OF HYE-MIN.

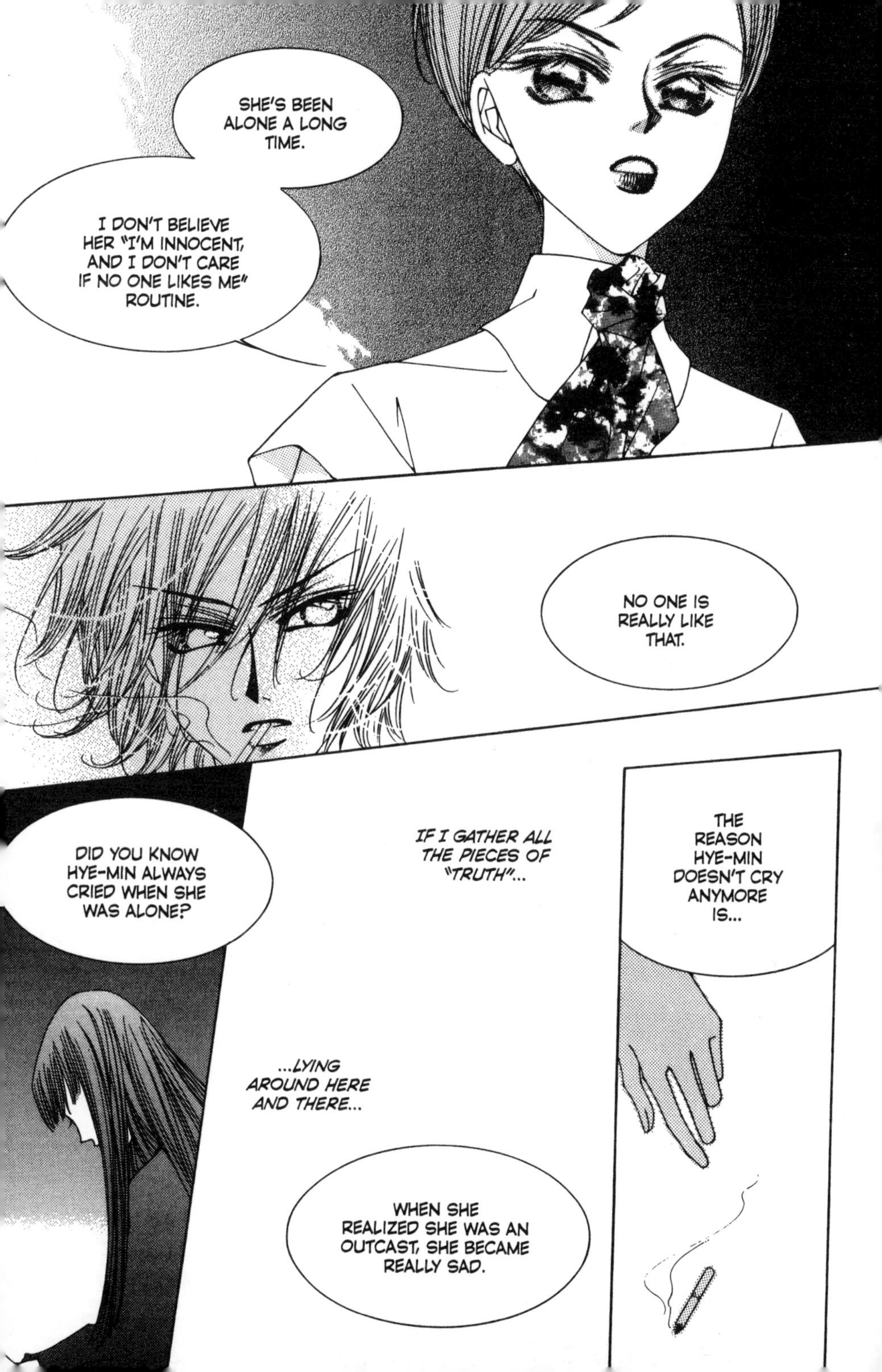
SHE'S BEEN ALONE A LONG TIME.
I DON'T BELIEVE HER "I'M INNOCENT, AND I DON'T CARE IF NO ONE LIKES ME" ROUTINE.
NO ONE IS REALLY LIKE THAT.
DID YOU KNOW HYE-MIN ALWAYS CRIED WHEN SHE WAS ALONE?
IF I GATHER ALL THE PIECES OF "TRUTH"...
...LYING AROUND HERE AND THERE...
WHEN SHE REALIZED SHE WAS AN OUTCAST, SHE BECAME REALLY SAD.
THE REASON HYE-MIN DOESN'T CRY ANYMORE IS...

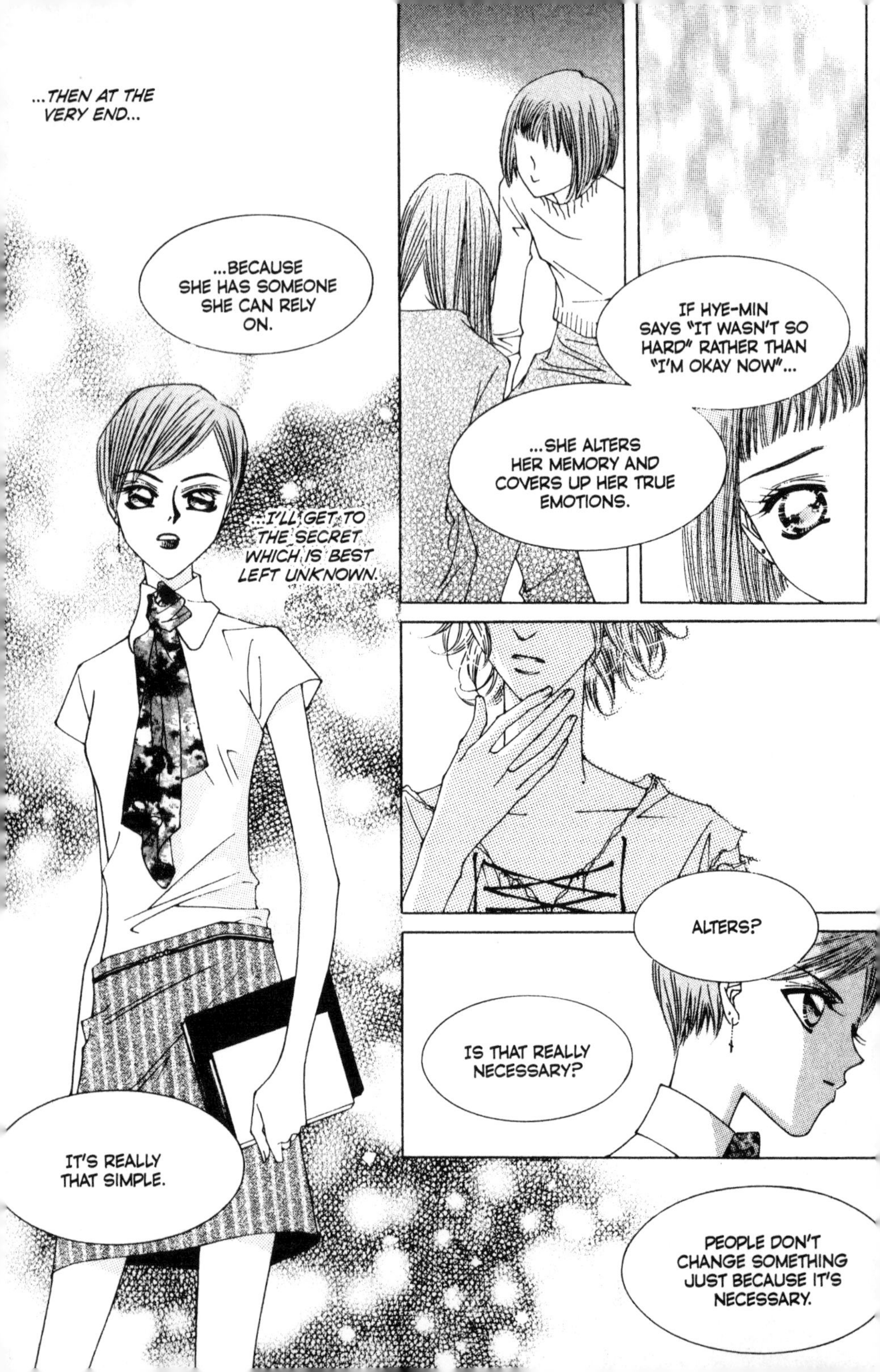
...THEN AT THE VERY END...
...BECAUSE SHE HAS SOMEONE SHE CAN RELY ON.
...I'LL GET TO THE SECRET WHICH IS BEST LEFT UNKNOWN.
IT'S REALLY THAT SIMPLE.
IF HYE-MIN SAYS "IT WASN'T SO HARD" RATHER THAN "I'M OKAY NOW"...
...SHE ALTERS HER MEMORY AND COVERS UP HER TRUE EMOTIONS.
ALTERS?
IS THAT REALLY NECESSARY?
PEOPLE DON'T CHANGE SOMETHING JUST BECAUSE IT'S NECESSARY.

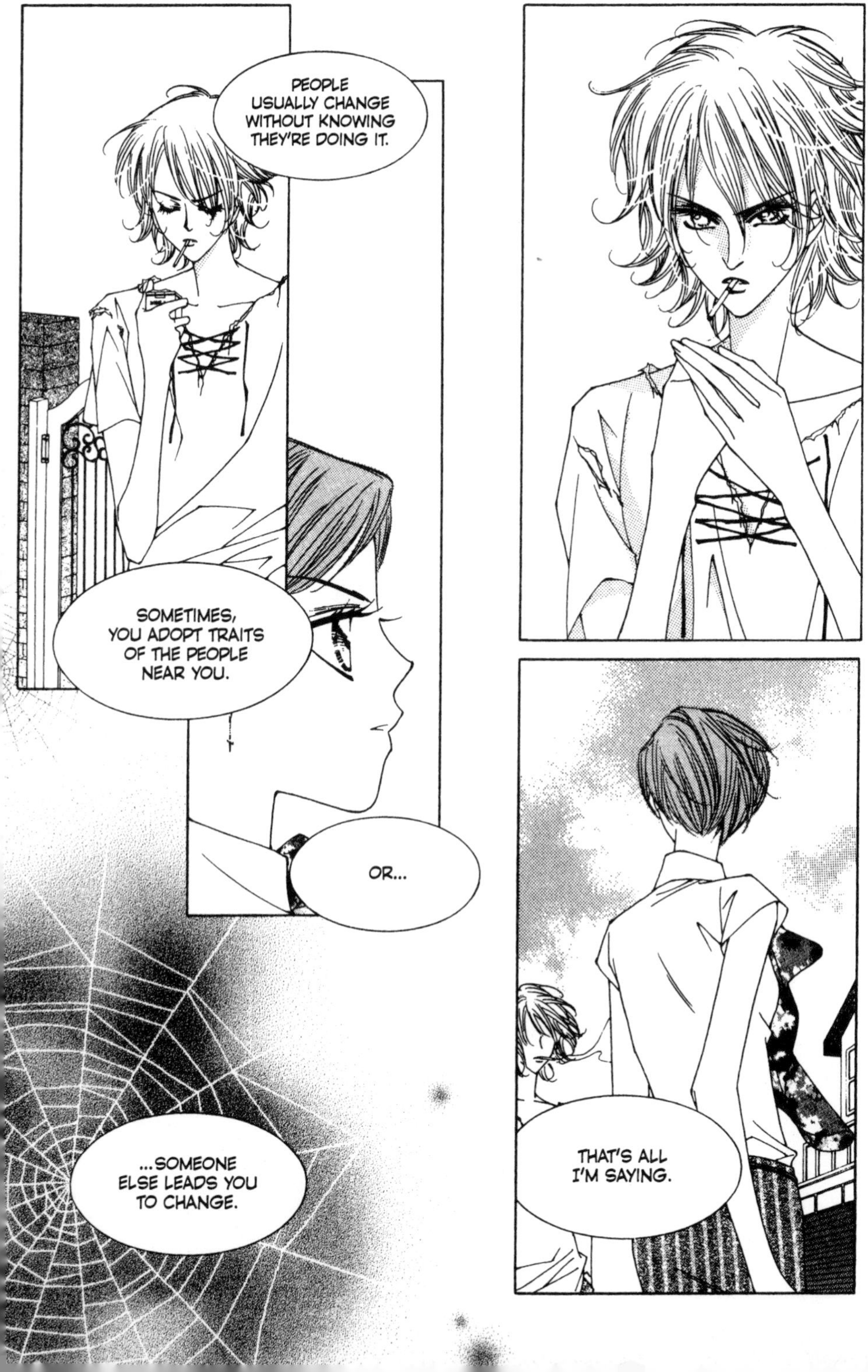
PEOPLE USUALLY CHANGE WITHOUT KNOWING THEY'RE DOING IT.
SOMETIMES, YOU ADOPT TRAITS OF THE PEOPLE NEAR YOU.
OR...
...SOMEONE ELSE LEADS YOU TO CHANGE.
THAT'S ALL I'M SAYING.

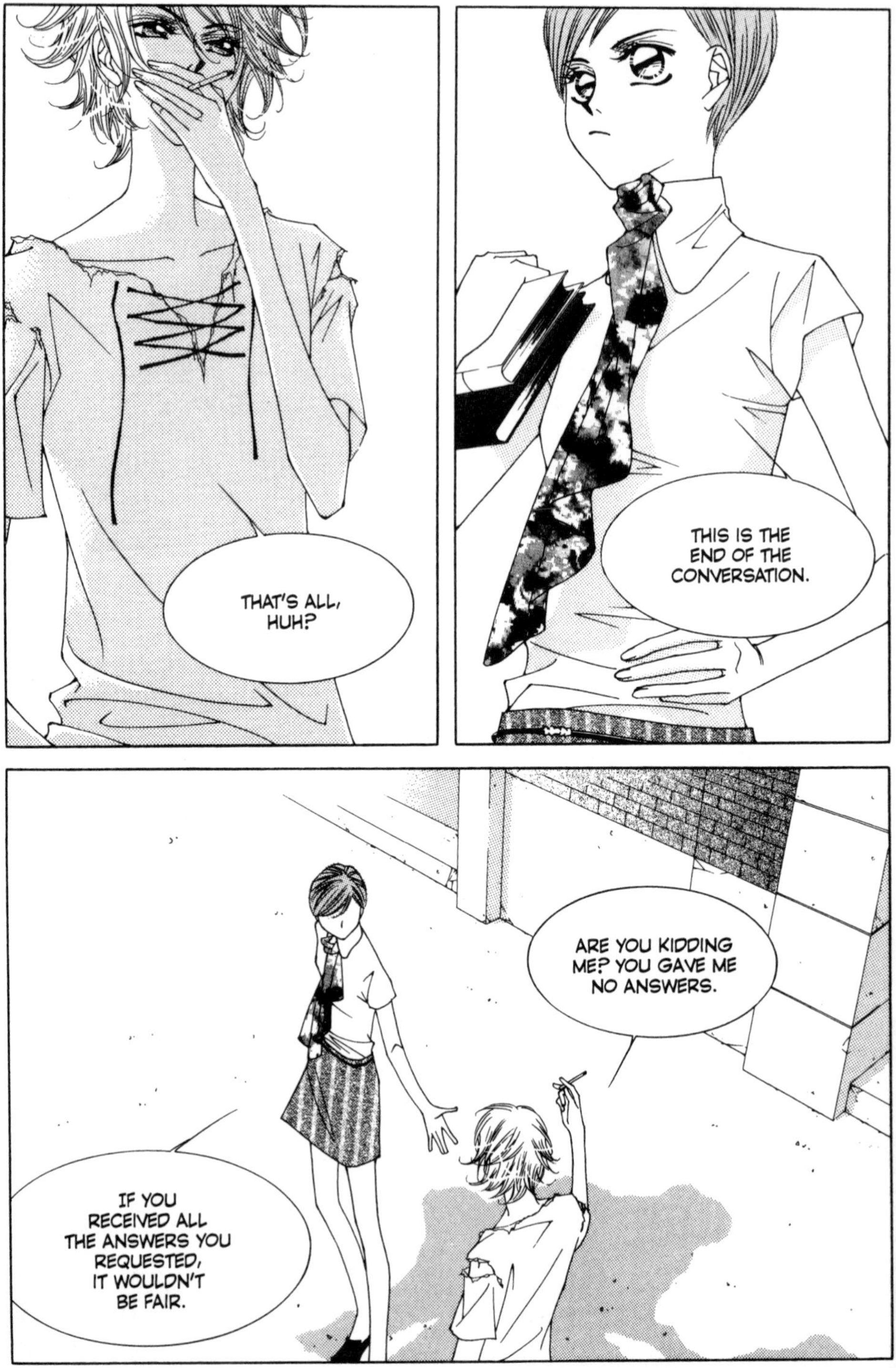
THAT'S ALL, HUH?
THIS IS THE END OF THE CONVERSATION.
ARE YOU KIDDING ME? YOU GAVE ME NO ANSWERS.
IF YOU RECEIVED ALL THE ANSWERS YOU REQUESTED, IT WOULDN'T BE FAIR.

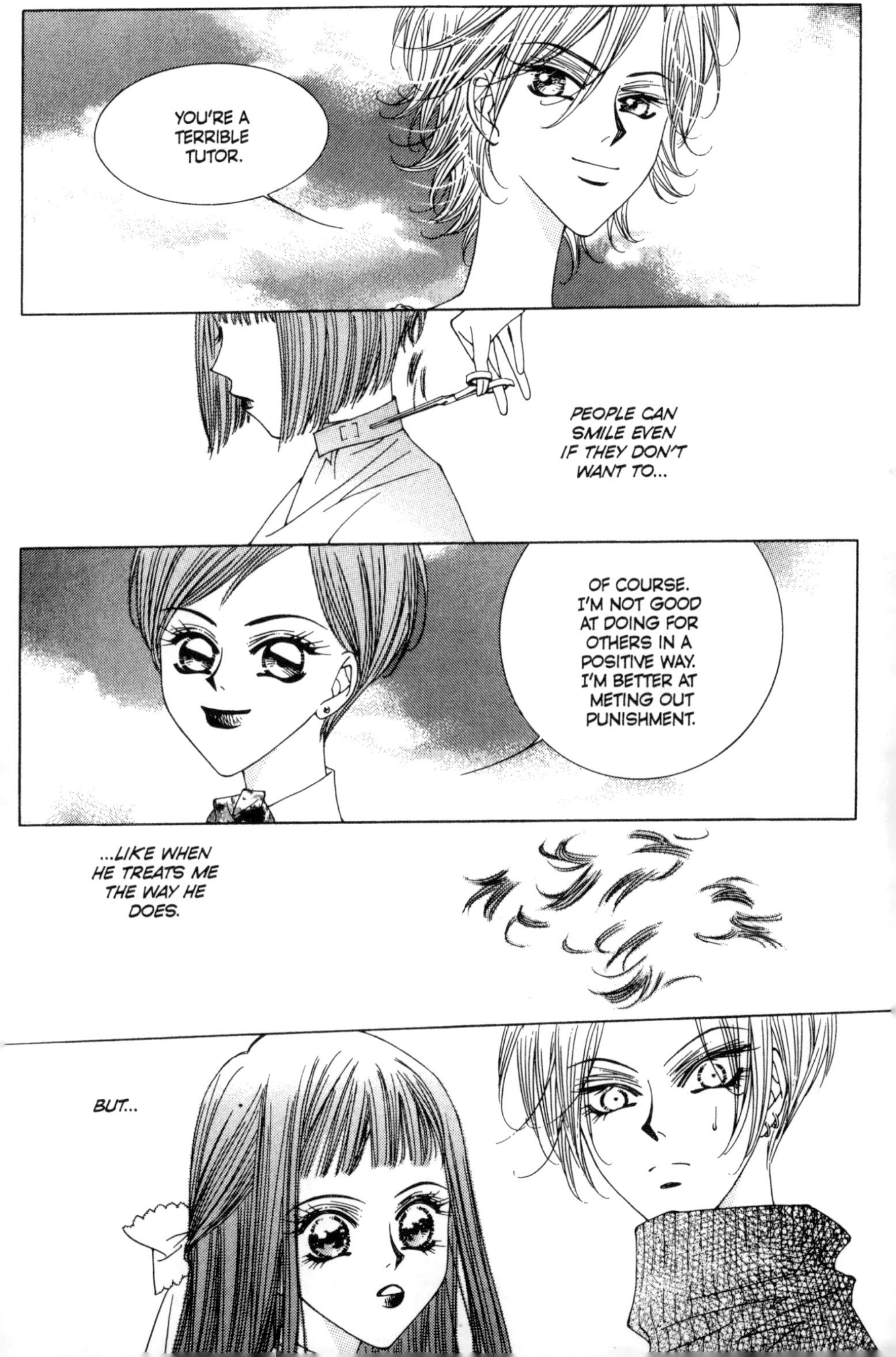
YOU'RE A TERRIBLE TUTOR.
PEOPLE CAN SMILE EVEN IF THEY DON'T WANT TO...
OF COURSE. I'M NOT GOOD AT DOING FOR OTHERS IN A POSITIVE WAY. I'M BETTER AT METING OUT PUNISHMENT.
...LIKE WHEN HE TREATS ME THE WAY HE DOES.
BUT...

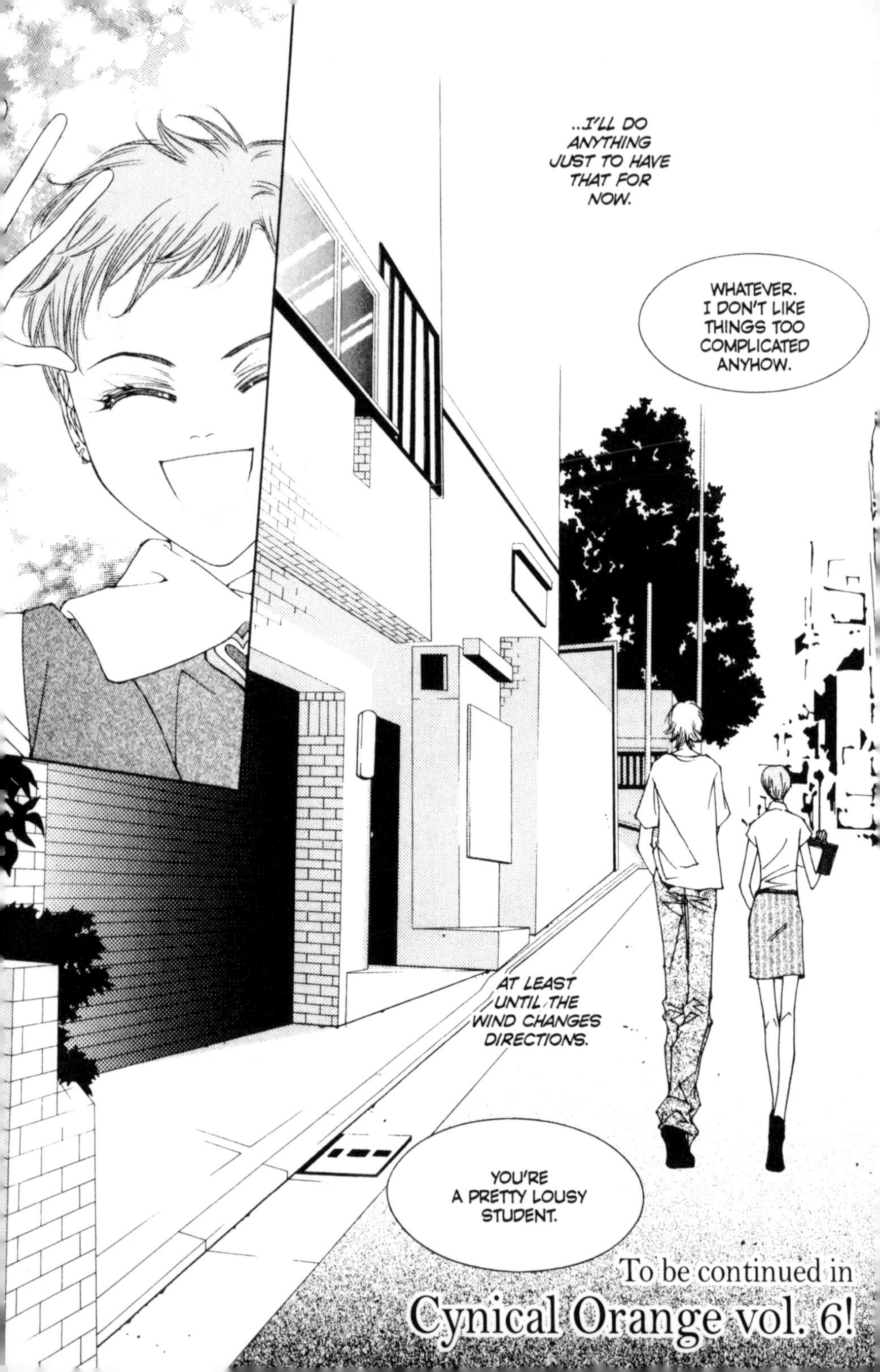
...I'LL DO ANYTHING JUST TO HAVE THAT FOR NOW.
WHATEVER. I DON'T LIKE THINGS TOO COMPLICATED ANYHOW.
AT LEAST UNTIL THE WIND CHANGES DIRECTIONS.
YOU'RE A PRETTY LOUSY STUDENT.
To be continued in
Cynical Orange vol. 6!

JUNE, DO YOU WANT ME TO TELL YOU HOW TO DOUBLE THE PROBABILITY OF YOU WINNING THE LOTTERY?
YOU BET! HOW?
BUY TWO TICKETS.
CRACK

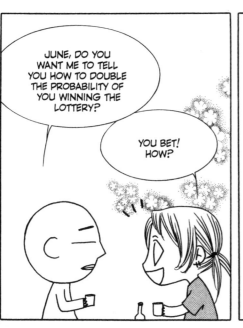

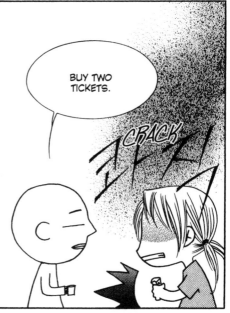

=BONUS TRACK=

PROBABILITY IS JUST A NUMBER. YOU CAN ONLY TRUST YOUR DESTINY. ~IT'S ALL A MATTER OF FATE.~

THE WARDROBE OF AN EGYPTIAN QUEEN

WHY ARE THE COSTUMES OF SUCH LEGENDARY PERIODS SO FANTASTIC? THE ACCESSORIES OFTEN LOOK FUNNY AT FIRST GLANCE, BUT MOST OF THEM HAVE A GREATER MEANING, SHOWING A PERSON'S LOVE OF THEIR GODS. THE BIG FEATHER SYMBOLIZES AMON, AND THE DISC SYMBOLIZES THE GOD OF THE SUN, RA. EGYPTIANS CONSIDERED A SNAKE TO BE A DIVINE ANIMAL, AND THEY BELIEVED THE WINGS OF AN EAGLE PROTECTED A HUSBAND WHEN HE WAS AWAY FROM HOME. A TRADE-MARK OF THE EGYPTIANS WAS THE DARK EYE MAKE-UP THAT PROTECTED THEIR EYES FROM THE SUN. I'M SORRY THAT SUCH A BEAUTIFUL AND MYSTERIOUS CULTURE HAS FADED.

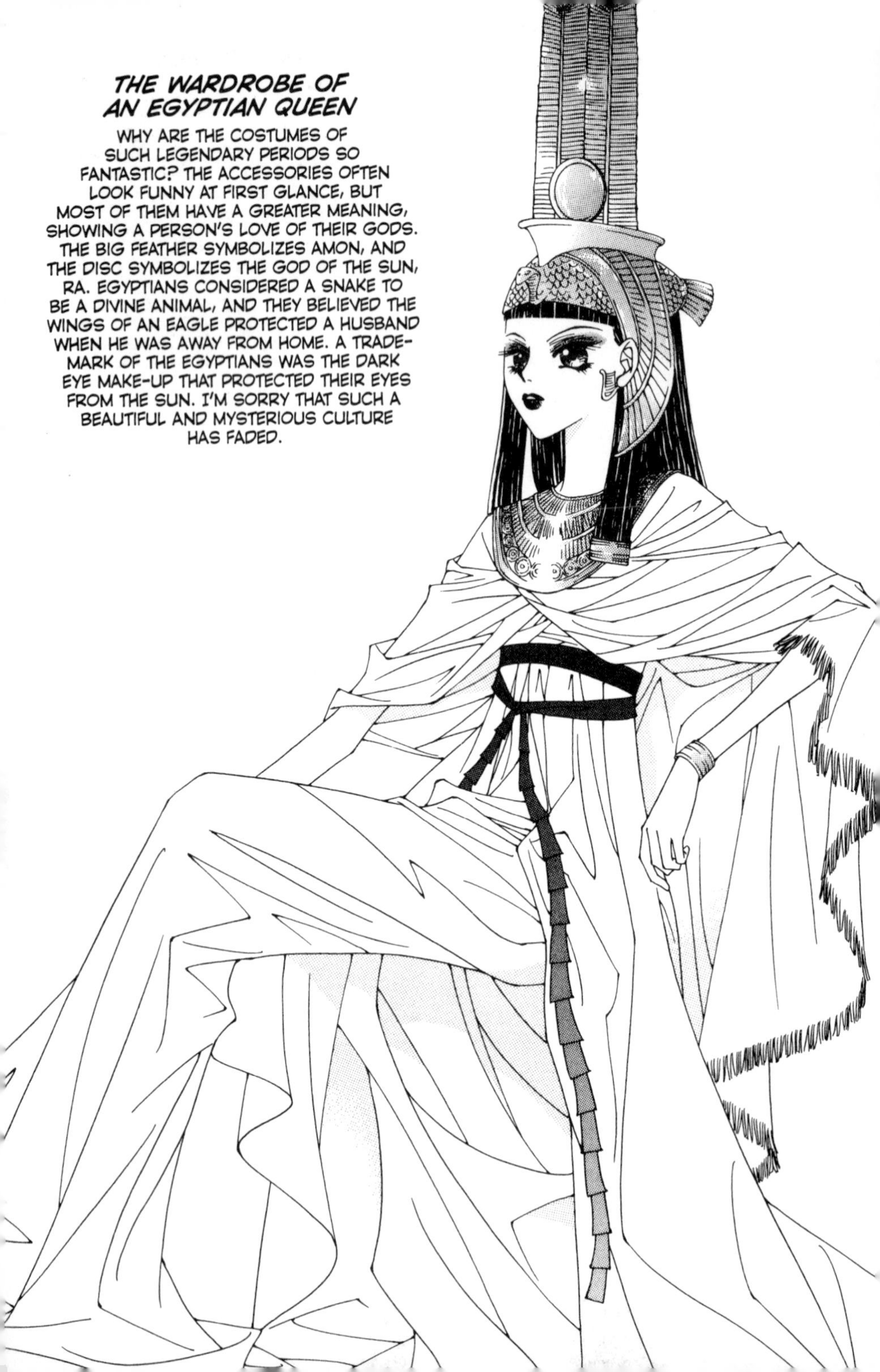

MEN'S FASHION DURING THE ROMAN REPUBLIC

IT'S ALMOST THE SAME AS A GREEK COSTUME. I FEEL THE GREEK ONE LOOKS A BIT MORE WORLD WEARY, WHILE THE ROMAN UNIFORM HAS MORE MANLY POWER. IT'S LIKE THE GREEKS DESIGNED FOR DELICATE AND PRETTY BOYS, WHILE THE ROMANS CONSIDERED THE LOOK OF GROWN MEN WITH MUSCLES. (THIS IS JUST MY PERSONAL OPINION.) THE TOGA IS A STAPLE OF ROMAN FASHION AND COMES FROM ETRURIA. THE COLORED SASH SYMBOLIZED THE RULING CLASS.

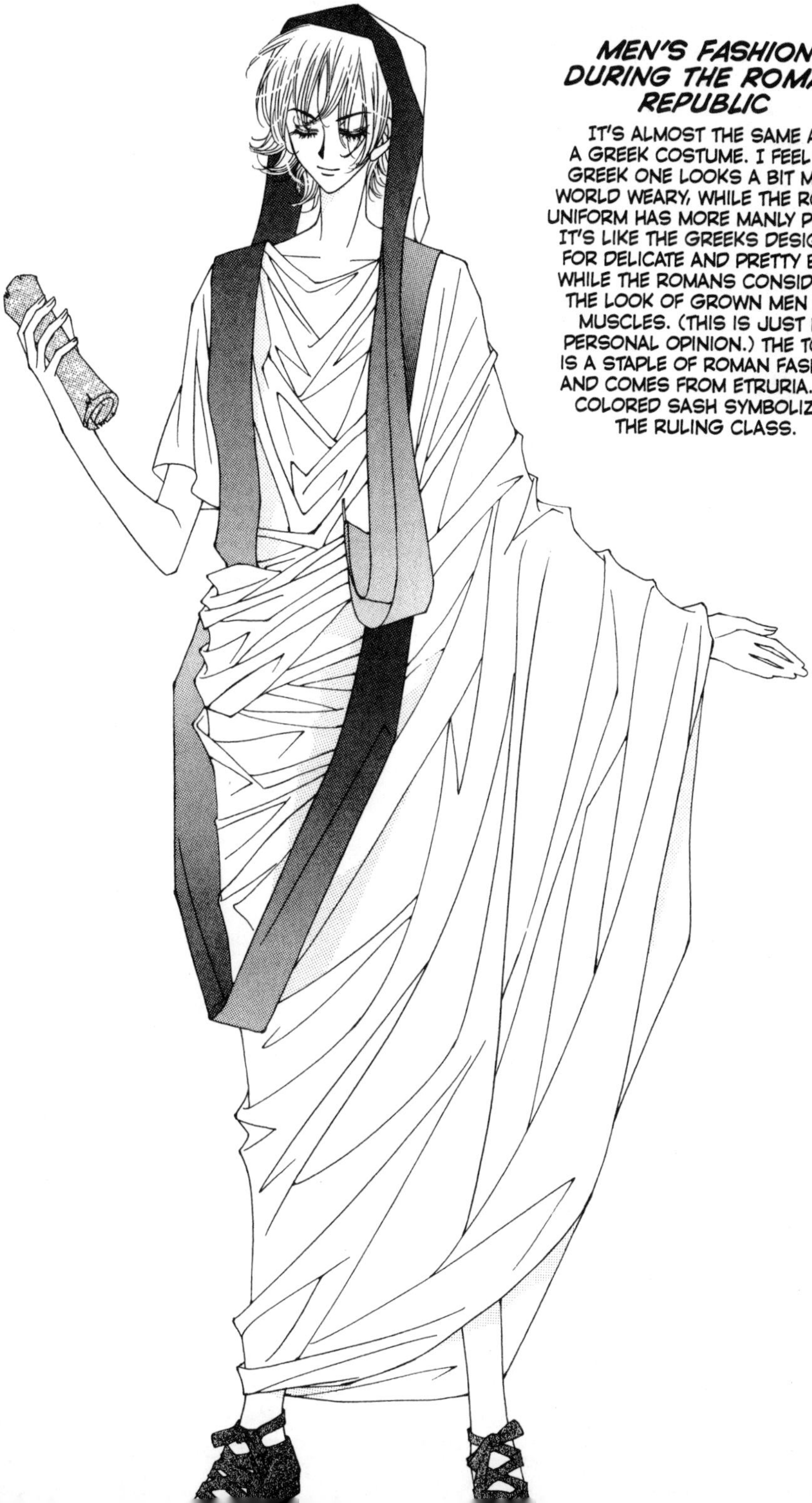

CULTURAL SHOCK

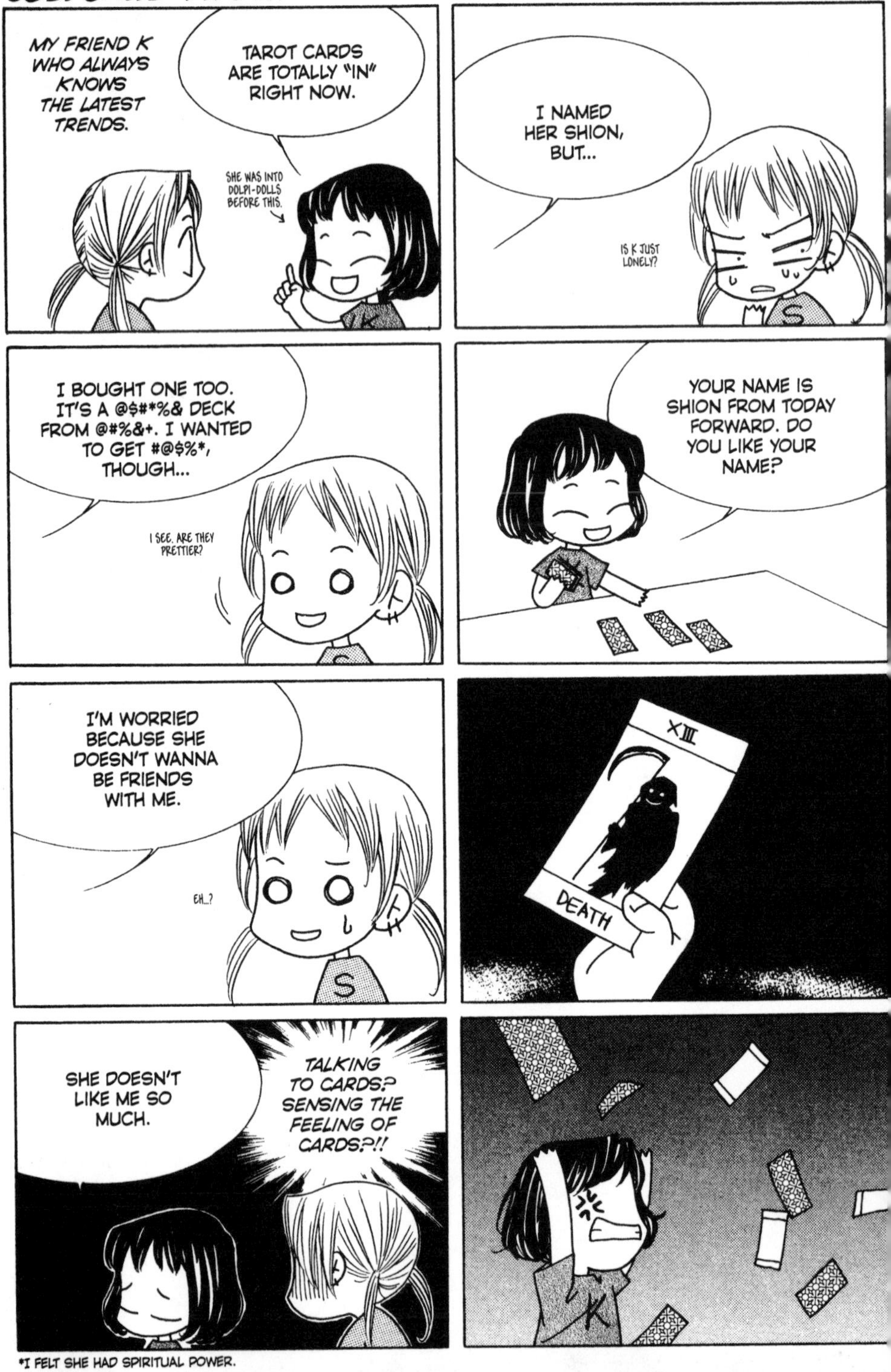
MY FRIEND K WHO ALWAYS KNOWS THE LATEST TRENDS.
TAROT CARDS ARE TOTALLY "IN" RIGHT NOW.
SHE WAS INTO DOLPI-DOLLS BEFORE THIS.
I NAMED HER SHION, BUT...
IS K JUST LONELY?
I BOUGHT ONE TOO. IT'S A @$#*%& DECK FROM @#%&+. I WANTED TO GET #@$%*, THOUGH...
I SEE. ARE THEY PRETTIER?
YOUR NAME IS SHION FROM TODAY FORWARD. DO YOU LIKE YOUR NAME?
I'M WORRIED BECAUSE SHE DOESN'T WANNA BE FRIENDS WITH ME.
EH...?
XIII
DEATH
SHE DOESN'T LIKE ME SO MUCH.
TALKING TO CARDS? SENSING THE FEELING OF CARDS?!!

*I FELT SHE HAD SPIRITUAL POWER.

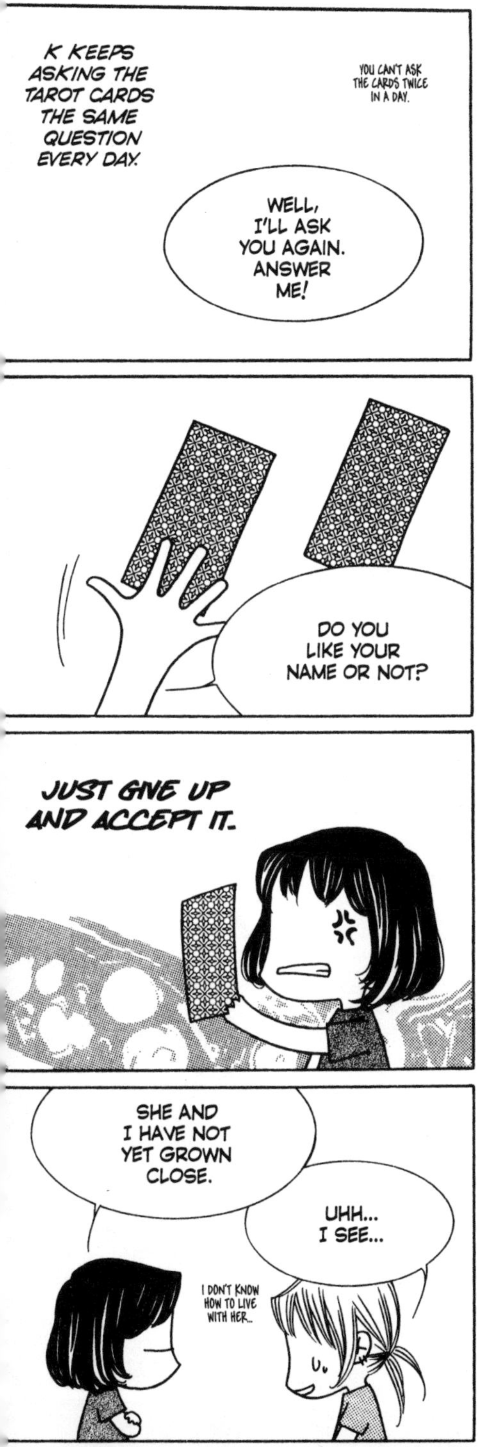
K KEEPS ASKING THE TAROT CARDS THE SAME QUESTION EVERY DAY.
YOU CAN'T ASK THE CARDS TWICE IN A DAY.
WELL, I'LL ASK YOU AGAIN. ANSWER ME!
DO YOU LIKE YOUR NAME OR NOT?
JUST GIVE UP AND ACCEPT IT.
SHE AND I HAVE NOT YET GROWN CLOSE.
UHH... I SEE...
I DON'T KNOW HOW TO LIVE WITH HER...

*I FELT LIKE I COULD UNDERSTAND, BUT I WAS STILL CONFUSED.

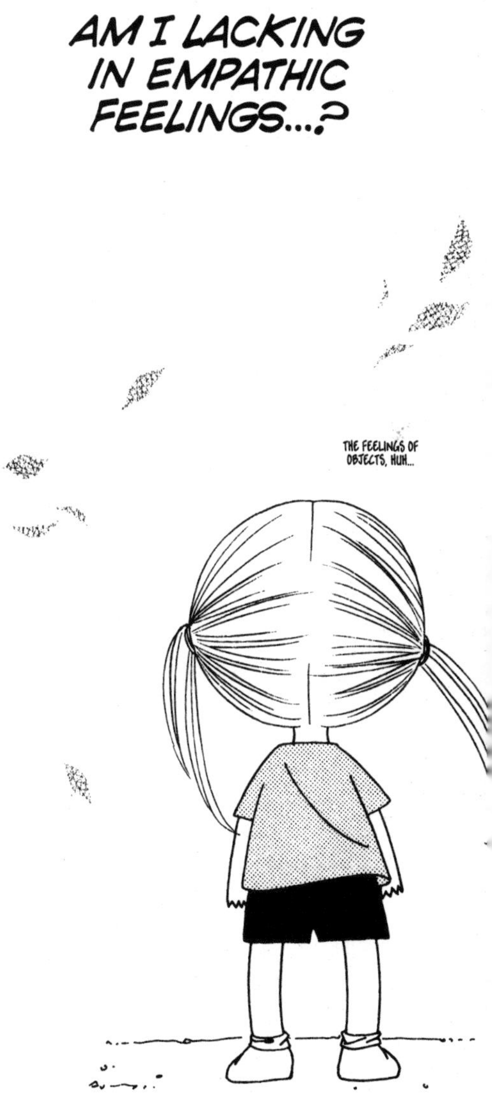
AM I LACKING IN EMPATHIC FEELINGS...?
THE FEELINGS OF OBJECTS, HUH...

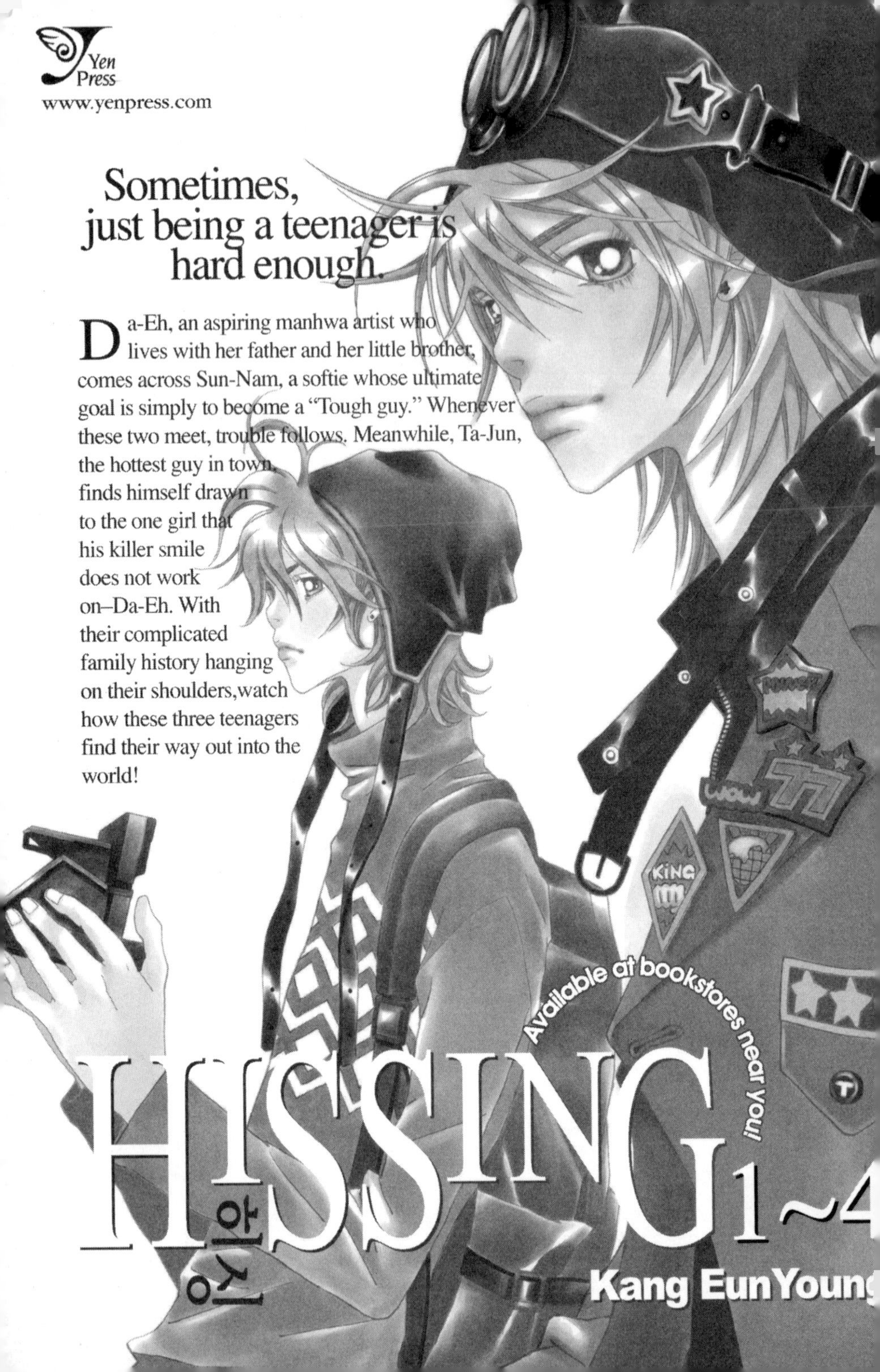
Yen Press
www.yenpress.com
Sometimes, just being a teenager is hard enough.
Da-Eh, an aspiring manhwa artist who lives with her father and her little brother, comes across Sun-Nam, a softie whose ultimate goal is simply to become a "Tough guy." Whenever these two meet, trouble follows. Meanwhile, Ta-Jun, the hottest guy in town, finds himself drawn to the one girl that his killer smile does not work on–Da-Eh. With their complicated family history hanging on their shoulders,watch how these three teenagers find their way out into the world!
Available at bookstores near you!
HISSING 1~4
히싱
Kang EunYoung

Becoming the princess . . . Isn't that every girl's dream?!

Monarchy rule ended long ago in Korea, but there are still other countries with kings, queens, princes and princesses. What if Korea had continued monarchism? What if all the beautiful palaces, which are now only historical relics, were actually filled with people? What if the glamorous royal family still maintained the palace customs? Welcome to a world where Korea still has the royal family living in their everyday lives! Only for this one high school girl, Chae-Kyung, is this a tragedy, since she has to marry the prince — who apparently is a total bastard!

Yen Press
www.yenpress.com

THE ROYAL PALACE

Goong

vol.1~3

Park SoHee

The Antique Gift Shop 1~5

Lee Eun

Available at bookstores near you!

Yen Press
www.yenpress.com

CAN YOU FEEL THE SOULS OF THE ANTIQUES? DO YOU BELIEVE?

Did you know that an antique possesses a soul of its own?
The Antique Gift Shop specializes in such items that charm and captivate the buyers they are destined to belong to. Guided by a mysterious and charismatic shopkeeper, the enchanted relics lead their new owners on a journey into an alternate cosmic universe to their true destinies.
Eerily bittersweet and dolefully melancholy, The Antique Gift Shop opens up a portal to a world where torn lovers unite, broken friendships are mended, and regrets are resolved. Can you feel the power of the antiques?

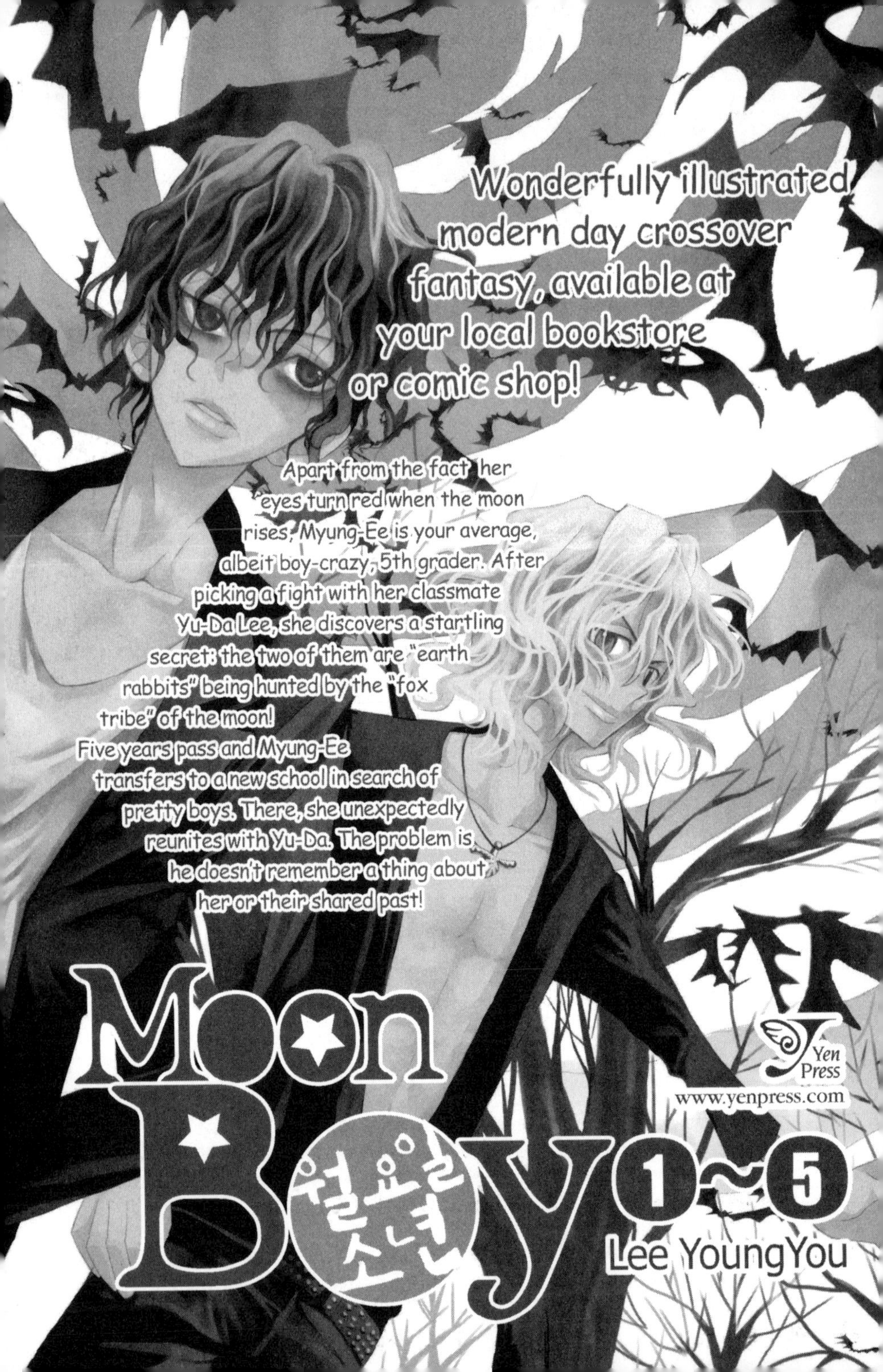
Wonderfully illustrated modern day crossover fantasy, available at your local bookstore or comic shop!
Apart from the fact her eyes turn red when the moon rises, Myung-Ee is your average, albeit boy-crazy, 5th grader. After picking a fight with her classmate Yu-Da Lee, she discovers a startling secret: the two of them are "earth rabbits" being hunted by the "fox tribe" of the moon!
Five years pass and Myung-Ee transfers to a new school in search of pretty boys. There, she unexpectedly reunites with Yu-Da. The problem is, he doesn't remember a thing about her or their shared past!
Moon Boy
월요일 소년
1~5
Lee YoungYou
Yen Press
www.yenpress.com

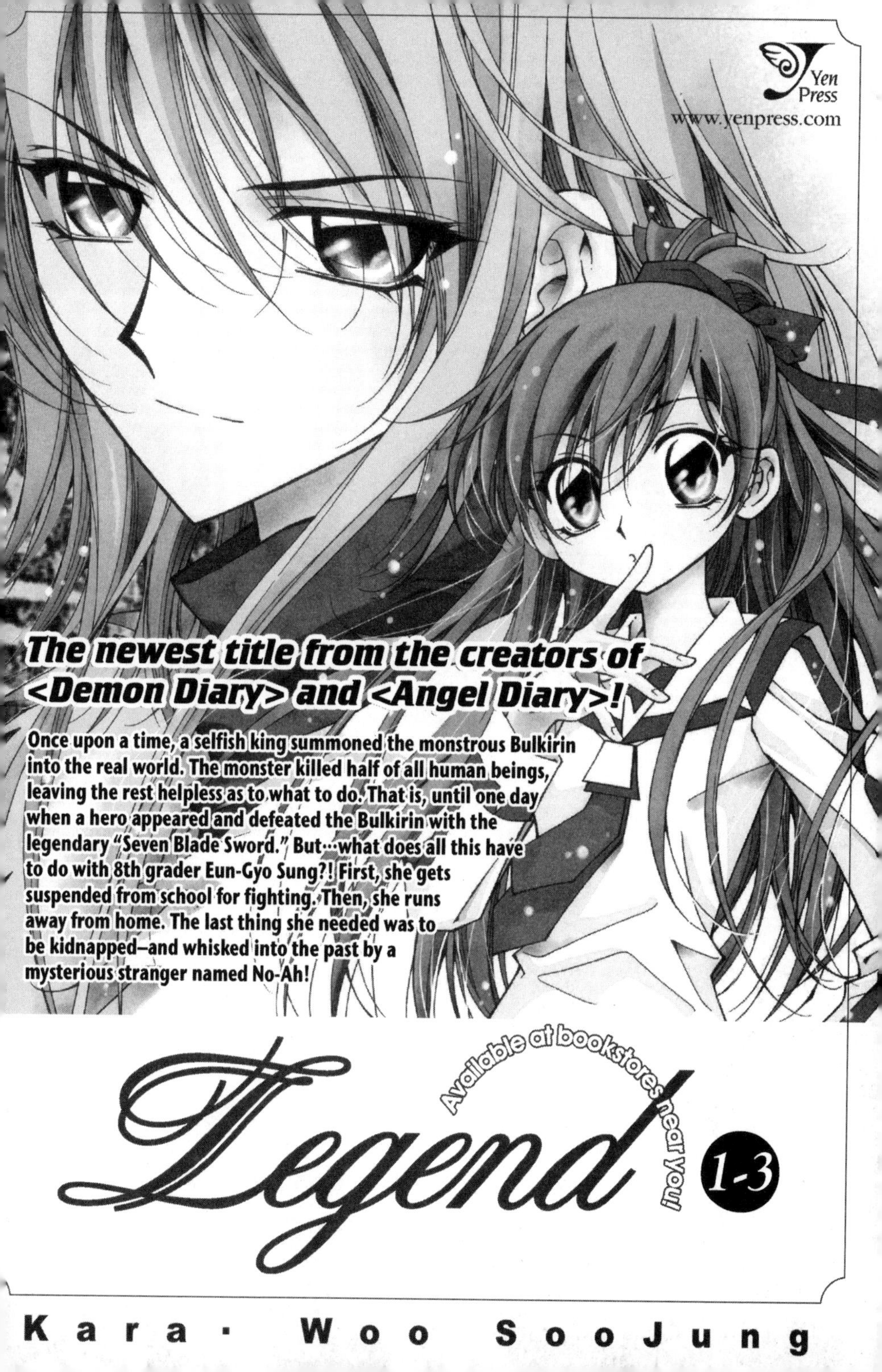
Yen Press
www.yenpress.com
The newest title from the creators of <Demon Diary> and <Angel Diary>!
Once upon a time, a selfish king summoned the monstrous Bulkirin into the real world. The monster killed half of all human beings, leaving the rest helpless as to what to do. That is, until one day when a hero appeared and defeated the Bulkirin with the legendary "Seven Blade Sword." But…what does all this have to do with 8th grader Eun-Gyo Sung?! First, she gets suspended from school for fighting. Then, she runs away from home. The last thing she needed was to be kidnapped–and whisked into the past by a mysterious stranger named No-Ah!
Available at bookstores near you!
Legend
1-3
Kara · Woo SooJung

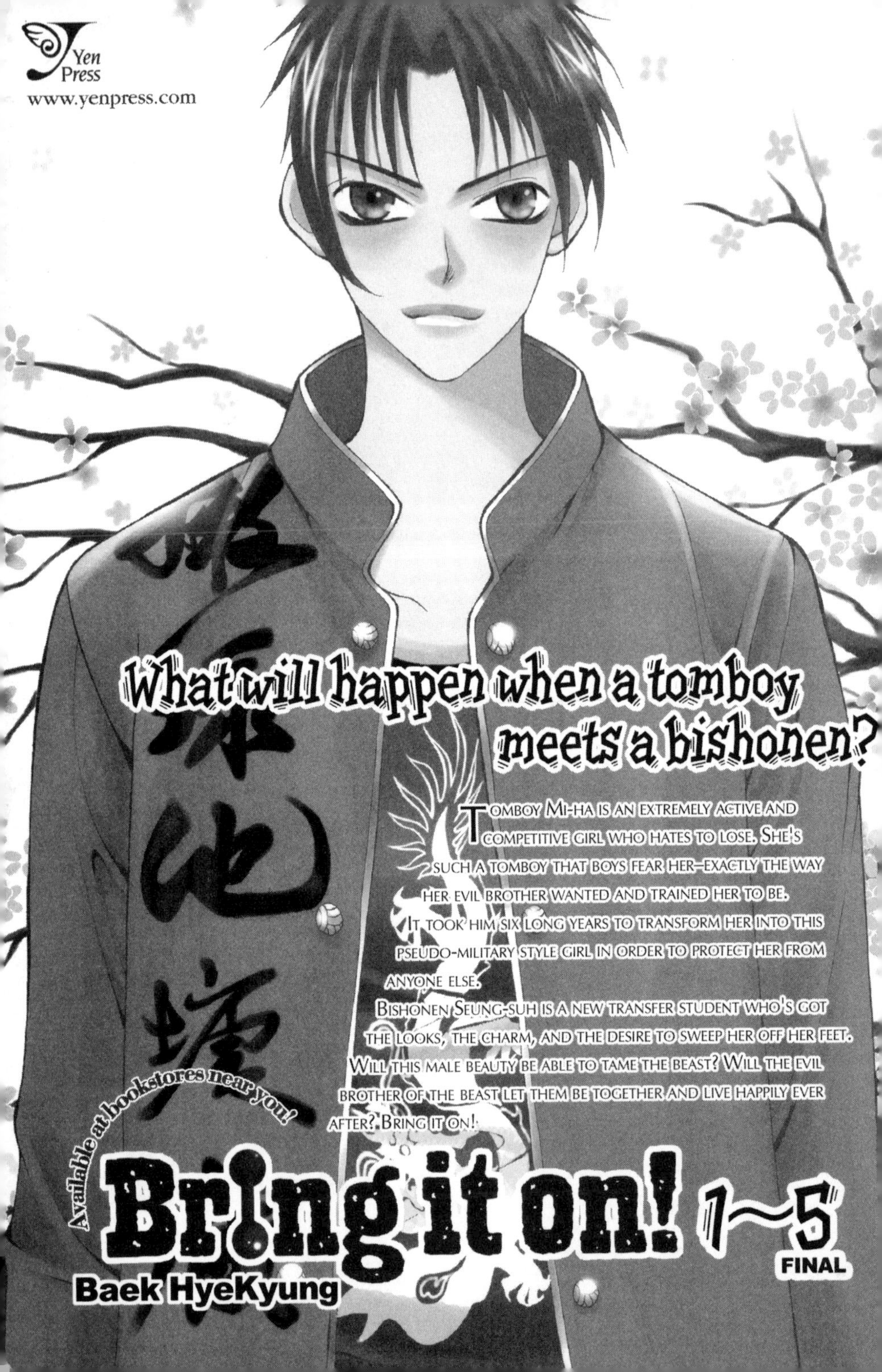
Yen Press
www.yenpress.com
What will happen when a tomboy meets a bishonen?
Tomboy Mi-ha is an extremely active and competitive girl who hates to lose. She's such a tomboy that boys fear her–exactly the way her evil brother wanted and trained her to be. It took him six long years to transform her into this pseudo-military style girl in order to protect her from anyone else.
Bishonen Seung-suh is a new transfer student who's got the looks, the charm, and the desire to sweep her off her feet. Will this male beauty be able to tame the beast? Will the evil brother of the beast let them be together and live happily ever after? Bring it on!
Available at bookstores near you!
Bring it on! 1~5
FINAL
Baek HyeKyung

Available at bookstores near you!

CHOCOLAT
1~6

Shin JiSang · Geo

Kum-ji was a little late getting under the spell of the chart-topping band, DDL. Unable to join the DDL fan club, she almost gives up on meeting her idols, until she develops a cunning plan–to become a member of a rival fan club for the brand-new boy band Yo-I. This way she can act as Yo-I's fan club member and also be near Yo-I,

How far would you go to meet your favorite boy band?

who always seem to be in the same shows as DDL. Perfect plan...except being a fanatic is a lot more complicated than she expects. Especially when you're actually a fan of someone else. This full-blown love comedy about a fan club will make you laugh, cry, and laugh some more.

11th CAT

Available at bookstores near you!

Kim MiKyung

1~4 & Special

Cute and charming, yet not
so bright little Rika is training to
become a real wizard. The first step is to find
a magic staff. Ah, that can't be too hard, can it?
As Rika and Eujen journey deep into the forest in
search of this wonderful magic staff, Rika loses her way.
She winds up in an unfortunate chance encounter with the
dark sorcerer who kidnapped the princess! Will Rika be able
to free the princess and become a real wizard? Follow this
cute fantasy story with Rika and find out.

The Cutest Fantasy You've Ever Met!

Cynical Orange vol. 5

Story and Art by JiUn Yun

Translation: HyeYoung Im
English Adaptation: Jamie S. Rich
Lettering: Terri Delgado

Yen Press
Hachette Book Group USA
237 Park Avenue, New York, NY 10017

Visit our Web sites at www.HachetteBookGroupUSA.com and www.YenPress.com.

Yen Press is an imprint of Hachette Book Group USA, Inc. The Yen Press name and logo are trademarks of Hachette Book Group USA, Inc.

First Yen Press Edition: October 2008

ISBN-10: 0-7595-2878-0
ISBN-13: 978-0-7595-2878-9

10 9 8 7 6 5 4 3 2 1

BVG

Printed in the United States of America